She pointed through the windshield.

Giles stopped the car. Behind the gates, framed by thick privet hedges, rose a monstrous and yet somehow beautiful piece of architecture unlike anything Giles had ever seen. A row of windows across the top floor of the house looked like nothing so much as eyes, staring madly down at them.

Everything inside Giles begged him to turn the car around and get Buffy out of there. There was evil here, massive, unbridled evil. Whatever was inside that house was unlike anything the Slayer had been called on to face in the past.

There was death inside.

"I'll go open the gates." Buffy unbuckled her seat belt.

Giles pushed up his glasses. "No! That is, they might be locked."

"And that's going to stop Supergirl," Xander said.

"I'll sound the horn," Giles said.

"I can take care of it," Buffy insisted, clearly amused. She gave Giles a lazy half smile and opened her car door.

That was when they heard the screams. Inhuman shrieks came from beyond that black gate, and after a moment, Giles felt almost certain that, somehow, the agonized wailing was coming from the house itself.

**Buffy the Vampire Slayer™**

Available from ARCHWAY Paperbacks and POCKET PULSE

**Buffy the Vampire Slayer adult books**

Available from POCKET BOOKS

# The Gatekeeper Trilogy
## Book One

# BUFFY
## THE VAMPIRE
# SLAYER™

## OUT of the MADHOUSE

CHRISTOPHER GOLDEN and NANCY HOLDER
*An original novel based on the hit TV series created by Joss Whedon*

**POCKET BOOKS**
New York   London   Toronto   Sydney   Singapore

An *Original* Publication of POCKET BOOKS

POCKET BOOKS, a division of Simon & Schuster Inc.
1230 Avenue of the Americas, New York, NY 10020

™ and copyright © 1999 by Twentieth Century Fox Film Corporation. All rights reserved.

ISBN: 0-671-02434-5

First Pocket Books printing January 1999

10  9  8  7  6  5

POCKET and colophon are registered trademarks of Simon & Schuster Inc.

Front cover art by Franco Accornero

Printed in the U.S.A.

For Lisa and Liz.
Thy will be done.

—C.G.
—N.H.

# Acknowledgments

Christopher Golden and Nancy Holder would like to thank: our agents, Lori Perkins and Howard Morhaim, and Howard's assistant, Lindsay Sagnette; and our editor, Lisa Clancy and her assistant, Elizabeth Shiflett. Our sincere gratitude to Caroline Kallas, Joss Whedon, and the entire cast and crew of *Buffy*. Thanks to our patient and supportive spouses, Connie and Wayne, for putting up with both of us.

Christopher would also like to thank Lucy Russo, and Nancy would like to thank the Babysitter Battalion: Rebekah and Julie Simpson, Ida Khabazian, and April Koljonen.

# OUT *of the* MADHOUSE

# Prologue

ALL THE FREAKS THAT LURKED IN THE SHADOWS OF THE Hellmouth were out in force that night, and all gathered in a single room for a horrifying ritual.

It was called Amateur Night at the Bronze.

Buffy Summers, the Chosen One, peered into the darkness, made somehow more dreary by the spotlights illuminating one band after another, each more hopeful and hopeless than the last. She had never seen the Bronze more packed. Each band had its own following, some well deserved and some merely fanatical. All of them crowded into the relatively small club.

The place was rocking. Buffy and her friends were fortunate to have found a table at all. The music wasn't all that bad, she was forced to admit. The sights were fascinating, to say the least, and the company was, as always, the best anyone could hope for.

It should have been a perfect evening. From the looks on her friends' faces, it was exactly that. For them. Oz, decked out in one of his nostalgic bowling shirts, held tightly to Willow's hand and babbled on earnestly about the fretless Rickenbacker the current band's bassist was playing.

Willow nodded brightly in response. They were still at that stage where everything they told each other was engaging. Buffy remembered that stage. Missed it. And wondered, briefly, if she would ever be in a relationship that lasted long enough to get past it. Perverse as it seemed to her, she liked the idea of being in love with a guy so long that she could start taking him for granted.

She missed it all, though. Missed getting dressed up for someone besides herself, and living in that delicious limbo of anticipation that having a real boyfriend was all about, not knowing what might happen next, and thrilled by the uncertainty of it all.

To the rear of the table, Cordelia and Xander sat close to each other—closer than Cordy would usually allow in public—and sipped their coffees. They just listened, sometimes to Oz and sometimes to the band on stage. Relaxed. Enjoying being together. Cordelia's cell phone was on the table, and every few minutes she glanced down at it. Finally she turned to Xander and said something, then flicked it shut and put it in her shoulder bag.

All four of them, the two couples, glanced around the club from time to time. Rumor had it that there was a major label A and R rep present for the monthly event, and they were all trying to figure out who it might be. Oz, after all, had his band to think of. The rest of these guys were competition for Dingoes Ate My Baby. No much, but competition nevertheless.

They were having a great time. They were seniors, after all. For the moment, the world belonged to them. Why shouldn't they enjoy it?

Perhaps, Buffy thought as she watched her friends, it really was a perfect evening. It was possible, however painful, that she simply didn't know how to enjoy just . . . being, anymore. Despite the fact that she'd been to the Bronze more often than math class, she felt oddly out of place, almost as if it were her first day in town all over again. It made her a little dizzy and more than a bit confused.

*They're all so innocent,* she thought. *They're all so young.*

Then she smiled grimly at herself. Maybe she'd passed innocent on the road of life a long time ago, but young she could still lay claim to. Sometimes it just didn't feel that way. Life was just starting for the rest of them. Who knew what fate had in store for them?

Buffy, on the other hand? Her fate was sealed.

Xander looked up at Buffy, saw her watching them, and smiled even as he knitted his eyebrows in concern.

"Okay, Miss Summers," Xander said, "penny." His hair was long again, more the way he'd worn it when she'd first met him almost three years ago. Still, his face was older. He'd lost his baby fat, that was for sure. If not his floppy sleeves and baggy pants. Cordelia, for all her sleek fashion sense—tonight it was a black Chinese dress embroidered with dark purple butterflies, sticks in her hair—had not yet been able to redeem him.

Buffy shrugged. "Put away your hard-earned cash, Xand. These aren't thoughts anyone should pay for."

He gave her a look. Slowly nodded. "Yeah," he drawled, "the band is bringing me down, too. Their only redeeming social value is that they're all girls." He snapped his head toward Cordelia. "And there'll be no physical violence from you. I saw you drooling at that drummer with the red hair two bands ago."

Cordelia rolled her eyes. "Oh, please."

"Was she not?" Xander flung at Willow, who glanced toward him and lifted her brows. Obviously, she had not been listening. It was a fairly common occurrence these days. One he was dealing with fairly well—accent on fairly.

Huffing, he squinted his eyes at Buffy. "Drooling, right?"

Buffy shrugged.

"Women." He sighed. "You stick together like peanut butter and fluff." Xander's eyes flashed with mischief. "Which, come to think of it, makes a sandwich."

"That's sick," Cordelia said. "You are disgusting."

"In your eyes, not necessarily a bad thing." He gave her a wink.

Cordelia looked up toward the ceiling as if her patience had flown toward the light fixtures like a moth. "Ooh."

Buffy smiled weakly, feeling sad and frumpy in jeans and a black spaghetti-strap top.

And the band played on.

*Fly away, let's run away*
*Let's start all over.*
*Let's kill time.*
*Let's unwind the threads of destiny . . .*

Oz shrugged and said, "They're not so bad."

"Yeah, for a band that sucks," Cordelia said. "And where did they get those clothes? That whole retro seventies thing is so over." She glanced at Buffy. "No offense."

Buffy tilted her head. She wanted to take offense. She wanted to rise to the challenge and lob something back at Cordy. But she couldn't seem to muster up the energy. She half smiled and took a sip from her iced latte. Where it had sat, there was a light condensation ring on the table. Iced latte. Nonfat milk. Her mother said she was getting awfully thin.

"Whoa." Cordelia frowned. "Are you sick or something?"

Buffy looked at her questioningly.

"Well, I didn't mean that as an insult, but you're usually so . . . defensive, y'know?"

*Let's kill time.*

"Heard from Giles?" Willow asked Buffy.

Buffy shook her head. "I told him to call only if there's an emergency." Finally she smiled. "You know, like if someone tries to spike the punch with extra ginger ale."

They all chuckled. Giles was at the annual meeting of the American Library Association, sure to be a wild rave loaded with massive potential for Buffy's Watcher to get all crazy.

"I miss him," Willow said simply. "I was thinking this morning about graduation and . . . y'know, after. It'll be weird not to walk into the library every morning to find out what the monsters are up to."

"We'll still hang with the G-man," Xander said quickly. Too quickly. Buffy watched Xander's face as he followed that thought through to its natural conclusion. After graduation, it seemed likely they would all go their own ways. Friendship or no, they had lives to lead. It would be hard to reconnoiter once they scattered to the four winds.

"I'll still see him," Buffy said quietly. "Every morning."

"No, because, you'll be . . . oh," Willow said. She looked pityingly at Buffy. "I guess you will."

"So, it's not like you graduate and get your Slayer's diploma?" Oz asked Buffy. "You just keep doing it?"

"You just keep doing it." Buffy made another ring on the varnished wood. "The Energizer Buffy, that's me."

"Drag." Oz nodded. "Sometimes Dingoes get tired of playing the same old songs."

"Name that tune," Buffy said. " 'In every generation, there is a Chosen One. She alone will stand against the vampires, the demons, and the forces of darkness. She is the Slayer.' "

"And speaking of demons," Xander drawled, "hiya, soul man."

Buffy looked over her shoulder. Despite her mood—and her life—her heart skipped a beat. Angel stood behind her, dressed in his signature black jeans, dark silk shirt, and duster. The dim lights in the Bronze underscored the paleness of his skin, which served to accentuate his dark eyes and high cheekbones. So handsome. Distant, now, where once upon a time he would have put his hands on Buffy's shoulders, leaned down to kiss the top of her head, perhaps her cheek, even her lips, in greeting.

Distant now. Careful. And unsure of his place among them.

Tonight, Buffy thought she knew that feeling quite well indeed.

"Angel," she breathed. "What's up? Is something bad about to happen?"

"Only if that band gives an encore," he said dryly, straight-faced, and nodded toward the stage.

Buffy brightened a little. Her life was strange, and filled with danger, but it had its compensations. She would rather have Angel in her life in some way, any way, than to lose him to darkness again. In a few months, her friends might very well leave Sunny-dale—leave her. Why would anyone want to stay? Someday, even Angel might leave. But for now, they were all here, together.

"Dance with me?" she asked Angel, sliding off her stool in anticipation.

She went to him and held out her hand. He took it, his fingers cold, and she led him to the dance floor. He gathered her in his arms; she lay her head on his shoulder and closed her eyes.

"Poor Buffy," Willow murmured.

The others acknowledged her sentiment with their silence. They all understood how difficult it was for her. Everybody applying for colleges, talking about their plans. Moving on. Growing up. What did she have to look forward to?

In some of the research she had done for Giles, Willow had found an entry in an early-twentieth-century Watcher's journal about the average life span of a Slayer. She had not shared the information with Buffy. In fact, she herself had tried to forget it.

It was, truly, the only piece of information she

could honestly say that she wished she had never learned.

Xander leaned forward as if sharing a secret, and though he spoke out loud, the deafening thrash roaring from the Carvin amps on stage was enough to keep whatever he might say secret. Willow could barely hear him, and she was only a few feet away.

"You said you were thinking about graduation," Xander said, his eyes indicating Willow. "It's been on my mind, too."

"On all our minds, doofus," Cordelia sneered, her lip curling in disdain. "It's only the single most important day of our lives. So far."

Xander looked at her, his face grave. Willow knew that look. It said, *Not now, Cordy.* Amazingly enough, Cordelia had apparently learned the meaning of that expression as well. She didn't interrupt again.

"It's not the most important day in Buffy's life," Xander explained. "To her, it's really just another day. Sometimes I wonder if she'd even have stayed in school if it weren't for pressure from her mom, and the convenience of Giles being right there."

"And us," Willow added.

"And us," Xander conceded. "Don't get me wrong, I feel horrible that she's so . . . trapped by the whole Slayer gig. But what she's doing, being the Chosen One, is so important to the world, that sometimes I wonder. I mean, if this is it, if we graduate and just, poof, there go the Slayerettes, will Buffy be the only one of us who continues to make a difference with her life?"

They looked at him oddly for a moment. There was a time when even the hint of philosophy or contemplation from Xander might have invited ridicule. Sometimes it still did. But not tonight.

Willow shrugged. "Have we ever made a difference?" she asked. "I mean us, really?" She looked at Oz. "You're new with this. What do you think?"

Oz raised his eyebrows. "I'm not sure there's one right answer to this question," he said sincerely.

"I'm not sure I want to know, anyway," Cordelia cut in. "I used to pray I would like, you know, get away from all of you and all the weirdness. Like I would drop you—"

"Or outrun us," Xander muttered.

She rolled her eyes. "Anyway, it hasn't happened. And now I'm all caught up in it just like you guys. So what do we do? List the Slayerettes Club or Scooby Gang or whatever under our activities in the yearbook and go back to the real world?"

"This being, of course, the unreal world," Xander said.

Cordelia gave her hair a toss, and regarded him intently. "Well," she said slowly, "it is."

Xander pinched her arm. "Ouch!"

"Don't be a baby, I barely touched you," he said. "But come on, Cor, are you saying none of this is important?"

"No." She shrugged. "It's just that it's not going to last." She looked around the table. "I mean, for us. We have *lives.*"

Across the room, Buffy danced with Angel.

"Poor Buffy," Willow whispered, so quietly she could barely hear herself. Apparently, though, Oz heard her, and put his arm around her.

"We're here, for now," he said. "Let's dance."

\* \* \*

Angel lifted Buffy's chin and gazed into her eyes with tender concern. "What's wrong, Buffy?" he asked.

She lay her head back on his shoulder, not daring to stare too long into his eyes. And it felt so good to have a shoulder to lean on, even if it was for just a moment; even if leaning on him was an illusion.

"Buffy?" he prodded gently.

She lifted her head, managed a smile, but she must have betrayed herself, for he didn't smile back.

"They're going to leave me," she said in a rush, biting back a choke of emotion.

He nodded. "But maybe not right away. Maybe not even soon."

She shrugged. "But eventually. And I don't blame them. They have to . . . to move on."

They danced for a few bars before he said, "I know it hurts. Believe me."

She flared, just a little, mostly because she was afraid she might cry. She said, "How would you know, Angel? You outlive everybody. You're always the one who does the moving on."

He shook his head. "It feels the same as being left behind. It hurts as much. It hurts more, Buffy. You haven't even been here three years. Spend sixty or seventy years watching someone you care for grow old and die, and then we'll talk."

"Oh." Her voice was small.

When the song ended, they went back to the table. Buffy saw the long faces of her friends and said, "Yikes. Where are all the shiny, happy people? Looks like this is my cue to take my depressing self home."

"No, Buffy, don't go," Willow said, brightening a little too easily. "We want to hang."

"Yeah, till we strangle," Xander added, patting her chair. "Pull one up, Angel. Grab a pint of O positive. Tell us vampire jokes. A bloodsucker walks into a bar with a parrot on his head . . . and?"

"Xander," Buffy chided. She picked up her crocheted bag and automatically checked inside for her weapon of choice: a very sharp stake. "G'night, boys and girls."

Willow stood. "Let's go, too, Oz. My parents are still after me about going out on school nights."

Oz nodded. "Buffy, lift?"

She looked at Angel, who said, "I'll walk you home."

Cordelia patted Xander's hand. "Us, too," she announced. "I have cheerleading practice at the crack of dawn." She rolled her eyes. "Why they continually schedule those things outside of school hours just baffles me. I mean, you would think they'd be more considerate. It's hard to look good at seven-thirty in the morning *and* be burning up with school spirit."

"Not for you," Xander said pleasantly.

Cordelia opened her mouth, an aggravated look on her face, and then closed it again, dumbfounded, as she apparently realized that Xander had just paid her a fine compliment.

They all left together, Buffy heading the parade with Angel in tow. On the stage, some poor fools were getting heckled for the crime of not realizing that grunge was so over there were kids in the audience who had still been in diapers when Seattle was the alt-rock destination of choice.

Outside, they swept past the new bouncer, the guy who'd replaced Bruno a couple of months back, and then turned right to trudge over to an alley which was the one spot where Cordelia and Oz could usually find a parking space.

Buffy lifted her face to the night breeze. She could smell the ocean, and for a moment she thought of Los Angeles and her long-ago life, when being the Chosen One meant you got a rhinestone tiara and a bouquet of red roses, not a lifetime's supply of holy water and enough garlic to open up your own Italian restaurant.

Under his breath, Oz was singing "Let's kill time," and Buffy realized that as bad as the band had been, the song was actually kind of memorable. In a melancholy way.

They were halfway down the alley when something scrabbled along the roof of the Bronze. They all glanced up at the thing, which darted along, leaving behind a shadowed blur.

In the distance, a woman started screaming.

Without hesitation, Angel and Buffy fanned out, flanking the others. She reached into her bag and pulled out a stake. She held it out to him, only to see him withdraw another stake from inside his duster. Buffy approved. A good workman comes with his tools, Giles had told her more than once.

"Help!" someone shrieked. "Oh, my God!"

Buffy's legs pumped as she covered ground almost as fast as Angel. Together they rounded a corner, sprinted toward a screaming woman. But Angel was in the lead, and the woman took one look at him and ran in the opposite direction. Buffy realized that he must be in full vamp face, but wasn't concerned. If the woman could run, she was basically unhurt. It was time to redirect their focus on whatever had attacked her.

Then Buffy heard the scrabbling noise from above.

The monster was back on the roof. Angel came up beside her, and they watched it as it rushed back across the tops of the buildings. It seemed to fly, or leap, almost like a flying squirrel, a long coat or cloak billowing out behind it.

"It's Batman," Angel said.

"I don't think so," Buffy replied grimly.

It was heading back toward Buffy's friends. Angel must have realized it at the same time, because as she broke into a run back the way they'd come, he kept pace with her. She rounded the corner again, and saw them standing, talking, where they had first seen the strange creature on the rooftop.

"Run!" Buffy shouted, closing the distance to her friends as fast as she could.

The shape soared into the air above them, cloak unfurling like giant bat's wings. Its head fell back as it sailed, and a plume of blue flames erupted from its mouth.

"Yow," Xander said. "Name that demon."

It landed heavily on the roof on the other side of the street, its hands making a terrible scraping sound like fingernails on a chalkboard. Buffy followed it with her eyes, but it was almost impossible to make it out in the darkness. It stood far back on the roof and seemed to regard them for a moment. Then it rushed toward the edge of the roof, passing beneath a series of overhanging lights so fast the effect was like a strobe.

"Run," Buffy said to the others. "Now."

Cordelia broke ranks first. With a tiny shriek she turned around and ran back toward the Bronze. Two mistakes in one. The first was running. The second was running *away* from Buffy and Angel.

The thing threw itself off the roof and dove after

13

her. More blue flame shot from its mouth, lighting up Cordelia's retreat as well as the thing itself. It was manlike, with a hideous, fanged mouth, black eyes like holes in its face, and pointed ears, and it was wearing some kind of white, oily armor.

Pretty, it was not.

"Cordy!" Xander shouted, racing after Cordelia.

"No, Xander!" Buffy cried, and sped up, her lungs burning now as she caught up to where Willow and Oz stood, trying to figure out what to do next. Buffy solved the problem for them. "Don't move!" she snapped.

Cordelia glanced back at Xander, then up at her pursuer and screamed.

Xander reached for Cordelia just as Buffy caught up with him. She grabbed his arm, holding him back, and yanked him hard out of her way. She was the Slayer. She was supposed to keep him safe. Keep them all safe. Xander lost his footing and went down hard. Buffy tried to leap over him, but her legs became tangled up in his fall, and she went down as well. It took her a moment to free herself. Buffy leaped to her feet as the creature settled down to the street between her and Cordelia.

It opened its mouth as if in a roar, and a volley of flame shot from its gullet and caught Cordelia on the back of her head. Instantly, her hair began to burn. Cordelia shrieked wildly, her hands flailing in utter panic. The thing reached out for her, and its talons snagged her dress, tearing the fabric. Cordelia barely noticed as she batted at her hair, but from one small scratch on her back, she'd begun to bleed.

Then Angel vaulted past Buffy. He reached Cordelia first and pulled her down onto the pavement, where he covered her head with his body, smothering the flames.

The monster turned to face Buffy. Inhuman eyes wide, it seemed to examine her. It lifted its right hand to its mouth and licked Cordelia's blood off the single talon with which it had scratched her. Buffy raised her stake. The thing ignored her, turning its attention back to Cordelia.

"Hey, ugly!" Buffy snarled as she went after it. "You're gonna hurt my feelings if you keep this up."

Then, somehow, Xander was in front of her, between Buffy and the monster, going after it. He reached out, got hold of its black cloak, and tugged. The thing turned, opened its mouth . . .

"Xander!" Buffy shouted, and tackled him. Hard.

Blue flame crackled as it jetted from the thing's mouth, burning the air above them as they tumbled to the pavement. A second later and it would have been Xander's face crackling with fire.

"Ow, damn it!" Xander shouted.

But Buffy was already up and swinging. She connected with the monster. It looked like a tall, thin man, and as it opened its mouth, she landed a savage roundhouse kick to the side of the monster's face. It howled and staggered backward, raking the air between them with hands that ended in thick, metallic talons. Flame vomited from its mouth.

Buffy ducked, bent sideways, and snapped her left leg up straight and hard, catching the thing in its midsection.

The thing was momentarily off balance. Angel rushed it from the side and slammed it against the metal siding of the warehouse behind it. It fell to one side, violently crashing into a line of trash cans, which spread their refuse over the sidewalk.

Quickly, instinctively, Buffy and Angel moved into position, trapping the thing between them. She looked at Angel; he nodded once at her, and they attacked from either side. But as they rushed it, the monster rose to its feet, bent its legs, and leaped up, soaring into the air. It landed on the hood of a Toyota fifteen yards away. Metal squealed and crunched beneath its weight.

"Oh, my God," Willow said, as she and Oz stared after it.

It sprang against the side of the building and crawled up it like a lizard, arms and legs scrabbling furiously. It reached the edge of the overhanging roof, grabbed it, launched itself up and over it, and continued on. In a few seconds it was gone.

The squeal of metal was like an echo of the thrash pulsating from the open door of the Bronze down the street.

Another squeal, like a horrid guitar riff.

Then nothing.

Catching her breath, Buffy jogged toward Cordelia. "Is she okay?" she called, passing Willow and Oz, who were also loping toward Xander and Cordy.

Xander was on his knees, cradling Cordelia's head in his lap. "Yeah, no thanks to you," he snapped, glaring up at her. "God, Buffy, I was *there*. Why'd you knock me down?"

"I was worried that . . ." she said, and then stopped. It had been reflex, pure and simple, that had made her push Xander out of her way. She hadn't thought about it. She had simply done it. The second time, she'd saved him from getting his face scorched. But the first, it was just . . . she was the Slayer.

"If you had just let me help her instead of making me scrape up my arms until they looked like hamburger meat, her hair wouldn't be falling out in smoking little clumps," Xander continued.

"Oh, no!" Cordelia wailed, clutching at her head. "No!"

Xander glared up at Buffy.

"No," Buffy blurted defensively. "I had to—" She held out her hands. "I've never seen anything like that creature before. I didn't want any of you getting hurt."

"I was doing just fine. It's not like I can't hold my own." He raised his chin, very angry, very protective as he cradled Cordelia's head. "God, Buffy, why don't you just get a life. Oh, right. You already have one. And this is it."

"Xander," Willow said, shocked, as she breathlessly joined the group.

Xander glared at Buffy.

She looked away, into the darkness where the monster had retreated.

Angel came up beside Buffy. "You did what you had to do," he said to her.

She slumped, turned, and started walking home.

Alone.

# Chapter 1

BODIES GYRATED, MUSIC POUNDED THROUGH PITIFUL speakers, drinks were poured, imbibed, or spilled in mass quantities. A watered-down gin and tonic in hand, Rupert Giles stood in the far corner of the room and took it all in, careful not to show his disdain. That would be unforgivably rude. This might be New York City, the capital city of rudeness, but that did not mean Giles had to behave in a boorish manner. Come to think of it, there were plenty of boors in London.

Surprised as he was by it, he was forced to admit, at least to himself, that he missed Southern California. At least a little bit. Certainly he missed Buffy and the other students with whom he spent so much time. But there was a certain comfort to the West Coast's laissez-faire attitude that he had begun to enjoy . . . and which, despite the bacchanalia surrounding him, the East Coast distinctly lacked.

19

In truth, great forces had conspired to bring him to Manhattan in late winter. Not the least of which was pressure from his employer, the principal of Sunnydale High School, to at least make an effort to become better versed in modern library science. It seemed the Dewey decimal system just wasn't good enough for some people anymore. In some ways, books weren't even the answer. It was all about information now, he thought sadly. And much of that information, however incomplete, however orphaned from any pedigree, was drawn from computers these days.

His only previous interest in computers had been generated by Jenny Calendar, the woman he'd loved. And that meager interest had died and been buried along with her.

The other primary reason that Giles agreed to attend this function—"Libraries 2000," sponsored by the American Library Association, among others—was the fact that many of the events were to be held in the Warwick Hotel, a grand old dame of a building whose granite and gargoyles looked down on 57th Street with all the haughtiness of Britain's proudest structures. He had stayed at the Warwick on one of his first visits to the United States, and recalled with pleasure an enormous mural of Queen Elizabeth knighting Sir Francis Drake in the downstairs dining room.

Indeed, in spite of his misgivings, Giles had managed to enjoy himself for the past few days, both with the other librarians he'd met and exploring New York alone. It was an extraordinary city. It was true, he'd discovered (or at least, hypothesized), that one could find literally anything in this city, if one knew where to look. The seminar had, thus far, been a relaxing escape from Sunnydale and from the pressures of his role as the Watcher.

He felt a bit guilty for having abandoned Buffy, even for a week, but she had nearly forced him to go, even instructed him on what to pack. He had disappointed her, he was sure, in his refusal to "go more cazh" and "leave all that tweedy stuff in the library, where it belongs." She also arranged for Cordelia to drive him to the airport, a trip he hoped never to repeat, given her penchant for checking her makeup in the rearview mirror. She had even supplied him with an ancient, weather-worn copy of *New York on Five Dollars a Day,* thoughtfully marking sights she imagined he might enjoy, and which, frankly, he had: the museums and a number of bookshops. It seemed fairly clear that Buffy had actually wanted him to go.

Who could blame her? He was, at least officially, an authority figure in her life. It would be nice for her to be free of him for a time. Still, Giles looked forward to returning home, and suspected that Buffy would be pleased when he did return. And, thus far, there seemed to have been no urgent crises requiring his attention at home.

Reluctant as he was to admit it, Giles was having . . . well, fun.

At least, he had been until he'd entered *this* room. The invitation, a splashy foldout from something called stacks.com, which was apparently an Internet meeting place for librarians, had announced a cocktail reception in the Cary Grant Suite of the Warwick Hotel. Well, seeing the Cary Grant Suite had proven an irresistible lure for Giles, and it was, indeed, something to see.

There was a large bedroom on either side of the

enormous parlor that served as a reception room. The suite was at the southwest corner of the hotel, and there were two sets of French doors that opened out onto an absolutely extraordinary balcony. It wasn't at all like any balcony Giles had ever seen, and certainly not something twenty-seven stories above the city. The enormous stone edifice was more like a large terrace one might see at a stately home in the Cotswolds. At least twenty-five feet wide, it ran the length of the Cary Grant Suite's outer wall. The granite color matched the sky; it was apparently quite chilly outside, and the forecast had called for snow, but so far none had fallen.

Giles wondered if he ought to escape to the balcony, despite the cold. It would be a welcome relief from the party. As a rule, the librarians who were attending the stacks.com "cocktail reception" were younger than he, and American. The men wore blue jeans and sneakers with their button-down shirts, and the women, perhaps eager for a chance to dress, wore tiny black dresses or silk pants.

With his gabardine suit and old-school burgundy tie, Giles knew how out of place he must have appeared. Even that was only a fraction of how out of place he actually felt. He brushed a hand through his slightly graying brown hair, then pushed his glasses up his nose for the hundredth time.

"Good Lord," he muttered to himself. "These are librarians?"

But if he were honest with himself, Giles would be forced to admit that it wasn't the dress or behavior of these people that had him wanting so desperately to retreat. Nor was it the fact that, with his love of dusty old books and getting lost in the stacks—ironically, the place he felt the most at home, and the polar opposite of the stacks.com party—he felt positively antique, though even the youngest person in the room was little more than a decade his junior.

No. Worst of all was how much they all reminded him of Jenny. With their sense of fashion and their technical knowledge and the confidence with which they spoke, moved, danced, even breathed, the people crowding the Cary Grant Suite gave him great cause for lament.

It wasn't exactly grief, or mourning. Enough time had passed that those wounds had begun to heal. He'd even caught his eyes roaming appreciatively from time to time. The thought had occurred to him that he might, at some point, meet someone else whom he would like to have in his life. Someone else to love.

But he still missed her terribly. Still ached to tell her little things that he'd discovered in his research and wanted to share, only to realize that he had no one to share them with. No one who could truly appreciate what such utter trivialities meant to him. It still hurt.

With a sigh, Giles edged around several people who were talking loudly together about a "chat room" where they'd apparently spoken with Frank Herbert, the author of *Dune*. Giles didn't have the heart to tell them that Herbert had been dead for years, and was dismayed that they didn't realize it themselves. Dismayed, but not particularly surprised. After all, it all boiled down to Web sites and URL's, not frontispieces and back matter. A pity.

He opened one of the French doors and let himself out onto the stone balcony, where a large group of people had already gathered. The sharp wind brought the scent of smoke. Instantly, Giles understood the hardiness of his fellows. Most of them were smokers, exiled to the frozen outdoors by law and the demands of political correctness.

With a shiver, he turned up the collar of his suit coat, and shoved his hands deep in the pockets of his gabardine trousers. In his room, he had a very nice pair of leather gloves, which he wished he'd brought. Exhaling, seeing his breath curl as if he, too, had lit a cigarette, his eyes scanned the cityscape, the lights and the activity far below. Sixth Avenue was bright with the electricity of life, vivid with every bit of excitement and bluster and spectacle that humanity could muster. That was New York City to him.

"Breathtaking, isn't it?"

Her voice was soft, her tone thoughtful, with none of the razor edge of the city in it. Giles blinked, glanced just to his left, uncertain at first if the woman was speaking to him. But he couldn't see her in his peripheral vision. Giles turned, and for a moment, he couldn't breathe.

She was divine. A tall, yet lithe woman with the most delicate features imaginable. Her faced seemed to glow, and though it might have been the neon burning in the city beyond, Giles chose to deem it some ethereal light. In either case, it made her look almost angelic. A splash of her honey-blond hair fell in a gentle wave across her face, while the rest was done up in a long, elaborate braid that fell down past her shoulders. It was unfashionably long, but Giles thought it quite lovely.

She wore a crushed red velvet dress with tight sleeves that accentuated the golden color of her hair. It wasn't the most daring dress he had ever seen, but the way it fell across her body, few women could have worn it well. She wore it very, very well.

The Watcher realized that he was staring.

"I'm . . . I'm sorry," he stammered. "Did, uh, did you say something?"

The woman smiled at him, and Giles felt himself offering a silly, lopsided grin in return.

"You seemed to be appreciating the city," she said. "I merely commented that it was breathtaking."

American, he presumed, because of her lack of accent. But an American who used the word *merely* in casual conversation! Giles felt himself falling rapidly into infatuation.

"Indeed it is," he said, after what felt like an embarrassingly long pause. "For such a depraved city, it certainly has its charms."

The woman smiled broadly, and laughed softly, comfortably. There was a sort of gentle lilt to her laughter that gave it the ring of authenticity. She meant it.

"There is always a certain charm in depravity," she said boldly, grinning at Giles.

As his cheeks flushed crimson, she turned her gaze away from him and out toward the city he had been admiring moments ago. "It is a wonderful place," she said. "Though I suspect most of the tech-head numb-skulls slobbering all over each other in the other room have rarely if ever even looked out a window."

Giles chuckled, dropped his gaze, then brought his right hand up quickly to keep his glasses from plummeting twenty-seven stories. He gave her a sidelong glance, and thought, whimsically, *It could be love.*

"Rupert Giles," he said, turning to hold out his hand.

With a firm grip, she shook it. "Micaela Tomasi," she said. "It's very much my pleasure."

"You must be cold."

She raised her face and nodded. "I am."

He gave her his suit jacket, and felt warmer than he had since landing at JFK.

That was the beginning. For nearly an hour, they spoke of New York, its culture and museums, its depravity, and then of other cities they'd visited or yearned to visit. They talked of books and bookstores, and Giles was astonished to find that she was aware of some of his favorite used bookstores, some so out of the way he'd nearly forgotten about them himself. From Avenue Victor Hugo in Boston, to Cobwebs on Great Russell Road, across from the British Museum in London, Micaela knew them all.

The party ended, the other librarians leaving very reluctantly. The bartenders in their white shirts and black vests left their posts. A man came with a noisy industrial vacuum cleaner, whose hum could be heard through the closed balcony doors.

Still, Giles and Micaela talked on. There seemed to be so much to say. A few minutes before midnight, Giles looked regretfully at his watch.

"I hate to bring this up, but . . ."

"Yes," she immediately agreed. "It is getting late. Perhaps we could pick up our conversation at breakfast?"

The Watcher nearly laughed out loud. In his experience, there was nothing like avoiding the discomfort of asking a woman out by having her ask first.

"I can't think of anything I'd rather do," he said with great certainty. "Shall we say nine o'clock, in the lobby?"

"I'll be there, stomach rumbling," she replied.

They walked together out to the elevator. When they had stepped in, and he had pressed the number 16, she chuckled to herself.

"Hmm?" he asked. "Did I miss something?"

"We're on the same floor," she said. "I was just thinking what a lark it would have been if they'd double-booked me into your room."

Giles blinked, blushed once more, but his only reply was a slightly embarrassed smile. His mind, however, was racing with the possibilities. So much so, that when they stepped off on the sixteenth floor, and Micaela turned in the opposite direction, he felt a bit of disappointment.

"Good night, Miss Tomasi," Giles said. "Sleep well."

"And to you, Mr. Giles," she replied, almost primly. Then mischief crept into her eyes as she said, "Pleasant dreams."

As he walked down the hall toward his room, Giles whistled jauntily, his jaw muscles already somewhat sore from the smile that threatened to stretch his face for eternity. Somewhere, he heard a phone begin to ring. Around the corner, he heard a door open. He reached the juncture in the corridor, rounded the corner, and was nearly barreled over by a broad-shouldered man wearing a Yankees baseball cap.

" 'Scuse," the man grunted, but didn't look up; his face was obscured by the bill of the cap.

"Yes, well," Giles said, affronted. "Perhaps if you watched where you were walking . . ."

But his reproach was lost on the man, who had already hurried around the corner. Grumbling slightly, Giles turned back down the corridor. Only then did he notice that the phone was still ringing. The sound was coming from the open door of room 1622, just down the hall.

His room.

The phone stopped ringing as Giles rushed to the open door, eyes darting about with caution. He pushed the door fully open and flicked on the light. The place was a shambles. Many of his things were in tatters, the clothes thrown about the room, drawers open, mirror shattered. A thief, he realized immediately. Searching for valuables. And the phone ringing? A signal, perhaps, from a cohort, lying in wait to warn the burglar should the room's registered occupant return.

It had just happened. The phone, the sound of a door opening.

The man in the Yankees cap.

Giles ran from his room, sprinted along the corridor and around the corner. Down the hall, he saw the stairwell door swinging shut under the glowing red EXIT sign. The anger that began to build inside him was a distant memory, but all too familiar. There existed within Rupert Giles a man capable of great bouts of rage. It didn't matter if the thief had actually stolen anything, for Giles had little of value with him save for a few antique books.

No, it was the principle of the thing. The violation.

The anger boiled up inside him and his heart pounded as he reached the stairwell door. Giles gripped the knob, twisted it, and flung the door open hard enough to bang loudly against the cement wall inside. Instantly he started down the steps, holding lightly to the handrail as he moved his feet rapidly. At the next landing, he began to slow. He could no longer hear the running steps of the man he pursued. At the fifteenth floor he paused and listened carefully.

The door behind him sprang violently open, and Giles had only just begun to turn around when he felt a pair of powerful hands slam into his back. Flailing wildly, he fell forward and tumbled down the cement steps, striking his head several times.

He cried out.

But his cry was cut short as his head slammed into the landing, and he crumbled into unconsciousness.

"Rupert?" The voice was distant, and Giles drifted up out of the blackness inside his head for only a moment. He tried to focus on the face above him. The woman, the honey hair. He knew her, but her name escaped him.

"Honey," he whispered, looking again at her hair.

"I've called for help, Rupert," she said. "The ambulance is on its way."

Then he slipped into darkness again, retreating from the pain.

\* \* \* \* \*

Buffy didn't like being in the library without Giles. Never mind that they were on school property in the middle of the night without anyone's permission. When Giles was with them, such nocturnal visits might be suspicious, but they'd find a way to explain them. Buffy didn't want to think about having to explain how she'd come to have a key to the school. Still, her disquiet had little to do with the potential for discovery and consequences.

She'd been in trouble before.

No, her agitation had more to do with the hollow

feeling in her gut. The library was Giles's province. He was the Watcher, the holder of knowledge, the man with the books. Being here alone had Buffy reflecting on what things might be like without him. The thought didn't sit very well with her. She needed Giles: he was the backbone of everything the Slayer stood for. He was such a huge part of her life, not merely because he was her Watcher and her friend, but because as long as Giles was around, she could remind herself that no matter how lonely the life of the Chosen One would become, she was not completely alone. Not as long as she had Giles.

The place just didn't feel right without him there, presiding over the stacks, caring for his dusty leather volumes.

Seated at the study table with the green glass lamps, Buffy sighed and slammed shut a book entitled *Dragons and Fire Demons* which had given her exactly jack in her search for the identity of the bizarre creature they'd encountered earlier that night.

"We need Giles," she said, not for the first time.

Oz sat opposite her at the oak library table. He looked up from the book he had been skimming, raised his eyebrows, and nodded. "He's the man."

"Hey!" Willow balked.

She sat in the hard wooden chair that Giles had begrudgingly allowed to be placed in front of the small desk upon which the library's computer sat. The computer, which Giles had once called "that dread machine." But Willow was a hacker *par excellence.* At the moment, the dreaded hacker was glaring at them in consternation.

"I can be the man sometimes," she said, then

faltered. "If . . . I were a man. You know what I mean. Giles has way too much monster trivia stored in his brain, and we could sure use him right now. But I'm not too slouchy in the research department."

Buffy shook her head, a slight smile on her face.

"You're pretty amazing, Willow," Oz said. "There's plenty of times you've helped in ways Giles couldn't. But he *is* the Watcher, y'know?"

"She knows, Oz," Buffy said, then turned again to Willow. "Don't go all Xander on me, Will. You know you're a major asset to the team."

Willow grinned. "Yeah, I am, aren't I?"

"Even a greater asset if you could figure out who this fire-puking moron is," Buffy added with a sigh.

"Oh, is that all?" Willow asked innocently. "That's easy."

She slid her chair back to let them get a look at the computer screen, upon which there was a frighteningly accurate sketch of the creature they'd battled earlier.

Buffy's eyes widened. "That'd be him."

"According to legend he's called Springheel Jack," Willow explained. "First known sighting was in London in 1837. Apparently he mostly assaulted women. This sketch comes from the London *Times* of February 22, 1838. The assaults went on for years, kind of sporadically. In 1845, he attacked a prostitute in broad daylight, in front of witnesses."

"Not a very careful monster, is he?" Oz asked.

"Or he's just not afraid of getting caught," Buffy replied.

That gave them all pause for a moment. Then Willow went on.

"In 1877 almost an entire English village got a good look at him. There's a record of an appearance in Liverpool in 1904. Then he seems to have disappeared for almost fifty years. Next time he shows up is, believe it or not, in Houston, Texas. Let me check the date . . ." she turned back to the computer a moment. "Okay, June 18, 1953. Since then, not a peep."

Buffy was thoughtful a moment, and Willow and Oz were both watching her, waiting for her to decide their next move.

"Why Sunnydale?" she asked.

Willow shrugged. "It's the Hellmouth. Don't all the nasties get around to visiting eventually?"

"Big demon tourist spot," Oz agreed goodnaturedly.

"Yeah, but he hasn't popped up since 1953," Buffy argued. "I mean, why now?"

Their contemplation was interrupted by movement up in the stacks. They'd come in that way, through the back door, to avoid being seen coming through the school's front entrance. As they all looked up, Xander emerged from among the bookshelves.

"Hey," he said, too subdued by far for Buffy's tastes.

"Hey, Xand," she said.

"How's Cordelia?" Willow asked quickly.

Xander nodded slowly. "She's going to be okay. The docs want her overnight, just to make sure she isn't in shock or something. They couldn't quite get why she was so freaked over her hair. They must not have teenage daughters. Anyway, she's fine, really. It looked a lot worse than it was. And she's already set up an appointment with her hairdresser in the morning."

"That's a relief," Oz said.

Buffy glanced at him, wondering if he was being sarcastic about Cordelia's hairdresser appointment, or sincere about her medical condition. It was hard to tell with him sometimes, his wit was so dry.

As Xander came down one of the short stairwells into the reading area of the library, Buffy stood up and walked toward him. She stood awkwardly and looked at him.

"Listen, Xander, I'm sorry about tonight," she said. "I just . . . I've had a lot on my mind lately, and I guess I just don't want to lose you. Any of you."

Xander paused, not meeting her gaze for a moment. Finally, he looked at her, and Buffy knew from that look that he was still angry.

"I understand, Buffy," he said. "That doesn't mean I'm not pissed about it. One of the only reasons Giles doesn't get all wacked about us hanging with you is that you've always been real clear that we're not a liability. That we can hold our own.

"Looks like that was all just talk, huh?"

Buffy's eyes widened. "Not at all!" she protested. "I just . . . I can't believe I have to explain this to you."

"Explain it to yourself," Xander said angrily. "We're supposed to be a team, Buffy. Maybe we're not all the Slayer, but we all have a job to do. Why don't you just do yours, and let the rest of us take care of ourselves. We can do it, you know."

"Xander," Willow said tentatively, as Buffy stood speechless between them. "Buffy's saved our lives more times than I can count."

"I know that, Will!" Xander said, throwing his arms up in exasperation. "And only an idiot or a jerk wouldn't be grateful. I am. All I'm saying is, if we're a team, Buffy ought to start acting like a team player."

He stared at her, without malice, but with an anger that hurt her deeply. She knew Xander was her friend, knew he cared greatly for her. That only made it worse.

Buffy sighed. "I'll take it under advisement," she said, trying for levity but only succeeding in causing Xander to shake his head in surrender.

"If you guys are busy," said a voice from above, "I'll come back later."

They all turned to look up into the stacks, where Angel now stood, his duster torn, looking much the worse for wear.

"What happened to you?" Xander asked.

"Ran into Rocky the Flying Squirrel again," Angel explained. "He's fast, I'll tell you. There've been two more attacks. He seems to be working his way across town in a straight line. Shouldn't be too difficult to catch up with him."

Buffy exchanged a glance with Xander, who turned his eyes away from her for a moment. When he looked back, the anger in him had disappeared. He nodded to her, and she hoped that meant things were all right between them.

"What are we waiting for?" Buffy asked.

"Not for me," Willow said, and Buffy turned to look at her. "Sorry, Buffy, but I'm already going to get flak from my parents. I've got to go home."

Buffy glanced at Oz. "You guys can manage?" Oz asked.

"We'll find a way," Xander said, his sarcasm obvious.

Oz ignored him. Willow, however, gave him a nasty look, and then she and Oz left together.

"So," Xander said. "What's the plan?"

Buffy bit her lip. "Well," she said. "Seems like the only way to catch this guy is to sneak up on him."

"Sneaking," Xander agreed. "Excellent plan. And Dead Boy is ever so good at sneaking."

As they walked out the library's rear door together, Angel turned to Xander. "Don't call me that," he said menacingly.

"Dead Boy," Xander replied.

Robert Hanrahan slept peacefully aboard the fishing trawler *Lisa C.* Mort Pingree was at the helm, and so Hanrahan had allowed the gentle waters to lull him to sleep. The smell of the Pacific and the motion of the water were as much a part of his life as the land. More so, in fact. The ocean was truly the only place that Robert Hanrahan had ever felt at home.

At the helm, Mort Pingree was also feeling a bit sleepy. He'd been rocked to sleep when it was his watch before, and Hanrahan had never found out. Which was good, because if the boss ever found anyone willing to take Mort's job, he'd have been fired long ago.

Grumbling under his breath, Mort poured another cup of the disgusting black sludge that Hanrahan called coffee. In a little while, he'd wake the boss to take over until just before dawn, when they'd drop the nets and try to get first crack at the morning's pickings. For now, though, it was just Mort and the sea. He looked to the distant shore and saw a few lights still burning in Sunnydale. Mainly streetlights, he thought. Everybody with a decent job was fast asleep.

Mort Pingree hated being a fisherman. Hated the sea. The ocean, whatever. But it paid, and he wasn't exactly qualified to do much of anything else. What he hated most, actually, was the smell. It took days to get rid of entirely, and he didn't remember the last time he'd had several days off in a row.

"Damn fish," Mort grumbled, and sipped his coffee.

Then spilled it all over his chest as something bumped the *Lisa C.* Mort swore, but not too loudly. The coffee hadn't been hot since sundown, and he was more curious about what they might have run into. Setting the cup down and wiping his fingers across the stain on his shirt as if he actually had a napkin in his hand, Mort took a few steps starboard to peer over the side of the boat. The ocean was black, and he couldn't see anything.

"Mort?" he heard Hanrahan snarl from below, as the old fisherman stomped up to the deck. "What the hell've you done now? You trying to run us aground?"

"We're nowhere near shore, or anything else for that matter," Mort snapped at his boss. "Look for yourself!"

Which Hanrahan did. And Mort was right. He peered out into the darkness at nothing. Nothing out there at all.

Something slammed into the boat again, and it began to tilt, hard to starboard. Hanrahan lost his footing, slipped in fish guts Mort had never gotten around to cleaning up, and slid right off the deck of the *Lisa C.* and into the water.

Mort Pingree screamed as huge tentacles lined with razor-edged suckers whipped across the deck and the helm, gripping the trawler in a crushing embrace. One of the tentacles lashed across Mort's abdomen, the suckers tearing his belly open on impact.

By the time the *Lisa C.* was hauled beneath the waves, Mort Pingree was already dead.

Meloney Abrams kept telling herself it was only another year. Another year of waiting tables at The Fish Tank, suffering the gropes and the leers and the come-ons, and she'd have enough money to hit the road, go to L.A., maybe even go to community college or something. Whatever. Just out of here. Somewhere she could make a fresh start.

Sexy blues poured out the door behind her as Meloney stepped out of the bar. There were only a few customers left, so Dickie had let her take off a little early. Even paid her tonight so she wouldn't have to come in on her day off tomorrow to pick up her check. Maybe he wasn't all bad, she thought. Even if he did try to get her alone in the back room just about every time she worked.

What else should she expect, Meloney wondered. He was a guy, after all. In her experience, at least, they all had to *try*.

With a shake of her head, Meloney started walking toward the lot where she'd parked her tank, a 1982 red Ford Granada. She figured someone could come after her with a cruise missile and the car would come through just fine.

She never made it to the car.

A fluttering sound behind her drew Meloney's

attention, and she turned to see a man standing about twenty feet away. The strangest looking man she'd ever seen. His body and face were a sick-looking white, and his eyes looked like bullet wounds. Working at The Fish Tank, Meloney had seen a couple of bullet wounds in her life.

The sleazeball wore a cape.

"Back off, scumbag," she said bravely. "I don't need a stalker, okay?"

The sleazeball opened his mouth, gave a creepy laugh, and with the laugh, a bit of blue flame shot from his mouth.

Meloney screamed, and ran for her tank.

That fluttering came again, she glanced over her shoulder, and the creep was gone. She slowed her pace, uncertain now, and then the fluttering came again, and a thump as the creep—the thing, whatever it was—landed in front of her, blocking her path.

It was inhumanly fast. Its hands lashed out, one gripping her throat, the other, with claws like needles, slashing open her clothes.

It tore out her heart.

"No!" Buffy screamed, but she was too late to do anything except warn Springheel Jack.

As the thing turned toward her, Angel's powerful arms locked around the pasty-faced killer, and its sunken black eyes widened in surprise.

"You vicious, sadistic freak!" Buffy roared, and gave Springheel Jack the hardest backhand she could muster. The weird, oily white skin of its cheek split under the blow, black bone showing through and a bit of blue fire leaking out.

"You should try not to be so predictable in your

patterns," Xander told the thing, then released the trigger on Buffy's crossbow.

Springheel Jack tried to break Angel's grip, but the crossbow bolt slammed into its chest . . . and was deflected by the weird armor it wore.

"What the . . ." Xander began.

But the monster only smiled at them, pointed teeth showing, and opened its mouth to burn them.

Buffy hit it again, even harder, and several of the thing's teeth broke off. "Stop that!" she said, and then pulled out a stake. "Maybe this calls for a more close-up approach."

"Hurry, Buffy," Angel groaned. "Bastard's a lot stronger than he looks."

Buffy gripped Springheel Jack's face, forced its mouth away from her, and raised the stake, hoping the strength of the Slayer would be enough to pierce the thing's armor. Thinking maybe, if all else failed, she could just break its neck.

It crouched, pulling Angel down with it. Buffy lost her grip, and for a moment, her balance.

"Buffy, grab it!" Xander shouted behind her.

Springheel Jack shot upward with such speed and strength that all Buffy could do was stare in astonishment. Angel held on as tightly as he could and was carried up with the thing. It arced up and came down hard on the roof of The Fish Tank and out of sight.

"Angel!" Buffy cried in shock and horror.

On the roof, nothing moved.

"Oh, man," Xander whispered.

"Angel!" Buffy shouted again.

Then he was there, standing on the edge of the roof, staring down at them. Angel scratched his head, then dusted off his pants.

"He's gone," the vampire said grimly. "Just seemed to disappear."

Oz had parked his van half a block away and was walking Willow to her house when the perfectly cloudless sky split with thunder so loud both of them were forced to cover their ears. It roared through the air, almost as if someone were firing a hundred cannons just above their heads. Oz could feel it against his chest, pounding against him. It sounded as though the sky were collapsing in an avalanche.

"Whoa, Chicken Little," he said, as the echo of the incredible thunder rolled in waves across town.

"Yeah," Willow agreed. "The sky is falling."

## Chapter 2

*The Court of King Francis I of France*
*Fontainebleau, 1539*

SHE WAS THE WIFE OF HENRI, WHO WAS THE HEIR TO THE French throne, but to Richard Regnier, the alchemist, Catherine de' Medici would always be "the Little Florentine." Her court at Fontainebleau was entirely Italian, made up for the most part of fellow Florentines exiled from their native land by her kinsman, Cosimo. Her courtiers were her Medici cousins, Lorenzo, Roberto, Leone, and Piero. Her troubadour sang to her in Italian.

Catherine suffered and hated with the hot-blooded temperament of her nation. Regnier had never witnessed such torment. Such rage. That elemental nature in her both worried and mesmerized Regnier as he stood in her ornate private chapel, watching her. Catherine lay prostrate before a cedar statue of the Virgin, sobbing and pleading in her fine Italian brocades and jewels, her dark hair braided into a coronet that had come undone. He was an unwilling witness

41

to the shattering of what was left of this desperate woman's heart.

Desperate she was, indeed. Astrological charts had been ripped to shreds and strewn like rushes across the mosaic floor. A stinking pile of ashes smoldered on a small marble table to the left side of the statue of the Holy Mother—an animal sacrifice—a sorcerous act banned by the Church and outlawed by His Majesty the King. The air reeked of evil, treachery, and blasphemy. Sin blew through the chamber like an icy winter breeze. But Catherine de' Medici sensed none of this. She was a princess, not an alchemist, nor a sorcerer. She was an innocent.

All her life she had been a pawn. The daughter of the legendary Lorenzo de' Medici, she had been orphaned by both parents before the end of her first month of life. Then she'd been shut up in a convent before her eighth birthday, with no little girls to play with, no toys, no dolls.

Civil war erupted in Florence when Catherine was eleven, and her family's enemies sought to kill her or, at the least, ruin her chances for a princely marriage by destroying her reputation. In the dead of night she had been smuggled by her kinsmen to another nunnery, and then to Rome.

There, she had nurtured in her heart an innocent young love for a gallant named Giuliano. As soon as her handlers heard of it, they spirited her back to Florence until, when she turned fourteen, she was brought to France to marry the son of the king. It ought to have been a new beginning, free of the politics of Florence. Life as a princess. But after the wedding, portions of her agreed-upon dowry had been withheld from her new family. There being but minor political advantage to the match—and now, no financial gain to be had—it was on the lips of the French courtiers that she would be sent back to Florence with all the scorn due a penniless and ugly little orphan. Only through the kindness of her father-in-law, Francis I, had she been allowed to remain rather than being cast aside. The king announced that she was a submissive, sweet girl, one free of ambition and pride. Such a pleasant young lady could remain in his household.

But six years into the marriage, her husband, Henri, was madly in love with another woman, and Catherine had not produced a child.

Now, as the alchemist watched, circumstance ripped the veils of submission and sweetness from Catherine's face. And veils they were: she had never been that sort of girl. She had merely played a part in order to survive. For years. It astonished Regnier that one so young could possess such self-control.

As he felt for his wand, hidden within his generous sleeve of black velvet, Regnier's gaze returned to the pile of ashes. His heart beat angrily within his matching doublet. A rabbit had been used, perhaps, or some other small and helpless creature. The act was vile, bespeaking familiarity with the black arts. It shocked him that she would take part in it. Yet who would not turn from the divine if, when so sorely burdened, one was met with only silence from a God who never answered prayers.

Grimly, Regnier put his hand to the hilt of the rapier at his waist. He knew who had led the tragic lady in these forbidden devotionals. Who guided her along the treacherous path of the dark world, promising her what she wanted most in this world if she would favor him and raise him up. Who bled her of her reason and discretion and went so far as to urge her to have him, Regnier, murdered in his bed.

The sorcerer, Fulcanelli. He was a base, grasping man. He was cruel and heartless. But he was Florentine, and as the former advisor to Catherine's dead father, Fulcanelli held sway over her heart. He was, in a way, all that she had left of her lonely, frightened childhood. Her only link to the parents she had never known.

Poor, poor Catherine.

The princess's sobs rose into shrieks of agony, almost of madness, and Regnier hastily stepped forward from the shadows and put his hands on her shoulders. He had not been eager to betray his presence, for she would resent it. He had innocently entered the chapel to cleanse it of evil influences, as he did every night prior to Catherine's celebration of evensong. She was not aware that he did so because he never told her. He was her true friend, and he had sought always to protect the Little Florentine, because it was right to do so, and because he pitied her so. But as he was French, and distantly related to Henri's mistress, she had never trusted him.

*"Madame,"* he said in French, "please, I beg of you, calm yourself."

"Regnier," she rasped, clearly shocked and mortified, "what are you doing here? Get out! Get out or I will have your head!"

"Your Grace, I beg of you," he murmured softly, urging her to sit up. "The palace walls have ears. Your enemies lurk everywhere."

"My enemy is this body," she wailed miserably, punching herself in her abdomen with doubled fists.

"This barren, treacherous body." She wrenched away from him, fell to the marble floor, and surrendered once more to her misery.

Regnier persisted. "Let me call for your women. You need rest. You are much overwrought."

For a moment she was silent. Then her shoulders moved, and he realized she was laughing silently.

*"Much overwrought?* My husband seeks to put me aside because I have borne him no children. I shall be sent to another convent, or worse yet, made to serve her who takes my place like a slave. And you say I am much overwrought."

"You are yet his wife," he pointed out.

"And I am yet childless." Her voice dripped with bitterness and frustration. "Motherless, fatherless, and soon to be without a husband."

"No, it can be prevented," he said. "It must be."

"By you?" She laughed hollowly. "You're the king's lapdog. A mere alchemist and nothing more." She burst into fresh tears. "Though you have promised me a hundred times that you would help me, you have done nothing."

He was ashamed. He didn't know why his conjurations on her behalf had not succeeded. He had fasted, prayed to the gods of old, venerated the proper saints, performed more rituals than the pope had said masses. And still, this poor lady had no *petits enfants.* He suspected, though he had no proof, that Fulcanelli thwarted him. He also suspected, though he had no proof, that Fulcanelli himself was responsible for the princess's unhappy situation. In fact, it was his opinion that when Fulcanelli decided that the time was right, this lady would have no trouble conceiving.

"You don't even look like an alchemist," she added.

"You're a gallant, playing a role." She spoke with a challenge in her voice, as if begging him to dispute her opinion of him. It was true; he usually wore the clothes of a French nobleman among the other members of Francis's court. Only in private did he don the midnight-blue robe and pointed hat spangled with stars and comets that had been bequeathed to him.

"No, lady, I am a mage of some power," he assured her. "And I seek to serve you. And for now," he said, speaking aloud, "you must take heart. You must protect yourself from danger."

He reached into his other sleeve and pulled out a beautiful golden ball encrusted with gems. At a flick of his thumbnail, the ball popped open. Within, a piece of vellum was folded in the shape of a cross.

"This is a potent talisman," Regnier explained as he took out the paper cross, "which I have prepared especially for you. I have inscribed prayers in Latin, French, and Hebrew upon it. I beg of you to wear it always."

"Will it . . . ?" She cast down her gaze, unable to continue. Then she forced herself to speak. "Will it make me conceive?"

He was piteously sorry for her. "It will protect you from harm, and nothing more."

"But to be protected, I must be . . . I must fulfill my duty," she said slowly. "Surely God himself understands that." She raised tearstained eyes to him. "I am without hope, if I have no children."

"Did not God hear the cry of Rachel?" he asked gently. " 'Give me children, or else I die.' "

The tears began to flow once more. "Do you have any idea, *monsieur,* how many times my priest has recited that verse to me?"

He lowered his head. "I beg your pardon. I do not mean to patronize you."

She placed her hand on the crown of his head, much as one would give a benediction. It was a majestic gesture, which made him all the sadder for her. She had the makings of a fine queen; however, he was far from certain she would ever become one.

"It is kind of you to think of me at all," she replied in a shaky voice. "Though I must ask myself if you have been sent to smooth the way for my repudiation. Make me more compliant and obedient so that I'll withdraw without summoning my zealous kinsmen to my cause. You know we Italians are famed for our vendettas."

He was chagrined, and wondered if he had in some way revealed his less-than-favorable opinion of her exclusively Italian court.

"Not at all, dear lady." He hesitated. "Though I would caution you not to go up against the king of France. You know that your marriage is unpopular with the people."

"With whom is it popular?" she asked with scorn. "Answer me that, sir, and I'll go to my father-in-law and ask him to make you a duke."

It was on his lips to say, "It is popular with me," but that was untrue. He would say it as a reflex; he was a seasoned courtier, and such pronouncements flowed from his mouth with practiced ease. But she was too intelligent. She had spent too much of her life as an observer for him to be able to lie successfully to her.

"I know not," he replied.

"And now I know that perhaps you are a friend," she replied, studying him anew.

He touched his hand to his chest. "I desire to be so,

*madame.* At the very least, the life of my master, the king, would be easier if I could in some way help his daughter-in-law with her difficulties."

"There is that." She rose with difficulty, waving him away when he moved to help her. "No," she said. "I have two feet, and I must use them."

"My admiration for you grows." He was most sincere.

"Then you are the only man in France who admires me."

She sighed heavily. She was indeed, less than beautiful. Was this poor girl unfortunate in every area of her life? Her husband's mistress, Diane de Poitiers, was a goddess.

"Leave me now," she said regally. "I must compose myself. No one must know of my private agonies." She looked at him meaningfully. "For six years, I have been a dutiful, submissive wife. I have never raised my voice. I have never begged my husband to love me. I have caused no trouble."

"I shall cause you no trouble," he assured her. "In all ways, I shall endeavor to help you."

She extended her hand. He kissed the air above it, bowed, and left her.

For a moment Catherine stood silently in the growing gloom, gazing in the direction in which Regnier had taken his leave. Then she shivered, suddenly cold, and wrapped her arms around her shoulders. The room darkened, as does the forest when the sun retreats behind the tallest trees. She felt a twinge of fear and looked around herself, as if to determine the cause. She was shivering with cold.

"He is a weak fool, and he will do nothing to help you," said a voice behind the statue of the Virgin.

Clad in a black robe decorated with crimson half moons, the sleeves reaching down to the floor and slashed with scarlet, Giacomo Fulcanelli glided toward her. His beardless face was weathered yet curiously unlined and even striking, his features distinct and well-formed. He had a lush mouth and dark eyebrows that contrasted sharply with the white hair streaming over his shoulders. His eyes were a startling crystal blue. His left hand, which was withered, he held against his side. It had gone bad, he had once told her, because the left chamber of the heart is the side which contains magick, and his had been so filled that his veins had overflowed with power. She believed this entirely. She had seen the effects of his power firsthand.

In his right hand he carried a cylindrical shape draped with a black cloth. Something inside scrabbled frantically.

*"Maestro,"* Catherine breathed, curtsying. "I didn't realize you were in the room."

"I heard enough."

He crossed the room and set the covered cylinder down on a marble table that matched the one littered with ashes. She frowned at the hidden object, having no wish to repeat the sacrifice they had made an hour before. It had completely unnerved her and sent her reeling into the crying spell Regnier had witnessed.

"So," Fulcanelli continued, laying a caressing hand on the drape, "you seek to replace me."

"No, not at all." She blinked, startled by his accusation. "He came unbidden."

He sneered at her. "And you wept in his arms. Have you lost all faith in me?"

Catherine played nervously with the rings on her fingers. "Of course not, *maestro*. It is simply that *Signore* Regnier has offered his help. Should I not accept aid from whatever quarter I find it?" She hesitated. "A starving man would eat either a fig or a joint of meat, would he not?"

He closed his eyes and sighed heavily. "How little you understand, Catherine." He and he alone dared to speak to her with such familiarity. Even her husband referred to her as *Madame*.

He stretched his hands to either side, then brought them together as he spoke. "Magick is complex, and only a master sorcerer can properly use it. If you allow that ignorant courtier to interfere, he might well impede the progress of my efforts." Fulcanelli glared at her. "In fact, I sense that he may already have done so."

"What?" she asked in a tiny voice. "What do you mean?"

"A soul whispers near my ear." He cocked his head and touched his earlobe. " 'I desired to be born to this lady,' it is telling me. 'But my way has been prevented.' "

His eyes widened. "And now it departs, flying toward Heaven."

"No!" she cried, staring up at the ceiling. "No, call it back!"

"It is gone." He extended his arms toward her. "Poor child. It was a son."

She covered her eyes with her hands. Swiftly he drew her into his embrace and urged her head down on his chest. "Turn that man away. Better still, persuade your father-in-law to exile him from court. He is a menace to you."

She wept against his chest. He stroked her hair. It felt so wonderful to have someone to hold her, touch her, comfort her.

"Better yet, have him killed," Fulcanelli said. "It would be the best thing you could do. That is, if you truly want children. Do you, little princess?"

She gazed up at him with fresh tears. *"Si,* you know I do."

"Well, then." He smiled at her. He eased her away from his chest and put his arm over her shoulders. Together they walked toward the draped cylinder.

With a flourish, he unveiled the object. Within, a tiny kitten batted at the bars of the round cage.

"No," she protested, her blood running cold.

"Come now. Let's not falter now, shall we?" Fulcanelli smiled. "The streets of the town are filled with cats. But there is not one single royal child in the royal nursery." He began to open the cage. "Do I speak the truth?"

*"Si,"* she breathed, "you do."

He pulled the kitten out by the scruff of the neck. It was gray and scrawny. A stray, she tried to tell herself. Something that would starve on the streets.

Something that would have died soon anyway.

\* \* \* \* \*

When classes let out the following day, Buffy and her friends gathered in the library to discuss Springheel Jack. A small debate had arisen over whether Jack qualified as a demon or was some kind of non-demonic monster or ancient species. Xander suggested an alien origin, and the others largely ignored him. The way Buffy figured it, if you added aliens to the mix, things just got crazy from there. As if they weren't crazy enough as it was.

Yet, in spite of all the other things that ought to have been on her mind, Buffy was mainly concerned about Giles. She had been trying to call, and later to beep him, without any success. The last two calls, she'd keyed in the school's number, so he'd be able to figure out that they were in the library. At the very least, he ought to have phoned her back.

So when the phone did ring, at about four o'clock, Buffy leaped from her chair, ignoring the others, and dashed for it. After all, how many calls did the library get after school hours?

"Hello?" Buffy said into the phone.

"Buffy?"

"Giles. Listen, I thought we'd worked out the beeper thing. That's why I gave it to you. Where have you been all day? I've been trying to——"

"Buffy . . ." Giles's voice was very faint.

"Our connection sucks," she said, positioning the phone against her ear. "I can barely hear you. Look, I'm sorry to interrupt your wicked-crazy fun, which I'm sure you're having with all the other, um, wicked-crazy library people, but weird stuff is happening. Willow thinks the sky is falling, and . . ."

"Buffy," Giles said again.

Something in his tone stopped her. She looked at the others, who immediately went on the alert, and said, "What's wrong?"

"I'm in hospital," he said simply. "I was . . . I was pushed down some stairs."

"Oh, my God." Buffy sank slowly into a chair. Her entire body went numb. "Giles, are you all right?"

The others stared at her, the anxiety on their faces bordering on outright fear.

"I'm afraid I neglected to tuck and roll," he said slowly. "I've got . . . I have to stay here." He sighed. "I'm rather muzzy, I must admit. I have what is so charmingly referred to as a 'morphine drip' protruding from my forearm. Ugly little beast, but quite effective, actually."

Buffy cleared her throat. "Morphine? Oh, my God, Giles." She closed her eyes. "How bad?"

"I'm all right. A bit black and blue around the edges. A few ribs cracked. And a ghastly headache."

*Brain damage,* Buffy thought, bulleting ahead. An operation. He could die on the table. Oh, God . . .

"But enough of that. You had an emergency of some kind?" he asked her.

"What? Oh. It's not important. What do the doctors say about—"

"Tell Giles about Springheel Jack," Xander spoke up, a look of concern on his face.

"Uh-uh. No way," Buffy insisted, covering the phone for a second. "Giles? We're okay here. We'll figure it out. You just get better."

"But Buffy," Giles protested. "If you're in danger, I must help you figure out what—"

"We'll deal. If things get too hairy, we'll call you back, okay?"

Buffy interrogated Giles about his condition for several minutes longer before hanging up the phone. She didn't mention Springheel Jack. Not at all. Though she knew they would likely benefit greatly from his help, in view of his current condition she kept silent. He would be up in an instant and on his way home, and probably do himself more damage than the jerk who pushed him down the stairs. Buffy couldn't afford that. She needed her Watcher all in one piece.

"So what's the diagnosis?" Willow asked, her concern obvious.

"He's banged up pretty badly, but other than that, I'm not sure," Buffy said with a frown. "He fell asleep talking to me," she told them. Then she bit her lower lip. "But not before he told me that someone ransacked his hotel room."

They all looked at each other.

"I'm going to New York," Buffy announced.

Xander raised a hand. "Oh, Buffy? Springheel Jack? Major weird stuff? Sky falling?"

"Hospitals have security. Okay, not like prisons. But security." Oz shrugged.

"Something's going on around here," Xander added, with a little less conviction. "We need to figure out what it is."

"I thought *you* could take care of things like that on your own," she snapped at him. "What do you need me for?"

Xander blinked and lifted his chin. "You want to start?"

She nodded at Willow. "Take care of everybody."

Willow nodded back, confidently, then blinked and pointed at herself.

"Buffy—" Xander began.

She headed for the door.

Buffy's mom wasn't home from work yet. But the fact that Joyce wasn't home was both a relief and an inconvenience. Buffy needed money for a plane ticket, and she needed to gently explain why she was headed off to the big city during the school week. Joyce was getting used to Buffy's life as the Slayer, but in many ways the Chosen One was still her one and only little girl. And most mothers did not take kindly to notes that read, "Dear Mom, Gone to NYC to check on Giles. He's been hurt. Love, Buffy."

What else could she do? Giles was not just her Watcher. He was her friend.

But what exactly could she do for him in New York? Make sure no one else pushed him down a flight of stairs. Try to find out who broke into his room. Figure out if this was a Hellmouth kind of thing or a New York City kind of thing. After all, it was actually possible that Giles was just a random victim.

She called the airlines, and was put on hell hold. She sat there, rifling through the kitchen trying to find one of her mom's credit card receipts from which she could read off the number—not a very nice thing to do but she didn't have much choice. It would take forever for her to pay her mom back, but she'd just have to understand.

She waited and waited, growing angrier and angrier, and had just brought the phone over to the fridge to search for snacks when the house began to shake violently. A seasoned Southern Californian, Buffy's first thought was of an earthquake and she ran beneath the transom in the kitchen, grabbing onto either side of the jamb as she was thrown back and forth.

Thunder blasted through the air so loudly it made her dive to the floor and cover her ears and shut her eyes tight. It was as if a grenade had just exploded in the room. The floor rolled. A thin crack formed in one wall. Glass shattered. Her body thrummed with the noise, and Buffy felt like she was being pummeled in the chest and gut and back by it.

Then it was gone.

She lifted her head and opened her eyes.

Buffy hung up and looked around at the kitchen. The teakettle, normally on the back burner, had slid to the floor. Her mom's spice rack was knocked over. The smell of caraway seeds permeated the room.

She tidied up, feeling odd, almost as if she were a guest in her own home. The sense of not belonging had seemed to dog her lately—first at the Bronze, and now here—and she didn't like it.

Then she heard the splat of thick raindrops. Made sense with the thunder, she figured, if that was real thunder this time and not Hellmouth thunder.

Idly she glanced out the window.

Odd round shapes were tumbling from a sunny sky.

Shapes whose legs flailed spasmodically.

"Okay . . . ?" Buffy whispered, and opened the kitchen door.

It was toads. Dozens . . . no, hundreds of large green toads, plummeting toward the grass, and the sidewalk, and the blacktop.

She made a face, said, "Eew," and sighed.

Exactly how a Slayer was supposed to attack a rain of toads was beyond her. The key was to figure out what was causing it, and she was not at all sure they'd be able to do that without Giles.

Poor Giles.

# Chapter 3

Xander stood just inside the door to Mr. Frankel's office, shifting uncomfortably from foot to foot. The man was sifting through some files on a table by the window. Outside, the shadows had grown long. It was almost five-thirty, and it would be dark soon.

Finally, out of patience and wishing he were anywhere else, Xander cleared his throat. The guidance counselor turned abruptly, startled as though he expected trouble in his office. For a moment, Xander wondered if that was just because he was a guidance counselor, or because they lived on the Hellmouth, and who knew what might happen in this school after hours. The memory of Jenny Calendar's murder was still fresh after a year. And it didn't help that another guidance counselor, Mr. Platt, had been savagely murdered just a few offices down earlier in the school year.

"Ah, Xander, come in!" Mr. Frankel said, with

exaggerated hospitality, once he'd seen that no threat was forthcoming. "I'm happy to see you here on time. Happy to see you here at all, in fact."

With a shrug, Xander stepped into the office and dropped into the chair in front of Frankel's desk. The mousy little man had a furry caterpillar of a moustache, as if that could somehow make up for his rapidly receding hairline. Xander had never liked him, but he thought that might have been more because he was a guidance counselor than because of his horrible geekiness. After all, Xander knew from geeks. Or at least, he used to. Back when he cared what people thought about him. He'd since learned that there was more to the world than the opinions of the general public.

"I, uh, was really sick for a couple of weeks, Mr. Frankel," he said lamely.

"Yes, well that didn't seem to impact your attendance record, did it?" the man asked, eyeing Xander closely.

"My parents don't like it if I miss school, but they wanted me to come right home. Anyway, I don't know what the big deal is. I'm set, Mr. Frankel. I haven't robbed any banks or purchased any high-powered weaponry, so . . ." Xander began to stand up.

"Please, Xander, sit down." Frankel pointed to the chair. "You know, there are only two other students who haven't come to see me yet about their plans for after high school, and one of them is your friend Miss Summers."

"Good luck there," Xander murmured.

"I'm required to speak to all the students, Xander. It's my job. You put me off as long as possible, and then asked me to meet you at a time you thought would be too inconvenient for me. Well, it was. I usually have dinner at six o'clock. Instead, I'll be here. But I am here, and so are you, so let's talk. Why waste that time?"

"That was my question," Xander replied.

Mr. Frankel picked up a folder from his desk. Xander's school record, Xander deduced, from the fact that his name and the word *transcript* were on the tab. "You know," the guidance counselor said, eyebrows raised, "your grades really aren't as bad as you seem to think. And I see here that you were accepted at several of the schools to which you applied. Is it simply a matter of not having decided which school you'd like to attend?"

"I have a plan," Xander lied.

The man looked at Xander. "Would you care to share that plan with me, Xander?"

"No. Actually. Not at all."

He shrugged. "I can't force you, but you realize the kind of limits you place on your future prospects if you decide not to . . ."

Xander stood up. Frankel blinked.

"Look, Mr. Frankel, I appreciate your interest. You've done your job, okay? You got me in here, we talked about my future, and all is right with the world. You have no idea what my life is like, what I'm like, what my plans for the future are. That means you don't have enough to go on to even offer an opinion of what I ought to do with that future."

The counselor stared at him with his mouth open in a comical little *O*. He half-rose, sputtering an argument of some kind.

Xander walked out. Graduation was only a few months away, and he was going to graduate, that much was certain. For the moment, it was enough.

That's what he told himself anyway. But in his mind, he carried an image of Buffy, and the question, *What would happen to her?*

And to whatever "us" there was?

"Buffy, what is going on?"

Giles still sounded weak, but not nearly as disoriented. Obviously the docs had scaled back the painkillers. Buffy still felt bad for him, but she was glad that he would, at least, be aware enough to call for help if anyone tried to go after him again.

"It isn't important, Giles," she said, cradling the phone as she swallowed the last of the french fries that constituted her evening meal.

"As of yesterday, it was an emergency," he said stiffly. "If you don't tell me what's going on, I'm only going to become more agitated."

Buffy sighed. "I'm more worried about you right now than I am about Sunnydale," she said. "You still don't have any idea who pushed you, or why?"

"Not a clue," he confessed. "But what is—"

"I wish I could come out there, but I just can't. Not right now. Just do me a favor, and try not to get killed. It would be a major hassle to start breaking in a new Watcher now, y'know? Training you was hard enough," Buffy teased.

"Yes, of course," Giles said gruffly. "I'd hate to put a new Watcher through what I've been through with you."

Buffy winced. She had begun the teasing, hoping to

distract him but also warn him of potential danger. And she was glad that his intermittent sense of humor had returned. But his comment cut through her own levity, brought her to a place of pain and sadness. They'd all been through a lot, but Giles had suffered so much, from the grisly murder of Jenny Calendar to his own torture at Angel's hands.

Deep in Buffy's heart, there was a part of her that felt the blame for all of that. And in that same dark place, she wondered if Giles blamed her as well. His words spoke to that part of her, and though Buffy knew it was useless to contemplate, the mere idea hurt her.

Giles must have sensed her discomfort. "That was a joke, Buffy," he said, his voice haggard. "Now, please, what's going on?"

Buffy sighed. "Weird stuff keeps happening. Willow calls it 'strange physical phenomena.' Apparently it's nothing new. It's all happened before, scientists don't know how to explain it, yadda yadda yadda."

"What sort of 'stuff'?"

"There've been reports of balls of fire, rain of toads—that was fun—let's see, supposedly this major thunder is called skyquakes, which sounds like breakfast cereal."

Buffy hadn't mentioned Springheel Jack. And she had no intention of doing so. A guy like him was a threat and a danger, and that was sure to worry Giles. She needed her Watcher back, sure, but she needed him back in action, not back in traction.

"Bizarre that these things should all begin to happen at once," Giles mused. "Taken one at a time, they would be odd occurrences, but nothing we couldn't chalk up to the sort of magnetic pull that the Hell-mouth has on all things out of the ordinary or unnatural."

"But Willow says this things *are* natural, or at least, some people think they are," Buffy argued.

"Well, it is true that no one has proven them to be of the supernatural, so science may simply have not had any opportunity to study them yet. Are you certain there isn't anything else? You seem quite preoccupied."

"I'm not the one in the hospital. When are they going to let you out?" Buffy asked. "Not that I'm rushing you. The important thing for you is to rest and get better, and try to keep your eyes open for the mad down-the-stair-pusher in case he tries again."

"I think it's likely to be several days, Buffy," Giles said. "I'll let you know when I've spoken to my doctors again."

They said their good-byes and Buffy hung up the phone. Her mind was awhirl with the chaos of the past few days, and she knew there was only one way to settle it down. The dreaded *R* word: research. She was supposed to rendezvous with the others at the library just after dark.

With her concern for Giles battling with the weird-nesses of the Hellmouth for her attention, Buffy picked up her black bag and went to the drawer where she kept some of her supplies. The way things had been lately, who knew what they might come up against. Besides, a smart Slayer was always prepared for anything. She shoved holy water, a pair of stakes, and spiked brass knuckles into the bag along with two notebooks, her history textbook, and a handful of pens, most of which she was certain would not work.

That done, Buffy pulled her hair back and slipped a scrunchie onto her ponytail. Again, because she had no idea what to expect, she had decided to put on the workout clothes she often wore when sparring with Giles. Sneakers, navy sweats, and a baby-blue tank top, with a light sweatshirt to cover it all.

She snapped off the light as she left the room, and was halfway down the stairs before she heard her mother's voice coming from the kitchen. And not just her voice, the sound of her laughter.

"Oh, Merrilee, it's so nice to hear your voice!" Joyce Summers said happily.

Buffy smiled. Her mother was talking to Merrilee Moody, an old college friend who still lived in L.A. She was glad her mom kept in touch with Merrilee, whom Buffy had always liked.

"Yeah, freshman year was a blast," Buffy's mom said, that tone of happiness still in her voice. "What was that guy's name, who used to walk around in nothing but a hat? Right, Moondog! You used to egg him on constantly! Don't lie to me, Merri, I was there!"

At the bottom of the steps, Buffy turned to go into the kitchen, but what her mother said next, and the tone of her voice, stopped her short.

"Oh, I'm so glad Janet's daughter is going to USC. Where are they going to get the money? A scholarship? Oh, that's so nice. She's an incredible girl." There was a pause. "No, I don't know what Buffy's going to do."

Joyce Summers's voice had gone cold.

"Well, you know, she's a big girl. I guess she's got to make those decisions for herself."

Distant.

"You know what? It's her life, really. I try to set an example, give her the best advice I can, but after that . . ."

Buffy walked into the kitchen. Immediately her mother perked up, smiled at her. "Hi, honey. It's Merrilee. Do you want to say 'hi'?"

"No time," Buffy said pleasantly, doing her best to cover the sadness that had come over her while listening to her mother's conversation. "Gotta jet, meet Willow at the library."

With a raised eyebrow, Joyce scanned her daughter's clothes, then covered the phone's mouthpiece with one hand.

"Is that really where you're going?" she asked. "We agreed you'd be honest about things."

"Library," Buffy nodded, then raised her fingers to slash an *X* in the air above her chest. "Cross my heart."

Joyce smiled. "Have fun," she said.

As Buffy walked out the front door, she was barely able to make out her mother's next words to Merrilee.

"She's going to the library," Joyce Summers said, her voice a bit warmer. "That's got to be a good sign." And then her mother laughed, but it sounded almost like a sob.

Buffy sighed. Mom had been in denial ever since Buffy had told her the truth. She just couldn't ever truly accept the idea that Buffy was born to be the Slayer, that it wasn't some crazy whim, and that as much of a burden as it placed on her day-to-day life and her future, she couldn't change herself. It was what she was.

Destiny. What a bitch.

* * *

Sunnydale High was a spooky place at night. Like any other building that was usually bustling with life, with people, there was something eerie and haunting about it after dark, when all that life was gone. Lights still burned in some of the classrooms and offices, but only enough to cast shadows inside and to throw a menacing glow from the windows, like the flickering flame inside a grinning jack-o'-lantern.

Xander had been in the school after dark dozens of times. Maybe hundreds now. But he'd rarely been there alone.

He was glad he didn't have a key. Not that it was all that fun to be standing in the dark behind the school waiting for Buffy to show with *her* key—and in fact it was probably more dangerous. But Xander didn't see the relative safety of the school as all that much of a comfort. Besides, the inside of the school hadn't always turned out to be a safe haven in past crises.

"Any time now," Xander said to the darkness around him.

"Getting a little jumpy?" the darkness replied.

"Yaaa!" Xander shouted, and stumbled backward a few steps as Angel emerged from the shadows, a mischievous smile on his face.

"Sorry, did I startle you?" Angel asked.

Xander looked at the vampire, angry and embarrassed. "Don't *do* that!" he snapped.

"Where's Buffy?"

"Do you see her?" Xander gestured around them. "No."

"Then she's not here, is she?"

Angel glared at Xander, but Xander wasn't intimidated. He'd gotten over his fear of Angel once he'd accepted the fact that Dead Boy was really back on their side. Granted, it was like having a pit bull around who might turn rabid at any time, but for the moment, he was their pit bull.

"We've got trouble," Angel said at length.

"How new."

"You know where Dorado Road passes over Route 17?" Angel asked.

"Yeah. I've seen some homeless people dragging shopping carts down under the bridge there," Xander said, remembering.

"Not anymore," Angel said darkly. "I heard on the radio that some of them have relocated and others disappeared. The ones who weren't fast enough probably got eaten. The ones who got away claim there's a monster under there. And earlier tonight, a guy riding his bike over the bridge was grabbed and dragged under."

Xander made a face. "Eaten?"

"Where's Buffy?" Angel asked, exasperated.

"What?" Xander threw up his hands. "A guy can't express a little disgust when a fellow human being gets chomped on by some beastie?"

"It's probably a troll," Angel explained. "They live under bridges."

"Whatever!" Xander rolled his eyes. "Let's go," he said, and began walking away.

"What about Buffy?" Angel asked, surprised.

"She's got a whole town to worry about." Xander turned and looked at him. "There's a lot more going on here than one grubby little troll. Can we handle this thing, or can't we?"

Angel considered that for a moment. "I guess if you had a weapon."

But Xander was already moving away. After a moment, Angel caught up.

It had taken them more than half an hour to walk all the way to Dorado Road—including a few minutes to stop by Xander's house and pick up his Louisville Slugger. When they arrived, they found the street deserted. The police had put up a detour after the attack earlier in the day.

"I'm surprised they aren't down there with flashlights and shotguns right now," Xander observed.

Angel looked at him oddly. "The Sunnydale police? If we're lucky, they'll go down in the morning, and they'll still get their heads bitten off."

Xander glanced at the baseball bat in his hands and sighed. "And they have guns. Great. Shall we?" He moved to the side of Dorado Road and was throwing one leg over the barrier there, prepared to slip down under the bridge that crossed over Route 17. Cars and trucks rumbled by far below, their headlights cutting the dark.

Angel grabbed his shoulder, stopped him from going down.

"You want to walk into his lair, in the dark, under the bridge, without so much as a flashlight?" Angel asked.

Xander blinked. "No?"

"No," Angel replied.

"So?"

"Taunt him. Draw him out," Angel explained.

"You mean tease him. Like insult his mother or something?"

Angel shook his head in disgust. "Something like

that," he said. "You stay over here, I'll start on the other side." He walked across Dorado Road and stood at the barrier, cupped his hands to his mouth, and shouted, "I'm crossing your bridge, you ugly bastard!"

Xander looked over the edge on his side, at the ground where it fell away and sloped down toward Route 17. Where the ground dropped past the underside of the bridge, there was only darkness. He didn't even hear anything moving, and wondered if Angel even knew what he was talking about. It wasn't as though he'd actually seen a troll. Could be a garden-variety serial killer as far as he knew. Or just drunken fools tumbling down the incline and into traffic. Could be . . .

"Ah, what the hell," Xander muttered to himself. Then he raised his voice. "Hey, you skanky, stinky, ugly little . . . troll! Trip-trap, trip-trap, here I come over your bridge. Billy goat gruff is here, pally!"

He waited, watching the shadows beneath the bridge. Still nothing moved. After a long pause, he turned to look at Angel, who was still staring down on his side of the bridge.

"Dead Boy!" Xander called. "Are you sure about this thing? I mean, if you wanted to spend some quality time with me, I would've penciled you in, y'know?"

Angel narrowed his eyes. "I've told you not to call me that."

With a deafening, furious roar, the troll leaped up from behind the barrier and landed on Angel. The vampire rolled, getting out from under the thing, and then they were up, alternately throttling and pummeling each other.

68

The troll was, as predicted, quite grubby indeed. Ugly. Skanky. Stinky. It wore the most ragged clothing Xander had ever seen, and where he could see its skin, it had a leathery hide, with disgusting matted fur in places and horns in others. Definitely grubby. It was not, however, and much to Xander's chagrin, little. Not little at all.

"Xander!" Angel shouted, even as he slammed a fist into the troll's face so hard that Xander thought he heard something crack. The troll roared in pain and anger, and brought both fists down hard on Angel's shoulders, driving the vampire to the pavement. It raised one huge hairy foot and tried to stamp on Angel's head. Once again, Angel was too fast.

"How 'bout a little distraction, Xander?" Angel asked, in full vampire face now.

Xander didn't respond. He felt his hands sweating on the grip of the bat where he'd wrapped sports tape at the age of nine. Angel and the troll kept hitting one another, and it was getting ugly. Angel's cheek was split and bloody, though probably already starting to heal. The troll was bleeding from its mouth, and Angel had snapped a kick to its gut that knocked the wind out of the thing for an instant. Angel tried to take advantage of the moment, but powerful swipes from the troll's hands kept him back.

The fight moved along Dorado Road, onto the overpass, and Xander kept following, waiting for an opening. The blows became more and more vicious, until Angel was forced to retreat momentarily, farther along the overpass.

"What the hell are you waiting for?" Angel snarled at him, yellow eyes glowing in the dark.

The troll lunged at the vampire, and Angel grabbed

it by the matted fur on its head and brought his knee up hard into its jaw. The troll stood up straight, howling in pain and frustration.

"This!" Xander said.

With the bat raised at his shoulder, his legs spread apart just like he'd always been taught, Xander stepped into the swing like he was going to smash one right out of the park. The bat whipped through the air and connected with the troll's skull with a satisfying crunch. Blood sprayed from its thick, misshapen nose, and the Louisville Slugger snapped into two jagged pieces.

The troll, rocked by the impact, stumbled backward, clutching its face and nose. It hit the barrier over Route 17, and then tumbled right over the edge.

"And that one's outta here," Xander muttered as he and Angel went to the barrier and watched the troll fall end over end until it slammed onto the pavement of Route 17, where it lay, limbs at odd angles.

"Take your sweet time, why don't you?" Angel said angrily.

Xander didn't look up. He was staring at the dead troll. "You arguing the results?" he asked.

"So that was your plan all along?" Angel asked. "Use me as bait until you can get your shot in?"

"As far as you know," Xander replied, straight-faced.

When he looked up, Angel was staring at him, eyebrows drawn together in anger. Xander couldn't help it, he started to laugh. Just a chuckle at first, then a full-on giggle fit. Angel started to say something, but then the grim set of his mouth turned into a slight smile. As it did, his face changed, metamorphosing from vampire to human. Or as close to human as Angel would ever get.

Xander stopped laughing. "Man," he said. "Do you have any idea how creepy that is?"

But Angel wasn't listening. He had looked over the edge of the bridge again and his eyebrows were raised in surprise.

"What?" Xander asked, concerned.

"He's getting up," Angel replied.

Sure enough, when Xander looked down, the troll was pulling itself to its feet. Unsteadily, it glanced up, glaring at them from one hundred and fifty feet below. It opened its mouth and began to roar . . . and the roar was cut off as the troll was silhouetted in the oncoming lights of an enormous tractor-trailer.

Xander and Angel both turned away, wincing, but Xander didn't think to cover his ears. The truck's air horn bellowed as it passed beneath them, and the wet crunch as it collided with the troll, pulping the monster against its grillwork, was audible all the way up on the Dorado Road bridge.

In his mind, Xander could almost hear Cordelia say, "Eeee-uw!"

When they glanced back down for the final time, there was nothing left of the troll but a bit of blood. Farther up Route 17, the truck was beginning to pull off to the side. Xander didn't envy the guy who'd have to clean off the front of that grill.

He picked up the pieces of the broken bat and examined them carefully. After a minute, he let them fall with a clatter to the pavement.

"Damn," he said softly.

"What is it?" Angel asked.

"Just another piece of my childhood shot to hell," Xander said lightly. "I guess some day I'll look back nostalgically on the slaughter of demons and bloodsuckers and stinky trolls, but somehow, I thought riding bikes and camping out in the backyard and playing ball with Dad were supposed to be the things that stay with you."

For a long while, as they walked back toward the school, neither of them said anything. About halfway there, Angel broke the silence.

"Nice swing," the vampire said.

"All in the follow-through," Xander explained.

"Just can't summon up that Willow magick tonight, huh?" Buffy asked.

Willow shrugged and stared at the computer screen. "My wand's all magicked out, I guess."

Oz raised his eyebrows in sympathy. "Sucks, huh?"

"Okay," Cordelia said, her voice quaking. "You guys have been avoiding this subject long enough. How does my hair look? Really?"

Buffy studied her face, looked at her hair, which, now that she'd had it cut and styled, really didn't look at all bad. It was shorter than usual by several inches, but it would grow back quickly. She thought about teasing Cordelia, patronizing her, but realized that the girl's hair was sacred territory.

"It looks fine, Cordy, really," Buffy said sincerely. "It's a good look for you. More mature."

Cordelia only stared at her, near tears, and tried to see her reflection once again in the glass set into Giles's office door. "Oh, you're just saying that to be nice. It's horrible, isn't it?"

"Just saying that to be nice?" Willow asked. "Buffy?

To you?" She blinked, reconsidered her words. "Um, what I mean is . . ."

But Cordelia wasn't listening.

"Let's move on, shall we?" Buffy asked. "We've found references to most of the weird things that have happened, but nothing to link them in any way."

"We might have more luck if you told Giles about Springheel Jack," Willow pointed out.

"Not until I have to," Buffy said.

"I'm thinking 'have to' is just around the corner from 'we got nothin',' what about you guys?" Oz asked, his face expressionless.

"Well, there's nothing we can do tonight," Buffy said, a shade of surrender in her voice. She massaged the back of her neck. "We're not getting anywhere. I vote we just bag it for tonight, and I'll go out and do some patrolling."

"With all the stuff that's going on, you shouldn't go alone," Willow noted. "We'll all go, but maybe we should wait for Angel and Xander."

"Wait no more, fair maidens," Xander announced from the upper level, where he and Angel stood, having come through the back door. "Or, should I say, fair maidens and lycanthrope-in-need-of-a-shave."

Oz ran a hand along his stubbly chin. "Out of blades," he said.

"Whee, doggies. You must go through 'em like a hog through flapjacks," Xander replied happily, as he and Angel walked down into the reading area where the others were gathered.

They all stared at him.

"He watched that *Beverly Hillbillies* marathon on Nick at Nite," Willow explained.

"God help us all," Buffy said dryly.

Cordelia rushed toward Xander, sobbing something about her hair, and he took several quiet moments in a corner to gamely attempt to reassure her that she didn't look like a troll.

"Trust me," he said. "I know."

Buffy looked at Angel, who nodded. "That's where we've been," he explained. "A troll was preying on people from under the Dorado Road bridge."

"But you killed it, right?" Buffy asked.

Angel was quiet for a moment, eyes downcast. "Actually," he said slowly, "Xander killed it."

"With my spear and magic helmet!" Xander cried, in his best Elmer Fudd.

Buffy raised a hand. "Okay, conquering hero, just deflate a second. We were just trying to figure out what to do now. I vote for patrol, since research isn't going anywhere. This troll thing only proves Willow's right. There's way too much for me to handle alone. I guess we should split up."

"I'll stick with Angel Eyes over here," Xander said, patting Angel on the back. "We make a good team."

Even as Cordelia moved to stand with Xander, Buffy blinked in surprise. Xander hated Angel, but he'd rather hang around with him than with her. It was a brutal revelation. *Obviously,* she thought, *whatever issues Xander and I have aren't completely resolved yet.*

She let her hands fall with a slap to her thighs, then glanced at Oz and Willow. "Okay," she said, "guess you guys are with me."

After the insanity of the previous few days, the rest of the night was surprisingly uneventful. Buffy came in fairly early, for her; her mom nodded pleasantly and told her she'd made some enchiladas for dinner; and Buffy had actually gotten to watch a little TV.

Later, as she climbed into bed, she felt unnerved by the lack of activity. It ought to have comforted her. Instead, it only left her with an ominous sense of foreboding.

*What's next?* she wondered as she drifted off to sleep.

Fifteen miles south, at a beautiful public beach, the remains of Mort Pingree and the *Lisa C.* washed up on shore.

# Chapter 4

A DEPRESSING FACET OF THE LIFE OF A WATCHER appeared to be that one spent quite a lot of time in the hospital, either as a visitor or as a patient. Even more depressing was the fact that one hospital significantly resembled another, whether it was the institution in London containing the bones of the Elephant Man or St. Bartholomew's in Manhattan, where Giles now lay in room 327. They shared a number of common factors: shiny beige floors, dull, pastel walls, gray metal beds, and remote-controlled access to two or three truly frightful channels of daytime television.

It appeared that programs about people unwittingly marrying cousins or receiving makeovers which, frankly, made them look rather identical to one another, constituted the bulk of the average television addict's mid-morning fix. If these were the sorts of things Xander's mother watched, then Giles was truly sorry for the boy.

A book, a book, his kingdom for a book.

In the next bed, separated by a curtain that divided the room into two lengthwise halves, his roommate, recuperating from some intensive surgery of an undisclosed nature, stirred and moaned in his sleep. The man had done little else since he'd been brought in.

With a heavy sigh, Giles flicked the remote, then paused, interest piqued by the announcement of a news break. Various fires, car accidents . . . hmm, at noon an interview with a man who claimed he had drowned on the *Lusitania* and had no idea why he was now in New York City. That might be worth a look.

"Rupert?" queried a soft voice at the doorway.

He turned his head.

Framed in the doorway, Micaela Tomasi was a vision in a filmy crimson and black dress that tapered to calf length, her blond hair loose around her shoulders, wild and lovely.

She hovered on the threshold. "Am I disturbing you?"

"Not in the least." He couldn't stop himself from a quick comb-through of his hair with his fingers. And the inevitable readjustment of his glasses on the bridge of his nose. Until Buffy and the others had taken to teasing him relentlessly about the habit, he'd not realized that he did it so often. Now he was acutely aware of all his actions as Micaela entered, carrying a bouquet of red carnations.

"Oh, how lovely," he said, smiling at her.

"Thank you." She preened a little, even though they were both pretending he was talking about the flowers. "The nurse is looking for a vase. And here's something else." She opened a black bag rather like Buffy's Slayer satchel and pulled out a book.

"I'm afraid it's nothing fancy," she said.

He took it from her. It was an omnibus of Sherlock Holmes mysteries. "Thank you so much." He flipped through it. "It's been ages since I read Holmes. How thoughtful."

He clicked off the television as she pulled a chair up to his bedside. She was wearing a deliciously spicy perfume. "And how goes the conference? If I recall the schedule correctly, you're missing the keynote speech by someone from the Smithsonian."

"How are you?" she asked, ignoring his question. "Do they have any leads yet?"

"Leads," he said tentatively. He had not told her he'd been pushed, had he? Only that he had fallen. He wasn't sure. He might have said anything while he'd been semiconscious. Including telling her she was incredibly beautiful. "Well, not as yet."

Micaela sighed. She fanned her fingers and looked down at them, then folded them in her lap and leaned slightly forward. "We're not alone," she said quietly, as if guessing the cause of his reticence.

"My roommate is asleep," he assured her. Cocking one ear, he waited for a moan and nodded when it was made. "You see? Quite unconscious."

She took a breath. "I need to talk to you."

He looked at her oddly, then raised his eyebrows, imploring her silently to continue.

"Rupert, I'm from the Council," she said, as if in confession. "I was sent here to warn you."

For an instant, his disappointment was palpable. Then a slight embarrassment took its place—she had encouraged their flirtation, even begun it—followed by anger. Jenny, too, had not been exactly what she had seemed. Fellow teacher, beautiful techno-pagan, yes. But also a Gypsy assigned to spy on Angel, to make sure he continued to suffer for the crimes he had wrought against her people.

"To warn me about what?" he asked with asperity.

"Please," she said. She put her hand over his. "Don't be angry with me for not telling you right away. You see . . ." She shrugged and smiled faintly. "The Council are so stodgy and peculiar that, well, I never expected to be so immediately . . . taken with you."

Giles sniffed angrily, looked away. "You have a gift for fiction, apparently," he huffed.

"No. I mean it. Think about it, Rupert. I work for the Watchers' Council. I'm a Watcher myself. In training," she added, with a tinge of humility. "I don't exactly have a lot of chances to . . . talk with interesting men on the balconies of swank hotels in cities like this one. I was . . . I just wanted to be a girl for a little while before we got down to business."

"And the nature of that business is?" he prodded, although the wind had been blown out of his sails. He wanted to believe her. Her smile was so frank and so appealing. He, too, had enjoyed being a . . . boy for a little while.

"The nature of that business is . . ." she said, looking sad and growing distant, as if their moment were over before it had actually begun. "Watchers are being murdered. Sought out and attacked. We don't think it's random."

"Good Lord. Who's died?" he asked quickly.

She made a face. "People you know and care about. Marie LaMontagne. Julian Spring."

"Dear God." He shook his head, mourning the passing of his colleagues—good, decent people. In their younger days, Julian and he had gone pub-crawling a few times. Marie had the best memory of any Watcher he'd ever known; she'd been able to dredge up obscure facts from the history of Slayers and the Watchers' Council on a moment's notice.

"As you're the Watcher of the current Slayer, we believe you're a prime target."

He took that in. "I was pushed down a flight of stairs."

She nodded. "Who knows what more might have happened if I hadn't heard the commotion?"

"It was a lucky thing indeed that you were staying on the same floor," he said, then caught himself. Luck obviously had nothing to do with it. The expression on her face confirmed that thought.

A middle-aged woman in a set of brightly colored scrubs bustled in, and Micaela immediately rose and faced her. As the Slayer's Watcher, Giles knew a fighting stance when he saw one, though the nurse didn't notice at all.

"I had to hunt around," the nurse said, smiling pleasantly. Her accent was pure Brooklyn. "We got a celebrity on the ward. Do you know who T-Minus-Ice is? He came in last night with multiple gunshot wounds. There are so many flowers for him. We're taking loads down to the fourth floor. That's oncology." She took the flowers from Micaela and plopped them unceremoniously in the vase. "Terminal cases."

"How thoughtful," Giles drawled, eyeing the lop-sided arrangement in the green glass container.

"I'm not supposed to tell you about Mr. Ice," the

nurse said conspiratorially. "But you didn't seem like the type to go autograph-hunting, you being British and all, so I figured it would be all right."

He smiled politely, beginning to feel a bit ragged around the edges. He was tiring. He felt sore around his rib cage and more than a little concerned about Buffy's recent secretiveness. The doctors were taking their time releasing him, and Giles had nearly reached the point of simply getting up and leaving.

"Indeed," he replied, and the nurse smiled in return.

She brushed past Micaela and squinted at his IV bag. "How's the pain? Need a shot?" She made as if to push him on his side. Since the removal of the morphine drip, he had been receiving his painkillers in a most undignified portion of his anatomy.

"No, thank you, Sister," he said, then corrected himself, "I mean, Nurse." In Britain, nurses were called "Sister," as if they were nuns.

From the other bed came another moan. The woman shifted her attention to him and said to Giles, "Just push the call button if you need anything, honey."

"Thank you. I shall."

She bustled behind the curtain. "So, Mr. Russo, how are we?" she asked.

There was no sound.

"He's still out," the nurse announced. "Lucky for you. When he wakes up, he's gonna be a real pain in the a— . . . a real pain."

She emerged from the curtain, pulled it back into place, and breezed out of the room.

After a beat, Micaela said, "I'll be acting as security

for you. Can you think of what they might have been trying to find among your belongings? Any special objects?"

He thought a moment. "I purchased two books yesterday, older texts."

"Could you tell me the titles?" she inquired, sounding very official, almost detached.

*"Cursed Objects.* The Covey edition. I've been looking for it a long time," he allowed. "Also, a volume on haunted places in New York. Probably not too useful, a bit too Hans Holzer, if you know what I mean."

"For general consumption," she filled in.

"Yes, but one never knows when one will find a gem."

She smiled at him. "I couldn't have said it better myself."

He smiled back. "But neither was taken."

"Well, that's good. It would be terrible to lose the Covey." She checked her watch. "I need to get back. I'm expecting a fax from the Council and I need to see what the police report has to say."

She crossed to the bouquet of flowers and fluffed them in the vase, repositioning one of the stems, then stepped back to appraise her efforts. "I'll be back in a couple of hours."

"I'll look forward to that," he said sincerely, holding the book against his chest.

"Me, too." She cocked her head. "You know, there's no other way you and I would ever have met," she told him, gazing at him with that mischievous boldness he had found so charming. "As upsetting as the circumstances are, I'm certainly glad I've met you. You are something of a celebrity yourself, after all."

She laughed a most delightful, soft laugh. "Maybe I should ask you for your autograph."

He chuckled softly in return.

"Or for a date, when this blows over." She leaned forward and brushed his lips with hers. "After all, we haven't had our breakfast."

"Nor our pleasant dreams," he countered. His mouth tingled.

"Speak for yourself." She grinned broadly at him and straightened. "I'll be back soon. Be careful."

"I shall. You, as well. After all, you're a Watcher."

"Yes, I am."

She regarded him fondly. Then she left the room, a gentle memory of her perfume lingering behind her.

Giles smiled a moment.

Then he put the book on the nightstand, picked up the phone, and said into the mouthpiece, "I need an outside line. Long distance."

Giles phoned Council headquarters in London and was slightly irked to find that none of the actual Council members was available to speak with him. Instead, he found himself having a somber conversation with a man named Ian Williams, apparently some kind of assistant, who had only recently been assigned to the main branch.

He did not know if the Council, or this Williams, would inform Micaela that he had called to verify her story. If she truly had his best interests at heart, she would not care. Still, he wished he could have trusted her more fully to begin with.

However, Williams informed him that yes, she was there as security for him. And yes, Watchers he knew and cared about had been murdered.

And yes, they considered him to be in grave danger.

He picked up the phone and called Buffy.

"How are you?" Buffy asked Giles, cradling the phone against her cheek as she paced.

"They're dithering about something. Internal bleeding or some trifle."

*"Trifle?"*

"I must reiterate, Buffy," he continued, ignoring her. "If I'm in danger, one can only assume that you will be, too."

"Well, Giles," she said, shifting uncomfortably, "I usually am."

# Chapter 5

THE WEEKEND WAS VERY QUIET, SATURDAY AND SUN-
day passing without so much as a skyquake. It did
rain some in the small hours of Sunday morning, but
there was no thunder to speak of, and nothing but
water fell from the sky. Buffy ought to have been
relieved, relaxed.

She wasn't. Not at all.

To her it merely felt like the calm before the storm.

She sat in hurricane-eye silence in the back seat of
Cordelia's car. In the front, Cordy and Xander were
just as quiet. On the radio, the latest angsting female
rocker bucking for the Lilith Fair lineup droned on
about her personal tragedies. Xander hummed idly
along. The hostility between them had abated to a
dull dissatisfaction with life in general. The silence in
the car had nothing to do with that. It sprang more
from anxiety than anger.

News had traveled quickly through town by word of

mouth and by radio, and finally by television. Something terrible had happened at the docks. Something disastrous.

Cordelia's headlights cut the darkness. The crescent moon hung overhead. It would not be full for a few weeks yet, but Buffy thought of Oz. Then Cordy's headlights picked out a police car up ahead, blocking the road. A uniformed officer stood in the center of the road, holding both hands up, commanding them to stop. A moment later, Cordelia had braked and rolled down her window.

"What's going on?" she asked nonchalantly.

Buffy smiled. Cordelia didn't like to lie, but it wasn't hard for her to seem clueless when necessary. Still, Buffy had learned that there was much more to the girl than it seemed at first glance. She was a lot smarter, and a lot more courageous, than she would ever let on.

"Sorry, miss," the cop said grumpily. "Road to the docks is closed, probably until morning. Got a big mess down there, and we're only letting emergency vehicles past this point."

Almost on cue, an ambulance and a fire engine roared past them in quick succession, followed by a lumbering construction crane in much less of a hurry.

"Wow, it must be serious," Cordelia said, watching the flashing lights disappear around the corner ahead.

"It's a mess," the officer repeated.

Buffy tapped Cordelia on the shoulder and said, in a low voice, "We'll take a detour."

"Well, thanks," Cordy told the cop.

She guided the car into a U-turn and drove back toward the center of town. After a quarter of a mile, they turned north on Shore Road and pulled over as soon as the shoulder was wide enough for the car.

"You're sure about this?" Cordelia asked, anxiously glancing up and down the street. "If my car gets stolen . . ."

"I'm sure it'll be fine," Buffy reassured her. "But if you're nervous about it, just stay with the car."

Buffy and Xander got out, and for a moment, Cordelia remained behind the wheel. The engine ticked slowly as it cooled off in the darkness. There were no streetlights on Shore Road. This close to the docks, there were very few homes. Just over the rise to the west were warehouses and the ocean, but here . . . nothing.

"Wait up!" Cordelia said, and hurried to get out of the car. Buffy watched as she slammed the door behind her and clicked on her alarm. It chirped, confirming its vigilance. Then Cordy was rushing to join Buffy and Xander, and the three of them went over the rise together and soon found themselves walking behind a long row of warehouses and a cannery that had been closed since before any of them were born.

In the distance, they could hear sirens and the roar of truck engines.

One was tall and wiry, with dark hair and a beard shot with white. The other was bald, with a neatly trimmed beard and a startling face: one eye was pure, milk white and surrounded by a sunburst scar, the other was a dark brown, almost black. Both wore clothes selected to make their wearers completely forgettable: the tall one, Brother Galen, wore a fisherman's sweater and a pair of jeans. The bald, scarred man, Brother Lupo, had on a tailored shirt and a pair of gray Dockers.

They stood side by side in the darkness on the small rise just off Shore Road. From their vantage point, they could see the Slayer and her companions as the three trekked toward the site of the evening's catastrophe. Even as Galen and Lupo watched, the Slayer led the others between two large buildings and out to the wharf, where they turned to walk along the ocean. In the distance, the sky was lit by the flickering of fire and the flashing of emergency lights.

"Now?" Brother Galen asked respectfully.

"We go," Lupo confirmed. "But remember, Il Maestro has decreed that the Slayer be taken alive. We need her knowledge. He needs her power."

Lupo gripped Galen's jaw and turned the other man's head to face him. He stared into the other's eyes grimly. "You have a taste for violence, Galen," he said knowingly, intimately. "This is neither the time nor the place to indulge that taste."

"Yes, Brother Lupo," Galen said gently. "You speak for Il Maestro, and I obey his words."

Brother Lupo raised a pair of binoculars, though he could see through only one lens, and scanned between buildings for the Slayer. He found nothing.

"Quickly," he said. "But silently, Brother."

Together, they moved swiftly down the small incline to the back of a large green-gray warehouse, and then began to trot almost soundlessly along the cracked parking lot. After the next building, the two men turned toward the water. On the right, another warehouse, and on the left, the abandoned cannery, whose every window had been shattered long ago.

From inside came the whisper of wings, though whether bats or gulls, neither man bothered to guess.

The ocean washed against the wharf ahead, but when they reached the delivery road that ran in front of the warehouses, they stopped. Slowly, they turned the corner and looked south along the water, where a warehouse burned savagely. A large fishing trawler, mast buckled and hull breached, jutted from the side of the burning warehouse as if it had been impaled there. And, somehow, it had.

"Chaos' name!" Brother Lupo breathed, and stared in awe.

They saw the Slayer and her companions hurrying toward the site and set off after them, sticking close to the front of the ancient, deserted cannery.

"Beautiful, isn't it?" a voice whispered in the dark.

Even as Lupo began to turn, Brother Galen shrieked in agony. The thing that had whispered had used its claws to tear open Galen's belly, and even now, he frantically tried to keep his guts from spilling out, unaware that he was dying.

"You!" Lupo said, startled, as he stared at the creature. For he knew it, or at least, he had seen it before. The white, oily flesh, the black eyes like wounds . . . It was called Springheel Jack.

"This is not supposed to happen," Lupo said, shaking his head and gaping in horror at the killer and at the body of Brother Galen as it slid to the pavement with a wet slap.

"That's what they all say," Springheel Jack whispered pleasantly.

Then it opened its mouth wide, baring needle teeth, and vomited blue-white flame at Lupo's face.

"No!" Lupo screamed, and his hands came up

quickly, flashing past one another as if weaving something . . . and they were. Weaving a spell, creating a shield that turned the blue flame away from him.

"How did you do that?" Springheel Jack asked angrily. "How did you . . . ah, but no matter. I will split your rib cage, and your entrails will join the other's on the ground."

"Chaos' name, no," Lupo said, terrified as he watched the moonlight glint off the killer's talons.

Then, a shout: "Hey!"

Springheel Jack turned, and the Slayer was there with a brutal snap kick to the face that sent him reeling. Behind her, her male companion, the one they called Xander, stepped in toward the murderous fiend and swung a piece of lumber he must have picked up from the road or one of the buildings. The wood connected with a satisfying crunch, and even Brother Lupo winced.

The Slayer moved easily, her every muscle prepared for battle, a confident warrior, intent upon victory. She needn't have bothered, her companion kept after Springheel Jack. The board flashed back and forth, first from one direction, then another. With each impact, the monster reeled, falling back. It opened its mouth, tried to spit fire, and its attacker slammed the board against its head. It stumbled back toward the edge of the dock. Seeing that it could not fight, it crouched, prepared to leap away.

"Uh-uh," the Slayer's companion said, and swung the board with savage strength against the fiend's legs.

Springheel Jack grunted. As it fell, it slashed its claws out toward the boy who had humiliated it so. Talons tore just through the boy's shirt before the Slayer intervened. With a spin and a snap, she kicked

Springheel Jack in the chest with tremendous force, and the fiend tumbled backward off the wharf and hit the ocean with a splash.

"I had him!" Xander said, rounding on the Slayer.

"You did," the Slayer agreed. "But he almost tagged you with those claws. You did great, Xander. Teamwork, remember."

"Wow. Do you guys think he's dead?" asked the girl who had accompanied the Slayer and Xander. Cordelia, Lupo thought her name was. An appropriate appellation for one of such classic beauty.

"Not likely," the Slayer replied, then finally turned to Lupo himself, whom she had saved. "But I don't think he'll be back any time soon. What about you, mister? Are you okay?"

Xander said, "I'll check on the other guy. Maybe an ambulance . . . Cord, get out your cell phone, just in case."

The Slayer said to Lupo, "I think you're in shock."

For a moment, Lupo could only stare at her in awe. She was an extraordinary creature, just as all the legends said. But to see her this close, why, it nearly took his breath away. The Slayer. In a world where so many legends had disappeared into the mists of time, to see her there before him was one of the most sublime moments of his life.

"Hello?" the Slayer prodded. "Do you want to sit down?" Still he didn't speak. "Are you all right?"

"Sure, Buffy, he's terrific," the beautiful Cordelia said with great archness as she pulled a cellular phone from her purse. "He just saw some mons . . . monster-mask-wearing gang member on crack attack his friend." Cordelia looked at Xander. "So, 9-1-1?"

"I don't think so," Xander said, rising. He stopped

in front of the corpse of Brother Galen, perhaps shielding the exquisite young woman from the carnage.

"I'm sorry, man," Xander said to Lupo. His dark eyes were sad, his jaw set in a grim, somber line. "I, ah, think, well, actually, I know that your friend is dead."

"Oh, merciful heavens," Lupo groaned, his accent thick and noticeable even to him at that moment. Could they hear the lack of sorrow in his voice as well? "Dear Brother . . . my brother," he said brokenly.

"Your brother? Oh, wow, I'm really sorry," the Slayer told him sincerely. "I . . . we came as fast as we could."

"And quickly indeed," Lupo agreed, "or my life would have been forfeit as well." He lowered his head. "To that . . . gangster."

"Um, listen, we'll go tell the cops about what happened. Just hang out and they'll be down, all right?" Xander suggested, patting him on the arm.

"Thank you," Lupo said simply.

The Slayer stared at him, and for a wild moment he thought that somehow she knew who he was. He kept his head down, hoping he conveyed the proper posture of bereavement. In truth, he cared nothing for Brother Galen. But his frustration was growing into anger; he'd known Springheel Jack was in Sunnydale—the Hellmouth had drawn him—but was it mere coincidence that he had come upon them so far from the town's main residential area? The monster should have been hunting, and therefore, could reasonably have been expected to remain near the largest concentration of people.

Brother Lupo blinked, his reverie broken as he realized that the Slayer and her friends were moving away quickly, whispering and glancing back toward him in sympathy. When they had disappeared into the night, Brother Lupo counted to one hundred. Then he walked over to the cooling corpse of Brother Galen, picked up his feet and dragged him by his legs to the edge of the dock. His intestines trailed alongside him, leaving a bloody swatch on the pavement and then the wood of the wharf. The splash when the body hit the water was barely audible over the sounds of chaos from down the shore.

Lovely chaos, he thought, and then set off after the Slayer. It would be more difficult, now that she had seen him, but Lupo knew he must not lose track of her, or Il Maestro would see him damned to hell for eternity.

*The Slayer,* Brother Lupo thought. And then he whispered, *"Bellissima."*

"So, Buffy," Cordelia said idly, almost as if they weren't marching toward catastrophe, "do you really think Springheel Jack is still alive?"

"I don't think a little bath is going to hurt him," Buffy replied grimly.

"What?" Xander protested, holding his hands open like a preacher. "I kicked his ass! He's ghost, ladies. Gone. Poof."

Buffy shrugged lightly. "Let's hope so."

By then they had gotten close enough to the main dock area to see the scale of the destruction there, and the sight was enough to belay any further conversation on the subject. A pair of long docks that had once jutted far out into the water were nothing but splinters now. At least two ships that Buffy could see had been sunk, one with its prow pointing starward, and the other smashed into two large pieces which were nearly submerged.

Then there was the warehouse fire, and the boat that jutted from the blazing building like a broken sword from the chest of a fallen warrior. There were five fire trucks, three ambulances, and a score of police cars. Miraculously, the firefighters seemed to have the blaze under some kind of control, and it was rapidly diminishing in power. Buffy watched in awe. She'd always thought of firefighters as the true modern heroes. Men and women who faced death willingly every day to save the lives and livelihoods of others.

Wow.

They walked toward a tight knot of police cars. Xander and Cordelia hung back a moment, apparently unsure of how to proceed. Buffy urged them on with a tilt of her head, and they weaved through the cars. Just to Buffy's left, an older, white-haired cop who looked somewhat familiar—familiar enough for Buffy not to want to get too close to him in case he remembered her as well—was questioning a thirty-ish, dark-skinned dock worker whose arms were thick with ropy muscle. He was a clean-cut guy, and well spoken. The image of the old man of the sea with his pipe and a little too much to drink went right out the window.

"Let's talk about what you really saw, not these wild stories," the white-haired cop said emphatically.

"Do I look like a drunk to you?" the man demanded of the cop, and Buffy smiled, thinking about how much his words echoed her thoughts of a moment ago. "No, really. I've been working these docks since my fourteenth birthday. I've heard every tall tale from every fisherman and sailor who's come into port here for nearly twenty years. I know a fish story when I hear one, Officer, and so I can't blame you.

"But this thing was real, you understand? This really happened."

"Now, Mr. Curtis, don't get carried away," the cop said condescendingly. "I'm sure this was very traumatic for you."

"Damn right it was traumatic!" the man snapped. "But that doesn't mean it didn't happen. Look around you, you idiot! You ever seen anything like this before? Other than a hurricane or a tornado, what could do this? Hell, I don't know what it's called, but it's bigger than anything I've ever seen, and the tentacles on the thing are strong enough to do that!"

Mr. Curtis pointed to the boat jutting from the now merely smoldering building. Buffy's eyes widened as she considered his words. *Tentacles?* It sounded crazy, but he seemed anything but. And in Sunnydale . . .

"You watch the way you speak to an officer of the law," the old cop said angrily. "And as far as these cockamamie . . ."

The cop's eyes had fallen on Buffy, Xander, and Cordelia.

"You kids have a reason to be here?" the cop demanded. "Clear out of here, before I find a reason to give you trouble."

He was about to turn his attention back to Curtis when he blinked, then focused his attention on Buffy. "Hey," he said. "Aren't you . . ."

"Leaving!" Xander finished. "Absolutely. Right away. Great idea."

With his fingers tightly gripping Buffy's arm, Xander wrapped his other arm around Cordelia's waist, gave her a quick kiss, and then propelled them both back the way they'd come. Back toward Cordelia's car.

"Are we talking sea monster here?" Buffy asked when they were a good distance away, the ocean lolling gently against the wooden posts that supported the wharf.

"Sounds like it, yeah."

"Wait a minute, guys," Cordelia said, and they both stopped to look at her. She was staring down at a small pool of blood and a thin trail of it that led to the edge of the wharf, just above the water.

"Isn't this where that guy was killed just now? By Springheel Jack?" she asked.

Xander and Buffy looked around. Even as Xander agreed with Cordelia's assessment, Buffy crouched to look at the blood trail.

"Tell me that's Springheel Jack's blood," Xander pleaded.

"I don't think so," Buffy said. "Either someone came to help the other guy and he turned out to be a bad guy, or Springheel Jack came back."

"Or the guy you saved just dumped his brother's body," Cordelia added.

"Oh, sure. They're tourists with funny accents, and his brother is eviscerated by a monster, so hey, it's Dumpster time!" Xander said, huffing.

"He thought Springheel Jack was in a gang," Cordelia persisted. "You didn't exactly see him screaming hysterically?"

"No, because I believe that's your own private Idaho," Xander shot back. "You know, not everyone goes around shrieking at every little demonic thing that pops up."

"Oh, is that right?" Cordelia shot at him. "Mr. Macho Man?"

Buffy frowned, glanced at the two of them. She hated to admit it, for several reasons, but it was possible Cordelia was right. If the two guys were illegal immigrants, it was more than likely that he had not gone to the police, and had wanted to hide any evidence of his presence here from the authorities.

Before she could reply, the sky cracked open with a blast of thunder that rumbled through the air like a tidal wave about to crash down on their heads. They covered their ears a moment and just stood there.

With her hands clapped over her ears, Buffy let her eyes wander aimlessly over the black Pacific, moon-light flickering off the crests of each wave. Then something broke the surface of the water. Something huge, with massive tentacles or arms, and far too many of those for Buffy's tastes. It was the biggest living thing Buffy had ever seen, and she only got a glimpse of it. Of part of it.

"Oh my God," she said, as the skyquake echoed off into the sky. Xander and Cordelia followed her gaze, and they saw what she saw. "Now how in hell do I slay that?"

Giles slept fitfully and woke with a feeling of profound anxiety just after two in the morning that Sunday. He tried, with moderate success, to get back to sleep, but when his eyes fluttered open again and he saw that it was nearly half past three, he sat up painfully in his hospital bed. He quickly calculated the time difference between New York and London—

it would be half past eight there now—then picked up the beige hospital phone and asked for an outside line. He dialed the number he'd been using, and then listened to it ring on the other end: two, four, eight times. The Council would not be so unrefined as to have an answering machine, of course. What would their message say, after all? But at the very least, there ought to be a butler or maid already about at . . .

On the eleventh ring, a deep male voice answered. He recognized it as belonging to Ian Williams, the new assistant he'd spoken to earlier.

"Yes, hello. It's Rupert Giles," he said quickly. "Sorry to disturb you at this early hour . . ."

"Early here, Mr. Giles, but an ungodly hour where you are," Williams said. "Has something happened?"

"Precisely my question," Giles replied. "Your Miss Tomasi was here yesterday afternoon. She left about a quarter to two, and was due to return last evening by seven. She never appeared, nor did she phone with a message. No word at all. I've tried her hotel, left word for her, but there seems to be no sign of her. What with the news she brought me, I was a bit alarmed. I would look for her myself, of course, but I have one more round of tests tomorrow before the doctors will release me."

On the other end, there was only silence. Finally, a speculative "Hmm."

"Ian?" Giles asked.

"Disturbing news, Mr. Giles," the man said. "Disturbing indeed. I suppose we must fear the worst. You'd best check out with due haste, allowing for doctor's orders, of course. You might want to make a brief inquiry into Micaela's whereabouts, but if she doesn't turn up right off, you ought to head home straightaway. The Chosen One must be your first priority."

"Yes," Giles said, mind already racing with the nastiest of possibilities, for both Micaela and Buffy. "As ever."

He returned the phone to its cradle, but could not sleep. The man's words echoed in his mind.

*I suppose we must fear the worst.*

Giles thought of the twinkle in Micaela's eye, the way her hair shone, even without the sun. Her knowing laugh.

*I suppose we must fear the worst.*

The horror of it all was that Giles had experienced the worst. He knew what that might entail. His concern for Micaela went beyond mere fear, dread building upon dread, and far along the path to terror. And, given the odd way Buffy had been behaving, and the little she had told him about what was happening in Sunnydale, he was also concerned for the safety of the Slayer and her friends.

Suddenly resolute, Giles could remain still no longer. With a careful hand, he removed the intravenous needle from his arm and slid his legs over the edge of the bed. He still felt slightly woozy, and he allowed himself a moment before rising. Then, a deep breath, ignoring the pain in his head and back, and Giles stood up, decidedly uncomfortable in the cotton pajamas the hospital had provided.

He stood for a moment, unsteady, and then moved carefully to the closet where his clothes were hanging. His other things were still at the hotel, but the clothes he had been wearing that night had been laundered and brought to him here.

Giles reached for his shoes, bending to retrieve

them. A spike of pain shot through his back and neck to his head. Giles grunted and put a hand to his head, even as his legs went numb and buckled beneath his weight. He fell to the floor in a heap, his glasses skittering across the cold tile.

When his eyes flickered open again, he was back in bed and an unfamiliar doctor was shining a penlight into his eyes.

"Micaela," Giles croaked.

"Whoever she is, she can wait," the doctor said gruffly. "Maybe you're getting stir-crazy, Mr. Giles, and I can't blame you. But there's a reason you're still in this hospital. Maybe you'll listen to the doctors the next time."

Then Giles drifted off again and didn't open his eyes until long past morning.

In an extraordinary garden that rambled across the grounds of a palatial estate in Kyoto, one of the finest cities in the world, Kobo Sensei screamed.

He lay in the dirt of his garden, feeding the earth and the plants there with his blood, his very life. Kobo Sensei's time as a Watcher had ended many decades earlier. He was an old man now, and had dreamed often about dying in his garden, but in those dreams, he had slipped gently away from a world he had served long and well.

Nothing like this.

The blade split the flesh of his wrist and traveled lightly under the skin, opening him as he himself had prepared fish tens of thousands of times in his life. Once again, Kobo Sensei screamed.

But he did not give them what they wanted. He did

not answer their questions, only some of which he knew the answers to.

Except for his screams, Kobo Sensei was silent.

Around him, in a semicircle, stood seven men in dark cloaks, with hoods that covered most of their faces from view. Even with the little sun that still lingered in the sky, he could tell little of them from their appearance. Men of different complexions, sizes, and shapes, but all men. Beyond that, it was clear they knew something of magick.

And a great deal about pain.

The blade came down again, this time to a point several inches below his navel. Its tip pressed into Kobo Sensei's abdomen, split the skin, and again, began to travel up.

Mind and body growing numb, Kobo Sensei gritted his teeth and glared at his hooded torturers. He vowed to himself that he would not scream again, and Kobo kept that vow.

He was silent unto death.

# Chapter 6

WILLOW SAT IN THE SCHOOL LIBRARY, FEELING A BIT creeped. She was alone. With the books that lived there, true. And the library's trusty computer. Her only other company was the glow of the green glass study lamp and the comforting tapping of the keyboard. It occurred to her that if she could remember the name of the hospital Giles was in, she might be able to hack into his medical records and find out exactly what was wrong with him. Any medical terminology she was unfamiliar with would certainly be available on the Net.

Her job had proven to be a complicated one. It would be fairly easy to discover the nature of each phenomenon or monster they had encountered over the last week, but what Willow wanted to know was if there had been other instances where they had all appeared at the same time. Entering SPRINGHEEL JACK,

SKYQUAKE, SEA MONSTER, she told the search engine to locate only those matches containing all five words.

*No matches found.*

"Oh, bother," she said, frustrated, and deleted SEA MONSTER. Or maybe SKYQUAKE was the problem. Maybe there was another term for it they hadn't thought of.

She left the search and clicked on her bookmark for the Library of Congress subject headings index. SKY-QUAKES wasn't listed at all.

Yawning, she frowned and squinted at the screen. It had so been listed. She'd checked.

She sat back and thought a moment. Typed SKY QUAKES, with a space between the two compound words.

Nothing.

Then she glanced up at the clock. She was startled to see it was much later than she'd imagined. If she left now, she would get home right on time. After all, she could resume her search once her parents went to bed, on her home computer. Except that the school's local area net was behind the firewall, meaning that she couldn't access it from home. So she'd have to save more searching in Giles's files for tomorrow.

Pushing back her chair, she grabbed her book bag and turned off the computer. Then, hesitating a moment, she turned off the study lamp as well. The library was drenched in darkness, illuminated only by the light in the hall. The school at night was not a friendly place.

She had nearly died in the school at night. Back when he was evil, Angel had ambushed her and would have killed her, if Buffy hadn't stopped him.

But tonight Angel was with Buffy, patrolling for more unexpected visitors. Though Willow now stood firmly on the side of welcoming Angel back into their midst, that thought comforted her very little as she walked right beside the very spot where he had held her captive, laughing and squeezing her neck.

Then she was outside, at the top of the steps. She inhaled deeply. The library always smelled of dust and a little bit of mildew. Tea sometimes, too. She smiled softly at the image of Giles in his office, holding a steaming cup in one hand while he turned pages with the other.

She missed him. They needed him.

She wanted him home, now.

And she never wanted anything bad to happen to any of them.

Cordelia came up for air and said, "Xander, this is serious."

"I know," Xander assured her, "and I'm taking it very seriously."

They were parked at Makeout Point, a discreet distance away from the other cars—okay, she was dating Xander, but she didn't have to hang a neon sign around her neck, did she?—and as usual, Xander wasn't listening to a word she was saying.

Exasperated, she gave him a slight push in the chest. Her expensive Smash Box lipstick was slathered all over his face.

"What?" he asked, panting slightly.

"College," she said. "How many times have we been through this? Xander, if you don't go, you'll end up working for minimum wage."

"No, no, Cor." He smiled at her. "I intend to go

right past Go and live on the streets. I'll lose all my teeth and I'll write you love poems on the walls of the public urinals. Can you just hardly wait?"

"Listen, moron." She stared at him. "My parents are probably going to ship me off to Switzerland. Or maybe San Diego. It might be nice if you tried to go to the same place as me. But you can't if you don't apply."

"Hey, I applied to lots of schools. And I got accepted at a few. A couple."

She made a face. "All those colleges you applied to are lame. My parents would never let me go to any of them."

"Switzerland." He looked at her as if she were insane.

She shrugged. "Yeah."

"My parents can't even spring for a wild fling on the Matterhorn at Disneyland. How on earth am I going to get to Switzerland? Besides, I don't speak . . . Swiss."

"And it *is* a girls' school," she mused, seeing his point. She brightened. "Okay. San Diego. Or maybe a nice private college on the East Coast."

"Okay, here's a thought." He fluttered his lashes at her. "Why don't you stay here with me and go to community college?"

"It's beyond me why you aim so low," she said. "You're capable of so much more."

"Yeah, and I'd like to prove that to you right now." He put his arms around her neck and pulled her close to him. She felt his warm breath on her cheek and her heart caught. "And as for aiming low . . ."

"*Xander.*" She shook her head. "Why do I even *try.*"

Suddenly his grin vanished and he looked at her very seriously. For a moment, there was silence. And then he said, "Cordelia, I'm really glad you try. It helps that you . . . y'know, believe in me."

"I didn't say that," she replied defensively.

He smiled. Kissed her.

She kissed him back.

After all, there were a few months left until graduation.

Cordelia had begun the arduous task of reapplying her makeup by the glow of the interior dome light while Xander played a private drum solo on the dash. Her words were almost incomprehensible as she smoothed on her lipstick, but Xander translated: She was making him promise to go see Frankel the guidance counselor again.

"Okay?" she asked, popping the cap on her lipstick and dropping it into her purse.

"He hates me," Xander said, only half kidding.

"I'm sure he doesn't. Besides, it doesn't matter. He's there to help you. He's a servant of the taxpayers."

"Right. Or else he really wanted to be an astronaut, but they were full up."

She fluffed her hair. "How do I look?"

"Innocent and beguiling."

"Good." She smiled at him. "Let's go home."

"Your wish. My command. Miss Chase, start your engine."

Cordelia thrust the key in the ignition and turned it. The engine roared.

"Ooh, tiger girl," Xander gushed.

She narrowed her eyes at him. "One more crack and you're walking."

Xander held up his hands. "I'm saying nothing."

"See?" she said airily as she fishtailed down the mountain. "You *are* smart enough for college."

# Chapter 7

### *The Court of King Francis I of France*
### *Fontainebleau, 1539*

THE LIGHT BREEZE THAT WHISPERED THROUGH THE gardens at Fontainebleau carried a bit of a chill with it, and as Richard Regnier strolled deeper into the sprawling flora, he felt a nearly overwhelming urge to turn back. With a brief glance at the trellises and arches that made the labyrinthine garden about him, Regnier set his jaw firmly and strode on. *It might well be that a grim destiny awaits,* he thought, *but a Regnier never hides his face from the winds of change.*

He knew well where he walked; these were paths he had trod nearly his entire life. Word had come by messenger under the seal of the Dauphine herself. Catherine de' Medici requested his company in the rose garden just after sunset. There were, in fact, many expanses of cultivated roses on the grounds, but Regnier was familiar with the princess's habits. The spot to which she referred was a sculpted bit of garden, an oval clearing surrounded by dense rose bushes, with a small alcove also carved from the bushes themselves at its center, like the pupil of a scarlet eye. Yes, Regnier knew the way well enough. Thus, he followed the path swiftly, mind and body poised to act in his own defense should the note prove a ruse, despite the Dauphine's seal.

A high trellis thick with hanging grapevines blocked Regnier's view of the sculpted roses until he came abreast of the rose-latticed archway that led into the odd clearing, the bloody red eye of the storm. He stepped beneath the arch and into the darkened oval, with only the moon to light his way. Twined roses spread out on either side until they joined like lovers' hands on the side opposite the entry arch. At the center, the alcove had a visitor.

Regnier exhaled with a bit of relief when he saw that the Dauphine had indeed come to meet him. Catherine de' Medici had never been beautiful, but her tragic heart and troubled soul had always allowed her the gentle illusion that sympathy engendered. Now that illusion had dissipated, and her plainness had revealed itself as merely ugly. The illusion was gone, indeed, but to be replaced by what? Regnier studied her face for an answer, and then he saw her eyes. The Little Florentine began to open her mouth, but even before she could speak, Richard recognized the fury in her eyes, and knew that he was undone.

"Thank you for coming, magician," she said, her French impeccable and startling for its rarity. "Mine was an odd invitation, I know."

But Regnier was not soothed by her seeming benevolence.

"Please, *madame,*" he protested. "I know not what madness Fulcanelli has been whispering into your sweet ear, but by your demeanor alone, I can see that you are greatly disturbed."

At that, Catherine de' Medici laughed, and Regnier knew he had no hope at all. But before he could even decide whether to continue to argue logic, or to retreat as swiftly as possible, he felt the presence behind him, and turned to see Fulcanelli standing beneath the rosy arch. The sorcerer's withered hand was tucked against his ribs, but even that obvious weakness only seemed, somehow, to make him more formidable. And from behind the rosebush where Catherine stood, a pair of Fulcanelli's acolytes emerged.

"You are a base deceiver, a devil of the worst kind, Richard Regnier," Catherine de' Medici said, her anger palpable. "You turned your ear to my secret prayers, and twisted them, thwarting me with every breath. I can only imagine that you are in league with the harridan who has so completely bewitched my husband."

Regnier held his hands up, about to protest once more, but then thought better of it. Instead, he rounded on Fulcanelli, rage furrowing his brow.

"Demon!" he hissed at the crippled man. "You cleave to this woman and pledge fealty to the house of de' Medici, and all the while you construct the most evil plots your wicked mind can conceive. She is already under your sway! You have all the power you desire! What can you possibly gain from preventing her the simple joy of motherhood?"

Fulcanelli dropped his head, shook it sadly, and smoothed imaginary ruffles in the crimson and black cloak that he wore.

"Dear, demented Richard," Fulcanelli sighed. "You seek to thrust your guilt upon another, but it is plain for all of us to see. *Madame* has already decreed your fate, and believe me, it is far kinder than another might have been."

For a moment, Regnier could only stare, open-mouthed, at the sorcerer. Then, slowly, he began to turn back to face Catherine. But even as he turned, Fulcanelli's acolytes fell upon him. Regnier's right hand began to glow with eldritch flame, but too late. A heavy cudgel struck his temple, and he fell to the ground as though he were dead.

This was, in fact, Catherine de' Medici's first impression.

"I commanded that he not be killed!" the Dauphine protested immediately.

"Please, lady," Fulcanelli said gently, gliding across the clearing toward her. "These faithful friends have been about such unfortunate work in the past. They would never take a life in error."

Catherine knelt at Regnier's side and laid her hands on his chest. She seemed relieved to feel the rise and fall of his chest beneath her fingers, and Fulcanelli frowned at her concern.

"You will see him safely to a merchant vessel, and deliver the purse I have provided to the captain for his passage to wherever that ship next sails," the Dauphine ordered.

Fulcanelli merely bowed his head obediently. "So you have commanded and so shall it be done, Your Grace," he agreed. "Though I know not why you would spare one so evil, so duplicitous."

The princess glanced up sharply at her advisor. Her eyes roved quickly over the acolytes as they began to lift Regnier from the hard earth of the clearing. Together they stood in silence, Dauphine and sorcerer, until the two men had passed beneath the rosy arch and out of the clearing. At last, when the two were alone, Catherine narrowed her eyes and glared at Fulcanelli with a distrust she had never before allowed.

"I have had my fill of killing, Giacomo," she said evenly. "With Regnier gone, you have your wish. If I chose correctly in believing you, perhaps I will also have my wish. But I will not buy my future and my child with more blood. If God does not see fit to give me a babe, I refuse to seek my solace elsewhere. Whatever comes, I am through with death and blood."

"We are, none of us, through with such things until we breathe our last, Catherine," Fulcanelli said darkly. "But I will respect your wishes, and not trouble you with such suggestions any further. I only pray that you will bear the heir that your husband so desires."

With her predicament stated so baldly, Catherine flushed deeply, angrily, and said nothing. She pushed past Fulcanelli and followed the winding path that led from the garden labyrinth. The sorcerer stared after her for some time, his upper lip curled back in distaste. Slowly, however, his expression changed, and a smile began to bloom on his face.

"You will give your prince a son, my dear," Fulcanelli whispered to the night. "But not yet. Not until it pleases me, and nurtures the seeds of chaos."

Several hours after he departed the gardens, Fulcanelli strode across the moonlit grounds toward an antiquated stable where the Dauphin's pasture horses were kept. When they had aged too greatly for display, Henri ought to have sold them or fed them to the army, as far as Fulcanelli was concerned. That he was soft enough to put the creatures to pasture only reinforced the sorcerer's belief that he was unfit to rule. But Henri's father, Francis, still sat on the thrown.

Fulcanelli had time to alter the course of French history.

The pasture stable was remote enough that it had become a sort of staging area for some of Fulcanelli's more questionable practices. There was often a stable boy about, even that late at night, particularly when it rained and the stable offered the only shelter around. A bottle of wine and a loaf of bread were usually all that were necessary to pay the lad to keep away for a time. That and the implicit threat that Fulcanelli represented. He was a sorcerer, after all, and the boy was rightly terrified of him.

This night, the boy was nowhere to be seen as Fulcanelli approached the massive side door to the stable. He slipped the latch and passed through in utter silence. Upon his entrance, the horses stamped and whinnied in their stalls, but the sorcerer ignored them. What he sought was at the back of the stable, where the structure was wide enough for the horses to be bathed and brushed, several at a time.

Two of his acolytes, Giovanni and Francesco, stepped from the darkness of the stable and bowed in silence.

"Regnier?" he asked.

"Aboard ship, and thus your vow to the Dauphine is fulfilled," Francesco reported. "The captain was quite pleased to have the passenger aboard, and just as pleased to promise his death as soon as they are in open seas."

Fulcanelli steepled his fingers beneath his chin and nodded slowly. "Very good." He dropped his hands, cocked his head, and glanced past them into the darkness. "And the other matter we discussed?"

The two men exchanged a dark look, and it was Giovanni who spoke. "Luciano is dead," he said bluntly. "She took his head before I could spill the ashes you supplied into the air."

"The spell worked, though?" Fulcanelli confirmed. "The ashes put her to sleep?"

"She sleeps even still," Francesco said, and then stepped aside to allow Fulcanelli to pass.

The sorcerer moved deeper into the stable. On one wall a lantern hung. Fulcanelli passed his hand across it, and the candle within ignited with flame, blazing brightly and throwing its illumination across the stalls, startling the horses. And ahead, where the structure opened wide, a body lay flat, arms and legs jutting out to form a star. A pentagram.

The girl was beautiful, her hair a dark red that was uncommon in France and even rarer in the sorcerer's native Florence. She was naked, and perfect, but Fulcanelli's eyes did not stray to the glow of her flesh. Such idle pursuits held no fascination for him. Instead, he gazed upon her face, at the troubled expression that had surfaced there, though her mind was deeply submerged.

His withered left hand tingled and itched, and he held it tight against his body. With his right, he withdrew a blade he had chanted spells over each night for twenty-seven years, awaiting this very opportunity. In his heart, he had never imagined it might actually come to pass, but here she was. Fulcanelli's heart raced.

"You will both be well rewarded, my sons," Fulcanelli said quietly, without taking his eyes away from the naked girl on the cold ground.

He crossed the half dozen steps toward her, a man entranced, and fell to his knees on the hard-packed earth. Gingerly, almost lovingly, he placed the razor edge of the blade against her breastbone, nestling the tip between the ridges formed by two of her upper ribs. Then he began to chant. The ritual took several minutes, during which time the girl did not move, save for the gentle rise and fall of her breathing. When Fulcanelli was through, he lowered his head in supplication.

"For chaos," he whispered, tears beginning to stream down his cheeks. "For entropy."

With all the considerable power in his right arm, the sorcerer and alchemist Fulcanelli forced the dagger through skin and muscle. Blood spurted from the wound and splashed his robe, adding more crimson on the ebony field of his sorcerer's garb. Her eyes flashed open, but she did not scream.

Then it hit him, the power flowing up through the blade. His flesh sang with it, crackling as though he'd been struck by lightning. Fulcanelli threw back his head, and began to scream, not in pain but in triumph. With the ritual his research had provided, the lifeblood of the Chosen One, of the Slayer, lent him a power even he had barely dreamed of. Power that would allow him to continue to build the foundations of a scheme that would one day bring chaos back to Earth, chaos unending.

"Delicious," Fulcanelli hissed.

Lightly, he brushed the red hair away from the dead Slayer's pretty face.

\* \* \* \* \*

Oz scratched his stubbly chin idly as he sat on a stool in Starbucks. Iced cappuccino wasn't much of a breakfast, but after a night like last night it was a necessary evil. He rubbed his hands over his face, wishing he felt more awake. Instead, it only reminded him how tired he was. When a guy spent three nights a month as a werewolf, and a lot of others helping his girlfriend and her buds hunt monsters, it could get pretty tiring.

When the phone had rung at just after nine, he'd thought for sure it would be Willow. That would have been okay.

Instead, the voice on the other end belonged to Devon.

"Dude, are you asleep?" Devon asked.

"You mean at the moment?" Oz answered.

Devon didn't get it. Nor did he apologize. Instead, he babbled on about needing to get together this morning. Since it wasn't all that far from his house, Oz suggested Starbucks. He had the unusual need to get caffeinated, and he knew that Devon practically lived on the stuff.

Now here he sat, twelve minutes past ten—twelve minutes past when Devon ought to have shown up— and no sign of the Dingoes' front man. *Probably saw some girl on the street he couldn't resist making a play for,* Oz thought, with no animosity. That was just Devon.

Six minutes later, as Oz noisily drained the last of

his iced cappuccino, Devon walked through the door. Oz watched him scan Starbucks quickly. When Devon spotted him, the singer nodded his head and sidled over to the table, pulling up a stool. Devon ordered the biggest, blackest coffee he could pronounce the name of. Neither of them mentioned Devon's tardiness because, honestly, it didn't really bother either one.

"What's up?" Oz asked.

"Oz, man, we gotta talk about the band," Devon said gravely, still nodding.

"Why? Have the record labels finally seen the error of their ways and cut us a fat money deal?"

Devon frowned, looked at Oz as though the idea were even more absurd than Oz thought it was.

"Okay," Oz said. "Fame and fortune isn't our topic for the day. Spill, Dev. What inspires you to drag me to your caffeinated world at this unholy hour?"

Devon nodded once more, and then abruptly the nodding ceased. He ran a hand through his hair, pushing it behind his ears.

"There was a Winner Take All Battle of the Bands at Crestwood last weekend, man," Devon said, eyes looking everywhere but at Oz. "The pot was twelve hundred bucks. I was there, man. The guys who took that pot home, they were the total definition of suck."

Oz raised his eyebrows, still mostly in the dark, but a bit concerned that he knew where this was going.

"That cash should have been ours, Oz," Devon said. "But you know why we aren't twelve hundred bucks richer today?"

"Can't win it if you ain't in it," Oz said bluntly.

Devon just pointed at him, to signify that, yep, that was the right answer. Oz felt the weight of that finger as if it were an outright accusation. The band were his brothers. Other than Willow, playing with Dingoes was about the most important thing in his life. But ever since the whole werewolf thing, he'd had to clear three nights out of his schedule just to make sure he didn't kill anyone. Add that to the moral weight of protecting the town from demons and vampires . . . Oz just couldn't look the other way when the horrors started descending on the Hellmouth. Or erupting out of it. But that didn't sit well with the Dingoes. Mainly because they didn't know about it.

Resentment had been growing among the other members of the band. He'd felt it, but he'd been fool enough to believe that they would take his regular absences in stride. Whenever he could—and with the full moon, he always could—Oz gave sufficient notice, two or three weeks in advance. When that meant a Monday or Tuesday night, it wasn't any big thing. But as time went on, and the missed opportunities began to accumulate, he had found himself growing more and more distant from the band. Now this.

"Dude, we're just wondering where the band falls on your priority list, y'know?" Devon asked. "I think it's a fair question."

Now it was Oz's turn to nod.

"Very fair," he agreed. "The answer is 'very high.' I'm in it for the long haul, Devon. I've just got some things going on that . . ."

"Things going on for like a year," Devon said, and

for the first time, Oz sensed some hostility there. "Ever since you met Yoko."

Oz glared at him.

"Oh, I mean Willow," Devon drawled.

With a grunt, Oz pushed his empty cup away and stood up from the stool. "This conversation is over, man. You want to find a new lead guitar player, that's cool with me. No hards, all right? But my not being available all the time, that's my fault. I think laying it on Willow is an insult to her, and an insult to me. And honestly, it's beneath you."

As Oz turned, Devon reached out to stop him.

"Whoa. Oz, chill," he said. "This isn't like you."

Oz sighed. "Well, it isn't like you to be such a numbskull." He paused a moment, then shrugged and sat back down at the table. "Listen, Dev, it's a little personal, okay? A few nights a month I'm . . . I'm in a program. Sort of therapy, but with pretty strict ground rules."

Devon's eyes went wide. It was almost as though he'd been frozen in place. Then a kind of empathy began to creep across his face, an understanding that went beyond anything Oz might have expected from him. It wasn't that Devon was stupid. But he spent most of his time in a small cocoon of Devon-ness and was rarely able to comprehend any priority or opinion that he didn't share. Finally, and so slowly Oz didn't notice at first, Devon began to nod.

"We cool?" Devon asked.

"Super cool."

Devon sucked back his coffee, pushed back his stool, and hopped to his feet. "See you at practice later, then, all right?" he said, as if the whole conversation had been some sort of performance that they had now completed.

"Yeah," Oz agreed, then glanced up at the clock. It was almost eleven o'clock. "I should be going, too. I'm a little late for school."

Devon laughed at that, and then boogied out the door. Out on the sidewalk, he turned and waved, smiling. With half a smile of his own, Oz shook his head in amazement at how quickly the crisis had passed. Devon and the other guys expected certain things from him, and as long as he delivered, things were pretty copacetic.

It made him think of Willow, and all the things she was going through with her parents, and college. He figured Xander and Cordelia were probably having the same problem. The so-called grown-ups had it all figured out. They had a plan for their kids, even if the kids didn't know what their own plan was going to be just yet. The parents had expectations, and that put a lot of pressure on their kids to fulfill those expectations.

Buffy had it worse, in a way. She had her mom, and she had Giles, too. One telling her she couldn't be what the other insisted she had to be. They both had expectations, and she didn't want to disappoint either one.

And Oz? Oz had the Dingoes.

"I don't know," Xander said, and shrugged. "I mean, I don't want to sound all *Dawson's Creek,* but maybe I'm just lashing out at you when it's other things that are bothering me."

Buffy laughed, shook her head. "Okay, Mr. Self-analysis, what are you buggin' about?"

They sat together at a small table in the Bronze. It had been dark less than an hour, but the others still hadn't shown. Buffy was actually glad to have the time with Xander. They'd agreed to take at least a few hours off from combating the veritable minefield of weirdness that Sunnydale had become, but there were things she and Xander needed to address together that had been shoved aside for too long.

"Maybe I'm just asserting myself," Xander said gravely.

Buffy tried not to laugh again. She managed to just get away with an affectionate smile.

"Forget it," Xander snapped.

With much effort, she forced the smile from her lips. "No, really. I'm sorry. Seriously, though, you don't have much trouble asserting yourself. Anymore."

"Well, see, that's where the problem comes in. It's this whole business of choosing a path for your future. I just . . . I don't know what I want from life. Not yet. Not really."

Buffy looked at him more closely and saw how profoundly this was actually bothering Xander. There was always more to his thought process than rapier wit and a craving for snack food, but he was generally content to allow it to seem otherwise. For the most part, Xander seemed to enjoy being the class clown, so to speak. And he was naturally funny, no question. But there was an unspoken acknowledgment among those who cared for him that at times his wit was merely a defense mechanism to mask his insecurities, anxieties, and frustration with life.

Pretty common, actually, for teenage boys.

But here, in this moment, the mask was down.

Buffy reached out and laid her hand over his on the table. "Nobody knows," she told him, searching his eyes. "Really. I mean it. For all the horror that I have ahead of me, in one way I guess I'm lucky. I don't feel lost. I have a purpose. Probably a very short life span, but a purpose, anyway."

"But everyone's supposed to have a purpose," Xander protested. "Well, except guys like John Bogart and Dave Rheingold. Thing is—and I guess this is it, really—my parents know I don't have it all figured out, and they act like I'm still a kid, like they're just going to figure it all out for me. But I am going to figure it out. At some point. Maybe I don't have all the answers now, but it's up to me to find them, not my parents."

Buffy remained silent, just letting Xander talk. She wondered if senior year was this hard on all of them. She imagined Willow, at least, knew what she was going to do with her life. But then she thought of Oz, and realized that Willow might not have it together either.

"I'm not sure how this all connects to me," Buffy said at length.

Xander shrugged, offered a self-effacing grin. "Me either. I do think you went overboard the other night. Just a little too enthusiastic for the NFL. I know that I probably overreacted a little, and I know you have a lot on your mind too."

"We all do, Xand, and it isn't like I'm without blame."

"Don't flatter yourself, darlin'," he said in a passable Elvis. "Nobody said you weren't to blame."

"Gee, thanks," Buffy said.

They laughed, and then just sat and appreciated the comfortable silence between them, even as a neo-goth band called Black Rose fiddled with their instruments on stage.

"They sound good," Xander said after a while.

"They haven't started playing yet," Buffy informed him. "They're still tuning up."

"How can you tell?"

Silence again, and it was good.

"Y'know, I've been meaning to ask you something," Xander said suddenly. "All these funky new party guests we're having, not to mention the bells and whistles, does it seem like the countdown to New Year's Eve to you?"

Buffy looked at him, frowning. "You mean, do I think the increase in the number of wacked-out happenings in Helltown means we're building to something big?"

"Pretty much."

Buffy smiled her most innocent smile. "What ever gave you that idea? The thought never crossed my mind."

"Thanks," Xander said. "Your sincerity is comforting. You've been trying to figure out how to stop that sea monster. Maybe you could just ask him real nice, tell him he'll be happier somewhere else."

The smile disappeared from Buffy's lips in an instant. Over Xander's shoulder, she saw a man standing at the entrance to the Bronze. He was staring at her, but she didn't need his attention to recognize him.

"What is it?" Xander asked, even as Buffy watched

the bald man turn and stride out past the club's bouncer.

"Come on, Boy Wonder." She grabbed Xander's hand and pulled him up to follow her. "You want some action? It's your lucky night."

"So, what are we fighting?" Xander asked, rubbing his palms together. "Spooks, bloodsucking fiends, or things that go bump in the night?"

"How 'bout bald, scar-faced guys who disappear after getting attacked by Springheel Jack and taking their brother's corpse?" she asked.

"Is that multiple choice? 'Cause I do much better in the essay section. More room for improvisation."

But by then, Buffy was leading him out the front door of the Bronze. She glanced both ways, and caught just a glimpse of the pale bald pate of the mystery man as he disappeared around a corner up ahead.

"Oh, man, not again," Xander complained at her side. "You do know this is a trap, don't you?"

Buffy offered that innocent smile again. "A trap? You're joking."

Xander grumbled a bit, then rolled his eyes. "Okay, I guess I asked for this."

Together, they jogged along the side of the warehouse into which the Bronze had been built. At the alley, they paused to survey the area.

"Gone," Xander observed.

"Yeah," she said. "Right."

Side by side, they stepped into the alley. Beyond a pile of wooden palettes and an enormous blue Dumpster, a car was parked, lights out, about thirty yards away.

Xander frowned. "Maybe we should wait for . . ."

"And put even more of us in danger? I think we'll handle this ourselves."

"Your call," Xander said.

But when he reached the stack of wooden palettes, he took a moment to work a board free. Xander didn't mind fighting, really, but it was always comforting to have a thick piece of wood in your hand if you were going to have to bash someone's head in. Or, at the very least, prevent the same from happening to you.

The danger was tangible. It hung around them like thunderheads just before a storm, like the moisture that soaked the air and promised not only rain, but a torrential downpour. Yet, in spite of that, Xander felt the wood in his hands and the presence of Buffy at his side, felt his muscles tense and thought, *Now this is right. This is the way it should be.*

Maybe she was the Slayer. And maybe he wouldn't be in Sunnydale forever. But as long as he was, they were a team. All of them.

As if that thought were their cue, the doors of the sedan opened. The windows were darkly tinted, and the dome light did not go on, but the full moon was bright enough to pick out the blind white eye and bald head of the man they'd been pursuing, the man they'd saved from Springheel Jack. He had been in the driver's seat. The other three were very ordinary looking, with the exception that they, like the bald man, wore long, navy-blue greatcoats that looked too warm for the weather.

Oh, that and the fact that the one who stepped out from the passenger side looked an awful lot like a . . .

"Vampire," Buffy whispered.

Before Xander could reply, she whipped her hand under the hunter-green silk shirt she'd been wearing open and untucked over a tank top. From the waistband of her pants, at her lower back, she withdrew a nasty-looking stake.

"What, you had a feeling?" Xander asked, as the four men began to walk toward them, *Reservoir Dogs* style.

"A good worker always comes with her tools," Buffy replied.

"And thank you, Giles," Xander said, holding the length of wood in front of him.

"We meet again, Chosen One," Baldy said, his voice a lot more menacing than Xander remembered it.

"Last time, I saved your life," Buffy reminded him, as though it might make some difference.

"Indeed, and in return, I give you yours," the man said. "Provided you come with us without an argument or a fight."

"And if I don't?"

The man's milky-white eye seemed, somehow, to focus along with the other. He stared at her.

"You will come with us, willingly or not. But if you fight us, your friend will die."

Buffy seemed to hesitate a moment. Xander snorted in derision. They might have her over the barrel if they threatened his life, but he didn't plan to give Buffy a choice.

He moved fast enough to surprise even himself. Before the bald man, the vampire, or the others could even credit the idea that he was attacking them—and without the Slayer—Xander waded in and slammed the length of wood against the vampire's head. Jagged board tore vampire flesh, and blood ran from the wound as the vampire roared and spun to face Xander in full vamp face.

"Lupo?" the vampire snarled, apparently awaiting his orders.

The bald man—Lupo—nodded his head. "The Slayer is to be taken alive. The boy is your supper."

The vampire laughed. It was a thin, gangly creature, but Xander knew better than to underestimate it. In fact, he knew just what to do with it.

"Vampire," he said cordially.

The thing lunged for him.

"Meet Slayer," he added, and dove out of the way.

Buffy stepped in, spun into a high kick that connected solidly with the vampire's jaw. There was the crack of breaking bone, and the vampire grunted in pain. It turned on her, but it was too late. Buffy slammed the stake home with both hands, and then let it go.

The vampire exploded into a cloud of dust even as Buffy and Xander squared off against the three remaining attackers, all of whom seemed human. The two men behind Lupo started forward, one toward Buffy and one toward Xander. Xander cringed, shouted, "No, please don't kill me." The man grinned and reached for him, relaxed by Xander's apparent fear into thinking how simple this kill would be. Xander sprang up with every ounce of strength he could muster and swung.

And missed.

A fist jammed into his gut, and Xander doubled over. The goon slammed him hard into the side of the building, and it was then that Xander saw the flash of a dagger in the moonlight. His left hand shot out, grasped his attacker's wrist, and he balled the right into a tight fist and popped the guy in the jaw so hard that he thought he heard one of his own fingers snap.

The dagger clattered to the alley, and Xander picked it up. Its owner got his footing again, and came toward Xander with an evil grin, in spite of the dagger.

Which was when Buffy grabbed him from behind, having made short work of the other goon, and drove him headfirst into the grille of the sedan, smashing one headlight and probably fracturing the man's skull.

Then they were side by side again, staring at the man the others had called Lupo. Xander had thought for sure the guy would be scared of Buffy now, realizing he'd gotten himself into something he didn't have control of.

If he was scared, he didn't look it. Lupo still had a smile on his face.

"It has been my pleasure to watch you, Slayer," Lupo said. "And a joy to see the courage you inspire in those around you."

"Great," Xander said. "Even when I actually get to kick some ass, you still get the credit."

Buffy didn't respond. She was staring at Lupo, and Xander saw why. The scarred, blind-white eye had begun to glow with an arcane blue light.

"Tch," Xander clucked. "Why does it always have to be magick? I hate magick."

"I'm not much of a sorcerer, actually," Lupo said. "Even so, I advise you to capitulate."

Buffy went after him. She was standing still one

moment, and the next she was flying across the dozen or so feet that separated them, one hand out to grab hold of his navy coat and the other balled into a fist to pummel him mercilessly.

The roar from above made her falter.

She looked up just in time to dive out of the way as a huge beast with white fur landed on the pavement between them with a thud. It landed on its feet, its long white tail waving behind it, and Xander's first thought was that someone had mated a mountain gorilla and a polar bear. When it let its head fall back and opened its mouth to roar, Xander felt a surge of nausea and fear run through him.

*This thing is why Cro-Magnon men lived in caves,* he thought, and stumbled backward toward the mouth of the alley, searching for some kind of weapon so that he could try to help Buffy.

"Slayer," Lupo said happily, "this is a Wendigo. I have called it here to take you. It has only the basest of instincts. All it knows is that you are not to die. Beyond that, I cannot control it."

Then Lupo pointed at Buffy.

"Her," he said.

The Wendigo bellowed again, green eyes flashing against white fur. Its mouth was lined with yellowing fangs, and its tail slammed the front quarter of the Lexus and caved it in.

"Xander, run!" Buffy said. "Find Angel!"

For a moment, he thought to argue with her. Was she just trying to protect him from this thing? But then common sense kicked in. Buffy needed major backup, and he just wasn't going to cut it.

Xander Harris had never run so fast in his life.

\* \* \*

Seconds after Xander took off out of the alley, the Wendigo sprang at Buffy. Its arms were incredibly long, its talons razor sharp, and its tail whipped dangerously from side to side. Buffy had only one place to go . . . forward. She jumped at the Wendigo, inside the reach of the huge beast. Deadly it might have been, but still, it was only an animal, and an animal could be taken by surprise.

Once.

She stepped in, slammed an open palm up into the thing's jaw and heard a satisfying clack as its teeth slammed together. Its head snapped back. Buffy slapped its arms away, then drove killing blows into its chest once, twice, three times. The thing staggered back. Buffy knew this was her only chance—she was only going to get one—and she spun into a kick that would break the Wendigo's neck.

It was impossibly fast.

It grabbed her leg out of the air, fingers clamped on her ankle so hard she felt the bones grinding together, ready to snap. The Wendigo roared in pain and triumph, and held her upside down by one leg. She saw the way its eyes narrowed as it looked at her, trying to decide what to do next. She wondered how hungry it was, and then started kicking, trying desperately to break free.

No chance. She was going to die.

The sound of a horn split the night. The Wendigo looked up in abject terror, dropped Buffy unceremoniously to the pavement—she barely turned in time to save herself from some massive cranial trauma—and then the beast turned and sprinted away down the alley.

Buffy began to stand slowly, painfully, but then she

had to dive behind the Dumpster as the sedan roared from the alley and out into the night. She thought about trying to pursue it, but quickly realized how ridiculous the idea was at that moment. Once again she stood, dusted herself off, and then turned toward the mouth of the alley, expecting to see Angel and Xander, at the very least.

The last thing she expected to see was the huge, shaggy man with antlers sprouting from his head who sat high on a black steed with fire jetting from its nostrils.

"Roland?" she sputtered, stunned to see the Lord of the Hunt, with whom she had allied herself once before.

Then she thought of the horn, and the fear in the Wendigo's eyes. It had been terrified of the sound, because that signified the arrival of the Wild Hunt, a group of supernatural stalkers who would run it to ground and take its head as a trophy.

"What's . . . what's happening?" Buffy asked, incredulous. "Please tell me the Hunt isn't . . ."

When Roland spoke, his voice was deeper than she recalled. More of a growl than real words, but she understood well enough.

"I am here alone," he assured her. "The Wild Hunt rides less often now, with me as Erl King. And we would not come back to Sunnydale, regardless."

"Then how can you be here?" Buffy stared at him, saw the small fires that burned in his eyes, and shivered, remembering the boy he had once been.

"I came after the Wendigo," the Lord of the Hunt said. "And I came to warn you. It was called, yes, but it was only able to come through because things are falling apart, Buffy. As things will do. Entropy claims all, in time. But now is not that time, and yet the barriers between worlds are falling. You fight the creatures of Hell, but you have learned that there are other places. Old places, now only myths and legends, which still exist."

"Like the Lodge of the Wild Hunt," Buffy said.

"Yes, very like it," Roland agreed. "A thin veil separates the world you know from all the things the world doesn't believe in anymore, the things that should not or cannot be, and some that never were."

"I don't understand any of this," Buffy said. "It's just too much."

"Know only this, then," Roland said, and he cocked his head as if listening to some far-off sound before continuing. Finally, he said, "There are holes in the fabric of things, tears in the veil, and there are things which do not belong in this world which are slipping through that veil."

"Like the Wendigo."

"Yes," Roland agreed. "And like me."

There was a brief moment of awkward silence before he said, "I will retrieve the Wendigo if I can. And I will keep the Hunt in check. They will not trouble you. The rest is up to you."

"But I don't understand," Buffy complained. "What's causing it? I mean, how am I supposed to know how to put all these crazy things back where they belong? I can't just keep killing them, there are too many. I have to stop them from coming through."

"The legends my father told me as a boy said that there was more to being the Chosen One than mere killing," Roland said. "We each have our destiny to fulfill, Buffy. Yours is to stand between your world and the darkness, to be certain the sun comes up each day. You are the Chosen One.

"You will find a way."

Without another word, Roland spurred on his steed, and the fire-breathing ebony stallion galloped past Buffy into a dead-end alley and simply disappeared.

# Chapter 8

Two days after he had attempted to leave and collapsed, Giles was still in the hospital. After that incident, he was seized with a strange sort of lethargy. He lay in his bed, dozing fitfully, often waking with a start and the dreadful sense that something terrible was happening.

He dreamed. Some of his dreams were delightful images of himself in another sort of life, freed from the encumbrance of his position as Watcher. He saw himself with a beautiful woman with honey hair—Micaela—the two of them fussing over adorable twin boys on a Sunday outing at the London Zoo. He looked younger, more carefree, as he munched an ice lolly and admired the animals with his family.

Other dreams were nightmares: monsters of all sorts rose from the Hellmouth and overran first Sunnydale, and then the world. Tens of thousands of innocent people were slaughtered by a hideous army of the undead; not an army, exactly, but legions of incarnate evil; hordes of mindless creatures killing everything in their path.

As Giles lay in a pool of sweat and moaned, he saw Buffy's friends cut down, one by one: Xander, hanged and disemboweled; Willow, burned at the stake; Cordelia, sliced to ribbons, her skin peeled away inch by excruciating inch; Oz, weighted down with chains and tossed into an icy river.

And then, most horrifying of all: Buffy herself, bound within a pentagram, a knife piercing her heart, and a figure looming over her, laughing.

"No," Giles panted, waking himself. He struggled to sit upright, but the effort was too great. It was as if a weight pressed against his chest; he had a vision of a hideous creature perched atop him, pinning him down.

Soft laughter echoed through the room. Giles listened, his heart pounding. It seemed to be coming from behind the curtain, the one that separated him from Mr. Russo.

After a few moments, the laughter died away. Giles tried to reach for his glasses, then for the call button for the nurse, but he couldn't move. He could scarcely breathe.

Seconds ticked by; then, after some span of time, he dozed. As he came slowly to, he heard the laughter again. Something brushed his foot, like fingertips draping over his toes as someone glided past his bed.

He tried to frame the word *Sister,* then reminded himself that here they were nurses. But he couldn't say anything.

Then he thought he heard the sounds of a struggle behind the curtain.

With monumental effort, he managed to turn his head.

Backlit as if by a brilliant moon, two figures were thrown into silhouette on the curtain. One was hunched over Mr. Russo's bed, choking the very life out of the one who struggled. Giles blinked as the figures blurred in and out of focus.

"No," he rasped.

The room spun crazily as he extended his hand toward the violent scene. The only sound, other than his own tortured whisper, was the desperate choking.

From somewhere deep inside himself, Giles found untapped reservoirs of strength. He catapulted himself out of his bed and grabbed the curtain with both hands. But the effort took too much out of him, and he sank to the floor, taking the curtain with him.

There was no one behind the curtain.

Mr. Russo's hospital bed was empty.

Footsteps rushed in from the hallway. The overhead fluorescent flicked on.

Someone put an arm around him. He looked up, expecting to see the night nurse. Instead, he was greeted by the sight of a young man with sandy blond hair, who said, "Mr. Giles, Mr. Giles, are you all right?"

"What . . . what happened to Mr. Russo? Who are you?"

Just then someone else raced into the room. As the young man helped Giles to his feet, the newcomer, a woman in scrubs, said, "Mr. Giles, you shouldn't be out of bed." Then she glanced past him to the fallen curtain and said, "Oh, dear. Did you need to use the bathroom? You should have used your call button."

"No, I did not," he protested, as she came around to his other side and together with the sandy-haired man, they half led, half dragged Giles back to his bed. "There was a man there, attacking another . . ." He trailed off, his sense of discretion taking over. "I had a nightmare."

"Not a surprise, with your fever," the woman said. She huffed. "Where's Lopez? Off sneaking down to the Coke machine. Oh, well, your nephew here can help us."

Deftly she smoothed the sheets and fluffed Giles's pillows as the other man sat carefully on the side of the bed. Giles frowned up at him; the man's silent gaze pleaded with him to say nothing.

The nurse continued, "Now, you just slip into bed and I'll call the doctor in to check you over. You had a bad fall."

"Nothing hurts," he assured her. "I'm fine." And he was; he felt better than he had in . . . days. The lethargy had dissipated; the surreal sense that he was witnessing terrible events rather than having bad dreams was gone.

"Now, now. We'll be the judges of that." She wheeled over the electronic temperature gauge, slipped a plastic cover over the thermometer, and popped it in his mouth. "Leave that in, all right? I'll be back in less than a minute."

As soon as she left the room, Giles pulled the thermometer out and demanded of the young man, "Who the hell are you?"

"Watchers' Council," the man replied in a whisper.

"They sent me to replace Micaela. Ian Williams caught me up on the whole business."

"Still missing?" Giles asked unhappily.

The man nodded. Giles noticed now that he looked exhausted. His face was pasty and there were rings under his eyes. "We think someone's been trying to keep you here."

"Trying . . ." Giles frowned. "Please, give me my glasses." He couldn't think if he couldn't see.

"With magick or with poison," the man went on. He handed Giles the glasses. "Either that, or they were trying to kill you slowly enough that it wouldn't raise any attention. My name's Matt Pallamary," he added, extending his hand. "I'm very honored to meet you, sir."

Giles sighed to himself and shook the man's hand. "I'm sure the pleasure is mine," he said politely. He gestured to the empty hospital bed across the room. "I was absolutely positive I saw that man murdered."

"He died yesterday," Pallamary informed him. "His corpse was wheeled out of here while you were delirious with fever."

"Poor man. Was there any evidence of foul play?"

"No. I heard one doctor whispering 'PPPBBB' to a nurse." When Giles shrugged in ignorance, the man translated, " 'Please put pine box beside bed.' Terminal, in other words." He moved his shoulder. "My aunt is a doctor. She tells me these things."

"How very ghoulish," Giles commented.

Pallamary continued. "I brought you a rose quartz. In fact . . ."—and now he stammered with acute mortification—"I . . . I had just gotten back here when you fell. I can't help but think it was my fault, sir. If I hadn't left to go get it—"

"Nonsense," Giles cut in, more sharply than he'd intended. Truth be told, the mention of rose quartz had broadsided him. After Jenny's death, Willow had given him Jenny's rose quartz and told him it was purported to have healing properties. Perhaps he should have brought it with him to New York.

"I've got to get out of here," Giles said. "I must return to Sunnydale at once. If someone's trying to keep me here, it doesn't bode well for the Slayer."

"Of course, sir."

"Tell that woman I want to be discharged at once." With determination, he threw back his covers.

"But, Mr. Giles, it's the middle of the night."

He started to swing his legs over the side of the bed. "Then I'll simply walk out."

Pallamary frowned. "Please, sir, there're just a few hours until morning. They'll be more accommodating then. Besides, you have had a bad fall, and it is possible you were hurt."

Giles said, "That doesn't matter."

Pallamary very gently blocked his way. "I'm very sorry to contradict you, but it does matter. As you say, the Slayer may also be in grave danger. You need to be in good shape in order to help her."

Giles paused. There was that. He didn't know if Pallamary had an inkling about the strange goings-on in Sunnydale. Buffy had been growing more and more evasive in their phone conversations, and Giles just knew that things were worse than they seemed. With Watchers being murdered, and odd happenings by the Hellmouth, Buffy would need him nearby. Something serious was going on, and Giles was determined to find out what it was. Still . . . he was a practical man by nature.

"All right." Giles sighed heavily. "I'll wait until morning. But then I'm leaving. And you'll drive me to the airport, yes?"

Pallamary inclined his head. "It would be my pleasure, sir."

Standing on Dead Man's Walk, which overlooked the ocean, Angel thought about the impending sunrise and wrestled with the desire to linger and watch it. Not wrestled, exactly. He didn't have a death wish. But a part of him yearned for it, accompanied by a fleeting bravado that urged him to dare it, in the same way that a human might fantasize about stepping off the lookout for the thrill of terror that would surely accompany the act.

Angel knew he could not stay for the sunlight. But he had compensations. The brightness of a blue summer sky, the shimmering of a dew-colored spider web, the sparkle of sunbeams on the ocean white-caps—none of these could compare with the brilliance of a soul. And while most of the world walked around completely ignorant of the fact that souls were real, Angel fully comprehended the reality—and the gift—of possessing one. He knew he enjoyed a state of being beyond both human existence and vampiric immortality, and that he might be the only individual ever to do so.

There was a beauty inherent in that, as well as an almost unrelenting loneliness. The darkness, and the dawn.

Staring once more at the horizon, he turned to go. The Kraken was not going to show its face—or its tentacles—tonight. Angel had very much wanted to check it out for himself, see what they were up against, and he had come up to the lookout with the hope that it would be visible from this height. The waning moon had still been casting a good deal of light on the nighttime water. No such luck, however.

He began to walk back down the path, his boots occasionally crushing a piece of ice plant lodged in the sandy soil. The soft night breeze brought the tang of salt with it; idly he licked his lips and thought about a restful day in the darkened rooms of the mansion.

Then he heard an almost subaudible growling; it rumbled toward him as if it came from something moving beneath the ground.

Angel stopped, looking left, right, then in a small circle. The growling sound increased in volume, as if it had reached the surface now. It was coming from the left, he decided, moving toward the sound. Then it seemed to switch, echoing off the rubble of what had once been a ruined lighthouse, but could not even be counted as that any longer.

After a couple of minutes he gave up. He had no time to investigate. Aware that in the last few days the others had been ambushed several times, he continued down the path with greater care. Every muscle in his body went on full alert, ready for a fight.

Squinting, he crouched and bent forward. There were tracks in the sand like the long, deep ridges from the tires of an off-road vehicle. Yet the tracks were smooth, without patterns. Something in the depressions sparkled in the flashlight beam; he knelt on one knee and scooped up a sample, examining it. It looked like bits of glass.

He wished he had more time before sunup; he

would like nothing better than to follow the tracks. But he didn't. He reluctantly left the ominous growling and the footprints behind on Dead Man's Walk.

Giles's hospital-assigned physician was none too pleased to learn that his patient was determined to be discharged. He tried to talk the stubborn Englishman out of it, but in the end there was nothing to be done.

"You're crazy to just walk out, so soon after that fever, but this isn't Bellevue. Even crazy people can't be kept here against their will," the man had said to Giles.

Giles had failed to see the humor in the doctor's statement, and rather gruffly thanked him for his care. Then he turned to Matt Pallamary, whom he regarded as little more than a sincere young man who might one day make a decent Watcher, but was not one yet, and said, "The hotel first, and then the airport, yes?"

Pallamary brought his car around—it was a ubiquitous Camry—and came around to the passenger door, opening it with a flourish while the hospital volunteer who had wheeled Giles to the curb helpfully put on the wheelchair's brake and flicked back the footrests.

After so many days in hospital, the Manhattan air seemed refreshing, even pleasant; Giles thought to mention that fact to Pallamary as he gingerly slid into the passenger side of the front seat and allowed the volunteer, an elderly gentleman, to fasten his seat belt for him.

The reason that he did not mention it was because he noticed that beneath the console for the music system was a small, plastic sort of cubbyhole affair. And in the cubbyhole was the distinctive paper bookmark that was packed with each purchase from one of the bookshops he, Giles, had visited.

As Pallamary came around to the driver's side, Giles surreptitiously fished out the bookmark and examined it.

On the back was written "Room 1622."

Giles's room number.

Before Pallamary opened the door, Giles slipped the bookmark back into place.

Pallamary sat down, put on his seat belt, and shut the door. Pleasantly he said, "Well, that's over with."

"Quite." Giles said, "I just had a thought. I'd appreciate it so much if you would drive me straightaway to the airport, then go back and collect my things and send them on. I'm most eager to return to the Slayer, and it's quite possible I can route myself through a couple of different airlines in order to get to her side as soon as possible."

"Oh." Pallamary looked nervous. "But, um, those are your private things, sir, in your room, I mean. Would you be comfortable having a stranger going through them?"

"A stranger already has," Giles said, feigning surprise. "Didn't they tell you? A most peculiar volume was stolen from my room. It was called *Convergence: Massed Supranatural Phenomena.*"

Pallamary pulled away from the curb and wove the car into the heavy New York traffic. Around them, car horns blared at one another and bicycle messengers dodged bumpers with astonishing grace.

"But I thought nothing was taken," Pallamary said slowly.

"Oh, no, quite a few things were filched," Giles assured him. "Didn't Micaela tell you?"

"Well, yes, now that you mention it," Pallamary conceded, "she did tell me about that book."

Giles's blood ran cold. This man was not from the Watchers' Council. Giles didn't know who he was, but he most assuredly knew who he wasn't.

"Oh, look," he said, pointing to a Dunkin' Donuts. "I fancy a cup of decent coffee. How about you? You must have had your fill of hospital cuisine, same as I."

"Oh. Yes," Pallamary said uncertainly. "Yeah. It was terrible stuff."

"Pull over then," Giles suggested. "I'll run in. Cream and sugar?"

"Yeah." Pallamary looked concerned. "That'd be great." He frowned. "If you feel up to it."

"I feel fine. Honestly," Giles announced. "Just hungry."

Pallamary pulled over, double-parking, as was the custom in Manhattan.

Giles got out of the car and walked with an unhurried gait toward the doughnut shop. He smiled and waved at Pallamary, who was watching him with a wariness that gave Giles pause. Suppose they were being followed?

He went in and said to the young shopgirl, "I beg your pardon, but I was wondering if you have another exit?"

She blinked at him, as if waiting for the reason he wanted to know. But when he offered nothing more, she said, "Well, there's the one for deliveries."

"Excellent. I'd like to use it." He smiled at her graciously. He had discovered that in America, his accent opened doors—as it were—which were locked to others. "Please."

"Um, okay. It's back there."

She gestured to her left.

Giles turned and held up a finger to Pallamary, then pointed to exactly where he was going. He hoped to give the indication he was off to use the loo. He couldn't see if Pallamary saw him or nodded back. The sun was glinting on the Camry's windscreen.

Giles slowly sauntered toward the alternate exit.

The airport terminal was buzzing with travelers when Buffy arrived with Xander. Fortunately, they didn't have to wait long before Giles's plane touched down.

"Hi," Buffy said, rushing toward him as he emerged from the pack of passengers coming in on the New York flight. She hesitated when she saw the bruises on his face and the cut above his right eye, then hugged him anyway. He didn't look too good in some ways, but in others, he had never looked better. As in: he was here, and she needed him big-time.

And she had missed him and worried about him more than she could have imagined.

"Ooph," he groaned as she gave him a quick squeeze, then smiled faintly as she gazed at him in concern and let go of him. "It's good to be home." He looked past her to Xander. "Where is Cordelia?"

"At your place. We planned a party, just for you." Buffy brightened. "That you're paying for, because we're all broke."

"Hey, G-man," Xander said, coming forward and offering his hand. "Welcome home."

"I told you never to call me that." Giles shook his head.

"Yeah." Xander smiled. "Think you did. Sorry."

Xander took Giles's single bag, and Buffy fell into

step beside her Watcher. "So, you haven't been able to figure out who Pallamary is working for?"

Giles had called her from the airport to give her the full rundown in case something happened to him on his way back from Sunnydale. As in, his plane blowing up in mid-flight.

"Sadly, no. I take it that you were equally frustrated in your quest to discover the identity of the men who attacked you outside the Bronze?"

"Nada." Buffy gazed at him. "Are you really okay? Or did you jump ship because of all the weird stuff going on around here?"

"Hey, he looks okay, doesn't he?" Xander asked. "C'mon, Buff. Never look a gift Giles in the mouth. Or whatever."

They walked outside. Oz was parked in the passenger loading zone, and as they neared the van, Willow burst out and ran toward Giles.

"You're here!" she cried. "I am soooo happy!"

Buffy said quickly, "Don't hug him too hard."

"Oh." Willow looked abashed. "I wasn't going to hug him at all. Although I would have liked to." She made an apologetic face at Giles. "I didn't think it would be respectful."

"I'm glad to see you, too, Willow," he said.

Willow asked, "Where's your luggage?"

"In New York. It's a long story."

Willow nodded. Buffy figured that by now Willow was used to long stories. She hoped Giles hadn't lost anything valuable to him.

"Now, Buffy, don't you think it's time I got the full story about what's been going on around here?" Giles asked. "Rains of toads, skyquakes, mysterious attackers, the Wendigo . . . and why is it I'm certain you're leaving something out?"

"Well, there's Springheel Jack," Xander volunteered.

"Dear Lord," Giles said, eyes widening. "What else?"

Buffy huffed at Xander. "Narc," she said. Then, to Giles, "Well, Angel thinks he ran into a Tatzelwurm. Whatever that is."

Giles put one contemplative finger to his lips. "The Tatzelwurm, you say?"

Buffy looked for confirmation at Willow, who nodded. "Yeah, probably. Rumbling, growling, indentations, glass in the sand?"

"Good Lord." Giles smacked his forehead. Buffy wanted to tell him not to do that. He was smacked up bad enough as it was. "The Gatehouse."

When Buffy and Willow just stared at him, he said, "The Tatzelwurm—there's only one—is said to have been locked up inside the Gatehouse."

"Only it's not," Buffy guessed. "That was a pretty easy one, Alex. I'll try Less Obvious Observations for two hundred. Meaning, what the heck are you talking about?"

"Of course." Giles was flushed. His eyes were shining. Buffy wondered if there was some kind of medication he was supposed to take, but had forgotten to.

He walked ahead of them and gave Oz a wave. Popping open the passenger door and taking Willow's seat, he said, "Oz, hello. Please take me to the library."

"Giles," Buffy protested. "Party."

"No. I've got to get to the library straightaway. I think I've got the answer, Buffy." He almost smiled. Maybe it wasn't medically related after all. He did get that jaunty, way-jazzed look when he was jamming on the knowledge.

Giles let them in. Xander went off in search of snack food. Willow and Oz stood together as Buffy hung idly beside the return cage, where Giles kept his books of most secret stuff. Also weapons. She eyed a new, super-powered crossbow with interest while he rummaged around, then said, "My God. They're missing."

He came out of the cage. "I have two volumes on the legend of the Gatekeeper, and neither is here."

Buffy shrugged. "Maybe you put them somewhere else?"

"Took them home to catch up on them?" Willow suggested.

Giles shook his head. "No. I distinctly recall placing them in the box on the right-hand side of the top shelf. One of them bears a line drawing of the Gatehouse on the cover. It's quite lovely. The Gatehouse itself is a replica of a Florentine villa from the time of the de' Medicis. Sixteenth century, as I recall."

"Me, too," Buffy said archly. "Sixteenth. I'm positive."

He ignored her, crossing the room to his office. Curious, Buffy followed, gesturing for Oz and Willow to join her. They hung in the doorway as Giles pulled an NFL phone card from a stack in his desk and began to punch numbers into the desk phone.

"He's playing the horses," Buffy told Willow and Oz. "Gatehouse in the sixteenth."

Willow looked at Buffy and tried to smile. But her gaze was glued to Giles. She murmured, "I tried various combinations of key words—like Tatzelwurm—in your database but I never got a Gatehouse."

"Even so, I applaud your efforts, which I'm certain were exemplary," Giles said, then sat in his chair and cleared his throat.

*"Ja, guten Morgen,"* he said in German. *"Frau von Forsch? Hier spricht Giles."*

Margarethe von Forsch was a second-generation Watcher, and she deeply admired Rupert Giles, who was at least third-generation. She was a somewhat disheveled and matronly German academic who, growing weary of waiting for an opportunity to guide a Slayer, had lost herself among the volumes of folklore at Goethe University in Frankfurt am Main. Several of her own studies graced the private library of the Watchers' Council, an accomplishment of which she was quite proud.

Now, having been awakened from a deep sleep, she listened intently as Herr Giles quizzed her on the legend of the Gatehouse.

"According to the stories, the Tatzelwurm was most assuredly captured by the Gatekeeper and kept within the house," she said, nodding, though the handsome *Engländer* could not see her. *Thank goodness,* with moisturizer all over her face and her hair in old-fashioned curlers.

"In Boston," he said.

*"Ja.* Even so. All the evidence points there."

"Very good. *Vielen Dank."*

"Wait! You must fill me in," she said unhappily,

and gamely trying out her American slang. "I'm dying to know what's going on."

"Later, Frau von Forsch. I'm sorry, but I've much to do."

"You promise you will tell me?" she asked.

"I promise."

"Then, until later."

He said, "Indeed."

He disconnected first. Slowly she hung up.

"Well, friend Giles," she murmured, "what are you up to now?"

"That is precisely what we would like to know, also," said a voice in the room.

She cried out as a figure stepped from the shadows behind her open bedroom door. Dressed in a monk's robe, it was very tall, and its face was hidden from her view. It glided toward her as if it had no feet.

The air surrounding it crackled a deep blue.

In its right hand, it hefted a thinly tapered, jagged blade.

"You will tell us," it promised.


Giles hung up and looked at the trio of young people standing behind his chair, Buffy standing slightly in front of the other two.

"Well," he said, "we must devise a way for some of us to go to Boston. Buffy, for certain."

Buffy eyed him. "Boston."

"Yes." He nodded.

"In the middle of the school year."

"I know it's going to be a stretch," he conceded.

"And we're going because?"

"I believe we're needed." He took in the three of

them, and was struck by the strange dichotomy of their young lives. He would have to think of a clever ruse indeed to spirit Buffy and possibly a number of her cohorts out of Sunnydale, since telling their parents and school officials the truth—that the Slayer was needed to thwart an evil menace of a supernatural nature—was clearly out of the question.

"Who's needed?" Xander asked. "Us? 'Cause, y'know, I might be best put to use as a blunt instrument. Monster comes up, Buffy can just pick me up and beat the thing to death with my rigid, screaming form."

Giles rolled his eyes heavenward. "Xander, please. I don't have time to figure out what's happening to the Gatehouse and coddle your fragile teen male ego at the same time.

"Angel must stay behind, of course. It's too dangerous for him to travel by plane. In my absence, it would seem that Willow ought to remain in Sunnydale as well. If I cannot bring my library with me, having you here as home base is the next best thing," Giles told her.

Willow beamed. "And, if, y'know, there're any more big huge spookables, I may be able to help with some of the spells I've been researching."

Giles frowned. "You'd best take care with such things, Willow. I know I don't have to warn you. You're a sensible girl. But magick is not to be trifled with. Have a care, and only cast spells you are confident that you are prepared for."

Willow nodded.

"Of course, Oz will want to stay with you," Giles said, talking to himself now. "I suppose it will have to be just Buffy and myself. Pity. If the Gatehouse is in as much jeopardy as I believe it is, we could use all the help we can get."

Xander cleared his throat. "Um, hello? What was that about my fragile teen male ego?"

"Oh, yes, Xander, I apologize," Giles said. "Your help will be greatly appreciated."

"It's a plan, then," Xander said, nodding. "And, y'know, though she's not real keen on coming to anybody's rescue, I have a feeling the lovely Miss Chase won't want to miss this. She can scare the bad guys off by showing them her American Express bill."

Giles's mind was whirling with suspicions and fears, worries and wonders, and so, when he happened to glance over and see Buffy staring quite intently at him, he was momentarily taken aback.

"Buffy?" he said. "What is it?"

She raised an eyebrow. He recognized it as her patented sarcastic look. "In the midst of all your grand travel plans, you left something out. Boston, why?"

"Something has gone terribly wrong at the Gatehouse," he said.

"Oh, in *that* case, I'll start packing," she said dryly.

"I guess this means no party," Willow ventured.

"I still need to go home." Giles smiled at her. "I have one further question for Frau von Forsch. Let me give her another quick ring, and then we'll leave. All right?"

"Sure," Buffy said.

She turned and left his office. Willow and Oz followed her.

Giles heard Xander say in a loud voice, "Boston? Is

anyone else thinking Boston Massacre? 'Cause, y'know, Boston Tea Party would be nice. Maybe we could say we're all going to a reenactment of the revolution. Or a big spelling bee."

All of which gave Giles pause. Not a reenactment or something as obvious as that, but a history contest of some kind. He could convince the school's principal of that, say it was sponsored by the ALA or something. And the parents would love it.

Giles dialed von Forsch's number in Germany. Figuring she was still awake, he had thought to ask her if she might fax him whatever pertinent information she had about the Gatehouse, since his own research texts were gone. *Stolen?* he wondered. Was that what they had been looking for in his hotel room in New York?

He let the German woman's line ring ten times, but there was no answer. He waited two minutes—he could wait no longer—and dialed again.

No answer.

He waited two more minutes.

Still no answer.

Finally, he dialed an international operator. After an interminable wait, he was informed that there was a report of some kind of interruption of service at the residence of the party he was attempting to reach.

He closed his eyes as fear for her washed over him.

He dialed the Watchers' Council.

"Yes, Giles here," he said softly, when the phone was silently answered. "Please check on Margarethe von Forsch. Immediately. I'm afraid . . ." He could not finish.

And then, as he listened, his blood ran cold. For he

was being informed of the death of Kobo Sensei, the Japanese Watcher who had lost a Slayer. The sorrowful old man had assisted Giles in saving Buffy when a Chinese vampire named Chirayoju had possessed Willow. Now he was dead.

He had been slowly and brutally tortured to death.

And now no one was answering at Frau von Forsch's house.

"Giles? It's time for that one last hurrah," Xander called to him. "We're having mini-pizzas straight from the dairy case."

"Yes. Coming," Giles said shakily.

He rose and went to join the others.

Cordelia was in heaven, or the closest thing to it if you weren't at Neiman Marcus: the Sunnydale Mall was having a gigantic blowout sale, and she had found an amazing pair of shoes in a store she would not usually have deigned to enter. But tonight, on a whim, she had gone in after she'd picked up the supplies for Giles's homecoming party, and there they were: her size, her color, and way beneath her price range.

"Yes, Virginia, there is a Santa Claus," she breathed, hopping deliriously onto the escalator.

Cordelia preened. She knew she looked great in her black jeans and red velvet tank top with crisscross straps. Xander said red was her best color. Also blue, green, and yellow.

She carried her prize to the parking lot and flicked off her car's security system. She had one hand on her door before she remembered that very strange things had been happening lately—or, to put it more accurately, more strange things than usual—and that

Buffy had cautioned everybody to be on their guard. A chill shot through Cordelia. For all she knew, the earth could open up right beneath her feet and suck her down. Or a pack of trolls could rush her and carry her off to a nearby bridge.

Or when she opened the door, her car could blow up.

Crazy, all of it. But suddenly Cordelia just couldn't shake the feeling that she was being watched.

She swallowed and looked anxiously over her shoulder. Her stomach clenched. For a moment she stood frozen, unsure if it would be better to get inside the car or stay out of it, go back to the mall or what. Things didn't look too creepy in the parking lot, although there was a clump of men in dark clothes standing near the exit, and maybe they were staring at her, but that wasn't abnormal at all. They could just be waiting for the bus.

She peered into her car, first at the front seat and then the rear. *Looks okay.* She would have to get in and go pick up Xander eventually, because soon the mall would close.

And besides . . . the hair stood up on the back of her neck . . . the clump of guys in dark clothes could not possibly be waiting for the bus. Their dark clothes were nice clothes, and in Southern California, no one who had nice clothes ever took a bus. Buses were for people who couldn't afford cars. Period.

More frightened now, she opened the door and slid in, slamming the door and locking it as quickly as she could. She jammed the key in the ignition and peeled out of the lot, realizing she was calling attention to herself but too frightened to slow down. Her car fishtailed as she reached the street and she hung a left, then closed her eyes in frustration because Xander's house was the other direction.

She hung a very wide U and jammed back down the road, suddenly finding herself irritated with Buffy. If she'd never met Miss Thing, she probably wouldn't be in danger right now. Never mind that Buffy had saved her life time and again, and that it was the Hellmouth that drew all the evil things to Sunnydale, not Buffy herself. She was here to slay them.

But if she, Cordelia, hadn't been friends with Buffy . . .

—Suddenly Cordelia shrieked in abject, visceral terror—

. . . there would probably still be a pasty-faced monster with black holes for eyes sliding headfirst from the roof onto her windshield.

A monster vomiting torrents of flame that were already melting the glass.

Gathered around the runestone, the men in the parking lot of the Sunnydale Mall stared at the glowing characters as the black pebble shimmered and spun in Brother Dando's palm. It trailed purple, silver, and blue-white light as it searched the environs for the Slayer. Finally it came to rest and pulsed crimson, a dark, silent heartbeat.

"Northeast," Brother Isimo said, nodding to the others. He was dark-skinned, with long, gray hair that tumbled over his shoulders and a distinctive scar etched within the hollow of his cheek. "The Slayer walks the night."

Brother Dando smiled. He was very small, nearly a dwarf, yet he was the most powerful among them. He could crush a man merely by wishing it. "That is good. We can proceed."

Brother Isimo nodded. "Her mother is not an ally. Her Watcher continues in captivity in the hospital."

Brother Dando whispered to the runestone, "There will be no rest for her from us. There will be no haven for her from us. No safe place from us. No asylum from us."

"No asylum," the others intoned.

"We must make haste," Brother Kukoff ventured. He was the youngest among them, in terms of his abilities. Yet he was almost sixty-eight years old. "Il Maestro waits for his victory."

"Indeed, brother," Brother Dando said. "We must please Il Maestro in all things."

"In all things," the group chorused.


"Oh, my God, oh, my God," Cordelia cried as she lost control of the car, drove over the sidewalk, and strafed a row of trash cans.

Spread-eagled across the windshield, Springheel Jack threw himself against the melted web of glass. He was wild to get at her. His grin told her that. And his horrible, black eyes.

"I've marked you!" Springheel Jack hissed through the flames. "Once I've left my mark on the prey, the prey must die!"

Cordelia winced, and for the first time in days, pain flared up in the slowly healing scratch on her back where the monster had slashed her. Then she screamed again as he lifted one hand from his grip on the metal stripping above the windshield and began to tear at the melted edges of the hole in the windshield.

The car veered to the left; Cordelia was not so much

driving as holding onto the wheel in sheer terror. Her foot was frozen to the accelerator and she had lost all knowledge of how to control the vehicle. All she was capable of doing was screaming and holding on.

She kept going, kept her foot on the gas; she had no idea where she was going, and in fact couldn't even think coherently enough for such a notion to occur to her.

Again, Springheel Jack belched fire, but she jerked the wheel enough to unbalance him, and the flames torched the passenger seat, setting the upholstery ablaze. Cordelia screamed and somehow, in her blind panic, slammed on the brakes.

Springheel Jack tumbled roughly from atop the car.

Cordelia didn't see where he landed, couldn't see him even now, but somehow she pulled herself together enough to understand that she should make a break for it, now.

She put the car in reverse and floored it. The stink of burning rubber clashed with the stench of superheated chemically treated fabric. She batted at the fire ineffectually, sobbing.

Then she slammed on the brakes and shifted into drive. She pushed the gas pedal to the floor and the car leaped forward.

If he was out there, she would hit him. She would run the hideous bastard over if it was the last thing she did.

The car hummed, then roared, as it barreled down the street. She had to roll down the window to clear the smoke; she could barely see out the windshield; and she had a brief, horrible thought: *What if I hit someone else?*

But she hit nothing. She bulleted along, going as

fast as she could, daring that monster to step in front of her car.

He didn't show.

Yet somehow, Cordelia felt no sense of relief. She still felt those bottomless, black wounds that were the creature's eyes boring into her.

He was still out there.

# Chapter 9

Willow was painting her toenails Rosetta Stone and listening to the new Keb' Mo' CD, trying to relax. Between all this Boston stuff and the pressure her parents had been putting on her lately to choose a college, she was a bit on edge. It was either relaxing in her room making her toes pretty or a wild *Thelma and Louise* weekend in Vegas with the girls. And since the whole Vegas thing might cause, oh, just a little problem in the parental area, she'd settled for Rosetta Stone.

The thought of college, of leaving, made Willow glance around her room. She was practically an adult. Not a little girl anymore, but nobody would know that from the frilly way the room was decorated. Lace. Floral patterns. Wherever she ended up going to college, Willow promised herself one thing: no stuffed animals.

Well, maybe one. And her bunny slippers.

*Yup,* she thought, *I'm a rebel.*

A rebel. Which was why she'd slunk off to her room after a brief and accusatory conversation with her parents. Xander's mom had happened to mention to Willow's mother that Xander was going to Boston for a national history fair. Giles had concocted a wonderful cover story—Willow had even helped—but it had come back to haunt her. Her parents now thought she was either not doing well enough to go to the fair or purposely staying home to be with Oz.

There was just no winning sometimes.

In truth, she was a little creeped out at being left to essentially hold the fort. She didn't want the responsibility, really. But she'd deal. She always had. And she'd have Oz to help her. Then there was Angel. Not quite as comforting—she still got a bit creeped out around him at times—but at least he was strong, durable, and really, really hard to kill. Of course, Oz was really hard to kill as well, him being a werewolf and all.

Willow let her freshly painted piggies dry and watched the clock. She'd planned to see the others off down at the airport, and it was almost time. Buffy and her mom were going to swing by and pick her up.

She passed her mother in the hallway, but didn't stop to chat. It would only be more pressure tactics about college or suspicion about her not going to Boston. With a sigh, she trotted down the stairs, blew her father a kiss before he could rise from his chair, and was out the door.

The streetlights flashed by above the car, casting shifting shadows on the dash and seats. Buffy looked out the passenger window, watching the night. Watching the people, more than anything else. A young guy in gym clothes ran in the opposite direction, headphones covering his ears. He was a honey. A white-haired couple, holding hands like youthful lovers, walked a pair of black poodles. A woman in a dark business suit swung a leather briefcase idly at her side.

Just people in the night. In the shadows. With no idea what real darkness was like, no idea what real dangers lurked in that dark.

Unnerved, Buffy turned to face forward and realized that they were almost to Willow's. Her mother turned left onto a side street. Buffy glanced at her, noted the grim set of her jaw, and wondered again if asking her mother to drive her to the airport had been the wisest course of action. For the others, it was hard to lie and get away with it. Buffy thought that telling her mother the truth was, in a lot of ways, much more difficult.

The airport was twenty minutes away, and they were already running late. The only saving grace was that the connecting flight out of LAX, the red-eye to Boston, didn't leave until forty minutes after the puddle jumper arrived in L.A. As long as the plane didn't take off without them, they'd still be all right.

Joyce Summers nearly missed the turn onto Willow's street. When she realized it, and began to back up to make the turn, Joyce cursed under her breath. Again, Buffy glanced at her mother's face, even as Joyce sighed deeply.

"Mom?" Buffy asked, all possible questions in that one word.

Even as she started watching house numbers, Joyce took a breath and said, "Buffy, this is getting so serious. Cordelia was *attacked.*"

But Buffy heard a question in her mother's voice that Joyce had not put into words.

"I'll be back, Mom, I promise," Buffy insisted.

Joyce nodded. "I know, honey. I do. But it's just . . . well, you're leaving again. I can't pretend I'm happy about it."

"Mom, this is a little different, don't you think? You're driving me to the airport. It isn't just me, either. It's Giles and Cordelia and Xander. Which, you know, should be loads of fun. You have Cordelia's cell phone number. Plus, it's for a few days, a week at best. After that, Giles really wouldn't be able to explain our absence. Someone would check on us.

"Trust me. We'll be back. *I'll* be back, and soon."

Joyce smiled wanly. She began to speak, only to have Buffy cut her off.

"There's Willow."

"We're half a block from her house," Joyce observed. "I hope nothing's wrong."

"You want my guess? Probably nothing out of the ordinary for a teenager barreling toward high school graduation," Buffy offered.

"Graduation, what a beautiful word," Joyce said dreamily. "You don't know how many times I was afraid you wouldn't make it."

Buffy smiled to herself. No matter what, her mother wanted exactly what Buffy wanted: for her daughter to be a normal teenage girl. The real difference was that Buffy was just a lot more realistic about the possibility of that ever happening.

As in: none.

"I'll be there, Mom," she said. "I might be late. I might put my gown on inside out, but I'll be there."

"You'd better," Joyce said, but this time, she didn't look at her daughter.

The car slowed to a stop and Buffy reached back to unlock the door for Willow. After she'd climbed in the back seat, Mrs. Summers accelerated again, and Buffy saw how relieved to be getting away from her house Willow seemed.

"Thanks for coming to get me," Willow said to Buffy's mother.

"Any time, Willow," Joyce replied.

"Cool," Buffy said. "Now anytime you want to go out with Oz, my mom can pick you up and just take you over there!"

Joyce shook her head in amusement. Willow, on the other hand, only managed a particularly lackluster smile.

At the end of Willow's street, Angel sat in the driver's seat of Giles's battered Citroen and drummed his fingers in syncopated rhythm with a Pearl Jam song on the radio. His musical tastes were broad, though they ran more toward the classical. Still, he could appreciate almost any kind of music. His voice almost a whisper, he sang along.

Giles had debriefed him on his suspicions regarding the people who were killing Watchers, and apparently hunting Buffy as well. Since the Watcher himself was not going to be in town, he had given Angel the use of his car for the duration of the Boston trip. As they'd discussed, the first thing Angel did with the car was use it to follow Buffy. And, as expected, he hadn't been the only one.

The key now was to make sure that Buffy made it to the airport without anyone tailing her. Giles thought it was a good idea for their destination to remain a secret. If they could keep their enemies in the dark while on this trip to Boston, it would make things go a lot more smoothly. It might also give them time to find out exactly who was behind those attacks.

But as Angel had explained to Giles, there might be other ways.

Headlights flashed across Angel's face, bathing him in white brilliance, causing him to look like nothing so much as a walking corpse. Which was, of course, very nearly what he was.

"Try not to be seen, Brother Taggart," Lupo said dismissively. Taggart was a good driver and had done an admirable job of tailing the Slayer thus far, but on these small side streets it was almost impossible not to be noticed. Thus far, Taggart seemed perfectly capable of the impossible, having stayed far back from the Slayer's vehicle and made subtle movements when necessary.

When the vehicle had slowed so that the Slayer's companion might enter, Taggart had turned right, made a quick course around the block, and emerged two blocks farther along the road, even as the vehicle carrying the Slayer made a three-point turn in the street and went back along the way it had arrived.

Taggart was good at his job. He'd served in MI5 for some time and killed people in the Falklands under orders that hadn't come from his superiors. Lupo enjoyed his company. It was a pleasure to be in the presence of a man to whom life was so pure. So simple. Taggart was a killer. Given the order, he did the job. No fuss. No argument. No guilt.

Brother Lupo felt that if Il Maestro had had a thousand such men, his plans might have come to fruition decades earlier.

Instead of now.

Far ahead, the taillights of the Slayer's vehicle—one of which glowed white through plastic Taggart had broken so as to identify the vehicle from a distance—turned left at the corner and then were gone.

"Don't lose them, Taggart."

"Sure and I'm not goin' to lose them," he replied in his thickly accented English.

At the end of the street there was a stop sign. Taggart, not wanting to risk any attention, for those were his orders, made a complete stop at that sign.

When a fist smashed suddenly through the driver's window, Brother Lupo shrieked in terror. He felt sick, for he was used to inducing that emotion in others. Before Taggart could react, strong hands dragged him from behind the wheel, arms shredded by the broken glass. Lupo watched the man's thrashing legs as they disappeared out the open window.

Then he jumped behind the wheel.

"Who are you working for?" Angel snarled, yellow eyes glowing in his feral vampire face.

"Ye want to know anythin', ye wanker, then ye've taken the wrong man. Ye can go to hell for all the good your shiny little teeth'll do ye with me," the man said, even as the men inside their car scrambled to get someone else behind the wheel.

The Lexus the man had been driving lurched forward with a squeal as someone else finally got sufficient control of the car to get it far away from Angel. But the vampire didn't mind. His job was done. Angel had held them up long enough that they wouldn't be able to trace Buffy tonight. They'd probably realize she'd gone to the airport eventually, but for now, that was the best plan they had.

"Tell me!" Angel snapped, and shook the man, who was dangerous looking by human standards. Angel wasn't concerned.

"Now, or I rip your throat out!" Angel demanded.

Tires squealed. Angel glanced up in time to see the Lexus, which he'd thought long gone, barreling toward him. The headlights blinded him a moment, and the red-faced thug he'd been throttling used the distraction to lash out with bone-crushing force, trying to break Angel's hold on him.

It did little more than piss him off.

Angel backhanded the thug across the face. The Lexus careened toward them both. With a mighty shove, Angel threw the thug clear and then dove in the opposite direction, hoping the moment's indecision would buy a precious second, enough time so that the driver would be unable to hit either one of them.

Tires blackened tar with a horrible rubber scream. Angel leaped to his feet as a thin, olive-skinned man leaned out the passenger window of the Lexus with a pistol in his hand.

"Taggart!" the olive-skinned man screamed.

The thug Angel had pulled from the car sprang to

his feet just across the street and began sprinting for the car. Angel snarled and ran after him. He was only barely aware of the pistol, of the danger of getting shot. He'd been shot before. The only thing that mattered was getting answers—finding out who these bastards were who wanted Buffy dead.

Buffy dead.

Angel was not going to let that happen.

He caught up with the one they'd called Taggart, grabbed him by the back of his collar, then spun him around, one hand gripping the man's neck and squeezing his throat mercilessly.

"Talk to me, you son of a—"

The gunman in the car squeezed the trigger, the pistol barked once, and Taggart's forehead exploded, spattering gore and gray matter all over Angel's face.

The tires on the sedan smoked as the car peeled away.

Angel only stood there, furious and frozen with astonishment. *They did it on purpose,* he thought. *Killed their own man, just to keep him from talking to me.* Sometimes he wondered if humans weren't, in their own way, worse than vampires. The demons who inhabited vampires were, after all, created to be evil.

Humans had a choice.

Angel was about to let Taggart drop to the pavement when he paused, stricken by the scent of fresh blood. On his clothes. On his face. His lips. It was everywhere, and Angel felt the hunger come over him in a way it had not for some time. He stared at Taggart's destroyed face, and then at the rough flesh of the man's throat.

Somewhere nearby, a police siren began its keening wail.

With a growl of self-loathing, Angel let Taggart's corpse fall to the pavement with a wet slap. He drew his sleeve across his face, wiping the blood away, and then he sprinted for Giles's car.

"Buffy, we really must go," Giles implored. "That's the final call for our flight."

The small airport was far from busy. The airline employee who had announced final boarding was staring at them, as if anyone could look intimidating in that silly blue uniform. Buffy nodded to Giles without responding. They were all there, all but Angel. Oz and Willow and Buffy's mother had all come to see them off, and Cordelia and Xander stood just behind Giles, attempting to get Buffy to hurry.

"I don't want to go on that little plane," she told Willow, who smiled and raised her eyebrows as if to say, "tough luck." "Thanks so much for your sympathy," Buffy told her.

This time they both smiled.

"If you want to make your connection in L.A., you'd better hurry," Joyce Summers said.

Buffy glanced up at her mother in surprise. Joyce hadn't talked much since they'd arrived at the airport, and seemed to hold herself at a distance from the rest of them quite purposefully. They looked at each other now, mother and daughter, and a kind of tacit communication passed between them. In a moment of intense clarity, Buffy imagined that it was the same silent message fathers had given sons for millennia as they sent them off to war. *I love you. Be careful. Come back to me.*

Buffy stepped forward with a rush of unexpected emotion and embraced her mother, kissing her cheek. "I love you," she whispered.

"Willow, if you have any questions at all . . ." Giles began.

"She knows how to reach us, Giles. You only told her twenty-seven thousand times," Cordelia huffed. "Now, please, I just want to get this over with as quickly as possible. God, who ever heard of flying coach?"

"Um, the ninety-nine percent of the airplane-riding population who can't afford first class?" Xander offered.

Cordelia stared at him. "It must be nice to have an answer for everything," she sniffed.

"Actually, it is."

They continued to bicker. Giles sighed, picked up his bag, and walked toward the open door to the gangway. Cordelia and Xander picked up their things as well.

"Xand?" Willow asked.

Xander turned to face her, and she hugged him quickly, obviously quite aware that both of their significant others were looking on.

"Be careful," she said.

"Hey," Xander said, softening, "you too. We're going on a field trip. You're here with the spookables." He glanced up at Oz. "Hey, Wolf Boy, watch out for her, all right?"

Oz only smiled, which didn't surprise Buffy at all. He wasn't the type to have his fur ruffled by Xander's presumption.

"Come on!" Cordelia demanded, and pulled Xander after her.

"You kids have fun, now," Oz called after them.

Then Willow stood before Buffy again, and the two girls shared a long, wordless moment. Finally they embraced. With Willow's arms around her, Buffy could not help but reflect upon all that had been happening the past week, and even before that. They were speeding uncontrollably toward the end of life as they knew it. Graduation. Everything would change then, and the thought of it had been wearing on them all.

Buffy had seen it in the way Willow hugged Xander, as if she were preparing to say good-bye. Even now.

"Bye," Willow whispered.

"Yeah," Buffy agreed, then gave Willow one last squeeze before breaking off the embrace.

"Bye."

On the plane, Buffy noticed that Giles seemed quite a bit preoccupied. Though Xander tried his best to lighten the mood, the Watcher frequently slipped away, his eyes drifting off to focus on some impossibly distant site, far beyond the walls of the plane. Buffy sat next to Giles, and Cordelia sat with Xander in the row behind them. After a time, Xander and Cordy began talking softly to each other. Glancing at Giles again, Buffy began to grow concerned.

"Houston Control to Giles," she said at length. When he did not respond, Buffy poked his bicep. "Giles."

"Hmm?" With a furrowing of his brow, he turned to look at her.

"Okay, I know you were out sick the day they taught Small Talk 101, but you're really starting to worry me. Are you sure you should have left the hospital so soon?" Buffy asked, genuinely concerned.

"It isn't that," Giles said dismissively, and looked out the window at the darkness.

"Then what is it?"

For a moment, Giles did not respond. Only stared out the window. After several moments had passed, he took a short breath and turned to face Buffy once more.

"It's a bit silly, actually," he said, but his face and his voice were sad, rather than amused. "You see, the Watcher I met in New York, Miss Tomasi . . ."

"That Micaela chick?"

Giles smiled wanly. "Yes. That Micaela chick. I didn't know her very long, but I grew quite fond of her in that time. Now, with her disappearance . . . well, there are several possibilities, and none of them are very appealing."

Buffy lay the side of her head against her seat, looking at Giles with understanding, but trying not to show what she truly felt. After the murder of Jenny Calendar, the woman Giles had loved, Buffy was concerned that he might be too wounded to be interested in anyone else. And now, here was someone who might have piqued that interest if she'd stuck around long enough.

"She might have just gotten called away on other Council business. If this Pallamary guy was a plant, who's to say if he would even know where she was supposed to have gone?" Buffy offered.

Giles raised his eyebrows. "It's a nice thought. But it seems to me that either she was in league with our enemies from the outset, or they've killed her, just as they have several other Watchers of late."

Now he turned to look out the window, and Buffy tried not to look too closely at his troubled reflection in the glass.

"I'm not sure which of those options would be more distressing."

**Chapter 10**

*Boston, October, 1666*

AND SO, HAD HE LEFT HELL BEHIND, TO STAND TRIUM-
phant upon these distant shores?

Richard Regnier, now an ancient man—in terms of
years, if not in ailments and the predicaments of
aging—stood dressed in a somber but elegant black
coat, his copious sleeves caught back by bands of
black. His leggings, too, were black. Only his wig was
white. He was in mourning for his beautiful young
wife, Giuliana, now dead these seven months. Amid
the vines of various indigenous gourds, he stood on
the foundation of what would soon be his new home
and bowed his head, savoring the new sensation that
filled him. For a moment, he could not put a name to
it, but slowly it occurred to him that this feeling must
be peace. Coming to the New World had been a good
impulse, then, if serenity could be found within its
boundaries.

Of an evening, if he stood on his hill and looked out
over the harbor, he could almost see, in his sorcerer's

way, the ghost of a crimson glow across the Atlantic. Mere weeks before, the Great Fire had burned the city of London to the ground. Before the fire, the Plague had descended upon the population, killing tens of thousands.

Europe's only salvation was that Fulcanelli had perished in the chaos he himself had wrought, and Regnier gave profound thanks for that. The monster's reign of terror was now surely at an end.

In 1559, the Little Florentine, having become Queen of France, had been made a widow. Her fifteen-year-old son, King Francis II, had mustered a great deal of courage and withdrawn royal patronage from the decadent wizard, now more brazenly practicing his sacrifices and seducing half the virgins at court. Publicly humiliating the man, Francis had driven Fulcanelli out, just as Catherine de' Medici had once sent Regnier away in disgrace. Francis had died just two years later. Of an ear infection, it was said . . .

His revenge accomplished, Fulcanelli had left France and cast his net of chaos and destruction over the whole of the continent. Wars raged. Epidemics decimated the population of the continent. Many were certain the growing horror signaled the end of the world and the triumph of Satan over God.

Regnier had believed they were not far wrong. He was unaware of Fulcanelli's grand scheme, if indeed there was more to it than power and devastation. But it was clear to him, even then, that the sorcerer must be stopped or the seams of the world would surely split. To that end, the Frenchman had pursued his archrival over mountains and glaciers, across steppes and down into caverns as deep and treacherous as the mouth of Hell. At every possible juncture, they had entered into combat, both physical and magical.

At last, nearly a century after Fulcanelli had been driven from France, Regnier had stopped him.

With Fulcanelli dead, however, Regnier felt lost in Europe. The New World beckoned. It would have been too painful to live out the remainder of his days in Europe, and magicians such as he had many days to live. Fulcanelli had been nearly two hundred years of age at his death. There had been much vigor in him even then. Regnier was not even one hundred thirty. Such were the life spans of those who engaged the other dimensions of existence.

*The New World,* he thought now, as he gazed out over the harbor and felt the salty breeze against his face. *And a new life.*

Though his house was only newly begun, his excitement was such that he had determined to spend the nights on his land in the small cottage the builders had erected for him. A fire had been laid by his servant, whom he had sent home, and he looked forward to an evening of solitude and books.

Accordingly, he had brought his valuables—his magick arcana, his grimoire, and his most precious and private possessions, including the locket he had given to Giuliana, the beautiful Venetian he had loved and married . . . and whose bones lay in Italian soil, so very far from him now.

He opened the trunk. The filigree locket lay on top. His heart caught as he opened it. With his finger he traced the oval of her face, the dimples on either side of her smile. A famed beauty, particularly in these days when blue eyes and blond hair were considered the most desirable of feminine qualities. In Italy, blonds were the most desirable of all.

Giuliana, his Giuliana, slaughtered while he was on a fool's errand. That wretched bastard Fulcanelli, that ignominious and vile creature, to take his revenge on so innocent a head . . .

Peace flew from Regnier's heart as if it knew it had no place there. He balled his fists as tears coursed down his cheeks at the memory of his lost love. He would never love so fully again, of that he was certain.

As he wept, he spied his journal, slipped carefully into the side pocket of his traveling valise. Such tales lay within as would astonish the staid and religious population of this young town.

Composing himself, he lifted up the journal and opened it, seeking solace among the pages. He had to remember this: though he had lost everything he counted precious in this world, yet had he won.

*2nd September, 1666*

*All the city rages with a terrible fiery aspect. Churches, public halls, hospitals; Troy herself did not suffer so. St. Paul's is utterly destroyed. The cries and lamentations of the populace are piteous to hear: children scream in panic; mothers wail for their babes; men shout orders to demolish the houses which still stand, in the hope of my Lord Mayor that the fire shall starve.*

*But this fire feeds like a fiend on the wicked. For the most wicked who ever walked this earth hands it morsels like a lapdog. I have seen Fulcanelli standing atop the Tower of London* with his black wizard's cloak about him. That he was waiting for me to espy him was clear by his broad, triumphant smile as I raised my fist at him and extracted my wand. On another day, I should have been more circumspect about my magick, but this was the end of the world. Thus, I drew lightning down upon him, causing a clamor among those around me, but he dispelled my weaponry with a wave of his hand. A moment later, he had disappeared from view as the smoke rose up from the burning city.

I despaired. For had it not ever been thus, that he taunted me and escaped my wrath? A merry chase he had led me for almost a century. Fulcanelli, base servant of the Fallen One!

### 3rd September

I have passed the hours of day and night in vigil and practice of my art. Today I shall find Fulcanelli, for I am certain he is yet within the city. I shall find him and I shall kill him.

### 4th September

In my pursuit of the fiend, I have witnessed many horrors, but none so powerful as the firestorm of London Town. I searched through the hellish scene ever more resolved to end the life of the one who had started this terrible fire.

I saw him—but a glimpse—then lost him to a huge cloud of smoke.

But such was my fury that I dashed into the smoke, casting spells to guide my way as if I were *blinded by the conflagration. My heart thundered with the certainty that I was but footsteps behind him, and then a wall of flame shot up around me. I was much injured, but I cared not, for the flames were blue, and this signified his sorcerous attempts to thwart my progress. I swore that this day I would kill Fulcanelli.*

*Through that wretched, doomed city he fled me. On Tower Street, Fen-church Street, and so many other paths and roads, I ran with a vitality no man could wield save with magick, until I reached the Thames, burgeoning with goods floating upon it, and men in boats, and people diving into the water as their clothing burned upon their backs.*

*And there, on a large and elegant ebony barge, I saw him. Perhaps a dozen monks of a sort had gathered round him as the oars pulled. They wore hooded black robes and I could not see their faces. I understood these to be some of his loyal followers and acolytes, the secret band he has seduced into his influence.*

*He stood in their midst, his back to me. But I spied his withered arm and his gray locks, and knew him as my nemesis.*

*Before he had a chance to act, I called the flames forth from my very fists, and they arced out over the water. The fire caught in his hair and his coat, and in an instant he writhed as a pillar of flame.*

*His followers began to shriek and run in all directions. I heard one screaming in the sorcerer's native Italian for water.*

*But the humanity in Fulcanelli had withered*

long ago, not unlike his atrophied limb, and he crackled and burned as a husk of evil. He was fully ablaze in a trice, and he whirled in a circle, a column of flame.

He turned round; perhaps in some way he was able to see me. And in the case that he could hear me, I shouted, "For Giuliana, and all the innocents you have butchered!"

One single blue flame shot weakly at me from the pillar of fire, and then he was no more, only smoke and cinders.

Half of his accursed band fell to the deck of their vessel, wailing and shrieking. The others turned toward me, and I could see by the subtle gestures of their hands that they were preparing to turn their own black magick against me.

I prayed to God, and to the wind, and capsized their vessel. With satisfaction I watched them tumble into the water. Their heavy black robes began to pull them down.

I would have run at them then, ensuring that each was dispatched, but at that moment a most beautiful child held out her hands. Her face was coated with soot and her long, dark hair was tangled and matted. She wore a singed nightshirt.

I lifted her up, and with a hard look at the sinking barge, I quitted the scene. Fulcanelli was dead; of that I was certain. If one or two of his depraved retainers survived, what did I care? They would prove no match for me.

21st September

Tomorrow I leave England and quit Europe. The New World beckons. Many others of my

*kinsmen have sojourned to the town of Boston,
and my runestones have directed me there also.*

*I leave with both anticipation and melancholy.
Yesterday I placed the lost child in an orphanage
in the countryside, and the nuns there were happy
to receive such a pretty and sweet soul. The
Mother Superior and I spoke together over a glass
of excellent porto. Incredibly, her order boasts of
a convent in Venice, and she had heard, through
her sisters, of the death of my adored wife (for
Giuliana was much beloved for her charitable
works).*

*She and I have therefore promised to corre-
spond. She assures me that she will keep me
informed of the progress of the orphan, whom she
has named Juliet, after my wife.*

*Of Fulcanelli's followers I have seen no sign,
and thus conclude that they have scattered.*

*Giuliana, you are avenged.*

*And my heart, though shattered and never to be
mended, is glad of it.*

> *Richard M. Regnier, Chevalier and Sorcerer
> Dover, England*

Regnier closed the journal and slid it into his coat.
He was cold; the twilight was bitter. Others—his new
neighbors—had remarked on the chilliness of the
season, but France had often been unseasonably cold.
Italy, never. Where Giuliana had smiled, there the
sun warmed all icy fields and frozen hearts.

He traced the shape of the foundation. It would be a
splendid house; even now, those Bostonians who

followed the staunch example of Colonel Winthrop, casting off ostentation and living simple lives, discussed the "palace" that would soon grace the hillside. He smiled to himself; palace it was not. He had lived in palaces. To his thinking it would be more like a villa, a lovely Italian country house such as Giuliana would have loved. Indeed, the decorations and the gardens would speak of Tuscany and Venice . . . and always, always, of Giuliana.

But for now, he had a humble cottage made of stone and wood, and a warm fire. It occurred to him that he might buy a little dog to serve as companion in this new phase of his life.

Smiling faintly at the notion, he bent down, hefted the trunk, and carried it to the cottage.

For two hours he read by candlelight a delightful account of the exploits of Marco Polo. He felt himself to be on a wonderful holiday, no longer vigilant, no longer responsible. In this extraordinary town, he could become an ordinary citizen.

Who happened to be a sorcerer.

Smiling, he felt his head drop to his chest, knew he would soon be drifting. For the first time in decades, he did not look upon sleep as a dangerous lowering of his defenses. Still, from force of habit, he wove spells of protection around himself to stave off potential lurkers in the dark.

He knew he ought to rise and change into his nightshirt, and from there crawl onto his simple cot. *In a while,* he told himself, and yielded to slumber, peaceful and serene.

\* \* \* \* \*

"Cool stuff," Buffy said hopefully in a loud voice, glancing at Cordelia for moral support.

"Oh, yes, very cool," the cavalry agreed, bending down and examining a row of snow globes with obvious disdain.

"We need postcards," Buffy continued. "And lots of other stuff. Requiring us to hang here for a while."

She touched a display of postcards featuring various famous landmarks of Boston—the Old North Church, the Bunker Hill Monument, the *U.S.S. Constitution*, and others—none of which they had actually seen in the hours since they had landed at Logan Airport. The visitors' information center, some historical societies, and a lot of gas stations, parking lots, and coffee shops had so far been the highlights of their first day in the city that was the heart of the Revolutionary era in American history.

Buffy was tired of being in the car, more tired of being terrified by Giles's driving in a car that actually had some zip—if not much—and eager for some fun before they got down to business. The car had turned out to be more trouble than help. Boston was a labyrinth of construction detours and one-way streets, curving alleys and double parking. The concept of finding an empty and legal parking space seemed almost laughable after a while, and Buffy wondered if they wouldn't have been better off on foot. Supposedly, Boston had an extensive subway system—what the locals called "the T"—and it seemed like they could get anywhere they needed to go by train.

No such luck. Instead, they double-parked along grassy commons or in front of rows of brownstones or restaurants and retail stores. It really was a maze, though admittedly, a very cool-looking maze. Despite the fact that it was still chilly in Boston this time of year, the more she thought of it, the more Buffy realized that walking around might be preferable just because they would get to *look at* the city.

But no.

Giles had established which area of the city the Gatehouse *must* be in, by virtue of its age and the fact that it was supposed to be set on a hill. Other than that, they were on their own. But Giles wasn't giving up. The car was illegally parked in a tow zone while they stood inside a weird convenience store, which also seemed to carry souvenirs and gifts. Giles quizzed the frumpy woman behind the counter about the existence of Ye Gatehouse—physically describing it and offering the name Regnier, but coming up empty. Buffy and the others had wandered up and down the aisles for nearly five minutes, and boredom was quickly setting in. As she glanced through the postcards, Buffy found one with a picture and some information about the Boston Computer Museum and thought of Willow. Since the plane had taken off, she'd done little else but think about Willow. And her mom. And Angel.

Xander ambled up to them with a pair of Paul Revere–head salt and pepper shakers. "It's no good, vixens," he said sadly, using the pepper as a puppet to speak to them. "Giles is absolutely positive that the Gatehouse is within blocks of this very spot and we must be off imeedjutleh."

"He does not talk like that," Buffy objected, then moved her shoulders and cricked her neck. "I swear, when I'm old enough to rent a car, the word *subcompact* will never cross my lips."

"That word has yet to cross my lips," Cordelia pointed out. "I'm thinking, why not a limo?"

Xander gave her a look. "Cor, do you have any notion how much a school librarian takes home after taxes?" His eyes widened as he spied the rack of postcards and pointed at a photograph of the harbor. "Ooh, taxes! Boston Tea Party! This is where it all went down."

"Yes, it's quite exciting, isn't it?" Giles said happily. He was carrying a large foldout map, which he was struggling to refold. "History surrounds us. And not a theme park nor some ghastly recreation containing a burger house in sight."

"Burger house?" Buffy drawled. "You said that, right?"

He blinked at her. Before he had a chance to respond, Xander said, "They're in the Dutch section of Boston. Burger houses."

"Not that we'll see any," Buffy went on. Then she caught herself and straightened her shoulders. "Which is fine, because we are here on a mission."

"I just hope it's not mission impossible," Xander said, stretching and yawning. "I didn't get much sleep on the plane. Do you guys realize it's still night at home? We could still be sleeping."

"If the world weren't hanging by a thread," Cordelia said. She gestured to Xander's salt and pepper shakers. "Are you getting those for your mom?"

Xander nodded. Though she didn't seem to have any affinity for the kitchen whatsoever, Mrs. Harris collected salt and pepper shakers. Buffy did not see the point. What good was stockpiling something just to put it on a shelf? Now, crossbows. Machetes.

Beautiful, handcrafted stakes. Those were things worth buying in triplicate.

"Right then, Xander," Giles said, folding up his map. "Please hurry and transact your business. The attendant has assured me that there's a house similar to my description not far from here, wherein resides a crazy old, ah, what did she say? Yes, crazy old coot. He's got to be our man."

"Our coot." Buffy smiled at him. "Hurray."

Giles did not smile back. "Buffy," he began, "it's possible that something is terribly amiss at this Gatehouse."

She shrugged. "We'll fix it. Then"—she rubbed her hands together—"sightseeing. We're three thousand miles from home. We ought to do something fun."

"Tea partying," Xander agreed.

"Shopping," Cordelia said, sounding a little wistful. "I've got to bring something home or my mom will kill me."

Buffy shook her head in disbelief. "Hey, want to trade moms?"

"You wouldn't want mine," Cordelia said. "Believe me."

"Yeah, Buff, 'cause your mom actually likes me," Xander said.

Cordelia looked indignant. "My mom likes you."

"Oh, yeah. Like cellulite." He gave her a sidelong glance. "I thought you didn't believe in lying."

"Well." She shrugged. "Maybe she doesn't like you as my boyfriend, but she doesn't *dislike* you as a person."

"Oh, I'm dancing on the ceiling now." He gestured at the window of the shop. Buffy turned and looked.

Still struggling with his map, Giles was halfway to the car.

"I'll go buy these family heirlooms. Then I suggest we follow that redcoat," Xander said.

"Next stop, weirdness," Cordelia said.

Buffy nodded to herself. "Hopefully," she replied.

## Boston, October, 1666

Richard Regnier woke with a start.

The cottage was dark and very, very cold. His candle was out, the fire, dying embers. Those were natural enough, if one has slept a long time. It was not the chill nor the shadows that sent a frisson up his spine.

It was the sure sense, developed over a lifetime devoted to magick, that something was horribly wrong.

He flicked his wrist and produced a small ball of light that hovered an arm's length in front of his chair. Cautiously he stood, his gaze traveling around the room, searching for an intruder. There was no one else in the room, at least that he could detect.

Still, he could not shake the feeling that he was in danger. He cursed himself for abandoning his habit of keeping his wand ever present at his side—with the death of Fulcanelli he had grown lax—and moved swiftly across the earthen floor to his traveling valise. He unclasped the fastener and grabbed up the wand. Regnier was capable of great magick without it, but the wand gave that magick focus.

There came a low rumbling, as if from deep within the earth. Regnier looked down at his feet. The rumbling grew louder. The cottage walls began to tremble and then to shake violently. Loud cracks ran up the walls of stone. The embers in the fireplace leaped out of the grate.

Regnier was thrown to the floor. He hit his head on the corner of his chair, and for a moment he was stunned.

As he sat up slowly on the rolling floor, something dark formed in the dirt. It was darker than the night shadows in the room, darker than any blackness he had ever seen. It absorbed the light around it, and yet he could still see it. Though he did not touch it, he sensed that it had form, substance.

The rumbling grew louder. He hunched over the puddle, if puddle it was, and held his wand over it, commanding it in Latin to do no harm.

Suddenly a high, frigid wind whistled through the cottage, so loud his ears throbbed. His belongings were flung against the wall. The pages of his books fluttered like panicked birds. Cold pierced him as if someone stabbed at him with a frozen sword. He cried out and repeated his incantation.

Unaffected by the gale, the puddle rose from the floor and hovered in a circle beneath his wand. Regnier examined it at the same time that he backed away, keeping a respectful distance until he could discern its nature.

There was a clap as if of thunder. The room exploded with light as brilliant as the sun. Regnier was thrown back hard. He slammed onto his back and immediately rolled to his side, covering his eyes.

Still the wind raged; he dared to pull down his hands and squint at the light.

It was gone.

The black circle had rotated so that it now hung vertically in the center of the room. The air around it seemed to shimmer as a pool of water broken by a stone or the movements of life beneath the surface. The texture of the world, the fabric of reality, seemed somehow false now. The circle was a flat, motionless, oily black, and the shimmering around it made it seem a scab on the flesh of the world.

Regnier struggled to his feet, his hair flying in the wind, and attempted to take a step toward it, but he could not move any closer. The circle expanded. The rippling air around it swirled with color, a gossamer rainbow frame around a portrait of deepest ebony. The air around this scar, this new wound on the heart of reality, glowed now a brilliant blue that jittered and vibrated. Once more the cottage's structure was assailed. Regnier's muscles tensed, his bones ached, and he felt that he might shake apart.

From the center of the circle a strange, hulking figure appeared, spilling from the oily blackness as though it were a babe forced unwilling and unaided from its mother's womb. It shrieked with a ghastly voice and then fell to the floor as it tumbled out of the circle.

At once the circle disappeared, taking all forms of chaos with it, save the creature it had disgorged. The rumbling ceased. The wind dissipated.

All was silent, save for the shrieking of the figure. Regnier approached it slowly, jerking when it raised three heads on one neck and clambered to its feet. It glared at him with three sets of red, luminous eyes and began to growl menacingly. Its body was like that of a dog, blacker than anything he had ever seen, even the circle whence it had sprung. Purple and black serpents writhed along its back, their tongues hissing at Regnier. Then its tail rose above the body, and a hooded cobra darted at him, spitting venom.

"Cerberus?" Regnier asked in astonishment. This was the dog of Hades, the hound that watched over the realm of the dead and forbade the living entrance to it.

The dog cocked its three heads and barked at him. Then it looked around itself, clearly terrified.

Regnier was bemused. The puddle had been some sort of portal, then, depositing this creature where it had no business.

Without warning, the dog sprang at him, all its teeth bared viciously. Regnier dodged it and immediately erected a magickal barrier that protected him from the beast. Cerberus collided with the invisible shield, then collapsed, stunned, to the shattered floor of the cottage.

With a small tremor as its only harbinger, the ebony pool began to reform only inches from Regnier's right foot. He moved away, fully expecting it to solidify, and to rise and shift as it had done before.

Instead, the puddle seemed to split in two with a thunderous snap, and the two halves slid in opposite directions. The cottage floor shifted with them, the walls themselves seeming to realign to accommodate this unnatural phenomenon. The air was split with a rending crack, and yet the building remained standing.

With a thunderclap, the duplicate portals grew even larger. From one, an odd creature, a beauteous lithe thing with the most gossamer wings, flew into the cottage, a spray of glittering dust trailing in its wake.

From the other a blaze erupted. The magician stepped closer to peer inside. Sweat poured down Regnier's face as he regarded the very threshold of Hell itself.

*1st January, 1668*

*In my hand I hold the letter. Today I should be glad, and yet I am filled with despair.*

*I have had word from Mother Mary John, with whom I have remained in contact out of my concern for the orphan Juliet, and to whom I have supplied funds for the girl's keep and future interests. This latest epistle, however, concerns not Juliet, but another child. A boy. My own son, by birth and blood.*

*While I was in the land of the Turk, lured there by Fulcanelli, Giuliana discovered her happy condition. By the time of my return, she already lay moldering in her grave. When Fulcanelli's acolytes overran our villa and our lands, I had thought all the servants massacred. With good reason, for I was unaware that Giuliana had engaged the services of a Signorina Alessandra, who was to aid in the care of the newborn.*

*Signorina Alessandra survives, however, and has recently arrived at Mother Mary John's convent as a novice, hoping to take her vows soon. It was only at mention of my name in connection with the girl, Juliet, that the Signorina told the story of her service to my family, and what came to pass after Giuliana's death.*

*My son still lives. Delivered even as the human devils in Fulcanelli's service pillaged my lands,* the boy was spirited away by Signorina Alessandra at the direction of my wife. A Catholic orphanage in Florence is all the home he knows.

I will write this night and request that Signorina Alessandra give up her dream of the convent and instead fetch my son from Florence and accompany him here, to me, to remain in my employ as his governess.

But my despair is palpable. The boy has never had a real home, and this house is not as I envisioned it in my dreams. My "palace" now stands, and its rooms are filled with monsters. If only I had been able to return the monsters when they'd come without the risk of tearing down that barrier between our plane and the Otherworld forevermore. Or if I had found some way to close the breach when it appeared, lo these fifteen months ago! But that chance has been lost, if ever I had it. The breach proved too large for a magician of my meager talent to close, perhaps too large for anyone to close forever.

Instead, I was forced to use uncommon magicks to seal it, and yet I must remain eternally vigilant. I employed the same magick I used to pen Cerberus that first, terrible night. These magickal barriers have taken form as rooms within my large house, thus keeping this breach a secret. With every stone, every beam of my enormous home, I infused my magick into the seal.

But I must guard the seal for the rest of my life, for it is a fragile thing. My dream of a peaceful life as an ordinary man is over.

*Inspired by the presence of Cerberus, I call myself the Gatekeeper.*

*And my little son, Henri, who comes to me now in innocence and joy, will one day inherit this terrible mantle.*

*Thus, I weep for him, for the son of Giuliana. For my son.*

*Dreadful, his legacy.*

*But it is his destiny. Fate has chosen the Regniers to guard the world from these evils.*

*Hell has found me once again.*

\* \* \* \* \*

The shimmering golden dome of the Massachusetts State House shone down from Beacon Hill in the blazing light of late morning. The Little Rental Car That Could circled Boston Common for the fourth time. In the passenger seat, Buffy glanced at Giles and noted the dark circles under his eyes. He hadn't been out of the hospital long, and already he had made two cross-country airplane trips and a less-than-relaxing search of a maddeningly designed city.

To their right, the green lawns of the Common sprawled out for blocks, gently sloping down toward what appeared to be a very populous business district. But to the left . . .

"Hey, we just passed Cheers!" Xander called out. Nobody responded.

After a moment Xander sighed. "Well, I thought it was cool. Better than another convenience store."

To the left, some of the narrowest streets Buffy had ever seen—little more than alleys, really—stretched up onto Beacon Hill proper. They were lined with beautiful old brownstones and other buildings that were even older. It reminded her of pictures she had seen of Paris.

Very much, now that she thought of it.

"It's got to be up there," she said, as Giles slowed the car for them to examine the street. "We've gone up every one of these streets, and this one looks like it leads to the highest point up here."

Behind them, horns began to blare.

"Giles, just turn already," Cordelia huffed.

Giles turned.

*The old buildings are probably all condos now,* Buffy thought. The sidewalks were cracked, the street cobblestone in some places. Cars were parked on either side so that there was only room for one car to travel the road at a time. *It must be a one-way,* Buffy thought, though she'd seen no sign indicating that.

The stone-and-mortar houses were beautiful, and undoubtedly very expensive. She could see through oversized windows that many of them were filled with wood and impeccably decorated. But the way they all seemed attached or built right onto one another, it seemed unlikely that any of them were this Gatehouse they were searching for.

"This looks like a nice area," Cordelia said, half to herself.

"A bit close, I would think," Giles pointed out. "Certain parts of London are like this, people living almost on top of one another . . ."

"What's wrong with that?" Xander muttered.

The narrow alley took a slight curve to the left, and Giles slowed the car slightly. They had nearly reached the apex of Beacon Hill, and soon they would start down the other side. There was a warren of alleys up here, but Buffy felt that they were near.

"I feel it," she whispered.

"Hmm?" Giles glanced at her.

Buffy pointed through the windshield.

"Giles."

"Oh, my God, Xander," Cordelia breathed.

"Good Lord," Giles echoed.

Giles stopped the car. Where Beacon Hill crested, the brownstones had given way to heavy black wrought-iron gates. They abutted the homes on either side, no inch of property unclaimed by someone on this valuable tract of real estate. But behind the gates, framed by thick privet hedges, rose a monstrous and yet somehow beautiful piece of architecture unlike anything Giles had ever seen.

It was a catastrophe, a sprawl of different styles— Queen Anne, Victorian, even some Medieval folly such as Strawberry Hill back in Britain. Chimneys towered over a section of mansard roof, and then a gabled portion, and a turret of exquisite beauty.

A row of windows across the top floor of the house looked like nothing so much as eyes, staring madly down at them.

Everything inside Giles begged him to turn the car around and get Buffy out of there. There was evil here, massive, unbridled evil. Whatever was inside that house was unlike anything the Slayer had been called on to face in the past.

There was death inside.

"I'll go open the gates." Buffy unbuckled her seat belt.

Giles pushed up his glasses. "No! That is, they might be locked."

"And that's going to stop Supergirl," Xander said.

"I'll sound the horn," Giles said.

"I can take care of it," Buffy insisted, clearly amused. She gave Giles a lazy half smile and opened her car door.

That was when they heard the screams. Inhuman shrieks came from beyond that black gate, and after a moment, Giles felt almost certain that, somehow, the agonized wailing was coming from the house itself.

Brother Lupo's milky eye glowed blue as he glared at the runestone in Brother Dando's shaking, outstretched palm. His fury was silent, but Brother Kukoff could sense the frustration emanating from his leader like an electrical aura.

He and the others stood in a circle on a sidewalk not far from the Slayer's home, beneath a gibbous yellow moon. He was tired of this place, and tired of all the walking and searching. He wanted to go home. But if they left without the Slayer, home was the last place they should go.

Brother Dando gave the runestone a tentative tap. It did not pulse. It did not move.

"The Slayer has not returned," Brother Dando said.

When Brother Lupo did not reply, Dando looked over at him. Lupo's bald pate looked like a bleached skull in the moonlight. His eye glowed eerily amid the shadowed hollows of his face.

With a grunt, Lupo gave the unsuspecting Dando a savage backhand, his knuckles splitting the flesh over Dando's cheekbone. The runestone clattered to the pavement. Breaking off a cry, Brother Dando stepped backward and instinctively crossed his hands in front of his face, gently touching his bloodied cheek.

The others swallowed hard. At one time or another, all of them had endured the painful results of Brother Lupo's temper.

" 'There will be no rest for her from us,' " Brother Lupo said in a low, dangerous voice, mimicking Brother Dando. " 'There will be no haven for her from us. No safe place from us. No asylum from us.' Your very words, Brother Dando. But we don't even know where she is, do we?"

Brother Dando had gone chalk white. "Brother Lupo, it's true, my incantation did not serve. But—"

"But what?" Brother Lupo advanced on him. "Are you saying that I am in some way at fault?"

"No, no, of course not," Brother Dando said quickly.

At that moment, a sound like a thunderclap made them all jerk. They glanced furtively around. What would it be this time, another troll?

Kukoff said quietly, "The Slayer has not returned, and for this reason the Hellmouth disgorges monsters of all sorts."

"Springheel Jack," Brother Isimo said in agreement. "Walking corpses. So many others."

"That's not why they come," Brother Lupo said angrily. He stared at each in turn. They all flinched from his gaze as if he had struck them, even Kukoff, who was last, and knew there was no blow forthcoming.

Brother Lupo whirled on his heel and stomped down the street.

The others hesitated for a moment, then gaggled after him like a flock of geese.

"Why, then?" Brother Kukoff whispered to Brother Dando as they hurried to catch up. "Why do so many creatures appear? Is it not because she is gone and she cannot protect this place?"

Nursing his jaw, Brother Dando placed the runestone in a small red satin pouch and put it in the pocket of his navy coat. "Il Maestro has many plans," he said. "He does not share them with all of us. Our task is to capture the Slayer."

Brother Kukoff was not comforted. "But we cannot control all these monsters. Not even Brother Lupo or Brother Isimo. And if we cannot protect ourselves, they will come after us just as they come after the people of this town."

He shivered, thinking of Springheel Jack. "We ourselves are in grave danger."

Dando set his face. "Better to face a horde of monsters and demons than to return to the Master empty-handed."

"Quickly now!" Brother Lupo called. He made a fist and swiped at the air. Kukoff felt a slap on the back of his head as surely as if Brother Lupo had stood directly behind him and hit him. He quickened his pace.

"The Slayer must return," Kukoff said to Brother Dando.

Brother Dando looked miserable and very, very worried. "The Slayer must return," he concurred.

*"With love's light wings did I o'erperch these walls,"* Springheel Jack whispered as he vaulted the gate in front of the Chase residence. Then he flew directly onto the roof and landed with a thud. He didn't care who heard or saw him. All he wanted was the girl who

lived here. "Cordelia," he whispered, and tasted her name on his lips. Though she was not here now, he didn't mind waiting for her.

Didn't mind at all.

Beneath him, a window opened and a man's voice trailed on the night air. "It's probably just a bird. Or a squirrel."

"No. Somebody threw something," a woman answered him. "Something big. Go up and see."

"On the roof? Now?" The man demanded.

"Yes. Now."

"Oh, for heaven's sake," the man said irritably.

The window shut.

Jack smiled. He decided to play a game.

If the man stayed in his house, he would not die.

# Chapter 11

Willow hefted her backpack. "Rosemary, thyme, my trusty homemade scapulars, and a mirror."

Oz frowned slightly. "The mirror is for . . ."

Willow shrugged. "You just never know."

Angel led the way out of his house and onto the lawn. Giles's car was there, along with Oz's van. Oz had been having trouble with his brakes, and, despite the fact that driving Giles's Citroen was sort of the automotive equivalent of riding a donkey, it was better than worrying about the brakes giving out.

"You okay?" Oz asked, as Willow slipped on her jacket.

She nodded. "Just tired." Then she shrugged. "It's hard not to tell them what's really going on. Buffy's lucky that she finally got to tell her mom."

"I'm not sure Buffy would agree with you," Angel said softly.

The three of them walked down the driveway toward the Gilesmobile.

"How many binding sites do we have now?" Angel asked. Willow inhaled and smelled honeysuckle. It was very sweet, and it reminded Willow of somewhere tropical. Like Hawaii. If they'd been playing Anywhere But Here, Hawaii would have been her location.

"Thirteen," she answered.

"Unlucky number," Oz said. He took her hand.

Willow shook her head. "Not always. It's a magickal number, though. I can't help wondering if there's some significance to it."

"Thirteen places where we've bound monsters and demons," Oz said. "Do you think you can learn to bind me? The chains are getting a little old."

Willow blushed a little. She said, "I could work on it."

He smiled. "My Sabrina."

"I'm not a witch," Willow protested. "And neither was Ms. Calendar." She thought a moment. "But we could use one. To tell you the truth, I'm not sure how much more of this I'm good for."

A short time later, Angel climbed up the embankment from beneath the bridge and shook his head. "Negative," he told Willow and Oz. He wiped his hands on his duster and stuffed his hands in his pockets.

"No trolls," Oz said, lowering the business end of his cousin's cast-off baseball bat onto his instep.

"No trolls," Angel agreed.

Willow slumped, put down her own baseball bat, and said, "This is bad."

"Yes, it is." Angel sighed.

There were trolls somewhere, and they were terrorizing Sunnydale. Although with the town's usual sense of denial, no one but the three of them acknowledged that the entire Nieto family—Mama, Papa, grandmother, and little José—had most likely been carried off by a band of ugly, hairy creatures camped out under the bridge by Highway 17. The description of the "kidnappers" on TV was merely "short-statured and dangerous."

"And all we can do to get them to show is insult them?" Oz queried.

"Better than confronting them in their lairs." Angel shrugged. "It worked last time." He pointed to the baseball bats. "Then Xander wailed the tar out of them."

"We're troll-less," Willow said.

"Hence, tar-less," Oz added.

"Maybe we could go after the Tatzelwurm instead," Willow suggested brightly. "Or . . . ooh, Springheel Jack, though I'd really like to pass on that guy." She made a face.

"How about the Kraken?" Oz suggested. In unison, Angel and Willow raised questioning eyebrows and shook their heads. "Yeah," Oz said, an earnest expression on his face. "We don't want to hog all the good monsters. We should leave some for Buffy."

Though he tried not to show it as they continued to drive around Sunnydale, Angel shared Willow's concern. An increasing number of supernatural beings had popped up in Sunnydale, and he, Willow, and Oz were quickly reaching their limit as to how much they could do to keep the creatures from causing trouble.

Trouble defined as the entire Nieto family still missing, as well as two toddlers and several high school students, and a number of family pets butchered. Also, six serious fires and the destruction of another building, this one blamed on a badly cracked foundation illegally allowed to pass inspection by a corrupt building inspector.

Not to mention the very large, very poisonous plague of spiders they had managed to thwart—in that case, by strategically setting some fires of their own.

As well as the shadow of a huge toad—easily as large as Buffy's house—which had outrun them and somehow evaded all of Willow's spells.

Then, of course, there were the men in long coats who kept popping up, and who, if left to their own devices, might manage to kill each other off, sparing Angel the chore. It seemed fairly obvious they were behind this influx of bad karma.

The confusion and the destruction reminded him of his old life, when he had run with his sire, Darla. Or even more recently, when he had lost his soul for the second time and reveled in trying to destroy the world himself.

He didn't appreciate such reminders.

But where once he might have thrown back his head and laughed, now he was very, very worried. Willow had cast a general binding spell, which, he was sure, was impeding even more dark forces from invading the town. But those which had already found some way into Sunnydale had not been "covered" by that spell, and she had been forced to use that same spell again and again, sealing off holes in the wall that separated their world from another.

Just to be safe, they had begun a regular patrol of the sites where breaches had already occurred, hoping to keep ahead of any potential problems. Part of this route was the area just down the street from the Bronze where they'd first run into Springheel Jack. The three of them got out there and walked around for several minutes before returning to the car.

They had just reached the Gilesmobile. Angel was about to suggest that Oz might like a turn at the wheel when a movement across the street caught his attention. Keeping his demeanor casual and unconcerned, he slid his glance toward the shadowed corner.

A man in a long coat was watching them. *One of them.* From his silhouette in the beams of an oncoming car, he looked to be holding a cell phone. As he stepped out of the sweep of the headlights, he raised his hand, and for one startled moment, Angel thought the man was waving at him.

Then he realized the wave was a signal to someone across the street. Angel's side of the street. Without turning his head, Angel glanced in the same direction.

Several yards beyond Giles's Citroen there was an alley. In Angel's significant experience, people didn't generally hide in an alley without a damn good reason.

"Willow," Angel said softly, unsure if she could even hear him.

But she did. Silently, she came up beside him. Angel heartily approved. She might not be the Slayer, but she'd spent enough time around Buffy and Giles that she certainly had the street smarts to hold her own.

"Some of our friends, up ahead," he murmured.

"Take the keys"—he slipped them into her pocket—"and get in the car. Oz, too."

"Hey, man," Oz protested under his breath as he caught up with them. "We can help."

"Start the car," Angel continued, "drive up to that alley. I'm going in there. With any luck, I'll be coming back out with company."

"Gulp," Willow said.

Her boyfriend looked satisfied, as though pleased he wasn't being cut out of the action. Angel understood. He liked feeling useful, too.

"Make sure the back door on the passenger side's unlocked," Angel added. "And that the other one is locked."

"Gotcha," Willow murmured.

"And you may have to ward off some magick." He gestured to Oz's guitar case. "Maybe put on those scapulars."

"Check," Oz said.

Willow unlocked the passenger side and slid in. Oz went around to the other side and did the same.

While they were doing that, Angel tore up the street and sprinted into the alley.

A large group of men, perhaps a dozen, emerged from hiding places and raced across the street. They were headed directly for the alley. Oz started the engine and looked at Willow. "Plan B?"

Angel was strong, and he was a vampire, but he looked to be outnumbered. Especially if there was magick added to the equation. Willow put on her resolve face and said, "We drive into the alley."

"My thinking also."

Oz floored it, because in Giles's car, there was no other way to make the car move forward. It lurched unsteadily, like a bedridden invalid trying to get out of bed, then picked up speed—relatively speaking— and staggered down the street.

Willow screamed as a man flung himself at her window, pounding on it. He was thin, with olive skin, and his face was contorted with rage.

Without a moment's hesitation, Oz cranked the wheel to the right, effectively knocking the man backward. He lost his grip on the car and stumbled back, going down hard on the pavement.

The car putted forward.

And stalled.

The man was up almost instantly. He stared after them and balled his fists. When he opened them, glowing spheres of green energy swirled above his palms. Sudden as cannon fire, the spheres rocketed toward Giles's car.

"Oz!" Willow cried. "Abandon ship!"

"What?" He looked over his right shoulder. "Oh."

He tore the key from the ignition and jumped out of the car at the same time as Willow. The magick spheres rocked the car, shattering the rear windshield, but that was all. Whatever their intention had been, killing the car wasn't a priority. Willow looked up and saw that two new crackling green spheres had replaced the others. She shouted her boyfriend's name.

Then she narrowed her eyes and focused. Giles's warning about not using spells she hadn't prepared was fresh in her mind, but against this magick, she couldn't think of anything to do but respond in kind.

Which was when Oz came around from the side of

the car and jumped the guy. With a knee to the gut and then a hard uppercut to the jaw, Oz took the sorcerer down. The man crumbled to the pavement with a grunt.

Willow raised her eyebrows. "Cool," she said, sounding something like Oz.

Angel was already on top of the building by the time the first of the attackers raced into the alley. Crouching, he counted at least twenty long-coated thugs—some of them sorcerers, if Buffy and Xander's assessment of them had been correct—stumbling over one another as they filled the alley and looked around for him.

"Dando, the runestone," someone called.

One of the thugs withdrew a small red pouch from his pocket.

"Cast a spell for the finding of a vampire," a man said, shouldering his way through the crowd. He was bald; one of his eyes was milky white.

"Yes, Brother Lupo," the one called Dando replied.

"If he is not found," Lupo went on, "one of you will die in his stead."

His followers looked at each other gravely. Angel would have liked the luxury of a smile, but he kept his attention riveted on the group.

There was a sudden squeal of tires at the end of the alley. Half a second later, the Gilesmobile shot into the narrow space, clipping a couple of the men as the others scattered.

"No!" Lupo cried. "Do not run!"

Police sirens pierced the night, growing closer by the heartbeat as the men picked up speed.

*"Bastardi!"* Lupo shrieked.

Angel nodded to himself, filing away this little tidbit of information: in all likelihood, Lupo was Italian.

Oz and Willow popped out of the car. Willow was waving her hands and chanting a spell of protection.

Angel climbed down some pipes on the exterior of the building and dropped to the car. The sirens were getting closer.

Behind the car were the two men Oz had taken out. Angel ran to them. One was unconscious. The other was trying to crawl away.

"Help me get them in the car," Angel called to Oz.

Oz grabbed the wrists of the conscious man. He was dark-skinned, with long, gray hair and a strange scar in the indentation of his cheek. He glared up at them and said, "I will kill you with my magick," and his eyes began to glow a sickly yellow.

"Oh, Will," Oz called.

Nervously, Willow began to chant something, she wasn't even certain it would work.

Then Angel reached around Oz and punched the man in the side of the head. He slackened and went limp.

"Better safe than sorry," Angel said. He gestured toward the other end of the alley. "From the sound of things, the police are going to be here any second. Let's get these guys in the car. One in the backseat with me, one in the trunk."

Willow found the latch for the trunk, which she had to hold open for them because it kept threatening to close. They put the other man in there. He was older than the one Angel had knocked out.

As Oz helped Angel dump the other man on the

floor, he drawled, "Looks like we culled the herd, Willow. Took out their oldest and slowest."

"Great," Willow said anxiously. "I'm not so crazy about sitting in a car with a couple of magick users, even if they are unconscious, old, or slow."

"We'll take them to the mansion," Angel said.

"So much for checking the binding sites." Willow sighed. "So many bad thingies, so little time."

Angel flashed her a sympathetic look. "Maybe we're about to figure out how they all got here. In which case, we can get rid of them."

Willow nodded at him.

As Oz drove to the mansion, he thought about the bad guys in the car, sure, but he was focused on Willow, and the problems she was having with her parents, and his certainty that some of those problems came from her being with him. Not for the first time, it occurred to him that the Dingoes might really go places. Might actually make it. In which case, where did that leave your friendly neighborhood teenage werewolf on the nights of the full moon?

"Oz?" Willow asked. "Are you okay?"

He smiled at her. "I'm with you."

When Willow smiled, she had the cutest dimples. "You're just saying that, 'cause you're hoping I'll put on my Eskimo costume for you." That was what she had been wearing when Oz had first noticed her.

"It makes me crazy," he agreed.

From the backseat came the sound of a fist making contact with flesh. Willow jerked.

Angel said, "Sorry. Didn't mean to interrupt."

Oz patted Willow's knee. "Sorcerers first. Then the Eskimo costume."

Willow estimated it was just after dawn, though with the way Angel had the house shuttered, there was really no way to tell. No sunlight, for obvious reasons.

She pushed herself against the space between the wall and Angel's strange stone fireplace and shuddered. The two men were tied to chairs, and they looked bruised and frightened. No wonder, with Angel in full vamp face, beating the crap out of them.

She didn't think she could take any more. She wasn't sure they could, either.

Oz held her hand tightly. Neither spoke. Oz looked a bit green, too, but a little steadier than she. He hadn't really been one of the Slayerettes when Angel had turned bad again, back into Angelus. He hadn't seen his cruelty. But Oz *had* seen what Angelus had done to Giles when he had tortured him for the secret to sending every single non-demon on the face of the planet straight to Hell. They all knew what Angel was capable of. The difference was, once upon a time Willow had been on the receiving end of that savagery.

Suddenly Angel looked straight at Willow. He said, "Willow, I know. But would you rather they were doing something like this to Buffy?"

She swallowed and cast down her gaze. Maybe she didn't have what it took to be a good Slayerette anymore. She would kill for Buffy. Had killed for Buffy, in fact. But this was . . . sickening.

Angel picked up the mangled hand of an older man, one of their attackers. Three of his fingers were broken. His face was torn and bleeding, his nose was pulped. His lip was split deeply and he'd lost several teeth. What was worse, however, were the wounds where Angel had used his own hands to tear into the man's back and chest and abdomen.

"A few more minutes of this, and I think I might have to get out the chainsaw," Angel said grimly.

He didn't smile. Willow wasn't sure if she wanted it to be a joke or not, wasn't sure what was worse: the idea that he might do it, or that he would find it amusing.

Suddenly, Angel held the man's left arm in his two powerful hands, and swiftly snapped the arm, breaking the bone, shattering the elbow. The man screamed.

"Please," the older man whimpered. "Stop."

Willow felt tears begin to burn her eyes.

"Don't be a fool, Kukoff," the other man said. "Il Maestro will kill you."

Kukoff laughed grimly. "Brother Isimo, we're dead already. Even if we say nothing, Lupo will kill us for Il Maestro. If this vampire doesn't kill us first." He looked up at Angel, his chin jutting proudly.

"We are the Sons of Entropy," he declared. "Harbingers of chaos. Agents of the apocalypse."

Angel crouched by the one called Kukoff, staring into his bruised and split and bleeding face. His nostrils flared and his lip curled back as he said, "That's quite a résumé. What the hell are you doing in Sunnydale?"

Brother Kukoff hung his head in shame. "Il Maestro does not reveal all of his plans to his acolytes. We are but one small part of his plan. A plan you can't even imagine. Chaos will come, fool, and even the vampires will have to bow to the Kings of Chaos, the Sons of Entropy."

"What plan?" Angel growled.

Willow looked away, burying her face in the crook of Oz's arm.

The one called Brother Isimo spit on Kukoff, who, in his turn, laughed at Angel.

"I'm . . . I'm not afraid to die," Kukoff said.

Angel snarled, yellow eyes blazing. He reached out quickly and grabbed the man's broken arm . . . and twisted. Kukoff screamed so loud that Willow's ears hurt, and now she was silently weeping on Oz. He held her more tightly, and she knew that he wasn't looking either.

"Wake up!" Angel snapped, and there was a slap.

Willow realized that Kukoff must have fainted from the agony. He spat blood as he awoke a moment later, and Angel growled low in his chest.

"I never said I was going to kill you," Angel whispered, just loud enough for them all to hear. "I'm not nice enough to do that."

"We are . . ." Kukoff began.

"Traitor!" Isimo shrieked.

Angel gave him a backhand that shut him up for a moment.

"We are nothing," Kukoff said. "A secondary force, sent to fulfill one small part of Il Maestro's plan. The plan is known in full only to Il Maestro, but when it is complete, chaos will flood the world."

"Like . . . Hell?" Oz asked tentatively.

"No, ignorant fool," Kukoff said, though his voice was weak. "Demons would destroy Earth. The reign of chaos will throw evolution and culture back a

thousand years. Two thousand years. The abomina-
tions of nature will walk the earth once more, the
children of chaos. And the Sons of Entropy will be
kings."

Willow stared at the monklike man for a moment.
Something was clicking inside her head, conversations she'd had with Giles and things that she'd read
during her research. These things he was so guardedly
referring to, they sounded just like the kinds of things
that were locked up in the . . .

"Oh, God," she whispered.

"What is it?" Oz asked anxiously.

"The Gatehouse," she said, her voice tinged with
horror. "They're going to take it over, or . . . or blow
it up or something."

Angel slapped Kukoff in the head. Blood spattered
the floor. "What's this?" he demanded. "What are
you guys planning for the Gatehouse?"

"I do not know," Kukoff said, eyes fluttering, barely
able to stay conscious save for the pressure Angel was
applying to his broken arm. "It is the key, that is what
Il Maestro claims. We are to claim it. The time is
right, now. The Gatekeeper is failing quickly, and we
have had his son Jacques, his only heir . . . removed."

Willow walked over to Kukoff and Isimo. She was
tempted to hit the men herself now. Anger over-
whelmed her so that she was barely able to speak.

"Where is the boy now?" she demanded.

"Is he still alive?" Oz asked, coming up behind her.

"I . . . I don't know," Kukoff confessed.

"But you can be sure that Il Maestro will kill him
when the time comes," Isimo added, proudly.

Willow felt the urge to strike him again, but then
she saw the blood in his right eye and the welt on his

forehead, and she just felt sick. She moved away from them, wanting only to be gone, now.

"No," Kukoff said, looking confused. "He will try to bend Jacques Regnier to his will. To our beliefs."

Willow looked at Angel, who shrugged and grimaced at her. They were both confused by this disagreement. Apparently, the man who led the Sons of Entropy really did keep his real plans to himself, if his men couldn't even agree on what those plans were.

Isimo's eyes shone. "You can't stop us. You may kill me, but our cause lives on."

"You still haven't told us why you're in Sunnydale," Angel warned.

Kukoff actually shrugged. "But I have. Our duty is less important, though still vital to Il Maestro's plan."

Angel stared at Kukoff. Willow watched the man's eyes, watched the sly smile that crept over his features. Finally, Kukoff opened his mouth again. "It is simple, really. We are to bring the Slayer back to Il Maestro, where he will cut out her heart and, like as not, eat it. There's power in the girl, and he wants it. Needs it."

"Well," Willow said, flustered and horrified, "Buffy's still using her heart, so, just forget it!"

"Tell 'em, Will," Oz said with a nod.

"You're such a fool," Isimo sneered at Kukoff. "Such a coward. I would have died before I told them so much as my name."

"It can still be arranged," Angel drawled, coming close to the man. He cowered, flinching as Angel raised a hand, then combed it through his dark hair.

A wind suddenly picked up outside, whistling along the vast corridors of Angel's mansion. Outside, branches battered against shuttered windows as if they were alive and demanding entrance. Thunder rumbled overhead.

In an instant, the lights flickered out and the room was plunged into darkness.

"Willow," Angel said.

Willow gathered her wits and said, *"To the Old Gods I give all supplication, and deference, and honor."*

There was a huge flapping of wings and an awful, distorted screech of a bird.

"No!" Kukoff shrieked. "Save me!"

The flapping grew louder. There was the sense of a presence above her, something deathly cold and evil. The vibrations of its flapping wings made her stumble to the right, away from the prisoners. Oz caught her in his arms and pulled her against the wall, where they sank together to the carpet.

*"I call upon you to protect all within these walls,"* she intoned.

"No! It has me! It is taking me!" Kukoff screamed. "Stop it!"

The creature screeched again. The wings flapped.

The lights went on.

Kukoff was gone.

Brother Isimo had been left behind.

With his eyes pecked out, and his tongue ripped away.

That he was dead was a blessing, in his case.

Willow swallowed hard. Oz slowly got to his feet and helped her to stand beside him. He looked at Angel.

"This is all information they're going to need," Oz

said. "Especially that part about, y'know, chaos reigning? That would suck. And the fact that this guy wants to eat Buffy's heart?"

Angel glanced at Willow. "You'd better call Cordelia on her cell phone."

The Gatehouse was screaming.

A hellish mix of shrieks rose and fell in a mad, frenzied chorus, and it all came from the house. The splintering of wood and the grinding of stone, the shrieking of nails being torn from centuries-old timber: the house was in agony.

A little shakily, Xander got out of the car and came up beside Buffy. He shivered unconsciously, cocked his head, and said, "Maybe we should have called ahead. I'm not sure they're up for company."

"They don't seem to be," Buffy agreed.

Xander went on. "Y'know, not that I would have wanted them to go to any trouble. But maybe they could have, I dunno, maybe exorcised the place first." He looked hard at Giles as the Watcher joined them in the street. "Okay, A: how come nobody else notices this, and B: are we still going in there?"

"To your first question, I would suspect the magickal properties of the Gatehouse somehow mask it from those unaware of its existence," Giles noted, examining the house with great interest.

"Wonderful," Buffy sighed. "So someone who didn't know it was here would walk right on by and not even see it."

"I suspect that is the case, yes," Giles agreed. "Powerful magick, that. Must have taken decades to construct that kind of spell."

"My other question, Giles," Xander reminded. "The one about fools rushing in, placing ourselves in great physical danger, ignoring the fact that the house is, well, let's face it . . . screaming!"

Giles pushed his glasses up and shrugged. "I'm afraid so," he said. "In fact, it's fairly obvious to me that we have no choice. We must enter."

"Then let's do it," Buffy said.

She climbed the fence, leaped over, and came back to open the gate for the others.

Suddenly a shrill buzzing noise rose above the din. With all the other noise, it did not strike anyone as odd until it trilled a second time. Xander and Buffy both stopped and looked at Cordelia. Giles raised an eyebrow.

"What?" Cordelia asked, obviously overwrought by the house.

"Do you want me to answer it?" Xander asked.

"Oh, God," Cordelia said, seeming relieved to have something other than the house to concentrate on. "I didn't realize it . . . oh, never mind." She whipped the thin cellular phone out of her small bag and flipped it open.

"Hello? Hey, Willow! Oh, God you should see this place . . ."

"What's going on? Is anything wrong?" Buffy asked quickly.

Giles moved toward Cordelia, body language clearly stating his intention to wrest the phone from her as soon as possible. But as she spoke, Cordelia began walking. Rolling their eyes, the others followed suit.

"It's like some carnival house of horrors," Cordelia

went on. "But the crazy thing is, it's right at the top of Beacon Hill, in the middle of the city, but it's got this magick thing where, if you aren't looking for it, you don't see it."

Cordelia paused a moment. Buffy, Xander, and Giles had passed within the gates of the Gatekeeper's home, into the shimmering magickal field which made the house and its grounds invisible to all those on the outside, save for those who knew what they were looking for.

Buffy glared at her. "Cor! Give me the phone!"

With a look of exasperation that said she couldn't handle more than one conversation at a time, Cordelia huffed and said, "Willow, hold on! Someone's having her latest tantrum and I think we both know who I mean."

She rolled her eyes, stomped through the gates, and handed the phone to Buffy. The Slayer put the tiny cellular phone to her ear.

"Willow, what's going—" She frowned, looked at Cordelia. "She's gone. Not even static."

"Maybe she didn't want to talk to you," Cordelia suggested.

"Or maybe some boogedy boogedy monster ate her up," Xander added. "Just jesting, of course."

Behind them, the house screamed.

"Did she say why she was calling?" Giles inquired.

Cordelia looked perplexed. "I didn't ask. I think she was just checking in, y'know. It is morning back home now, right?"

Frustrated, Giles and Buffy turned toward the house. Xander gave Cordelia a look, and she shot back one of her own. When he too had turned, she tried the phone and could not get an open line. With a shrug, she placed it back in her purse.

The four of them approached the house. As they mounted the steps, Xander paused.

"Uh, guys?" he said. "It's open."

"Solves one problem," Buffy replied.

She took the lead and pushed open the door.

Willow stared at the phone. "We were disconnected," she said, even as she began dialing again.

An hour later, they still hadn't been able to get through. The abruptness of the cutoff, and their subsequent inability to reestablish contact, had all three of them on edge.

"They could be in trouble," Willow said, for the twelfth time.

"And this is information they'll need, even if there's nothing wrong but problems with Cordy's phone," Angel added. "Of course, if that's all it was, why haven't they called back yet?

"Somebody has to warn them," Angel added. "As fast as possible. If we can't reach them, one of us has to go to them."

"I'll go," Oz said.

Angel nodded. "I have a lot of cash stashed away. You can use it to buy a ticket. You can park your van at the airport."

"Wait. No," Willow said urgently, then, "I'll go."

Angel shook his head. "I can't fight everything that's here alone. And you can't explain your absence as easily as Oz can."

"Since I'm basically a dropout already," Oz said.

"But . . ." She looked at Angel. "Why don't you go?"

He smiled kindly at her. "Will, we already know there's no way to guarantee that I won't land in Boston in sunlight. And a train or a bus would take even longer. And besides, you need to stay here and work your magick. Oz is the only one we can spare right now."

"Hey," Oz said mildly.

Angel led the way out of the room.

"What about him?" Willow said, gesturing toward the disfigured dead man in Angel's living room.

"I'll take care of him later," Angel said. "He's not going anywhere."

"Unless . . . flap, flap," Oz said.

Willow took his hand.

The Gatehouse swirled around Buffy and the others. There was no other word for it: the interior of the house bore no resemblance to any sort of reality. Walls appeared, disappeared. A huge, fanged demon dove at them, only to vanish. Flames erupted, then crystallized, sprinkling to the floor where they shattered into dried rose petals.

Above, there was no ceiling, only a free-falling canopy of comets and stars.

The moment the door had opened, they had been swallowed by the house, as if its magick had simply scooped them up. Buffy held Xander's hand tightly in her own, and she only prayed that Cordelia and Giles were likewise holding on.

A wave of magick passed over the room. It contorted. Convulsed. Then they stood in an angled chamber surrounded by mirrors, which exploded and buoyed them into a basementlike cavern, the floor of which was strewn with straw and pieces of wood. A filthy manlike creature with matted, waist-length hair was chained to the floor, gibbering and laughing.

Through it all, the house never stopped screaming.

"This isn't a Gatehouse, it's a nuthouse," Cordelia cried, holding tight to Xander.

"A madhouse," Giles concurred.

Buffy reached for his hand, and now the four of them formed a kind of circle.

"Not the place to book for the prom," Buffy shouted. She tugged on Giles's sleeve. "Maybe you guys should get out of here."

"What? And miss all the fun?" Xander bellowed.

"I want to miss it," Cordelia wailed. She had made an attempt at levity, but Buffy saw the fear in her eyes. No, not fear. Terror. She was close to tears.

There was a thunderous boom. The floor shuddered, then shook violently, then exploded as something burst through it. Cordelia screamed as Buffy pushed her out of the way.

At least seven feet long, it skittered toward them on four legs. Its body was cylindrical, and its head was all teeth, as far as Buffy was concerned.

"How astonishing. It's another Tatzelwurm," Giles said. "Be careful. It can—"

It launched itself into the air with a bizarre whistling sound.

"—leap," Giles finished.

"Duck!" Buffy cried. She jumped on Giles and pushed him to the floor. The worm sailed over him and landed with a thud. Immediately, it reversed direction and flung itself at them again.

"Cor!" Xander shouted, pushing her to the floor.

"Giles, how do we stop it?" Buffy asked, helping him to his feet.

"We could try staking it," he answered.

Then the section of floor he was standing on tilted sharply. Flailing, he fought to keep his balance as Buffy tried to grab him.

A wall appeared directly ahead of him.

He crashed through it, and disappeared.

"Giles!" Buffy shouted. "Giles, can you hear me?"

"Buffy!" Cordelia shrieked.

Buffy turned around. The Tatzelwurm had reared on its hind legs and was menacing Cordelia while Xander cast around. The places where it had slid along the basement floor were molten, a narrow channel of cement melted and fused again in its new shape.

The Tatzelwurm had slid over the man who had been chained to the floor. He wasn't a man anymore. He wasn't much of anything. What was left smoked and bubbled.

Buffy swallowed hard and glanced at Xander.

"Get Giles," he cried, eyes wide, his voice tinged with panic.

She gave her head a tiny shake. He frowned at her, bent down, and grabbed a piece of wood. He held it like a spear and jabbed it at the Tatzelwurm, which reacted by heating up its underbelly. It glowed a brilliant orange.

"Buffy, he's your Watcher," Xander urged, a weird mix of fear and courage coming over him now. "I can handle this."

"No, you can't," she blurted, and saw the frustration in his eyes. "I can't leave you," she tried again.

Then Cordelia said, "Xander and I can handle it, Buffy. You go help Giles." She said it with tears streaming down her face, but she said it.

Buffy turned.

Cordelia shouted, "No, wait, I take it back! Don't go!"

"Buffy, go!" Xander yelled at her.

Before she could reply, the decision was taken from her. The floor tipped even further. Buffy slipped over the edge of the canted floor and slid down until she, too, crashed through the wall.

A short time later, the world within the Gatehouse had begun to stabilize, somehow. The basement where Xander and Cordelia faced the Tatzelwurm was still the basement. Or dungeon, or whatever it was. As the floor was strewn with dry straw and one wall stacked with wooden crates, however, Xander thought the old ever-changing, barrel-o'-fun, house full of surprises might have been a better idea.

Where the Tatzelwurm crawled, it burned. Its underbelly glowed white-hot. The straw in the circle around Cordelia and Xander was on fire.

"Anyone for campfire tales and roasting marshmallows?" Xander quipped.

"Shut up, shut up!" Cordelia cried, even as she desperately tried to clear the floor immediately around them of straw before it could be set ablaze.

Xander faced off against the Tatzelwurm, which had grown quickly cautious. It seemed to understand that the sharp stick he held could harm it.

"Why hasn't it jumped?" he asked.

"Maybe heating itself up takes a lot of energy," she suggested.

"Must be a boy Tatzelwurm."

The thing started for them, and Cordelia shrieked. Xander jabbed the air with the stake in his hand, and the Tatzelwurm stopped once more. Steam began to rise beneath it as the floor bubbled with heat.

"Would you just keep your eyes on that thing!" Cordelia snapped.

Xander nodded. "Got it." He rubbed his eyes. "Smoke's getting to me."

"Yeah, me, too."

Her face felt like it was cracking, it was so hot. The smoke stung her eyes and tears ran down her cheeks. She wished Buffy would come back. With Giles. She wished the house would do something weird again so they would end up in a different room.

The worm rose up on its hind legs, twining around itself like a snake.

"It's going to jump!" she cried.

"Get back!" Xander shouted.

It struck then, propelling itself into the air. Cordelia scrambled backward, but she knew it was too late. The arc of the thing's attack would bring it down on top of her. Flames flickered to either side. As the smoldering belly of the Tatzelwurm came down toward her face, Cordelia realized she had nowhere to run.

"Cordy!"

Xander was there, stake in his hand, his arm wrapped around her. He held the stake up, elbow locked, and Cordelia knew in that instant that even if Xander impaled the thing, the molten heat from its body would kill him.

She smelled the Tatzelwurm's awful stench; felt the heat of its body as it plummeted toward them.

There was an explosion.

They stood pressed together in a tiny, airless room. The walls were covered with yellowed paper, an ancient floral pattern. In the corner was an old, rickety wooden wheelchair. A waltz played very faintly.

"Well, that was very nearly a disgusting way to die," Cordelia said, wrinkling her nose in revulsion.

Xander glared at her. "I'm sure I can come up with something more pleasant for you, Cor."

Cordelia huffed at him, as usual.

The wheelchair began to move.

At the airport, with the afternoon sun glaring through the windows, they faced each other. Oz said, "Hey, I'll be back soon."

Near tears, Willow tried to smile bravely, but she could only muster a sniffle. It seemed to her that no one who went to Boston was coming back.

"Take care," she pleaded. "Please call us."

Oz pulled her into his arms and kissed her. He held her for a long moment against his chest. She could hear his heart beating. She could feel the pulse in his neck.

"I'm sorry," he began, then shrugged. "You know."

"You don't ever have to apologize for who you are." She touched his hair. Tears spilled down her cheeks.

Then somehow he was gone, hurrying down toward a gate to catch the last plane to Boston. After the plane took off, Willow sat and waited several minutes until Buffy's mom hurried up.

"I can't believe it took that long to find a space." She smiled faintly. "Did Oz get off all right?"

Willow nodded. "We just made it in time. Thanks so much for driving us. Oz wanted to leave his van at Angel's, in case Angel needed it."

"Happy to do it," Mrs. Summers replied.

"That's so . . ." And then the reality of what was happening hit her: she'd been out all night, she hadn't recast her binding spells, and her parents had probably already called the police, despite Buffy's mom covering for her.

She must have looked upset, for Mrs. Summers murmured, "Oh, Willow," and pulled her into her arms. Willow couldn't help it, she burst into tears and let Joyce Summers rock her for a few comforting minutes.

"I'll drive you home now," she said.

In the car, Joyce suggested a wonderful, terrible lie to cover up for Willow's frequent absences: a friend of hers had run away from home, was living on the streets, and Willow was trying to urge her to go to the runaway shelter run by Connie DeMarco.

"It's the thoughtful kind of thing you'd really do," Buffy's mom said, smiling gently at her. "Your parents won't really be surprised."

Willow shifted uncomfortably. They came to a red light and she automatically looked out the window, looking for more men in long coats. They had a name now. The Sons of Entropy. Somehow that made them more terrible.

"Well, it's not something I'm really doing," she said. "But I can't tell them that. Any more than I can tell them that Oz is . . ." she trailed off. Had Buffy told her mother about Oz? "That he's a really good guitarist."

Mrs. Summers shook her head. "You kids definitely have it tougher than I did." She laughed shortly, derisively. "But then how did I know I was going to give birth to a vampire slayer? When you're a little girl, you think you're going to be a ballerina or a cheerleader. I guess."

She glanced at Willow. "What did you want to be when you grew up?"

"Marie Curie, discoverer of radium," Willow said dreamily.

Buffy's mom chuckled and shook her head. "Well, I certainly didn't. And Buffy . . ." She sighed. "Well, who knows what Buffy really wanted to be."

The light turned green. "Don't be too hard on your parents, Willow. They're just kids who grew up. You're a version of the dreams they had."

Willow was taken aback. "I hadn't thought about it that way."

"You're their chance to get it right." She made a face. "A weighty responsibility, I know. And unfair."

Willow shrugged. "I guess we have expectations of our parents, too."

Joyce nodded. "To always be right, and strong, and fair, and *there*. I'm afraid I haven't been there for Buffy much." She lowered her voice. "Angel told me to get out of Sunnydale. He said things might get worse before they get better. Do you agree?"

"Maybe," Willow ventured. "Are you . . . are you going to leave?"

She sighed and ran her fingers through her hair. "How can I? I need to be where Buffy is. Or can find me. When she comes back." She glanced from the road to Willow, and a single tear coursed down her face. "You do think she's coming back, don't you?"

"Oh, absolutely," Willow assured her.

There was a moment of silence between them.

"Hey, maybe I can do some of your research for you." Joyce moved her shoulders shyly. "I've taken some classes about the Internet. I'm sure there's something I can do to help."

"Oh, thank you so much," Willow said, as they pulled up to her house. "About the runaway thing. Do you think they'll believe me? I really hate lying to them."

Joyce smoothed Willow's hair away from her temple. "Sometimes the truth is so much harder to bear," she said softly. "If you think it'll help, I'll come in with you and talk to your parents."

"Oh, I . . ." Willow nodded gratefully. "I think it'll help. A little."

But the nice thing was, it helped a lot.

Joyce was feeling low by the time she got back to her house. Things were not good in Sunnydale. Her daughter was obviously in great danger. Willow was under a terrible strain. Even Angel was showing signs of extreme stress.

She hated this whole Slaying thing. If only there was some way Buffy could quit.

She remembered one night when Buffy was a baby. She and Hank had had a terrible fight—nothing new there. She was exhausted, and depressed, and had just managed to fall asleep when Buffy had woken up, squalling. Demanding to be fed.

Joyce had dragged herself out of bed and stumbled down the hall. As she pushed open the door to Buffy's room, she'd muttered, "I quit."

And then she had seen her perfect little baby, her daughter, and even though tears of exhaustion and anger were rolling down her cheeks, she smiled. Her heart filled with more love than she thought it was possible to feel. She would do anything for this baby.

She would kill for this baby.

Being a parent was like that.

Being the mother of the Slayer was like that.

# Chapter 12

"Giles!"

Buffy had called her Watcher's name over and over, to no avail. She'd tried to follow him, but the malleable house had thwarted her time and again. She had been dumped unceremoniously at the top of a long flight of carpeted stairs. When she looked around, it became clear that she had fallen from nowhere, from some nebulous pocket of chaos in the house.

The house had calmed some. She could no longer hear it screaming, but she was certain that what she did hear, a kind of whispering or hissing, was the sound of the thing breathing. As though it needed time to recover, or to gather its strength for another attack.

Yet, for whatever reason, the floor and walls seemed solid enough. The wooden planks of the ceiling were nothing more than that, now. Out the window at the far end of the hallway, Buffy could see that night had fallen, and she only hoped that whatever chaos was happening in here, it wasn't yet affecting the outside world.

"Giles!" she cried again.

There was no way for her to tell what floor she was on. From the top of the stairwell, she'd seen nothing more than a landing and a turn down some more stairs. The corridor was beautiful, if antiquated. Each room had an oak door, and Buffy studied the incredible woodwork as she walked along.

The doors were all closed.

"Xander! Cordelia!"

There was an echo, then, but it wasn't her voice. Instead, it was a kind of singsongy, mimicking voice that she could barely make out. There was no way to tell where it came from, either.

Buffy froze. She slid down to sit cross-legged on the floor and buried her face in her hands.

"God, I want to go home," she whispered to herself.

For several moments, she sat there, hoping against hope that something would happen. That Giles or Xander or even Cordelia would suddenly appear, maybe fall right through the ceiling and slam to the carpet next to her.

No such luck.

With a sigh and a grunt as she stretched the shoulder she'd bruised when she fell out of the air, Buffy rose and started down the corridor again, calling her Watcher's name. It was too quiet. Buffy could not believe that this was the same house as the thing that had come alive around them, sweeping them into a maelstrom of chaos and insanity. It seemed too . . . too real.

"Giles!"

Buffy paused. The hall was longer than she'd originally thought. *Maybe my depth perception is whacked,* she thought. *That fall may have given me a concussion.* She looked back the way she'd come, and the feeling grew even stronger. This was a big house. But she'd seen it from the outside.

There was no way a straight corridor in this house could be this long, or have anywhere near this many rooms. It was impossible . . . but everything in this house was impossible. Magic made it real. So, somehow, she reasoned, the house was much larger inside than it was outside.

Which was just great, seeing as how it made it even less likely that she'd be able to find any of her friends in the madhouse.

"The hell with it," she snapped, and reached for the nearest doorknob. Buffy had been a bit anxious about opening any of the doors, what with the freakiness of the whole house, but at this point she didn't think she had much to lose.

She turned the knob and pushed the door open.

Wind swept her face. A hard breeze filled with grit and heat, the baking dust of the west. From inside the room, the sun blazed down.

It wasn't a room.

Buffy felt her stomach churn, and her equilibrium was totally shot. She swayed on her feet and nearly pitched forward into the room . . . onto the hard-packed earth and scrub in front of her. The western plains stretched out for miles in the distance. Buffy squinted against the sun, felt her skin prickling with its merciless heat, and then closed her eyes, feeling the solid oak of the door frame under her fingers.

Somewhere close by came a rumble like distant thunder, but growing nearer. Buffy bit her lip and forced herself to open her eyes.

The dusty plains were still there. It took every ounce of her self-control to hold onto the door frame and poke her head through, into that other place. She glanced left, glanced right, and realized that the doorway she stood inside was just a hole in the world. Some kind of tear in the fabric of reality itself.

The rumbling grew louder, and Buffy looked off into the distance. A dust storm was rising, but something moved within it. The ground shook. The door frame trembled under her fingers. She narrowed her eyes, trying to make out what was in the huge cloud of dust, even as the sound began to separate itself out. It wasn't one sound, but many. Thousands.

It was a stampede.

Buffy watched with fascination as the herd approached, trying to make them out. Dark, hugely lumbering shapes moving at a pace far too fast for their size. Then she saw it—what the cloud had become. For it did have a shape, almost as though it had become a spirit, floating above the plains. The dust kicked up by those thousands of hooves had coalesced and formed itself into the huge spectral head of a buffalo.

Buffalo, she thought. But most of the buffalo were dead.

The stampede drew closer, impossibly fast. She could make them out now. And then Buffy knew, just looking at them. Bloody and rotted.

These buffalo were dead as well.

"Oh, my . . ." Buffy began to say.

A firm hand clamped on her shoulder, yanked her back, and shoved her to the ground. Buffy scrambled to her feet, spun to face her attacker, ready to take his head off with a roundhouse kick.

"That will be quite enough of that, I think," Giles said calmly, and reached into the other world, grabbed the knob, and pulled the door shut. The stampede's hoofbeats echoed for a few seconds before dissipating completely.

"Giles," Buffy said in relief.

Then she ran to him and threw her arms around him.

"I thought I'd lost you," she said, her voice fraught with emotion.

"Yes, so did I, for a few moments," Giles agreed. "I heard that awful noise and came running up the stairs, and there you were. The house seems to have settled on a shape, at least for the moment, hmm?"

Buffy sighed, let him go, and looked at him purposefully. "Great. Now what? What the hell is this place? You told us that the Gatekeeper's responsibility was to close breaches into this limbo realm where all the weird phenomena stay separated from us."

"And apparently, those things were kept here," Giles said idly, glancing about. Then he nodded toward the door he'd just closed. "That stampede, for instance. The unpublished journals of your Buffalo Bill Cody discuss visions he had as an elderly man. Those visions concerned herds of dead buffalo, whose spirits would not rest until the plains were wild again. Their species was decimated in the latter part of the nineteenth century, where once they were as common as deer."

"So they were more than visions?" Buffy wondered.

"Apparently. And apparently, the Gatekeeper does more than close those breaches, he . . . collects them, for lack of a better word. I'd suggest we don't open any more doors without being a bit better prepared."

Buffy stared at the door, then at Giles. "Good idea."

At the end of the corridor, something caught her eye, a flicker of light that didn't belong. Buffy looked past Giles and froze, her mouth open in a tiny, startled *O*. The window was gone. The night sky beyond it had been replaced by a swirling maelstrom of gray and flickering silver, weird blue and purple hues. The whirlpool expanded quickly, stretching from floor to ceiling and all the way across the corridor.

"Giles," Buffy whispered.

But he had already turned, alerted by her expression. Together they stared at the pool. Then, without warning, a dark figure stepped through it as though emerging from behind a waterfall. Silver strands of crackling magick swept off the figure like beaded curtains.

Its body was white oilskin. Its fangs glistened with the dim light of the hallway. Its eyes were dark holes, windows on the abyss.

It looked at them. "Excellent," it whispered, and when it laughed, blue flame spurted from its open mouth. Then it turned left and disappeared into an open doorway. Buffy heard footfalls on stairs, but they stopped abruptly. Somewhere there was a loud crash.

"Was that . . ." Giles began.

"Springheel Jack," Buffy confirmed.

"But how could he have traveled here so quickly?" Giles wondered aloud.

Buffy looked at him carefully, frowned. "You said yourself that a lot of things that are supposed to be in this house are showing up in Sunnydale. Like that Tatzelwurm thingie. Maybe there weren't two of them after all. Why there? I mean, it's the Hellmouth, right? But it's a big country out there, a big world, and Sunnydale is three thousand miles from here."

Giles's eyes widened and he nodded to himself. "Indeed. It would seem impossible, were it not for the extraordinary amount of magickal energy contained in this house. I would hypothesize that it is the single most concentrated source of magickal power in the world, an intricate web of spells, incantations, and wards that is constantly changing. Something of this magnitude will become utter chaos if left untended."

He turned to regard her gravely. "We must find the Gatekeeper."

Buffy blinked. "Giles, hello? I'm still lost. I can see the lure of the Hellmouth to creepy things. But what's the deal?"

"Well," Giles said tentatively, "I'm only just beginning to form a hypothesis myself. It's quite complicated. We know that the realm of the demons exists, and that the Hellmouth is the thinnest and most vulnerable part of the barrier between our world and theirs.

"According to the legend of the Gatehouse, there is at least one other realm, sometimes referred to as the Otherworld, where all manner of mystical and mythical creatures and things—things that might once have existed on Earth but have since become, shall we say, extinct—a world where such things still exist. The evolving natural laws of our world have somehow shunted them aside. This Otherworld is where they've been shunted to.

"The Gatekeeper, if my research is correct, is responsible for gathering and effectively imprisoning things which have somehow escaped the Otherworld—subverted the natural laws, you might say."

Giles seemed quite satisfied with himself. Buffy, though her head was spinning, thought she had actually caught most of his explanation. But there was still a great deal she did not understand.

"Okay," Buffy nodded. "But how are these escapees from the nuthouse traveling back and forth to Sunnydale? And why?"

Giles frowned. "Well, that's obviously one of the things we're here to find out."

"Oh, obviously," Buffy said. "Can we find Xander and Cordelia now?"

"Come then," he replied. "Time to find the others before they get in real trouble. The house seems to have settled down a great deal. Perhaps our presence alone is imposing order on the magickal matrix somehow? The insistence of our minds that this chaos does not belong. Hmm, we'll have to examine that possibility."

"You examine," Buffy said sharply. "I'll slay anything that tries to stop you."

Together Buffy and Giles reached the end of the corridor. The window had become nothing but a window once more. No more swirling magic whirlpool. Which was just fine with Buffy. Magick creeped her in a way vampires and demons never had. Vampires and demons were, at least, predictable. Magick could be put to use for good or for evil, and depending on the power of the witch or magician, there were very few limits on what could be accomplished with magick.

Sorcery could provide a person with their greatest dreams. It could also create the worst and most terrifying of nightmares. Buffy knew from nightmares, and as she and Giles turned to follow Springheel Jack's path up the stairs, she prayed silently that the Gatehouse would not be able to come up with horrors as terrible as those her own subconscious had created for her from time to time.

She thought it was a hopeless prayer.

Somewhere far above them, Cordelia screamed.

Buffy and Giles pounded up the steps side by side, and she was surprised that he was not breathing heavily. Her surprise lasted for two flights of stairs, and then even she had begun to labor under the strain.

"This is incredible," Buffy said, gazing up the stairs to the next landing. "The house goes on forever."

"Or it appears to," Giles said. "I doubt we'd have heard that scream if it came from much higher up. I think we ought to explore the next floor, unless we hear her again."

At the landing, they turned into the corridor. The Oriental carpet on this floor was beautiful, and Buffy had to wonder what she would see if she looked out the window, how many stories above the ground they would *appear* to be.

"Buffy," Giles said quietly.

He pointed.

Down the hall, one of the many doors stood open, and a pale lavender light shone out onto the walls and the carpet.

"We should check it out," she said with certainty. "We're not getting anywhere, Giles. We have to."

"Agreed," he said.

Then they heard Cordelia scream again. Upstairs.

"Damn!" Giles snapped.

Buffy spun and strode back out onto the landing, starting up the stairs. Giles started to follow, then took one last glance down the corridor at the open door before turning once more toward the stairs.

The stairs were gone. At the threshold that had once opened onto the landing there was nothing but wallpaper, and a beautiful painting of a schooner crashing on some rocks in a storm, despite the presence of a comforting lighthouse close by.

Buffy was gone.

"Dammit, no!" Giles snapped. "There must be some way to . . ."

He thought again of the theory he'd proposed only moments ago. They were somehow imposing order on this house, but they would not be the only forces present to do so. There were so many wills contending in the Gatehouse, usually reined in by the will of the Gatekeeper himself. If he had any hope of finding Buffy again, he would have to find the Gatekeeper first.

Cursing under his breath, Giles turned and strode down the corridor with new purpose. At the door that emanated purple light he turned in, opened his mouth to demand information on the whereabouts of the Gatekeeper, and then froze where he stood.

They were beautiful, and there were so many of them. Inside that door was a pleasant glade at dusk, a purplish light glittering from the wings of the things that flitted from flower to flower, from water to tree branch. They cavorted across large stones and danced on the gleaming surface of the pond.

*Sprites,* he thought. Or something very like them. Tiny, winged women, naked but for the sparkling butterfly wings that fluttered on their backs. Giles stood, almost hypnotized, almost as though they were the sirens of Greek mythology.

It was such a picturesque moment, it made him think of standing on that balcony in New York with Micaela, the way her honey hair tumbled over her shoulders. But that was the horrid city, and this was . . . this was paradise. He would have loved to have shared even a single moment like this with her, to have followed the path that their first meeting had set out for them . . . to learn if he could love again.

Giles felt despair rising within him as he thought of Micaela, and knew that in all likelihood she was dead.

As if it could sense the change in his emotion, one of the sprites noticed him. There came a high giggle and it flitted close to him. Giles smiled until its tiny little claws raked his cheek, laying the flesh open. Blood ran down his chin, and Giles snarled at the sudden pain and slapped a hand to his face.

The glamour was gone. He saw them for what they were. And what they were was horrible.

Buffy couldn't go back. The corridor where Giles had been was now gone. The only thing she could do was head in the direction of Cordelia's screams and hope that she would be able to reach all of them eventually. Giles was the Watcher: he ought to be able to take care of himself. At least, better than Cordy. Who was, after all, Cordy.

Besides, the guy they really needed to find was the Gatekeeper. Once she'd reached Cordelia, that would be her first priority. If they wanted to get out of this place in one piece, they had to find the guy who was *supposed* to be in charge.

"Off to see the Wizard," she muttered.

*Yeah,* she thought. *Now we know what Oz was like after the Wizard blew them off to take Dorothy back to Kansas.*

This landing was different from the two she'd seen. Rather than the corridor running sort of parallel with the stairwell, there was a single step up and then the corridor ran directly off the stairs, straight ahead. The hall was wide and there were portraits all along the walls. It looked like a fancy hotel, but at the turn of the century or something. It was beautiful. At the far, far end of the hallway, there was a window.

Outside the window, it was bright and sunny. The sky was perfectly blue. Buffy knew that in the real world, it was probably nine or ten o'clock at night. She decided to ignore the window. Nothing inside this house was real, not the reality she knew, anyway.

That didn't mean it couldn't kill her.

At the end of the hall, there was another stairwell. This one an incredibly wide, curving set of stairs that led down into what looked like an enormous foyer, the size of a small ballroom. Crystal chandeliers hung from the ceiling, and the floors were polished marble.

It ought to have been the fourth or fifth story. It was

obviously the first floor, and the long rows of glass doors and windows revealed that outside, the ground was covered with snow. A winter wonderland.

Nothing was impossible in the Gatehouse.

Behind her, a set of door hinges creaked loudly. Buffy spun to see several people emerging from a room behind her. Two men and a woman, all three of them completely naked. The men were opposites, one tall and thin, the other short and very, very muscular. Ripped, Xander would have said. And the woman was lithe, her body full and feminine. All three of them had thick black hair and eyes that were dark and shone at the same time, almost like an eclipse.

"Hello, little girl," the woman said. "I thought you might want to play."

"Or not," Buffy said to her, glaring at all three of them. "Now why don't you three head back to the Garden of Eden and grab some fig leaves to cover up, hmm?"

The tall man snarled at her, baring fangs. The burly, short guy hissed like a cat. The woman only laughed.

All three of them began to change, hissing as black fur sprouted all over their bodies. Buffy didn't even turn. She set her feet apart in a fighting stance, and held her ground.

It was a beautiful home, something he had never truly recognized while he was a captive here. And once he had torn the beating heart from the chest of its owner, the house would be his. Its many rooms would provides centuries of diversion.

But first, what was a home without a wife? Or at least a mistress. This girl, Cordelia Chase, was the first of his intended victims to have ever escaped his grasp. Once he had marked a target, they were never allowed to escape. This hunt had taken longer than any other, but he would still have her. Yet, something had changed. Originally he had planned to kill her. He might still. But there was something . . . arousing about a woman who could elude him.

A small rivulet of fetid drool ran down Springheel Jack's chin, and he grinned to himself. From somewhere upstairs he could hear his beloved screaming, and he vaulted the stairs nine or ten at a time, not discouraged by the knowledge that the house could not possibly have as many stories as he had climbed. There must be seven floors or more. Impossible.

It wasn't important. The only thing that mattered was the beautiful aroma that drifted down to him. He had caught Cordelia's scent the moment he returned to the Gatehouse, and now his entire body sizzled with a frisson of arousal unlike anything he had ever felt. Her scent, yes. The smell of her, and the dark odor of her terror.

That was what he loved best.

"Xander!" Cordelia screamed.

"Move!" Xander shouted, and then he shoved her aside as the wheelchair barreled toward him. Xander backpedaled as fast as he could, looking around the attic for something, anything with which to defend himself. There were heavy, dusty trunks and metal racks upon which hung ancient clothes that made the place look like a costume shop. An old spinning wheel sat in one corner, and next to it, a full length mirror on a wooden stand.

In the mirror, Xander could see an elderly woman sitting in the wheelchair. She seemed frightened as well, reaching out to him with one hand as she propelled the chair with the other. For a moment, he paused, but there was something else about the image in the mirror—the old woman was obviously dead. What little he could see of her, he could see through. The image was transparent, a specter.

"Gaaah!" Xander cried, and reached out for something, anything, to defend himself even as he backed farther away from the wheelchair.

Far to his right, Cordelia rose to her feet.

His fingers wrapped around something thick and cold, a metal pole. He pulled with all his strength, and only when it crashed to the floor between him and the wheelchair did Xander realize it was an old-fashioned birdcage on a metal stand.

He expected the wheelchair to stop.

It came ahead, slamming into the metal pole. Xander jumped back, his right heel caught on something, and he stumbled backward, arms flailing.

Cordelia screamed.

Xander felt a moment's resistance just before he crashed through the leaded glass window. The jagged, shattered glass tumbled all around him. His mind raced wildly, even as his hands whipped out once again, hoping for something to hold on to, anything to stop him from plummeting three or four stories to the hard ground below.

He tumbled onto the canted roof, rolling twice backward. His legs swept over and out into nothing but air, and his hands scrabbled at the edge of the roof.

Gripped. Caught the edge.

But only for a heartbeat, and then he fell fifteen feet to slam into a second level of roof that jutted out of the house, some kind of porch or patio that had been added later. His legs crumpled beneath him as he struck the slanted roof, and he tumbled once again, but forward now, and he tried desperately to stop his descent.

He saw brick. A chimney.

Then he struck it, hard, sending pain shooting up one knee and making him see stars as his right cheek bounced agonizingly off the brick.

But he stopped.

"Damn," he whispered.

Xander was splayed against the edge of the chimney. He'd slammed one knee into the brick and scraped his cheek, but otherwise he felt all right. His tongue probed his teeth, and though he tasted blood, all the teeth seemed fairly sturdy still.

"This is great," he muttered. "Now how do I get back inside?"

He sighed. "Not that I want to go back inside."

A scream tore the air above him, and Xander's eyes went wide as he remembered how he'd crashed through the window in the first place.

"Oh, God," he said, "Cordelia!"

He whipped his head around, craned his neck to look up, lost his grip on the chimney, and slid sideways over the edge of the roof, falling away into nothing, his scream so profane it would have made Angel blush.

He crashed into some shrubbery, branches scraping his abdomen and back through his shirt. His arms had tiny scratches all over them, his knee and face hurt from hitting the chimney, but as he pulled himself from the shrubs, he was happy merely to be alive.

Now he just had to make sure his girlfriend was still

alive as well. He stared up at the attic window he had crashed through. From here, it looked impossibly high. With a quick glance around, Xander realized that he was not actually outside the house, but in an internal courtyard. In truth, he was at the heart of the house. The house rose up on all four sides, but above, there was only the sky.

The gardens and trees in the darkened courtyard were overgrown, and when he followed the sound of burbling water, he discovered a vine-covered fountain at the center of the courtyard. Stone paths wound among the gardens, but they too were grown over, and it had taken Xander a minute to notice them.

Now that he did, he saw that though they meandered about, each one led to a set of French doors. Four different entrances back into the house. It seemed pretty likely that one of them would be open. If he was stupid enough to go back inside.

Stretching out his leg, testing his injured knee, he started for the French doors set into the house on the same side from which he'd fallen.

"As if I had a choice," he muttered. "I'll take boneheaded, suicidal boyfriends for one hundred, Alex."

From the trees behind him he heard a groan. Something moved through the overgrowth. Or rather, some things. For now he heard sounds coming from all around him. Xander moved along the path until he was roughly at the center of the courtyard, away from the vegetation. The moon shone down like a spotlight as the things came from the darkness of the wild garden.

They looked dead, but they weren't desiccated at all. Just filthy, matted people, almost like cavemen.

They were stooped over and grinning madly. As they grew closer, Xander realized that their skin was a greenish brown, and he realized that they weren't human anymore. If they ever had been. The one nearest to him was an old man whose beard was stained with blood.

"I want his eyes," the bearded, filthy thing said in a gurgling voice. "I love the way they pop in my teeth."

Xander sighed. "Ghouls," he said. "Why did it have to be flesh-eating ghouls?"

The wheelchair hadn't moved since Xander had tumbled out the window. For a time, Cordelia had been too frightened even to go to the window. When finally she mustered the courage, she could not see anything but a lower-level roof with glass scattered about and the tops of trees from some kind of courtyard.

She whispered his name, and then turned and rushed to the stairs that led down out of the attic. The door wouldn't budge. As she pounded against it, kicked the bottom, and twisted the knob madly, Cordelia began to cry. Tears streamed down her cheeks and she sobbed silently. In her mind she imagined the worst—imagined Xander broken and bleeding on the ground in the courtyard outside, jagged pieces of glass jutting from his corpse.

"No!" she screamed. "Please, someone!"

She pounded the door, bit her lip, felt the hot tears coursing down her face.

"Anyone!" she wailed.

Something thudded against the door.

Cordelia stared at it a moment before she said tentatively, "Buffy?"

With the shriek of wood and splintering hinges, the door was torn right out of its frame.

Cordelia scrambled backward up the steps toward the attic even as Springheel Jack came in after her.

He grinned, and whispered a single word.

"Darling."

# Chapter 13

Xander edged away from the ghouls—there had to be at least six of them—as he looked around for a weapon, an escape route, maybe even your friendly neighborhood Gatekeeper. No such luck.

He said to them, "Aren't you on, like, a special diet or something? Ghoul kibble? Gets rid of those special cravings?"

"I want his tongue," said another old ghoul as he crept from behind a tree trunk. His long beard caught against the bark, and as he jerked his head to free it, dead insects loosened from the matted hair and fluttered to the ground. "And the fat in his cheeks."

"Okay, winner of the gross-out competition," Xander said.

He turned and ran from the center of the courtyard toward the opposite set of doors.

He didn't get far. His foot caught on a thick tree

root and he went sailing through the air to land in a circle of rotten leaves and gray, waterlogged mushrooms.

Footfalls thundered behind him. He said loudly, "Hey guys, hear the one about . . . about . . ."

As the first hand grabbed at him, Xander fell silent. He had nothing to say.

"Oh, my God," Cordelia murmured, as she backed up the attic steps.

"No, not God. Simply your beloved," Springheel Jack said, smiling crazily at her. "Now come here, my darling. I want a kiss." He opened his mouth. His flashing, needle teeth gleamed, but something inside him was rotten, and she could smell his breath from where she stood.

Cordelia kept climbing. Then she ran into something. Half-turning, she realized it was the wheelchair.

The one with a ghost in it.

Springheel Jack came fully now through the door at the bottom of the attic steps and began to climb.

Cordelia swallowed hard and gave the chair a firm shove with her hip, urging it out of the way. It didn't move. She pushed again, her terror rising as Springheel Jack reached out a hand.

"Please!" Cordelia said desperately.

With a sudden jerk, the wheelchair moved backward of its own accord.

*I love a polite young lady,* the ghost whispered in her mind. *My name is Antoinette, girl. And I think I can help you.*

She glanced in the mirror. There was the old woman, her gray hair done up in a chignon.

*Springheel Jack has escaped from this house too many times. This was the last. You must use his own fire against him, girl. Use your wits to ensnare and entrap him.*

"Me?" Cordelia asked.

*The door,* the ghost said, her voice weaker now. *The fire.*

Cordelia turned to look back at the attic stairs. The door had already been destroyed, she thought. But then she saw what the ghostly old woman was talking about: there was a hanging door angled above Springheel Jack's head, much like a garage door. There was a rope attached to it, which was strung along the beams of the ceiling and through several eyehooks to fall straight down behind the mirror, where it was tied off on an old padded seamstress's dummy.

"My sweet," Jack said. He rushed for Cordelia. She ran behind the chair, felt terrible for using the old lady as a shield, remembered she was a ghost, and figured Jack couldn't hurt her anyway.

She still didn't get how she could use Jack's own fire against him. There was an incredible amount of old junk lying around, but Cordelia didn't have time to go through it now. Old clothes couldn't help her. They were so old they were practically nothing but rags anyway, just a lot of faded old fabric you might as well—

*Burn.*

Cordelia finally got it.

She just didn't know if she had the courage to do it.

"Cordelia, come for your kiss," Springheel Jack urged. He inhaled deeply, another smile spreading across his distorted face.

That did it. Cordy knew just how to use the monster's fire against him. She put her hands on her hips and sneered, "Are you crazy? Have you seen yourself in a mirror? You are in serious need of cosmetic surgery."

"What did you say?" he asked slowly, incredulously.

"I said that you gross me out," she shot back. And then she did what she hadn't imagined she could make herself do. She laughed at him, laughed from deep inside where her hysteria was hiding.

"How dare you!" Springheel Jack raged, and fire spewed from his mouth.

Cordelia felt heat on her back. Summoning her courage, she glanced at him over her shoulder. "How dare I what? Make fun of a clown like you?"

"A clown?" he sputtered. *"A clown?"*

He stared at her slack-jawed. Then he narrowed his dark eyes and more flame shot from his mouth.

Beside her, a rack of flimsy old clothes burst into a blaze. Like a trail of gunpowder, the fire traveled over other clothes, a row of hats, the aged wallpaper itself. Within seconds, half the room was engulfed in fire. The bed went up. The mirror shattered.

The flames were about to reach the rope that held the attic door in place.

Cordelia had figured out the old ghost lady's plan. Make him mad enough to set the place on fire with his raging bile, then trap him before he could get to her. But if the flames reached the rope before Cordelia herself could get downstairs . . .

"Will you be okay?" she yelled at the wheelchair. It rolled forward slightly just before the floor beneath it burst into flame, and it was engulfed. Cordelia caught her breath. She would have to take that as a yes.

"Okay, then." She sneered at Springheel Jack as he stood bewildered, surrounded on all sides by a firestorm. "Maybe you'll find a girl your type when you get to Hell!"

She turned to flee. Before she could reach the steps, the attic door shot downward with the force of a guillotine blade and covered up the entrance, effectively trapping her inside the burning room with Springheel Jack.

Cordelia screamed. Taking a step back, she looked up. The fire had reached the end of the rope which hung behind the mirror and it had burned all too quickly.

"Alone at last, sweet love. Come to me, Cordelia," Jack said softly.

Tears spilled down Cordelia's cheeks. She was actually going to die. Above her head, the rafters burned furiously. A huge plank of wood dislodged and careened toward her like a bomb.

She shrieked and jumped out of the way.

Now she was closer to Springheel Jack, who smiled at her and said, "We must hurry, my darling. We wouldn't want to burn to death before we have had one single moment in each other's arms."

"Heck, no," she muttered. The smoke was beginning to overwhelm her; she could barely see. Through slitted lids, she glanced desperately around.

The only escape was the window. She didn't know if Jack had figured that out, but that didn't really matter, did it? If she couldn't get to it, she was going to cook to death. But Jack was in her way.

Coughing, she took another step toward him. Her foot caught on something, and she glanced down. It was the iron center support for the padded seamstress's mannequin, now burned away. A little unwieldy for her, but it would have to do.

She hefted it and tried to assume the same fighting stance she had seen Buffy take a thousand times. Only now she was the fighter, facing a monster that had defeated Buffy.

She wouldn't cry.

She would *not*.

"Oh, my brave beauty," Springheel Jack said admiringly. "What a couple we'll make."

Then he ran at her.

Cordelia cried out and swung the support. He was too far away. She swung again, grunting with the effort. Her eyes bulged when she realized that she'd actually hit him, making hard contact with his left hip.

"You . . . bitch," he said, stunned, and opened his mouth.

She swung again.

The metal frame cracked against his face, and his head rocked back, his whole body thrown off balance.

Springheel Jack turned, snarled, and vomited flame at her.

At the same time that the floor gave way beneath him.

With a scream he disappeared, fire streaming toward the burning ceiling like a geyser. Terrified, Cordelia sobbed and held on to her weapon.

Then she picked her way through the burning room to the window, climbed out, and tried to hold on. But she was exhausted, and there wasn't much to hold on to, and she knew she would soon let go.

"Xander," she screamed. "Xander, where the hell are you? You got me into this and you better get me out or you're so dead!"

"You're making an awfully big production out of this, aren't you?" Xander asked, only moments after he had returned to consciousness.

The ghouls had carried him deep into the overgrown garden. He lay on the ground and fought not to cry out as he realized the grinning white blob he was staring at was a human skull.

There were more of them now. Perhaps a dozen in total, including two horrid-looking, stooped things, smaller than the others. *Ghoul children*, Xander thought in horror. *The whole family*.

"We have not eaten flesh in centuries," said the old guy with blood in his beard. He was actually rubbing his hands together.

"I'll disappoint you," Xander promised. "It's my stock in trade."

They had grabbed his arms and legs, and the oldest ghoul was trying to take the first bite. Xander kind of wished they'd bash his skull in first, but it looked like no such luck.

One of the ghouls said, "Is that smoke?"

And suddenly it was raining fire. Huge timbers slammed down around them, exploding into blazing grenades over their heads.

The ghouls holding Xander screamed and let go. Drained and injured though he was, he jumped up and ran for all he was worth. He dared only one glance over his shoulder, following the trail of flames as they spewed onto the fleeing ghouls. An overhanging wing of the house was on fire, and the ravaged section was falling into the courtyard.

If his geography was right, it was the wing of the house where he and Cordelia had been confronted by the ghost . . . the one with the window through which he'd crashed.

"Cordy," Xander breathed. Then he shouted her name, even as he cursed her under his breath. All the times he'd wanted to kill her, and here he was, once again, trying to figure out how to save her.

"I hate irony," he grumbled.

Stumbling, he reached a set of French doors and grabbed the handles, tugging with all his strength.

They were locked.

"No!" He slammed his full weight against them. "Cordelia!"

He slammed again, over and over. He was just about to abandon them and race to another set of doors when they opened.

A very old man in a black turtleneck sweater and olive trousers stood on the threshold of the house. Ragged and pasty-faced, his dark brown eyes were ringed with black circles. There was heavy gray stubble on his chin. He looked terrible. Maybe even worse than Xander.

"Fiend, are you with the Sons?" he demanded, then doubled over in a coughing fit that wracked his body. His fingers were sticklike, the veins protruding from the backs of his hands in a maze of blue and purple.

"Fiend? Me? Have you looked in the garden lately?" Xander shot back, pushing open the door.

The man wiped his mouth. There was blood on his

fingers, but he took no notice as he glared at Xander and straightened his shoulders. Suddenly, he looked younger, though still so old that a few decades would do little to diminish his decrepitude.

"Son of Entropy, I'm the one you seek. I am Jean-Marc Regnier.

"I am the Gatekeeper."

Buffy faced the three huge animals crouched in the doorway. The two men and the woman had completely transformed into black panthers, deadly and sleek. Their short black velvet fur covered rippling, jungle-deadly musculature. The tall man had become an immense animal, and a shock of gray ran down the spine of his shorter, more brutish companion. The woman was the smallest, but it was she who led the pack as they crept forward, low to the ground, yellow eyes always on Buffy.

All three of the enormous beasts bared their long, wicked fangs, growling deep in their chests.

The female swiped at the air, flashing savage claws capable of tearing an arm off with a single motion. Buffy's instinct for self-preservation screamed at her to get the hell away from them, but in this madhouse, she didn't know where to run.

The animals sprang through the doorway.

Without a second's hesitation, she launched a high side kick that took the female in the face, turning her away and blocking the charge of another. Then she leaped into the air and slammed down with all her weight on the hind end of the larger male. With a roar of fury he turned on her, crouching low, preparing to spring.

Buffy shifted into a fighting stance, looked at the

panther, and snarled in return. "I don't know if you can understand me or not," she said, "but here's a newsflash: if you three don't leave me alone, I'm going to kill you all."

How, she had no idea. She just hoped the panthers believed her.

Unfortunately, they didn't.

The animal she had attacked seemed wounded, though she knew not badly. He regarded her coolly and struggled to rise. The other two continued to glare and growl.

"Hey, I'm talking to you!" Buffy shouted. Beads of perspiration gathered on her temples as she pulled a stake from her belt. The Slayer was not supposed to show fear, but she had no other weapons, and she had never fought panthers before. Hyena people, yes. But not actual wild animals.

She held the stake point out and took one slow step toward them. Then another.

The larger male hissed at her. She felt at her belt, got another stake, and held it business-end in her left hand. Her mind raced, trying to formulate a plan if they should all charge her at the same time.

She didn't have the time.

As if on cue, they rushed her, growling savagely. She felt the sharp, numbing sting of a bite, had no idea where she had been bitten. Her head snapped violently back, and the gray-striped panther struck her chin with the back of his forepaw, almost like a slap. If she had not been the Slayer, the impact would probably have broken her neck.

She had a chance to get in a sharp jab to his paw before the animal drew it back. It roared in angry pain and lowered its head, its jaws wide open, and charged her.

She feinted to the left, then catapulted herself across the animal's line of approach, stake outstretched to make contact with its head as it launched itself at her. Her timing was good; the sharp point lodged in the panther's mouth, piercing its tongue and the inside of its throat.

The beast went berserk. As Buffy hit the opposite wall of the hallway, the huge head rolled left, right; it let out a roar that shook the walls.

Buffy would have loved the luxury of panic, but she could not afford to waste precious moments. She pushed her back against the wall and scrabbled to a standing position. The panther dropped to the floor and began wildly pawing at his snout. Buffy knew that within seconds he would recover and come at her again.

The female sprang, its powerful leap rocketing it on a direct path toward Buffy's head. Buffy dropped. The animal sailed over her head and rammed into the wall. The female panther turned even as it fell, attempting to redirect its momentum. Buffy drove her stake into the animal's abdomen. Blood spurted and gushed down her arm, spattering her face, as the animal thrashed on the floor.

The gray-striped panther began to slink toward her.

The wounded female rose halfway up, then fell back on its side. It lay along the corridor, its face away from Buffy. From the wound in its abdomen, blood spilled onto the carpet. But now the largest of the three, the one whose hindquarters she'd bruised, had regained its feet and was stalking her alongside gray stripe.

They moved in.

Without turning, Buffy slowly retreated. But as she moved to put as much distance between her and the panthers as possible, she ran into something as hard as stone. Her fingers reached backward and examined it quickly. It had to be another of the barriers erected in the house, weirdly misplaced as the house shifted once more.

As quickly and quietly as she could, she began to run her hands over it, searching for a latch, a door-knob, anything she could use to escape. Into what? That was a consideration, but not one she had the luxury of making.

As the two males slowly stalked her, preparing to pounce, Buffy saw the female roll onto its back. As Buffy stared, the animal lifted its head. Slowly the black velvet fur disappeared as its muzzle shrank back into a woman's face. As she panted hard, fighting for breath, she narrowed her eyes at Buffy. Blood burbled from her mouth.

"Don't bother running," she said. Then as she coughed up gouts of tissue and blood, her eyes rolled back in her head and she collapsed onto the carpet. Within seconds, she was fully human.

The other two panthers threw back their heads and howled. In unison they glared at Buffy.

They tensed to spring.

There was so much blood in Giles's eyes that he could barely see. The tiny monsters that raked his flesh were hideous, with black sticklike bodies and elongated stomachs. They plucked at him with long needle fingers and teeth that were longer still, and they shoved the bits of skin into their mouths as if they'd been starving for centuries. As they yanked off his flesh in strips, their stomachs grew, until those nearest him actually began to pop, disgorging rotten flesh which must have come from earlier victims.

Giles batted at them, but there were too many, and they came at him from all sides. It would have been easier to free himself from a swarm of wasps.

His instinct was to roll into a ball, if only to protect himself from further harm, but he knew that then he would be lost. He did manage to stuff his hands into the pockets of his tweed jacket, and he put his hand around the rose quartz Pallamary had given him at the hospital.

Giles had forgotten it was there. Now his first thought was that the quartz was cursed, and had helped to embellish, if not create, the havoc all around him. Perhaps if he got rid of it, the monsters would disappear.

Wincing against the pain it cost him to move, he tossed the quartz into their midst.

The air rent in two. A vortex of crackling blue energy took up residence in the center of the room, dervishing in a circle. It opened a portal—Giles saw it clearly—and black and purple light danced within.

Then the monsters began to be sucked into the black circle. In tiny, shrill voices, they flailed helplessly through the air as the portal pulled them in. They clung to Giles's clothes, his hair, his ears and fingers. To no avail: one by one they disappeared.

The rose quartz went with them.

After the passage of mere seconds, they were gone. Giles stood in the wood, catching his breath. So the rose quartz had been a protective talisman after all. He was surprised that Pallamary had given it to him.

Perhaps then, he had not been marked for death, but for capture, as had happened to him before. Then why were other Watchers being killed?

Having no answer, he moved painfully to the doorway, crossed the threshold, and slammed the door shut. Whatever madness still lay within the room would hopefully remain there.

For now, at least, he was not in immediate peril of his life. And so—as always—his next thought was of Buffy.

"I killed your girlfriend," Buffy said to the two panthers as they crept toward her. "And I'm an equal opportunity Slayer. Boys get no special treatment."

Gray stripe roared and sprang at her. Buffy twirled in the air and got off a roundhouse kick, connecting squarely with its jaw. The panther was enraged; he swiped at her with his left paw, then his right, but Buffy dodged out of the way like a prizefighter.

Still it came at her, darting forward, biting the air as she flung herself to the floor, rolled, then flipped to her feet.

Where was the other? Her eyes darted around, trying to keep a fix on both of them. Gray stripe could just be distracting her, setting her up for his big brother to come in for the kill.

"Buffy!"

It was Giles.

She called, "In the corridor!" and realized how stupid that was. This place probably had a kazillion corridors. "Stairway!" And a bazillion stairways. "Panthers!" Maybe he had found a map of all the rooms.

\* \* \*

Bemused, Giles stood before the door and placed his hand on the knob. From the sound of Buffy's voice, he could swear that she was on the other side. But was it a trick of the house? Some mismatched set of magickal variables he would be mortally sorry he had trusted?

If he opened this door, would something else try to kill him, and very possibly succeed?

He pushed up his glasses with a philosophical shrug. That didn't matter, did it? If there was the least chance that his death could save the Slayer, then he would die. It was that simple. One shouldn't take foolhardy chances, of course, but when faced with the possibility that one's sacrifice most likely would produce the end result, then—

*"Giles!"*

He opened the door.

The big panther merely watched as Buffy fought gray stripe; the Slayer understood it was waiting for her to get tired. Once she was worn out, it might join in. Or maybe it would simply claim the larger portion of the spoils, it being the big kahuna and all.

Buffy had no time to wipe the blood and sweat from her face. Nor the tears of frustration. If there'd only been this one panther to battle, she would have pulled it off. But there were two. Which meant, in reality, that sooner or later she was going to die.

Behind the beautiful cherry-wood door stood another beautiful cherry-wood door.

Giles was reminded of those American game shows where the picking of doors provided the highlight of the entire tawdry and tedious event. Or perhaps, more prosaically, of *Alice's Adventures in Wonderland*. So he opened door number two.

Covered from head to toe in blood, Buffy was struggling with an enormous black jungle cat.

Giles murmured, "Good heavens," stepped over the threshold, and grabbed her by the back of her shirt. He said, "Buffy, it's me," just as she whirled on him, prepared to defend herself.

At once she bounded toward the door, knocking him over the threshold and landing on top of him.

Then she jumped to her feet and slammed the door shut just as the enormous cat caromed into it. The door shuddered and bowed inward. Then all was still.

"Nice of you to stop by," Buffy said.

"Buffy, are you . . . injured?" he asked, horrified, his heart pounding with his fear for her.

"What? Oh." She looked down at herself. She was covered in blood, and there was a gaping wound just above her knee. The panther bite. Lucky thing he hadn't had a chance to really sink his teeth into her.

"I'll be okay. Eventually." The bite was starting to burn, now that she had the luxury of feeling pain. No joy there.

Giles cocked his head. "Do you smell smoke?"

"*Something's* burning," Buffy said worriedly. "We've got to find Xander and Cordelia." She started forward, then stopped and frowned at Giles. "Where are we?"

He shook his head. "I've absolutely no idea."

"What should we do?"

He thought a moment. "It seems that our presence has imposed some modicum of order upon the Gate-house."

"Just a little, though," Buffy said.

"Yes. That is the meaning of modicum."

"Uh-huh." She straightened her shoulders. "I knew that."

"It also seems that the house has been trying to reassert its disorder upon us."

"Drag."

"Buffy." He sighed. "I know you're trying to maintain your equilibrium, and I—" He blinked. "Perhaps that's it. Perhaps we need to establish even more order. You know, when I ran away to London to protest my destiny, we did quite a lot of, oh, meditating and such. Have you ever heard of transcendental meditation?"

She nodded brightly. "They played once at the Bronze."

"Just so." He managed a brief grin at her. "I do enjoy your sense of humor, Buffy. It's your timing I often object to."

"That's a load off. Okay, so trans and dental meditation, and I'm saying, 'huh?'"

He pushed up his glasses. "What I mean is that we should establish in our minds a sense of peace and calm. That we stand in the center of order and harmony. Perhaps this will radiate to the house long enough for us to find Xander and Cordelia."

"And put out the fire," she said urgently.

"And find the Gatekeeper."

"Who can put out his own darn fire."

"Are you with me?" he asked her, closing his eyes. "You've got to close your eyes and center yourself, listen to yourself breathe." He frowned. "You're breathing awfully hard, Buffy."

She gave him a tired half smile. "That's the house, Giles."

"Oh, dear." He looked worried.

She patted his arm with her bloody hand. "But don't let it ruffle your feathers. We'll calm it down, okay?"

"All right. Close your eyes."

## Chapter 14

STILL IN THE FUZZY STRIPED SWEATER AND YELLOW corduroy overalls she had worn to school, Willow met Angel a short way from her house. He was dressed for the night air in a black turtleneck sweater and his duster.

"Sorry I'm late," she said. "My father wanted to talk about my future again. I'm more interested in making sure there's going to *be* a future."

"I had no patience with my father's lectures when I was young. He didn't like my friends, either," Angel offered. "However, since most of them were drunken louts living off their inheritances, he might have had a point."

"Well, the closest thing Oz has to an inheritance— and he got it from his cousin—is three nights a months, he's a werewolf," Willow said defensively.

"The other twenty-seven, he's a musician. Which may qualify him as a lout. But he doesn't drink."

Her flashlight off, Willow moved through the darkness beside Angel, melting into the shadows, waiting. It seemed strange to her, being here with him. In addition to the horrors he, or the thing inside him, had perpetrated on her and those she loved, there was the feeling that she was here only as surrogate for Buffy.

Willow didn't like the way that felt. But with the others gone, she and Angel were all Sunnydale had left. She would do everything she could to make that count.

They crouched behind a large row of manzanita bushes. Beside her, Angel shifted his weight. He half turned, listening intently. In the yellow moonlight, his face was pale and his eyes brown, nothing like the savage face that it became when the bloodlust was upon him.

He blinked and touched her hand. Then he pointed to the deserted building they were observing. They were on the grounds of the ruined Delta Zeta Kappa fraternity house, where Willow recalled that Buffy had once gone partying with Cordelia, with disastrous results: the two of them had nearly ended up as sacrifices to the frat house's reptile god. The creepy thing had lived in the basement. Once Buffy killed it, the fraternity was disbanded; most of the current members went to jail and a large number of the alumni died mysterious deaths or killed themselves.

All in a day's work for the Slayer, Willow thought.

No one wanted the house itself. The college had let it go to ruin, ignoring the fact that they might get sued if somebody fell through the floor, and then someone had finally set it on fire. Now it sat like a blackened skeleton, hulking in the gloom beneath the full moon's glow. Ghost stories had sprung up around it, of course. Lots of them.

Stories Giles compiled faithfully, cross-referencing and cross-checking them to his heart's content.

"I swear there's something in there," Angel said. "Shambling around."

"Maybe it's, y'know, just kids or homeless people or . . ." Willow paused, looked at Angel hopefully, and then sighed. "Okay, it's some huge ravenous beast. But I can still be optimistic, right?"

Within the dreary ruins of the fraternity house, something snapped. Willow and Angel tensed. *Tree branch. Could be a raccoon.*

Beside her, Angel was on full alert. Willow rose up slightly, to get a better view. Mentally she ran over the binding spell she had been practicing. It was new, and it should work more quickly on larger things. Just to be on the safe side, though, she slid a stake from her belt and held it at the ready. Angel nodded, smiled grimly, and pulled one from inside his jacket.

There came a sudden flurry of noise, then a short, piercing scream. Then silence.

Angel said, "Let's go. Carefully."

As previously planned, Willow snaked to the left while Angel moved to the right. Keeping to the overgrown landscaping, they closed in on the house in two semicircles, moving into the darkness until neither one could see the other. Hopefully, no one else could see them, either.

Angel reached a stand of trees, rose up in their concealing shadows, and dashed toward the dilapidated structure. He ran up to the rotted porch, skirting a number of holes. What had once been the front door was now a gaping, charred maw that he ducked through, constantly testing the footing as he went.

Willow rushed up behind him. He raised his hand slightly to let her know he was aware of her, and together they charged into what had once been the living room. The back wall was completely gone. Tree branches draped with vines and deerweed bushes had grown into the space. If something was hiding from them, this was a good spot for it.

Back to back, they searched the room. Their shoes kicked up dirt and ash, and Willow had to fight not to cough.

After the circle was complete, Willow said, "Anything?"

"No."

They looked at each other. Angel was in full vamp mode, his eyes a golden yellow, his mouth drawn up in the rictus of a grimace.

"Well, *something* screamed."

Angel nodded and walked to the northwest corner, sifting through the debris with his boots as he made his way past the remains of an overstuffed chair. He bent down and said, "It was a raccoon."

"Was?"

He nodded. "Yeah. Big was."

"Anything I need to see?"

"Naw. But I'm going to boil it up for dinner later, if you're interested."

He rose.

Willow flicked on her flashlight. "Whatever killed

that raccoon knows we're here," she said. "We might as well see where we're going."

She aimed the beam at the staircase that led to the upstairs bedrooms. For the most part it was intact, though several of the stairs and the railing were gone.

A loud crash from the basement made them both freeze.

They looked at each other, then moved toward the nearer of the two doors leading to the basement. The stairs had been carved from rock, as had the entire cavernous basement, and Angel half-ran, half-flew down them. Willow trailed behind him. The ground was littered with debris.

Something smelled very rotten.

He growled and assumed a fighter's stance, saying, "Dead ahead."

"I see it," she said, capturing a figure in her flashlight beam.

It was vaguely human-shaped, crouched low. From the position of its hands and feet, it appeared to be facing them, but its face was in shadow. She advanced on it very slowly with a stake raised in her right hand—just in case—and Angel flanked her, shadowing her every move.

Lifting her hands, Willow began to chant.

They were almost on it when it bolted into the air and whirled around, flying straight at Angel. Its mouth was filled with fangs, its face was bloated and red, and its eyes glowed a sickening green. The way its head met its body didn't look right, as if the thing had a broken neck, and it stank like vinegar. The teeth flashed as it went for him.

Angel roared as he went for the thing. Somehow it

evaded him and hopped onto the crumbling wall of the deep stone well where the reptile god had lived. It bounced again, springing into the air, its teeth snapping.

"Is this thing a vampire?" Willow asked, staring at the monster.

"It's a *pennanglan*," Angel told her. "Similar, but not quite a vampire. I've never heard of them outside of Malaysia. It sucks the spinal fluid—"

The thing flew at them, and Angel and Willow split up, dividing the pennanglan's attention.

"More than I need to know," she snapped. "But what's it doing here?"

"Looking for dessert?"

Willow chanted more loudly and held the stake in front of her.

"Stakes work?" she asked.

"You have to destroy the head," he replied.

"I'd rather not have to get that close." She took up her chant again, though it didn't seem to have much effect.

It launched itself at Angel again. He dropped, and they both watched as the pennanglan sailed over his head and ricocheted off the opposite wall. Willow's eyes darted around the room, until she noticed that the chains the frat boys had used to bind their victims still hung from the rock walls. She scrambled over, grabbed a chain by its iron cuff, stood with her boot against the wall for more leverage, and pulled as hard as she could.

To her surprise, the chain loosened from the wall with no effort at all, and she tumbled backward onto her butt, then slammed onto her back, the wind momentarily knocked out of her.

"Willow!" Angel cried.

The pennanglan soared straight at her. The thing was hideous. Even as she struggled to get her breath back, she held the chain down at her side like a bullwhip. As the thing came for her, she stepped back, whipped the chain up and made it whistle through the air. Much to her amazement, her strike was on target, and the links wrapped around the creature's neck.

Willow pulled.

Its head came off too easily, with a sickening, slurping noise as its spinal column came along with it. The links of the chain tightened, then, on the thing's spine.

The pennanglan continued to fly. Its body lay on the floor, pumping fluids, but the bulbous, salivating head and spinal column came at her again, teeth gnashing.

"Angel!" she screamed. "What the hell *is* this thing?"

"That's what I tried to tell you," Angel said. "It doesn't need its body. When it hunts, it leaves the body behind. We've got to destroy the head."

Even as he spoke, Angel moved to block the thing's path. The chain was still attached, and as it went after Angel, the pennanglan stretched the links out to their full length, like a dog testing the limits of its run. Willow's stomach was churning with nausea at the sight of the creature, one of the most repulsive things she had ever seen.

The thing went at Angel, its teeth gnashing viciously. He moved so swiftly Willow nearly missed it. Angel whipped his stake up and slammed it right through the center of the creature's forehead.

It fell to the floor and didn't move.

Willow hugged herself and stared at it in horror. Angel went to her and put his arm over her shoulder. She twitched a moment, and then surrendered to his gesture of comfort.

"Buffy would be really proud of you," he told her.

"Is it dead?" Willow asked, still staring at the thing.

"We'd better burn it," Angel replied. "Just to be safe."

They did. The stink was awful.

# Chapter 15

CORDELIA HUGGED THE SIDE OF THE CHIMNEY TIGHTLY, tears flowing freely down her face, cutting lines in the sooty grime that had settled there. Above her, the topmost story of the house was ablaze with hungry fire. It licked out of the shattered windows and up through holes it had already eaten through the roof. Black smoke billowed around her. Fire crept down the outside of the house toward the secondary tiered roof where Cordelia clung, helpless and vulnerable. It slunk toward her, gripping the wood and shingles, as though it hunted her—as though it had a mind of its own.

A predator's mind.

The fire moved closer and Cordelia tried to scream, choked on the smoke, and settled instead for a whimper of despair that verged on surrender.

\* \* \*

Buffy and Giles were joined in a kind of circle, facing each other with their hands outstretched and clasped together. They had cleared their minds of fear, of anger, of the chaos of the house, and instead focused on the orderly things of their world. Buffy suspected that Giles was mentally sifting through the library's card catalog or something. For her, it was the simple act of cleaning her room, just the way she'd done it since she'd been a young girl.

A place for everything, and everything in its place, her mother would always say. So she focused on that. The ordering of her closet, the folding of her laundry, the making of her bed.

"Buffy." Giles voice was weak, as if he'd just woken from a long nap.

Her eyes fluttered open, and she found her Watcher gazing upward. He glanced around the corridor, and Buffy did the same. But the oddest thing had happened.

They weren't in the corridor anymore.

"What the . . . We've been shifted somewhere else again?" she asked incredulously. "I thought this was supposed to make things better."

"You misunderstand," Giles replied. "We haven't moved anywhere. Rather, it is the house that is shifting. And I believe we *are* making things better. Can't you feel it, Buffy?"

Amazingly, she *could* feel it. As she looked around at the room—a warmly decorated bedchamber with a brick fireplace on one end, high-backed chairs, and a canopied bed—Buffy had the inescapable feeling that this was right. Out the window beside the bed, she could see down into a large courtyard overgrown with a wild garden. A fountain at its center burbled weakly.

The house was even larger than they'd thought—even without magic—for it was made up of an enormous square with the courtyard at its center. The first two stories were somewhat wider than the upper two, and as she looked down, Buffy could see the shingled roof of the lower portion of the house jutting out of the wall beneath her.

This was real.

Out the window to her right, Buffy saw the fire blazing, billowing black smoke. That wing of the house was in flames. They had smelled the smoke before, but this fire was beyond what she'd expected. It was time to act, time to find Xander and Cordelia.

Just as she was about to pull her head back in through the window, Buffy heard a scream over the crackling of the fire. She squinted, staring at the blazing side of the courtyard. By the chimney on that lower roof, where the fire was quickly spreading, she saw Cordelia.

"There's no way to tell how long this lull will last," Giles began.

But Buffy was way ahead of him. She rushed past him, threw the door open without any caution whatsoever, and flew into the corridor. There were lamps along the hall that had probably once been kerosene, but now burned with Edison's greatest discovery. Various paintings hung at odd intervals, portraits and European cityscapes for the most part. The floor was wood, with a narrow Oriental carpet running the length of the corridor.

Buffy could actually imagine, for the first time, that somebody lived here. She wondered how much of the house would be left when the fire was through with it.

With Giles hard on her heels, Buffy bolted left,

running full-out toward the end of the hall, and the stairwell she knew must be there. It had to be. If she had to go the other way, the long way around the house, Cordelia would be dead before they reached her.

Xander stood in what appeared to be some kind of old-fashioned parlor. He was happy he'd closed the French doors behind him, even though the ghouls didn't seem to be coming after him. It was almost like they'd disappeared.

"Listen," he told the snappily dressed old man before him, "obviously you were expecting someone you don't like very much. I'm not him. If you're the Gatekeeper, we are looking for you, but only because Giles—he's the Watcher—thinks you've got yourself a little chaos leak in here. And I've been through your house, pal. He's right. Your magick needs some serious patching up."

The Gatekeeper's wrinkled face changed, suspicion creeping over his features. His white brows knitted together, and his eyes closed to slits.

"You are not with the Sons of Entropy?" he asked, his voice a dry rasp.

"As much as they might regret it, I'm the son of the Harrises of Sunnydale, California," Xander said. "And in case you didn't know, your house is on fire."

Even as Xander spoke, Jean-Marc Regnier, the Gatekeeper, shuddered. His head lolled to one side, his eyes rolled up, lids fluttering, and he collapsed in a heap on the floor with a single tiny gasp of breath.

"Oh, man!" Xander cried, kneeling at the old man's side. "Was it something I said?"

Regnier's lips moved, and Xander lowered his ear

toward the man's mouth. The Gatekeeper whispered one word.

"Cauldron."

Before Xander could ask him for clarification, a scream of utter terror broke the silence. Over the roar of the fire, and through the closed French doors, he recognized that voice.

"Cordy," he snapped, and leaped to his feet. Through the glass of the French doors, he could see her perched on the edge of the burning second-story roof of the Gatehouse.

"Oh, my God," Xander whispered.

He turned quickly and rushed toward the arched doorway that led from the parlor into what looked like an enormous foyer beyond. Before he reached the archway, someone stepped forward to block his way. Xander tried to stop but could not. He barreled right into the old woman in front of him.

Passed right through her.

The cold was startling. So frigid, in fact, that Xander convulsed a moment and nearly lost his footing. He managed to stay upright, but hugged himself tightly and breathed deeply several times as he regained his bearings. He should have knocked the old woman on her butt, he thought. How could . . .

*"Help him."*

"Ghaaaaa!" Xander cried, and stumbled back, even as the ghost materialized in front of him yet again.

For that's what she most certainly was. Spirit, specter, ghost, whatever. That was it.

"I don't have time for this," Xander muttered, staring at her in terror. "You can haunt me later, okay?"

He backed up, a quick glance confirming that

behind him was a wide double staircase that led up from the first floor.

*"The others are already on their way to help Cordelia,"* the ghost whispered.

Xander paused, studying the old woman's shade in detail for the first time. He thought he'd seen her in a portrait somewhere in this madhouse. Of course, in the portrait, he hadn't been able to see *through* her. And, of course, she'd had legs.

The ghost didn't have anything but a weird mist below the knees. She floated there in the hallway, looking at Xander as sternly as an angry grandmother.

"Were you the one in that wheelchair?" he asked, frowning. "'Cause I'd hate for there to be two of you."

*"You would not reach her in time,"* the ghost whispered. *"Even your friends will not reach her in time. The only way to save her is by saving him."*

"Him?" Xander asked. "The old guy, you mean."

*"He is my son,"* she whispered. *"Only he can control the house. Only he can save your friends. But you must bring him to the Cauldron."*

Xander bit his lip, staring at the ghost. He was nodding his head as though he were at the Bronze listening to a particularly righteous band. He bounced on the pads of his feet, energy coursing through him along with his fear and anxiety. What was the right thing? How did he decide?

*Come on, she's a ghost,* he thought. *Why should I trust her?*

A tiny, bitter, frightened voice inside Xander told him that she was right about one thing. His chances of reaching Cordelia in time, through this maze of a house, were almost nil. What other choice did he have?

Nearly running, he went back into the parlor and knelt again at the side of the fallen Gatekeeper. Without another wasted breath, Xander slipped his arms beneath the frail form of Jean-Marc Regnier, who seemed to have withered further in the intervening moments, and lifted him easily from the floor.

He turned to face the ghost, who shimmered now, flickering in and out of existence before his eyes.

"Okay, where's this cauldron thing?"

The ghost seemed to smile, before her face was creased once more with concern for the Gatekeeper. Her son, if she could be believed. Behind her, and around Xander, the walls seemed to become malleable again. Reality was flickering. The Gatekeeper moaned. Xander had never been good with math, but he could put two and two together. The old man was holding the place together. As he weakened, reality went on a coffee break. Which was bad. If the place was going to go wonky again, he'd never find his way to Cordelia, never mind some overgrown stew pot.

As if she'd read his mind, the ghost whispered to him. *"Close your eyes, dear boy. They will lie to you. My words, my voice will guide you."*

The room began to spin. Xander sighed, rolled his eyes, and then closed them.

"Why do I feel like I'm really going to regret this?" he asked aloud.

The ghost ignored his question. *"Quickly, now,"* she whispered. *"Forward twenty paces, then left and down the stairs. I'll warn you when we get there."*

"Yeah, unless I've got a practical joker for a ghost.

I've seen Charlie Brown fall for Lucy's taking-away-the-football gag too many times, lady."

But the ghost did not respond. After a moment, Xander began to walk forward, eyes firmly closed. From far off, he thought he heard Cordelia screaming once more.

Giles rattled down the steps to the third-floor landing as fast as he could go without stumbling. He held the railing tightly, and actually leaped the last two steps for good measure. Buffy had been a bit more direct about it: she'd actually jumped from the fourth-floor stair entrance to the landing between that and the third floor below. Then she'd done the same thing getting down to the third floor, lost her balance, tucked her head into a roll that brought her back to her feet, and she was off down the hallway before Giles had rounded that between-floors landing.

Now he turned right and began to run down the hallway, even as the lights started to flicker on the walls. Things seemed to wobble a bit, as though reality weren't quite certain of itself, and then they were righted. But there was no way to tell how long such a thing would last.

He was stunned by how little the fire seemed to have damaged the hallway. Buffy had stopped halfway down the corridor, and even now she stooped slightly to look out a window.

"Buffy?" Giles called.

"Oh, my God," she said, fear in her voice.

"The fire must be burning the outside of the house already, perhaps the floor just above as well . . ." His voice trailed off as he saw the smoke seeping through the seams of the wooden ceiling.

Buffy hadn't noticed. She was staring out the window. Giles bent to look out a window he was passing.

On the roof of a wing of the house that jutted out into the courtyard, Cordelia clung to the heated brick of a chimney that seemed to be protecting her from the fire. She had moved around behind it, putting it between herself and the blaze, and it was only pure determination, Giles was sure, that was keeping the poor girl from tumbling off the roof into the garden below. In fact, he wondered why she hadn't done exactly that.

For the fire was moving in. The entire roof was ablaze outside the window, and certainly the outside of the house must be as well.

The smoke began to thicken in the corridor.

"This is impossible, Buffy," he said anxiously. "Fire doesn't burn like this. It doesn't . . . choose its movements."

"I do," the Slayer replied.

She spun, ripped a large portrait in a heavy wooden frame from the wall, and swung it toward the window she'd been looking out of.

"Buffy, no!" Giles cried in alarm.

Too late.

The window shattered under Buffy's assault, and oxygen rushed into the hallway, carrying the blaze along with it. Flames roared into the corridor, and Buffy barely leaped out of the way without being scorched badly. As Giles watched, the fire shot out tendrils that seemed to caress the corridor's wooden ceiling almost tenderly. There was a shriek of stress from the wood, and the ceiling collapsed into the hall, blazing wood and furnishings from the floor above coming down with it. The two pieces of the fire joined like lovers too long apart.

Together, the flames began to consume the hall and everything in it.

Outside, Cordelia continued to alternate between screams and what Giles could now see were quiet sobs of surrender.

Giles ripped off his jacket. He could only hope that a second influx of oxygen would not cause the same reaction. The fire had found its entrance. Perhaps he could now create an exit. He wound the coat around his fist and slammed it against the window nearest him even as Buffy joined him. The window shattered and the Slayer used her sneakered foot to kick the rest of the glass free. The window, at the end of the hall, was away from the burning roof, but nothing out there was stable. It could all go up at any second, the blaze spreading as quickly as it had inside.

"You can't go out there," Giles said, and turned to the window. "Cordelia! We're here! You've got to make it to this window, or you'll have to jump!"

She only wailed louder. Buffy threw one leg over the edge of the window frame.

"You can't go out there," Giles repeated, more sternly this time, and clasped a hand on her shoulder.

Buffy winced, looked at him, and shook her head sadly. "Isn't that what I'm here for, Giles? Isn't that what we do? Slayers, I mean. My mom wants me to grow up and make something of my life, and you want me to risk my life to save the world. I guess you just can't please everyone, can you?"

Giles felt sick to his stomach, and not from the smoke.

"Buffy!" he snapped, aghast. "How could you . . .

you know it would destroy me if anything were to . . ."

She held up a hand to stop him. "It's the gig, Giles. I know that. One dies, another is called. I don't have to like it, I just have to do it."

With that, she slipped through the window and began carefully picking her way across the roof toward Cordelia, staying well clear of the burning areas even as she crab-walked backward across the shingles.

"Buffy? Oh, thank God! What are we going to do?" Cordelia shrieked.

Giles watched Buffy open her mouth to respond. She was perhaps twenty feet away from Cordelia. Then there came a loud crack like the snapping of a bullwhip, followed by several others. Where it burned, the roof began to fall in on itself. The chimney to which Cordelia clung tilted toward the house and began to crumble as it collapsed into the widening circle of flame and charred wood.

Walking with his eyes closed had taken some getting used to, but Xander had managed eventually. He remembered playing the game Marco Polo—which was sort of like hide-and-seek with your eyes closed—with Willow when they were kids. That's how she'd gotten the little scar under her chin. They'd been playing the game when her mother asked Willow to go get the mail, and she'd gone to do so—with her eyes still closed. And tripped over something in the garage, and fell, hard. And bled.

Xander had always kicked Willow's butt in Marco Polo.

With the ghost whispering in his ear, close enough for him to feel the coldness of her presence, Xander had made his way along several corridors and then down a flight of stairs that his unseeing mind reasoned must go to a basement or some such. He'd slammed the side of his head into a door frame only once, stubbed the toes of his right foot, even through the sneaker, twice, and, with the prone form of the Gatekeeper in his arms, knocked over something that shattered loudly.

But he'd made it.

*"Open your eyes,"* the ghost whispered.

Xander did. The room was extraordinary. A huge bedchamber with a canopied bed, an ancient writing desk, and a full-length, silver-backed antique mirror in one corner. Out the windows, he could see the garden in the courtyard and the burning portion of the house on the far side.

"But we went down . . ." Xander began.

*"Nothing is what it seems in this house,"* the ghost whispered. *"Not unless my Jean-Marc wishes it so."*

Xander saw movement on the burning roof, by the chimney, and then he couldn't look. Couldn't bring himself to watch it anymore. For that second, Cordelia was still alive. That was all that mattered.

He scanned the room. A tall spear was hung on hooks on one wall, along with several paintings. There were shelves of odd artifacts, intricately carved boxes that looked more like puzzles than anything else, statues and crystals, and what looked like a scepter or a wand.

"Okay, where's the—"

The word was going to be *cauldron,* but before he could finish, he saw the huge, black, iron pot in the darkest corner of the room, away from both door and windows. It was filled with what appeared to be water, and though there seemed nothing out of the ordinary in the room's temperature, there was steam above the water.

*"Put him into the cauldron,"* the ghost demanded. *"Do it now!"*

She was no longer whispering.

Another time, Xander might have managed a witty remark. He would certainly have felt reservations about what he was going to do. But he didn't have time for such luxuries as doubt.

He walked over to the cauldron, and as gently as he could, he lowered the Gatekeeper into the steaming water. Jean-Marc Regnier slipped into the iron pot, his head under the water, and air bubbles slid to the surface. Xander blinked and began to reach in after him.

*"Stop!"* the ghost snapped.

"He's drowning!" Xander replied. "He's going to die!"

*"No. He's going to live!"*

Cordelia didn't even hear Buffy scream her name. Over the pitch of her own terrified, final screeching, how could she? The chimney crumbled beneath her, and she wished frantically that she had found the courage to jump to the courtyard below.

As she slammed down onto brick and mortar and charred beams and blazing fire, an errant thought slid through her mind: her mother would be so disappointed if Cordelia burned to death. Closed-casket funerals meant it just didn't matter what the corpse was buried in.

The fire began to burn her, even as she fell, and Cordelia screamed in agony.

Then it was gone.

With a painful thump, Cordelia landed on a Persian carpet in front of a roaring fire, in a beautifully appointed room that seemed to be a library of some sort. Aching, she forced herself to sit up and examine herself.

"I . . . I don't . . . how can this just . . ."

She started to laugh. And it was this sight—Cordelia completely unsinged, but partially unhinged—that Giles and Buffy discovered when they came pounding down the stairs just outside of the library and burst into the room.

"Cordelia!" Giles said in shock and astonishment.

"Giles, how can this be?" Buffy demanded. "The fire. We both felt it. It was completely . . ."

"Real, yes it was," Giles agreed. "I don't understand it either."

"It's a miracle," Cordelia said, eyes dull with shock and lingering fear. "Or just magick."

Buffy and Giles had come deeper into the room to help her up. None of them were facing the door to the library when the new voice spoke.

"I beg to differ," the voice said. "It isn't ever 'just magick.'"

All three of them turned, still attempting to reorient themselves. The house was more normal now, though still palatial. The man who stood in the doorway was handsome, with rugged features and gray hair that was the only hint of his age. Buffy would have guessed he was in his early fifties, but he had an air of youth about him. Of energy. He wore olive trousers and a black turtleneck sweater, which only added to his debonair appearance.

"Though you are unexpected guests," the man said, "you are quite welcome in my home. In truth, were it not for you, the Gatehouse would still be in chaos, and I might well be dead."

Giles cleared his throat. "Indeed. Well, let me introduce myself at least," he said. "My name is Rupert Giles."

"Yes, the Watcher," the man said, then his eyes turned to Buffy, and they shone with crackling energy and confidence. "And you must be the Slayer, then. You have my gratitude, and my deepest respect. I am Jean-Marc Regnier, the current keeper of the gate."

"You're not doing a very good job of it, are you?" Cordelia said angrily. "Our whole town is filled with nasties that escaped your little zoo, and as for this place, obviously it's the maid's day off."

The Gatekeeper only smiled. "Ah yes. You must be Cordelia. My mother and your friend Xander have told me a great deal about you."

"Xander?" Cordelia asked, glancing around.

Buffy was also interested in Xander's whereabouts, but the mention of the Gatekeeper's mother intrigued her as well. They had yet to see anyone else in the . . . Buffy blinked. Behind the man, in the hallway, a ghostly woman seemed to hover briefly. Then she disappeared, and Xander came through the door behind the older man.

Cordelia gasped his name and ran to him. He held her close and kissed her hair. Then Cordelia pushed him away to arm's length and punched him hard in the chest. Xander's eyes went wide.

"How could you leave me in that attic by myself?"

she demanded. "God, I don't know why I put up with you!"

"Cordelia, I fell out the window," Xander snapped. "I almost got eaten by ghouls! And we'd all be dead if this guy hadn't taken a bath!"

They all stared at him. Xander shrugged.

"It's a long story," he said. "Ask the old ghost lady."

"Hmm," said the Gatekeeper. "Now that you've mentioned the ghouls in the garden, please excuse me a moment while I do a bit of the aforementioned housecleaning. It is, after all, the maid's day off." This last he said while smiling mischievously at Cordelia. Then the Gatekeeper lifted one hand, and it began to glow with a dark green light.

Quickly the crackling green light enveloped the Gatekeeper's body. He raised his other hand, so that he held both before him, palms out. Then he *pushed* something that was invisible to the rest of them. Throughout the Gatehouse, the sound of slamming doors echoed and rebounded until the house itself rumbled.

Then was still.

Buffy's eyes were wide as she looked around. Then she turned back to the Gatekeeper.

"They are all back in their rooms for the moment," the Gatekeeper said. "Though I've no idea how long I can keep them there. As it is, I will have to immerse myself in Bran's Cauldron at least once a day simply to stay alive and keep this house in order."

Giles mumbled something, looked at Regnier, and said, "The Cauldron of Bran the Blessed?"

"The very one," the Gatekeeper agreed.

"Great!" Buffy said happily. "Your life is back to

normal. Now maybe you can give us a hand with our town. It'll never be a suburban wonderland, but lately, things have been a little more . . ."

As she looked more closely at the Gatekeeper, Buffy's words began to trail off. The man's eyes had lost their twinkle. The luster of his hair, the prominence of his chin, the tautness of his skin . . . all had nearly disappeared. It was as though he were aging before their eyes.

"Mr. Regnier?" Giles asked, before Buffy could say a word.

"I need a bit of rest," the Gatekeeper said quickly. "Perhaps we can speak in the morning? You have come to me for answers, and for aid. The former I can provide. The latter I am afraid I will have to ask of you, rather than the other way round.

"But that will wait. My mother will see that you have rooms for this evening," Jean-Marc Regnier said weakly.

When he turned and walked from the room, the Gatekeeper seemed to have aged more than a decade.

But the house was stable.

"What was that all about?" Buffy asked.

"Perhaps the magick saps his ability to retain a youthful appearance," Giles suggested.

"I just know that's going to be my problem," Cordelia said sadly. "It's only a matter of time."

"Fine," Buffy said. "But what about this 'mother' thing? Has anyone seen someone else wandering around here?"

"Oh, I've met the keeper's mom," Xander said, nodding with obviously feigned exuberance.

"You guys are gonna love her."

* * *

The sky had only just begun to lighten when Micaela Tomasi slipped her legs over the edge of her bed and sat up, rubbing her itchy, watery eyes. Sleep had been an unfaithful companion the night before, teasing her with its nearness, touching her briefly, and then retreating altogether. It had been a warm night, and humid, and the light breeze that whistled through the open window of her room at the villa did nothing to alleviate her discomfort.

Still, it had not been the climate that stole any chance she might have had at sleep.

It had been the screaming.

Micaela lifted her lavender silk robe from the end of the bed, surprised that she had not kicked it off during the night, and slipped it on, tying it tightly around her waist. She looked out the window, saw the grounds of the villa, crumbling and overgrown with vegetation, years of neglect having taken their toll. In the distance, she could see the domes and spires of Florence, the gem of Italy, and she yearned to walk its streets once more.

But no, the Sons of Entropy would not allow her to leave them. Not now. They did not trust her, now. Not after the report that Matthew Pallamary had offered upon his return from New York. Little bastard. If he had his way, Micaela thought, she'd be dead already. Her only reprieve had come because Il Maestro was fond of her. He had personally taken responsibility for her when she was orphaned as a child. It had been through his machinations that she was adopted by a family connected to the Watchers' Council, his grand scheme all along that she should become a Watcher.

Now, at long last, the ruse was over and Micaela had been called home, to Florence, to be with the only man she had ever truly thought of as her father. He was not, of course, and considering his age, she wondered if any of his own children still lived. But to her he was more than Il Maestro. He was Father.

But the eyes of a child and the eyes of a grown woman are very different. Since she had returned, and under such extraordinary conditions, she had begun to see things differently. The Watchers' Council had trained her well. She had been enveloped and embraced by the respect and tradition and the burden that they all held so dearly.

It mattered to her.

Of course, her debt to Il Maestro was greater than any of her own petty emotions. Or at least, that's what she had thought before she met Rupert Giles.

It wasn't that she loved him. Not that. Though a part of her certainly had grown fond of him in a short time, and he was attractive, no doubt of that. His eyes were captivating, his proud chin and graven features enticing, and his mind . . . He was a man of extraordinary intelligence and courage.

Micaela did not love the Watcher. But neither did she want to see him hurt. All of the things that her father had taught her, the entire existence of the Sons of Entropy, was in question to her now. The Watchers' Council existed to preserve the order of the world, and the Sons of Entropy survived with only one purpose, to tear that order down brick by brick.

Before she even realized it, Micaela began to weep uncontrollably. She covered her mouth with her hands so that her sobs would not be heard. The stone walls of the ancient villa were little protection from those who might benefit from what they hear and pass on.

Her feet were cold on the stone as she stepped into the narrow corridor. Here, the dim light of impending sunrise had yet to throw its brilliance, and so she walked the hall in darkness. Several of the robed agents, the Sons, passed her in the hall. All bowed their heads in deference to her who was so favored by Il Maestro. When she reached the top of the long stone staircase that led down into the cellar, the guard did not even raise his eyes to meet her face.

From deep within the stone-cold heart of the villa, another scream tore the light from the morning, chasing the sun away as Micaela descended.

It was a dungeon. She had known that since she had first returned to this place two days earlier. Whether it had been used for that when she had lived here as a child Micaela did not know. But now, that was precisely what it was. Stone and mortar round all four sides, except where the stairs were built into one wall. Torches flickered in iron racks jutting from the stone, casting the room in a horrid, violent orange light.

Micaela shivered. It was as though she had stepped back in time. She was reminded of the Inquisition, and shuddered at the comparison. But it was accurate. She knew that.

The knowledge sickened her.

Chained to a wall on the far end of the cellar was Frau von Forsch, a frumpy German woman in her fifties who had been one of Micaela's teachers when she had become a Watcher. Two stout Sons in black robes attended her with long, tapered daggers. Blood ran freely from some of the many cuts that had been made in the naked woman's flesh. Other wounds had already dried to a brown crust.

But the cuts were not the worst. Far from it. For the torturers had also used the knives as brands, heating them over an open torch and then laying them against Frau von Forsch's flesh. There were dozens of burns on her body, blackened and bubbled, where her flesh had been seared.

Blade sliced flesh, and a small flap of skin hung from the older woman's abdomen.

Frau von Forsch screamed.

"Stop," Micaela said quietly.

The torturers did not hear her over the screaming.

She clapped her hands to her ears, closing her eyes tightly, tears streaming down her face, and shrieked her throat raw. "Stop it! Stop it! Stop it!"

Her screaming had become almost unintelligible, more agonized, if possible, than the captive Watcher's.

The torturers only stared at her. Then one of them reached up and pulled the hood of his robe back, revealing the so-sweet features of Matthew Pallamary.

"Hello, Micaela," Matthew said kindly. "Did we wake you?"

From the fog of near-unconsciousness, Frau von Forsch looked up, eyes fluttering. She blinked blood from her eyes.

"Mi . . . Micaela?" the older woman croaked. Then she tried to say something else, to warn Micaela off, but she could not even find the voice to do so. Her lips moved, and Micaela understood the word they formed.

*Run.*

Micaela only whimpered, then turned her eyes away. Her guilt was devastating.

"Let her down," Micaela said after a moment. "Let her down immediately. She has no voice. She cannot possibly tell you anything more."

In the silence, Micaela heard water dripping somewhere nearby. Or perhaps it was blood falling to the stone floor. The captive Watcher's chains scraped the wall. The torturers only watched Micaela, and after a moment, Matthew's face was split by a wide, derisive grin.

"Silly girl," he said. "We got the answers we wanted more than an hour ago. We're just having fun now."

By his eyes, Micaela knew that he meant it. The shriek that tore from her then was the sound of her soul crying out for salvation, for she knew in that moment that she was truly damned. She rushed at Matthew with her fingers hooked into savage claws. That laughing face was too much for her. He held up one hand to ward her off, but he had underestimated her. She easily slapped his arm aside, and the nails of her right hand tore furrows across his left cheek, little strips of flesh hanging loose as blood began to drip down them.

"Bitch!" Matthew screamed, and knocked Micaela to the floor with a brutal backhand, his knuckles shattering her nose. Blood spurted from her nostrils as she went down, and then he was on top of her. His fingers closed around her throat, cutting off her air. Micaela was still screaming, though it was a hoarse sound now and nothing more. She struggled against him as he raised his dagger over her heart.

"Weak-willed whore," Matthew snarled. "I should have cut your heart out when you were ten years old."

The blade began to descend. Micaela screamed hoarsely. Matthew grinned down at her, anticipating her blood.

His hand froze in a pool of dark light, the purple-black of a bone-deep bruise. Matthew looked startled a moment, staring at his hand and the dagger there. There was a sound unlike anything Micaela had ever heard, a crunch as though something fragile had been crushed under a terrible weight.

Matthew Pallamary screamed horribly, high and deranged, much louder than he had been able to elicit from Frau von Forsch the whole night through. The dagger clattered to the stone floor and Matthew crumbled onto his side, pulled into a fetal position where he cradled his shattered hand. He whimpered, his eyes wide with shock, and Micaela wondered if he would pass out.

"Hello, Father," Micaela whispered to the darkness of the chamber.

The deep, familiar voice came from behind her. "I broke every bone in his hand, my dear one. He won't lay a finger on you again. But I am growing greatly concerned."

She turned to face him, but her father, Il Maestro, was still swathed in the darkness of the dungeon. It was as if he could draw the shadows around him as a cloak. Or, more accurately, a shroud, for he was the closest thing to a walking dead man she had ever seen. His heart still beat, of course, but it was cold as ice.

"You know that I love you," Micaela said, and knew, in that moment, that it was a terrible truth.

"That does not mean you will not betray me," Il Maestro replied. "I had such grand plans for you, Micaela. Please do not make me have to kill you."

From the darkness, Il Maestro turned his attention to the torturer who had stood silent throughout the horror that had just passed. "You have learned the location of the Slayer." It was not a question.

"She and the Watcher have gone to Boston to find the Gatekeeper," the torturer replied, without lowering his hood.

A sigh escaped the darkest corner of the dungeon. "As I feared," Il Maestro said. "Contact my acolytes in Boston. Tell them we must abandon caution and move forward immediately. Also, tell them if they kill the Slayer before she reaches me, I will have their souls for my dinner."

"Yes, Maestro."

Micaela's heart raced. She knew what was to come.

"Back upstairs with you, daughter," Il Maestro said, suspicion still in his voice. "Do not leave the grounds without speaking to me first. And do not forget, in the moments when your heart begins to cloud your mind, that it was I who took you from nothing, who formed you into what you are today. I gave you your life, girl.

"I can take it from you as easily."

With a final glance at the bleeding form of Frau von Forsch, Micaela spun and ran up the cellar stairs, sobbing. Before she had returned to her bedchamber, the captive Watcher began to scream again. But this time, her screams were cut terrifyingly short.

It was the last sound that Micaela ever heard from the cellar.

Later that day, her father allowed her to bury her old teacher's remains.

But he would not let her pray.

* * * * *

*October 30, 1713*

*I am dying. At long last, the spectre of death stretches his loving hand out for me, and I willingly clutch at his bony fingers.*

*Nigh onto fifty years have I lived in this home, traveling by ghost roads to faraway lands, and with my own two feet over the cobblestone streets of Boston. Over those long years I have collected a great many oddities, stored now in this home. Things undead and unnatural, creatures of myth which no longer have a place in the world, but which have escaped the Otherworld.*

*The ghost roads have been an extraordinary help, of course, but traveling with the dead is an experience fraught with profound despair and, yes, even a little fear. When a soul is released from its fleshly prison, it travels along the ghost roads to its final destination, whether it be the House of Angels or the House of Demons. Heaven or Hell, or whatever the reality of each of those worlds may be. The entire Earth is criss-crossed with these pathways, an intricate web of paths for the ghosts of humanity.*

*But more things than ghosts travel those roads. For those roads connect more realms than the worlds of men, devils, and saints. The ghost roads* also form a path to the Otherworld, which I have been at pains to define herein, though I have very little of substantial experience with which to support that definition. When I travel the ghost roads, I am able to move about on the face of this Earth, but Heaven and Hell are closed to me, as is the Otherworld.

Many times I have explored the possibility of entering the Otherworld, if only to return the more dangerous of the monsters and other creatures who have escaped into my own world. But even if I were able to throw open some kind of door into that realm, I am certain I would be unable to control such an opening. The opposite of my intentions would occur, and all of Otherworld would flood the world.

Chaos would reign.

Thus, I am forced to keep the escapees from the Otherworld in a place where they can cause no harm, nor may they undermine the structure of modern culture and society. But as I have collected and made them my captives, I have had to make allowances for their presence in my home. Each new tenant has required a new room. An addition to the inside of the house, though unnoticed from without. Five decades of weaving spells and incantations, glamours and enchantments, so that this house is perhaps the single most intricate magickal construct the world has ever known. The sorcerors of ancient Egypt would be hard-pressed to produce something of greater complexity.

As it must be. For the world must be forever

kept apart from the limbo realm, the Otherworld, where such things exist. Just as the group of those called Watchers, in London, see to it that Hell does not engulf the world, so too must the Gatekeeper be ever vigilant to be certain the chaos of the Otherworld does not overwhelm it.

But the Gatekeeper is dying.

My poor son, Henri, will be the next to take up the mantle of the Gatekeeper. I only wish I could give him a choice, but the responsibility is too great. Henri is well schooled now; I sent him to England to be educated, and he chose to make a home there. Only lately has he returned to me. I have begun to prepare him for what he must face. As he must, in time, prepare a wife.

For I have cursed my entire family, all of my descendants, from now until the apocalypse comes at long last.

Upon my death, all of my knowledge, and all of my power, shall pass on to Henri. And upon his death, to his child. And so on, to each heir to the title of Gatekeeper.

As I answer the call of sweet surrender that I have so long ignored, my only regret is that the evil seed planted by Fulcanelli did not die when the sorceror himself met his end. Word has come from Europe of terrible deeds done in Fulcanelli's name by a band of rogue magicians and assassins calling themselves the Sons of Entropy. They are, it has been said, the lineage that has come down from Fulcanelli's original acolytes. They have founded a sect of chaos bringers built upon the foundation of his horrifying philosophy.

*This too, I have explained to Henri.*
*I lay down my sword and shield for the last time. Now the battle must be joined by others.*

*Richard M. Regnier, Chevalier and Sorceror*
*Boston, Massachusetts Colony*

Giles closed the journal only a moment before he heard the whisper.

*"Jean-Marc will see you now."*

Startled in spite of himself, he spun around quickly at the sound, and the book tumbled to the ground. The spine tore slightly upon impact, and a rush of guilt swept over him. What he'd just read was not merely a family heirloom, or some ancient artifact, but an extremely valuable resource for all those who would one day become Gatekeeper. Quickly he bent, retrieved the book, and placed it gingerly on an oak table.

When he returned his gaze to the ghost, he found her smiling at him.

*"It has been a very long time since we have had guests. It is pleasant to have you and your young friends here, Mr. Giles,"* she said.

Giles thought that she seemed a bit more solid now, her legs had even coalesced so that she did not lose her cohesion until halfway between knee and ankle. He wondered if it was the power of the Gatekeeper reinvigorating his mother's ghost, or the presence of so many individuals who could see her and thus reaffirm her belief in her own existence.

A debate for another time, perhaps.

"Thank you, *Madame* Regnier," he said with a slightly embarrassed smile. Giles was not completely alien to the concept of flirtation, but it had never been something he was adept at. Flirtation with a spirit was another thing entirely. It was not merely uncomfortable, but chilling.

The ghost of Antoinette Regnier floated through the library door and into the hallway. The others were off elsewhere in the house. They were supposed to be getting settled into their rooms now that the place was stable once more. Giles doubted that very much, however. He suspected that they were attempting to reach Willow or Oz, to find out what was happening in Sunnydale in their absence. Cordelia's cellular phone did not seem to be working, and Giles had suggested they step out beyond the magickal field that keeps the house hidden from the outside world. After that, they would likely explore what they could of the house. He hoped they were careful of what doors they opened.

Leading him, the ghost glided up the great central staircase with an elegance that he could never hope to achieve. Giles followed, eyes straying to survey the incredible furnishings in the home—the woodwork and tapestries, the paintings and the windows—but his gaze would not stay away from Antoinette for long.

No matter how many ghosts he had encountered in his time as a Watcher, they never ceased to fascinate him.

*"I should think you will all find yourselves quite comfortable here,"* Antoinette whispered. Or more precisely, she spoke, and the ghostly voice floated to Giles as if it had been spoken very quietly just behind his ear. *"If there is anything you need, please call out for me. I don't sleep, of course."*

They paused in front of the heavy door to the Gatekeeper's own bedchamber. The ghost put a finger to her lips and shushed Giles, as if one librarian and a ghostly old woman were going to make much noise. Then she passed right through the door, leaving Giles standing just outside it, feeling more than a bit foolish.

Should he knock? Just walk in? He chose both. He knocked twice, lightly, and then turned the knob and stepped into the room. There were some of the most amazing artifacts he'd ever seen before in that very room. But what drew his eye, of course, was the figure of the Gatekeeper, stretched out on top of the mattress with a dying man's abandon. His face was ragged and exhausted, his arms so limp Giles assumed the man felt too weak to move any further.

"Thank you for coming, Mr. Giles," the Gatekeeper said, and coughed several times during the sentence. "As you can see, I am in no condition to greet you. I have prolonged my life with magick for too long. Soon, I will pass."

Giles glanced at the huge black cauldron at the far side of the room, and at the long wooden spear, or lance, with an ancient-looking, battered metal tip that lay on the bed with the Gatekeeper, clutched in his old-man hands.

"The Cauldron?" he asked, and nodded toward the huge iron pot.

"Indeed," Regnier agreed. "One immersion used to buy me twenty years. Now it can barely give me the hours I need to speak with you. Even then, I am only able to retain control over the sorcerous matrix of the house by the power I draw from the spear."

Giles blinked, then looked more closely at the

spear. An idea occurred to him, and his eyes widened. Without realizing he was doing it, he actually took two steps backward.

"That isn't . . ." he began, then shook his head as if denying it would force the truth away.

Weakly, the Gatekeeper smiled. "All right. It isn't. Does that make you more comfortable?"

The Watcher swallowed, then reached up to rub his eyes beneath his glasses, settling the frame more comfortably on the bridge of his nose. Whatever else he had seen in this house, whatever else he would see, these two artifacts dwarfed it all. According to myth, the Cauldron of Bran the Blessed would restore vigor to a dying man, or even restore life to the dead. The only story Giles had heard of it surfacing had come from Gundestrup in Denmark. The Gatekeeper must have retrieved it from there.

The spear was something else entirely. Once, almost two thousand years before, the spear had reportedly belonged to a Roman soldier named Longinus. It was said that while Jesus was dying on the cross, Longinus had pierced his side with the spear.

Its powers had been debated for millennia, but certain things were known as facts. Anyone who held it in his hands could not be defeated in battle, nor killed by an opponent, as long as the weapon remained in his grasp. The legendary Emperor Constantine had, according to history, won thirty-seven military campaigns in a row, and died only when he had the misfortune to accidentally drop the spear.

It could not win a war, but it could make its owner the most fearsome warrior to ever walk the Earth. And, apparently, it could also lend a little of that strength to the ailing.

"Mr. Giles?" the Gatekeeper asked.

"Hmm? Oh, yes. Sorry. This is all a bit . . . overwhelming."

"I understand. But time is of the essence now."

Giles nodded. "Indeed. Though as you do not seem to have any family about, no heir, if you'll forgive me, I'm not certain what can be done to preserve the integrity of the Gatehouse."

The old man on the bed nodded only slightly, just enough for Giles to know that he agreed. "So you have read my grandfather's journal."

"Indeed. And with what is transpiring in Sunnydale at the moment, and your own obvious concern, I can only surmise that the Sons of Entropy remain active," Giles said, then paused a moment. He frowned, tilted his head, and stared at the Gatekeeper.

"Did you say 'grandfather'?" he asked.

"The Regniers are quite long-lived," the Gatekeeper told him.

"Remarkably so," Giles agreed.

Without warning, the Gatekeeper allowed a small but agonized groan to escape his lips as he pulled himself up farther on the bed. His eyes were squeezed tightly closed and his teeth clamped together. When, finally, he looked up at Giles once more, he looked as though he had aged another five years, and the desperation was clear in his eyes.

"You must help me, Mr. Giles," Jean-Marc said. "You are incorrect, sir. I do have an heir. A boy, eleven years old. I had sent him to school in England, just as my father sent me one hundred forty years ago.

"They've taken him. My boy, Jacques, is in the hands of the Sons of Entropy. To get him back, all I have to do is give up this house to them, and all its secrets. That is something I can never do."

"Still no call from Willow?" Buffy asked Cordelia.

"Well," Cordelia said, somewhat defensively, "I'm not going to sit out in the street just to get away from the anti–cellular phone magick that the stupid invisible house thing causes."

"We left her a message last night," Xander noted. "She knows we're alive and trying to reach her. But it's still too early to call there, Buffy. Her mom's going to want to know why we're calling at five in the morning, y'know. Give it an hour or two."

Buffy frowned, concern etched on her features. "I'm just getting worried. I didn't want to leave Sunnydale in the first place, and if anything happened to Willow . . ."

"Willow's a big girl," Cordelia said dismissively. "She can handle herself. Just take a breath, Buffy. We'll all go out and call in a little while, or . . . I guess you can just use the phone if you want."

Cordelia sighed. She didn't really want to loan her cell phone out to anybody. You just never knew who was going to call Greece on your dime. On the other hand, it wasn't as if Buffy knew anyone from Greece—or anywhere else more interesting than Southern California.

She took a long drink of coffee and tried to forget the events of the previous night. Cordelia was still completely freaked, but at least Xander had had the good sense to go out and get some breakfast for them. Okay, bagels and cream cheese and juice boxes weren't exactly the breakfast of champions, but any port in a storm, Cordelia figured. It didn't look like they'd be having regular meals for a while.

Xander was his usual cheery, sarcastic self, and Buffy was very quiet this morning—other than her usual grumpiness. Cordelia sipped the last of her coffee—Xander had also saved his own scalp by managing to find a Starbucks nearby—and picked up Giles's steaming cup. She slid out of her chair and started down the hall. They needed the Watcher's brain in fully functioning order, and as far as Cordelia was concerned, nobody could function fully at eight o'clock in the morning without coffee.

As she moved up the steps to where Xander had told her the Gatekeeper's chamber was, she was startled by the sudden appearance of the ghost of Antoinette Regnier on the landing above her. The dead woman's spirit seemed to be staring at her. Cordelia shivered, but did not look away.

"Can I help you with something?" she asked snippily.

*"If the worst happens, the Gatehouse must not fall. Jean-Marc will need a new heir,"* Antoinette Regnier whispered.

Cordelia's eyebrows knitted together. Slowly she held up one hand. At length she rolled her eyes, and spoke each word as if it were a sentence unto itself. "Do. Not. Even. Go. There."

She pushed past the ghost. In the corridor just outside the Gatekeeper's room, she heard the old man talking to Giles. Babbling.

"They are coming," Regnier said desperately, his voice rising in pitch. "It is too late. They are coming now. The Sons of Entropy are . . . they are close now. Any moment they could . . ."

Throughout the Gatehouse echoed the sudden sound of chimes—what passed for a doorbell in the enormous mansion.

"No!" the Gatekeeper screamed. "You mustn't let them in!"

Cordelia was turning into the open doorway, a tiny chill of terror creeping over her, when Giles exploded past her. His coffee cup flew from her grasp and popped open as it hit the floor, spilling pungent brown liquid on the carpet.

Giles didn't even slow down as he ran for the stairs. Cordelia followed him, picking up her pace and then scrambling down after him as fast as she could.

"What's going on?" she cried. "Giles, what is it? Who's coming? Shouldn't we . . ."

"No!" Giles roared.

At the huge double front doors of the mansion, Buffy was throwing back the locks as Xander sipped at a glass of juice. Buffy pulled the handle, and the door began to open.

"Buffy, no!" Giles shouted. "Don't let them in!"

Too late. As Cordelia watched in horror, Buffy threw the door wide.

"Xander! Buffy! Get back!" Giles screamed.

On the threshold, Oz raised his eyebrows, his eyes darting to each of them in turn.

"Did I miss something?"

# Chapter 16

"The Gatekeeper is dying," Giles said once again. It was a truth they were all having a very difficult time accepting. For if it was indeed true, the consequences would be unthinkable.

"Despite the power in the artifacts he has gathered here, it is only a matter of time—and not a great deal of time, I'm afraid—before he passes on," the Watcher continued. "When that moment comes, there must be an heir here in the house."

Buffy glanced at Cordelia, whose eyes widened as she held up a hand. "Don't even think about it."

"Man," Oz said unhappily, "I feel like I wasted a trip here. I could be a lot more help to Willow back home. I . . . don't like the idea of her being there by herself."

"Angel's there," Buffy offered.

"Only at night," Oz said. "But after Willow's call to

Cordelia got cut off . . . and, well, we had no idea you'd get this information from another source."

"How did you find this house, anyway?" Xander asked. "Didja sniff it out?"

Oz shook his head with a weak smile. "Cordelia told Willow it was at the top of Beacon Hill, and you could only see it if you were looking for it. I walked around awhile, but once I saw this place . . . well, hell, what else could it be?"

Giles cleared his throat, drawing the attention of the room back to himself. "Oz," he said, "we are grateful to have you here. Your information is more helpful than you realize. It confirms a great deal. Though this Fulcanelli character I've told you about from the original Gatekeeper's journals founded the Sons of Entropy centuries ago, it appears that Il Maestro, whomever he may be, has carried on Fulcanelli's crusade.

"If what you were told is true, the Sons of Entropy would use the Gatehouse to drop the barrier between our world and the Otherworld. Should that happen, all the myths and monsters and unnatural phenomena there would collide with our own world, sending humanity into a new Dark Age, overrun with supernatural chaos. It would undo a millennium of human progress."

"Okay, screeching halt, Giles," Xander said, frowning. "Why would anyone want that? I mean, okay, no more lines at the Burger King drive-through, but y'know, no more drive-through. It just doesn't make sense."

"Actually, Xander, I got the impression these guys think that when all this crap comes down, they're going to be kings or something."

"Like the warlords of old, or the feudal lords of old Europe," Giles said, nodding. "Il Maestro has obviously made some significant promises to them in that regard. What I wonder, however, is what relation this has to their attempts to capture Buffy, and possibly even myself."

"If they wanted you, it might have been to use you to get Buffy to do what they wanted," Cordelia suggested. "That's been an ongoing theme a couple of times, right?"

"Ever the mistress of unpleasant reminders, Cordelia," Buffy said. "Okay, let's say that's why they wanted Giles. And they've been killing off Watchers just to make sure they had as little opposition as possible, maybe keep the Council busy while they came after me and did their deal with the Gatehouse. Giles is right. If keeping the heir from the house is all they need to take it over, why do they want me?"

"You mean, other than the obvious?" Xander asked, a lascivious grin on his face.

Cordelia punched his arm.

"Why indeed," Giles echoed.

"Y'know," Oz said, "when Angel was making this one guy . . . talk, he said his boss would get a lot of power from Buffy. But I definitely got the idea that maybe there was more to it than he was saying. But not because he wasn't going to talk.

"He would have said anything right then," Oz added, and when they all looked at him with wide eyes, he went on quickly.

"Anyway, I think this Il Maestro guy has a lot of stuff going on that he doesn't share with his foot soldiers, y'know?"

"It may be," Giles agreed, "that the Sons of Entropy are operating on several levels, several arms of a master plan we have yet to perceive. Jean-Marc has also sensed their presence close at hand. They might very well be just beyond these walls."

With almost comic timing, Xander and Oz both glanced around at the interior of the Gatehouse's enormous dining room. They sat around a table that would have made King Arthur envious, but there were only the five of them. Six, if you counted the ghost of Antoinette Regnier, who appeared and disappeared at irregular intervals. She was keeping a close watch over her son, hoping to prolong the time before he would join her at last.

"How long can the Gatekeeper survive like this?" Buffy asked, and her eyes narrowed as she searched Giles's face.

Giles reached up his right hand to push up his glasses and massage the bridge of his nose. They were all very short on sleep now, and it didn't seem as though they were going to be getting any time to catch up. Not soon, anyway.

"It's impossible to say," the Watcher finally admitted. "Several days, I think. At least. Perhaps weeks, though I doubt that a great deal. Remember that the Gatekeeper's magick is all that is holding the complex mystical web of this house together. That places an extraordinary strain on him. If the Sons of Entropy are indeed nearby, there is no telling how stressful their next . . . visit may be."

"Correct me if I'm wrong," Xander offered, "but if all the house needs to have to keep itself going is an heir, couldn't we just pick somebody else? I mean, that's how the Watchers do it, right? One Slayer dies, and another is called, all that jazz?"

*"In the case of the Gatekeeper, the heir must be of the Regnier bloodline,"* the ghost whispered. *"There are no other Regniers. Jean-Marc's son, Jacques, is the last."*

"What if the kid's already dead?" Cordelia asked matter-of-factly.

Giles covered his eyes with one hand. Xander scowled, and Buffy shook her head.

"Cordy, we can always count on you for the sympathy factor," Xander noted, his discomfort obvious in his tone.

*"If my grandson were here, do you think I wouldn't know?"* the ghost whispered.

Oz shifted in his seat and raised his eyebrows. He wasn't the most talkative guy in the world, but he usually didn't speak unless he had something to say.

"Okay, call me crazy, but why don't we just go to Europe and find the kid," he said with a shrug. "I mean, it isn't like we have many other choices."

"You ever been to Europe?" Xander asked incredulously. "You want to find one eleven-year-old kid on the whole continent?"

"Have *you* ever been to Europe?" Cordelia asked him with a look of astonishment.

"We're not talking about me!" Xander protested.

Oz shrugged again. "It was just an idea. If the Sons of Entropy are trying to kill Buffy, they're going to keep coming after her. We track them down, and we get the information we need. Whatever it takes. We keep searching until we have the kid or the world ends."

Giles harumphed. "Despite his rather blunt explanation of our predicament, Oz does appear to have hit upon our only course of action."

There was a moment of silence in the room, and Buffy thought she could hear the ghost of Antoinette Regnier whining just slightly, as though someone had left a window open in her soul. Or perhaps she was just moaning with her grief and anxiety. Poetry wasn't part of the Slayer's job. Damn good thing, too.

"I'll go," she said. "Alone."

Giles began to protest, and Buffy saw the look of knowing, self-righteous anger that began to spread across Xander's face.

"Okay, someone has to stay behind on Hellmouth duty, and that would be Giles," she said quickly, then looked sternly at Xander. "You and Cordelia and Willow are not going to be able to go off on a jaunt to Europe without getting into all kinds of I-can't-answer-thats with your parents. I don't have that problem."

Then she looked at Oz. "We don't know how long this will take, and, frankly, you're a werewolf. Sure, we've got a few weeks to go, but again, who knows how long this will take."

"And Angel . . ."

Nodding, Giles interrupted. "Angel can't take the risk of flying. Too difficult for him to keep ahead of the sun."

It was Xander who spoke up first. "You can't go alone, Buffy." He pushed back the heavy oak chair, stood up, and walked over to the ceiling-high windows with the enormous drapes that hung down to the floor. He stared out the window.

"It comes down to this." He paused, then turned to look at all of them. Not for the first time, Buffy saw in his face, in his resolve and the proud jut of his chin, the man that Xander would become.

"Whatever my parents think doesn't really matter. If we don't get that kid back, their whole world is going to be turned upside down. Yeah, maybe they live on the Hellmouth, but like everyone else in Sunnydale, they somehow manage to get by without having to acknowledge how crazy that is. But if this Otherworld explodes into ours and we're overrun with monsters and legends and weird events, that's a little worse than having their son run off to Europe for a few weeks."

"Xander, you might not be able to graduate on time," Buffy warned.

Cordelia snickered. "Oh, please. Graduation? If we can't get the rugrat back here in time, there won't be any more school."

Buffy looked at her and blinked. She was always amazed by Cordelia's courage, existing as it did in spite of her amazing selfishness. Her courage was more of an afterthought.

"So back to the airport?" Oz asked.

It was the ghost who responded. She floated to the center of the room, nothing but mist from the waist down. From the center of the dining room table, Antoinette Regnier spoke imperiously, and for the first time, above a whisper.

*"There is a faster way,"* she declared. *"A mode of travel not open to all, but available to the Slayer."*

Then the ghost set her sights on Oz. *"And to the lycanthrope.*

*"Only beings touched by the supernatural in some way may travel the ghost roads and live."*

"Ghost roads?" Buffy asked. Though she wasn't entirely certain she wanted an explanation.

At the high window, Xander cleared his throat. He

stood with his hand parting the heavy drapes, staring out at the tall metal fence around the Gatehouse.

"Excuse me, ghost lady," he said. "Do you have a big Jehovah's Witness population around here? Lot of people trying to get you to join their religion?"

In an instant, Buffy was at the window beside him. She put a hand on Xander's shoulder, though whether to steady him or herself she was unsure. Outside the window, dozens of Sons of Entropy acolytes had already scaled the fence and begun working their way across the lawn.

"I don't think we're going anywhere," Buffy said quietly.

The shift in weather was sudden and extreme. Though the day had dawned with a clear blue sky and a tantalizingly warm pre-spring breeze—for Boston, anyway—atop Beacon Hill clouds began to form almost out of nowhere. Dark and pregnant with moisture, the clouds blotted out the sun within seconds of the moment Brother Julian led a dozen other acolytes onto the grounds of the Gatehouse.

"It knows we're here," he called.

"What do you mean 'it'?" asked Brother Cardiff, who stood a few feet behind him, just inside the fence. "You mean 'he' knows, the Gatekeeper knows."

Brother Julian ignored him. The Englishman was an idiot. The Gatekeeper and his progenitors had spun the web, but the house itself was the real power. It had taken the Sons of Entropy decades to learn what little they had about the house itself. Il Maestro had planned for nearly as long for this moment. The Gatekeeper had been dying, his strength sapped away with each passing hour.

Without the boy, the Gatehouse would be theirs. The boy might still get the magick of his forebears—a possibility Il Maestro was greatly anticipating—but the house would fall beneath their onslaught, and chaos would follow soon after.

That *had* been the plan.

The Slayer and the Watcher coming to the Gatekeeper's aid? That possibility had not even been planned for. Now, rather than attacking while the Gatekeeper was at his weakest, and the house's defenses were almost nonexistent, they had been ordered to move in immediately.

As the last of the acolytes led by Brother Julian cleared the fence—the monstrous house across the yard looking down upon them with furious window-eyes—the clouds moved in and sharp-edged hail the size of fruit began to pummel them from the sky.

"Attack, now!" Brother Julian cried.

Brother Cardiff launched himself forward, even as the ground rumbled and split. Brother Julian leaped over the rift that opened like a sinkhole in the earth before him, and Brother Cardiff helped him to his feet. The others followed suit, save for Brother Stefano, who fell into a sudden sinkhole which closed up again after him. The man's screams were cut off the instant the earth rolled over his head.

Brother Cardiff ran for the front steps of the house, only proving to Julian what an idiot the man was. Magickal fire crackled as Cardiff slammed into a sorcerous barrier that was part of the house's defense system. The man screamed, his hands went to his face, and he pulled away strands of melted flesh before crumbling to his knees in shock.

Hail crashed into Julian's shoulders and scalp,

cutting him where it struck. He ignored the pain. Lightning roared down from the sky and burned Brother Luciano where he stood, turning him to little more than bone and cinders in a way naturally occurring lightning never could have. They were dying.

"Enough!" Julian screamed.

Il Maestro had chosen him for this duty for a reason. Now it was time for him to prove his worth, to prove that Il Maestro had made the right decision. This very day, the blood of the Gatekeeper would run over his fingers and he would paint his face with the gore.

Now, though, Julian's hands erupted with a deep purple flame and he held them in front of him. The barrier that had melted the flesh from Brother Cardiff's face and chest was illuminated a moment. Julian chanted loudly in Latin and the purple flames seemed to solidify, almost as a weapon in his grasp. With the total focus of his mind, Julian held the crackling magick above his head as though it were a sword, and he brought it down, screaming with rage and the pain such concentration cost him. With a scream of wood and the shattering of glass, the house cried out in agony, and the barrier exploded in a shower of magickal energy that wildly altered everything around it. Brother François turned to stone.

A palm tree, flush with coconuts and drooping fronds, grew up to Julian's left in mere seconds.

Julian shielded himself, and channeled most of that energy down into the ground, and the earth shook. The magickal field that surrounded the property and kept the Gatehouse invisible to the world around flickered, but remained intact. It was not a defensive barrier, but a mere enchantment, a glamour of convenience. That would be the last thing to fall, or near enough to it.

Without moving any closer, Julian struck again at the breach he had made in the defensive barrier, this time turning the Gatehouse's own magick against it. The crackling blade of magickal energy he wielded slashed down into the earth. Dirt leaped from the ground in a straight line toward the double front doors of the Gatehouse. The stairs split in two.

The doors to the Gatehouse splintered and exploded inward.

The Sons of Entropy screamed in triumph.

Brother Malachy ran for the door. He had bragged that he would be the one to take the Gatekeeper's head, and he brandished a shining dagger in his right hand as he mounted the splintered steps. So arrogant was he that when the Slayer stepped through the shattered doorway with a long, thick shaft of wood that looked to have been the leg of a good-sized dining room table, he lifted one hand and tried to shove her out of his way.

The Slayer shattered Brother Malachy's arm with a single swing. The next one cracked his skull and left him drooling, hanging over the railing of the shattered stairs. Behind the Slayer, a dark-haired young man Brother Julian recognized from surveillance photos stepped out of the house, a second table leg clutched in his hands.

"No trespassing," the Slayer snarled, and set her legs wide apart to guard the entrance.

"Yeah," said the young man. "Beware of Buffy."

* * *

"Some of the Sons of Entropy are skilled with magick," Giles said. "The Gatekeeper will not be able to fend them off completely, not without help. Even we few may not be enough. We are out of our depth. Buffy will give them quite a battle, but she needs someone backing her up who is as hard to kill as she is. Plus, if the Gatekeeper can manage to perform this Ritual of Endowment he suggested, Angel's presence will be invaluable. After his fashion, he loves her. There is magickal power in that."

Oz nodded slowly. "I'll go," he agreed. "I'm not much good against spells and enchantments anyway. But how will I find my way?" Oz looked at Giles expectantly.

The Watcher could not blame him for being afraid, or for looking to him for answers. Giles usually had the answers, after all, or the ability to find them somehow. But not this time. On this day, the only answers they had came from a dead woman, and somehow, that was less than comforting.

*"How did Springheel Jack find his way?"* whispered the ghost of Antoinette Regnier. *"You focus on your heart's desire, on the destination you must reach, and you will find your way."*

"Okay," Oz replied. "But . . . how?"

*"The dead will guide you, if you get lost."*

Giles cleared his throat. "No offense intended, madam, but according to all the literature, the dead can be rather untrustworthy."

*"For a human, yes,"* the ghost replied. *"But the boy is not human, is he, Watcher? They will bear him no ill will, for he is cursed. In many ways, he suffers far more than those of us who may rest if we choose. There is no*

*rest for those bearing the mark of the wolf, bearing the stain of the supernatural.*"

"No rest for the wicked," Oz said, mostly to himself. "It's a party."

Then he clapped his hands together, stood up with a smile on his face that astonished Giles—though Oz continually astonished him—and said with great verve, "Let's get this show on the road."

*"My son is in pain. I shall return,"* the ghost said, and then simply evaporated.

"Boy, how'd you like to have her for a mom?" Oz muttered. "Talk about pressure. She makes Willow's mom look mellow."

"Yes, well, Willow's mother is alive, and unaware of the consequences that hang in the balance," Giles said, though he realized now was not the time for such a discussion.

"Oh, I'm pretty sure her priorities wouldn't change if she knew about the Hellmouth," Oz said, bouncing on the balls of his feet ever so slightly. "Well, unless it was an extracurricular activity that could help Willow get into a better school."

Giles pushed his glasses up on the bridge of his nose, and blinked several times. He realized that Oz was nervous, and sympathized. But they had no time for sensitivity or caution. They needed reinforcements.

"Oz?" Giles asked.

Oz nodded. "Right. I go, grab up Angel, tell Willow to hold the fort, and get back here like Ricochet Rabbit."

"I'm sorry?" Giles frowned.

"Never mind. American cartoon reference." Oz moved to the door that Antoinette's ghost had pointed out to them, and then he paused and turned to Giles. "What about Willow, Giles? I mean, is she really going to be all right back home alone?"

Giles considered lying. After a moment, he said, "I don't know, Oz. But if we fail here, none of us will be all right."

Oz's eyes hardened at that. Giles watched it happen. All the light, all the humor, went out of his eyes, and for a moment Giles thought he could see a glint of the wolf deep down inside.

With a twist of the knob and a hard pull, Oz yanked the door open and stepped inside. Giles stepped around the heavy wooden door, but by the time he looked inside, it was only a small bedroom.

Oz was gone.

Oz was insane.

Or, at least, in those first few moments, he'd thought he was. There was a vacuum around him, a pure nothing that brought tears to his eyes in an instant. He wept openly, panic making his mind reel as he wished for something to grab hold of, anything to give him a sense of place, of movement, of time . . . of just being.

*If this is heaven* . . . he thought, but he never finished the idea. There was no telling who might be listening.

No temperature, neither cold nor hot. No sound, not even his own breathing. And at first, when he tried to scream, nothing. No sensation, neither of falling nor of moving, nor of hard surface beneath his feet. The air around him was neither dark nor light, not white or black, but a kind of eternal gray, as if rain were on the way but the storm would never arrive.

Oz closed his eyes tightly and screamed into the abyss, tears streaming down his cheeks.

He knew this was it. This was part of the limbo that Giles had talked about, the gray world connecting Earth to Heaven, Hell, and the Otherworld. This was the ghost road. Or, at least, it was supposed to be.

The ghost road.

And as suddenly as he'd had the thought, he felt it beneath his feet.

He heard his labored breathing.

He opened his eyes.

The ghost road stretched out before him, conjured from somewhere within him or somewhere nearby, he didn't know. But it was solid, and that was all that really mattered to him. The gray air was thick and he could not see very far, though there were no obstructions to his vision. The road beneath his feet was hard and rutted like a dirt path, yet it looked more like chalk or crumbling concrete.

Now, from somewhere, he heard music. Distant music, with a static crackle that reminded him of a poorly tuned radio. Impossible, of course, yet there it was.

He could see nothing but the road, and the gray absence of life around him. No wandering souls, no rotting corpses. Oz had been uncertain what to expect from these ghost roads, but he had steeled himself for the worst. Or what he'd thought was the worst. In reality, those first moments of nothing had terrified him more than anything he'd come up against since he'd become involved with Willow and, by extension, with Buffy.

It was something the Slayer could not fight. Could not destroy.

Oz felt certain that what he had felt, in those drifting moments, was nothing less than death itself. Perhaps it had taken a moment for death to reassert itself, to realize it had no hold over him. It didn't matter. Whatever happened to him now in this cold, hideous limbo, as long as he knew that he was alive, he would be all right.

Oz began to walk.

Inside Giles's apartment, Willow pored over books she hadn't dared to open at the library, hoping to find stronger enchantments and bindings to place over the Hellmouth, and over Sunnydale as a whole. She had tried desperately to use magick to locate the actual breaches, but it was something she had not been able to master. Perhaps the Gatekeeper had been more naturally adept, had some kind of sixth sense. So a more general sort of protection would have to do, from Willow's point of view.

Still, though Angel had spent the previous night doing little more than fighting and killing things that shouldn't be walking the earth, he agreed with Willow that the wards seemed to be having an effect. Very few new creatures were appearing.

Giles's ancient radio was tuned to an old-time jazz station, and Willow didn't dare move the dial. It was so distant, she was afraid that she might never be able to find it again, and Giles would be crushed. Instead, she had found that the music delighted her. Rather than impeding her ability to focus, it calmed her considerably and allowed her mind to rely on intuition she might never otherwise have paid any attention to.

She wouldn't be giving away her CD collection just yet, but this ancient jazz music had promise.

Oz felt as though he had been walking for eons. Though he was not sleepy, and his legs were not tired, his mind was exhausted. *So tempting, the urge to simply lie down and close his eyes. The ground was hard, but if he strayed from the road to that gray nothing, perhaps he might find a comfortable place to rest.*

*What?* Oz shook his head. That was not the voice of his heart, the inner mind speaking to him. Those thoughts had come from elsewhere. Outside his mind. Outside of him.

*Leave him be, the lost one.*

"Who's there?" he shouted, head whipping about as he searched the void for life. Just the dread nothing around him, lulling him into surrender. Gray and endless.

Lost. The voice had said he was lost.

"Please!" he cried. "I can't be lost. Maybe you don't care what happens in the . . . other world now. Maybe it doesn't matter to you. But I think that if my friends fail, your world may be destroyed as well. Whatever it is you have here, it's ordered. It's all arranged by . . . by someone.

"If I don't make it, all that order could be destroyed. There'd be nothing left but . . ."

All around him, the gray dissolved into white, blinding light. The road beneath his feet shifted like the sand, and that too was white and burning. Oz shielded his eyes, blinked several times, but already the light was beginning to fade. He blinked, a rainbow on his retinas the first real color he'd seen since he had come to the ghost road . . . when? Hours ago. At least. Maybe days.

*"Don't say it!"* The voices were one voice, yet millions. The echo was inside his mind, slipping from cell to cell in his brain. Informing him on the most primitive level.

His eyes began to focus. Oz looked around, and he saw them. There in the afterburn, in the flash, as it faded. As it faded. So did they. Faces and bodies, whispering and wandering, some staring at him and some hiding their eyes. Some of them crying and some laughing. At first he thought there were but a few, but as those closer faded, he saw the others behind them. Behind them. And behind them. And behind them.

"It'll be chaos," he whispered.

Then he clapped his hands to his ears as the ghosts began to hiss angrily. It lasted only moments, though it seemed eternal. Oz found himself hissing as well, though he didn't even know if what came from his lungs was air, or if he'd somehow been . . . translated, into this world. More than ever, at this thought, he knew he had to stay on the path.

The blaze of light was still fading, his vision still not completely clear, when he looked up again, into the spectral faces of the multitude of dead souls.

He had their attention now.

Somewhere, a great distance from the path that he was on, and seemingly walking a trail of her own, he saw a familiar figure turn to regard him. Even so far away, he recognized her. Her skin and hair, so dark in life, now fading along with the rest of the world around him. Fading into whispers and shushing and wide eyes, curious and sad.

Impossible at such a distance, but when her lips

moved, mouthing words, he could see them very clearly. Could see the smile that played across her features and the light in her eyes. But when the words reached him, it was the whisper of the multitude, like a wave crashing upon the shore.

*I am free from my curse.* Her lips moved. The multitude gave her voice. *His curse is until the end of forever. Even though it would free him, he keeps chaos from coming. Light his way.*

Oz whispered her name, the Slayer who had lived because Buffy had died, and who had died that Buffy might live. "Kendra."

The dead were gone. The gray had consumed the light, and the road was solid beneath his feet once more.

In the distance, the music played, reminding him only then that it had been inaudible while the light shone. Far along the path ahead of him, it grew dark, and Oz thought he could see sunlight, and a tiny swatch of green.

He started to run.

Moments later, he saw a hole in the world ahead. Three-dimensional life stretched out in front of him. Through the gap he could see the sky and the sun, the grass and trees, and he thought . . . no, he *knew*, that he had made it. It was Sunnydale.

Though he'd slowed his pace, Oz smiled broadly as he strode toward the gap. Whispers trailed behind him, and he thought he heard the word *chaos* but he didn't turn. The dead would aid him now, he was certain of it. At the opening, little more than an archway that would drop him to the ground several feet below, he paused.

Something was wrong.

Oz leaned to the left. He could see the front of the high school where he was now spending his fifth year. Cars in the lot. School was still in session. Maybe the same day, even, despite the time that had passed for him.

But something was wrong.

He moved forward, and his nose rammed painfully against an invisible barrier. Blood spurted from one nostril and he cried out, then felt his face to see that it wasn't broken.

Dumbfounded, Oz felt the barrier ahead of him for weaknesses, but it was solid. He could see his goal, but he could not reach it. He didn't understand.

Then, in a single moment, he did.

And he whispered, "Willow."

Though Giles had done little to restock his kitchen after his return from New York, Willow had managed to find a single Earl Grey tea bag in the back of the cupboard. Tea was easy. Hot water. A little milk. Bag of herbs. She'd come to realize that, once you understood it, most magick wasn't all that much more difficult.

But there were consequences.

Willow was trying to stay away from the consequences.

*Wards and Talismans of the Ancients* lay open on the small desk on the other side of the room from Giles's tiny kitchenette. She hadn't dared explore the loft upstairs where Giles slept. Not only was it his bedroom area, but it was also where Angel had left Jenny Calendar's corpse after he'd . . . Willow shivered.

It wasn't something she wanted to think about.

Here in Giles's apartment, though, it was hard not to think about it. On the desk only inches from the book she was reading was a sphere of glass called an Orb of Thessula. It was that very sphere that she had finally been able to use to give Angel his soul back. To curse him again.

Sometimes Willow thought that it might have been a lot simpler if Buffy had just killed him. But when she had that thought, Willow forced herself to wonder how she would feel if Buffy had let the hunter, Gib Cain, kill Oz just for being a werewolf. When the animal came out of Oz, he wasn't any less savage than a vampire. That was why he locked himself up.

No, Willow needed Oz. And no matter what all the horrible things of the past year had done to their relationship, their friendship or whatever, Buffy needed Angel. Even just to be there for her. So she knew that even at the heart of darkness, it was possible to create light.

Willow let out a breath.

"Getting a little metaphysical, aren't we, Rosenberg?" she muttered aloud.

So the first time, she didn't hear her name.

The jazz music played on the crackling radio behind her, and Willow sipped her hot tea as she settled back down at the desk.

*"Willow."*

"Oh, God!" Willow snapped, spilled hot tea on her lap, and squeaked out an odd combination of pain and fear. Her eyes went wide as she stared around the room.

There was nothing there. Not unless it was lurking in the shadows.

"Angel?" she asked, as hopefully as she could ever ask to have him near.

*"Willow."*

She bit her lip. Her eyes began to fill with moisture as she whispered, "Oz?"

*"Whatever you're doing, it's keeping me out. You've got to let your guard down, just for a second. I can't come through until you do."*

"Oh, my God," she said, heart racing. "Are you . . . are you dead?"

*"No more than Springheel Jack. I'm traveling the same way he did. You've got to let me in."*

Mind racing, Willow reached to a pile of books and knocked several to the floor as she pulled out the one she thought she would need. The clock chimed in the hall, and for the first time she realized how warm it had gotten inside. Giles didn't have much by way of circulation from the few windows in the apartment, but she had persevered until now.

Willow paused a moment, her finger at the top of the page she would need to drop the wards, even for a moment.

*"What is it? You've got to get Angel. We need him right away. He's got to come back with me. Willow, what's wrong? Let me in!"*

She swallowed. Bit her lip again, and this time she wondered idly if she would draw blood.

"How do I know you're you?" she asked at last.

*"We don't have time, Willow. Everything hangs on this. They need me back there, but more importantly, they need Angel. Not just for his strength, but for some kind of ritual. We just don't have—"*

"Oz, if you're you, you know that doesn't matter,"

Willow said curtly, her heart breaking. "I can't drop the wards. Even if you are you, things will get in. They will. If I know it's you, I'll do what you say, but I have to *know*."

Willow sat and stared at the radio, feeling foolish as she realized she had been talking to the old Motorola with its bent antenna. It crackled again, static returning, and a voice she recognized as belonging to Louis Armstrong was singing something about the home fire, whatever that was.

Oz was gone.

For a horrible eternity that lasted only seconds, Willow wondered if it really had been Oz, and if she hadn't moved quickly enough. If they had lost, and it was all for nothing. Chaos would reign.

Willow began to cry.

From the radio, a blast of static. Then, four little words.

*"All monkeys are French."*

"Oz!" Willow cried, her smile filled with love and relief and still, some fear. He was still there, and it was Oz, indeed.

But what now?

Quickly, she began weaving the spell. The wards would be dropped for only a few seconds.

But there was no way to know what would come in through the breaches in that time.

No way.

Oz tumbled out onto the lawn in front of Sunnydale High. In a heartbeat, he was on his feet. Amazement swept over him as he realized he had done it, he had traveled more than three thousand miles in the space of an hour. Possibly less. Despite that, and despite the exhaustion he had felt while on the ghost road, Oz began to run.

He headed for Angel's house, wondering all the while how he was going to get Angel back to the Gatehouse without him getting burned.

Then he remembered. That was where he'd left his van.

Angel pulled on a clean black T-shirt. He took a long leather duster that Oz hadn't seen before and pulled it over his head as though trying to stay dry in a rainstorm.

"Let's go," said the vampire.

"Just like that?" Oz asked, slightly incredulous. "I mean, cool, but . . . it's pretty sunny out there."

Angel paused a moment at the door, glanced back at Oz. "You said Buffy needs me, right?"

"It's a little more complicated than . . ."

"It doesn't need to be," Angel interrupted.

He threw the door wide, grasped the edges of the coat closed in front of his face, his hands safely tucked inside the leather. With his head bowed, he stumbled toward the open rear doors of Oz's van and tumbled inside. Oz pulled the mansion's doors shut behind them, then slammed the van's back doors. He'd covered the windows as best he could, but Angel stayed covered as much as possible.

While Oz drove, from time to time he could hear Angel growling low and dangerous. By the time they reached their destination, he realized that the sounds weren't growls, but groans. Angel was in pain. At the school, Willow stood in the parking lot. Oz had called her at Giles's place from Angel's, and now here she was. If she was seen, her parents would find out eventually that she'd skipped school. It didn't matter. In the shadows of looming chaos, nothing mattered.

"Go to Buffy's house," Oz told her. "They might need you, and she'll be able to cover for you. Just for a few hours, though. If you haven't heard from us by then . . . it'll be over."

Willow nodded grimly, and spoke the words of the spell softly. Suddenly Oz could see the breach. It would stay visible just long enough for them to enter.

Angel moved quickly into the breach. Whatever might wait on the other side, he'd survived worse.

Oz stepped to Willow, took her hand in both of his, and kissed her, first on the lips, then on the forehead. Their eyes met.

"Come home," Willow whispered.

"Wherever *you* are, that's home," Oz replied.

Then he was gone.

"You mean you can't see them?" Angel asked, glancing around furtively, eyes never stopping on one face very long.

"I see them. But it's hard to focus on just one," Oz replied. "Unless they want you to see them, I guess. When they come close, when they're trying to communicate, then they're much more solid."

Angel could see the multitude, the endless parade of spirits who wandered the Otherworld, finding their way, in time, along the ghost roads to whatever came after. Heaven. Hell. Nothing at all, for some, perhaps.

He could see them all, all the dead. Just as they could see him, oh, so clearly. Oz could see them too, but perhaps not as clearly. They noticed him, but they let him pass unmolested. Angel, however, was something new to them. They reached out for him, their fingers passing through his flesh and making him shiver with a cold he had not felt since his blood was still warm.

They thought he was one of them, of course.

He was dead, after all.

"Get back!" he shouted, angrily. "Back!"

Then one of the spirits that had touched him flinched, stared at him in horror, and whispered to one of the others. Its voice echoed, as if they had all spoken.

*"Cursed."*

Angel almost smiled. *They don't know the half of it . . .*

Then the smile disappeared as a face ahead came into focus. The white mist all around the blanched surface of the ghost road had risen up around them.

*"Angel."*

The dead spoke his name, but it was only one of them whose lips moved. Her name was Theresa Klusmeyer. She'd died at his hands, his fangs at her throat as he made her a vampire. She was here because of him, still trying to find her way on the ghost road, trying to find her way to Heaven, or into Hell, if that was her destination.

"I'm . . . I'm sorry," Angel said gently, tentatively.

Oz stopped walking, reached back, and grabbed Angel's shoulder. "Just walk, man," he said. "Just walk."

Angel walked, and soon he came to realize that word had spread along the ghost roads. Others he had killed in his recent return to soulless savagery lined their path. Some part of him knew, then, what was to come. She would be there. Of course she would be there.

And she was.

Her dark hair so lustrous, the others seemed insubstantial. Her eyes round and gentle, and worse, understanding. Jenny didn't say a word as they passed, and when Angel tried to pause, Oz got behind him and pushed.

"We're almost there!" Oz shouted. "Just go, Angel, please! Buffy needs you!"

Angel took one last look at Jenny, then turned to face forward. There was a light ahead, and he walked toward it. After three more steps, he closed his eyes and simply let Oz guide him.

Ice-cold tears of blood ran down his cheeks, but Angel did not wipe them from his skin. They were damned little penance for the grief and terror he had wrought with his own hands.

"Almost there," Oz vowed.

"They're in!" Buffy screamed. "Giles, get back!"

Cordelia screamed as the Sons of Entropy crashed through the windows at the front of the house. The one in the lead, whose white hair and full beard gave him an almost saintly look, in spite of the bruise-purple magick that swirled in his hands, simply walked right through the front door.

"Up the stairs!" Xander snapped. "Get to the Gate-keeper!"

He shoved Cordelia, and she whimpered as she ran up the huge staircase toward the second floor. At the top of the stairs, the ghost of Antoinette Regnier waved her on, beckoning her to come nearer to the Gatekeeper, where he might protect them a bit better.

Xander, Giles, and Buffy were right behind her. She could hear their feet pounding the stairs. Could hear

Giles cursing and Buffy shouting taunts and jibes at their attackers.

"Giles!" Buffy screamed.

Cordelia turned.

Giles hung over the edge of the second story landing, holding onto Buffy's left hand. The Slayer herself dangled twenty feet above the marble floor in the foyer of the first floor. Below, the white-haired sorceror's hands glowed as he formed the magickal weapon he had used before. The others screamed at Buffy, one threw a piece of the shattered door at her.

The stairs had disappeared. The house had simply erased them. Or the Gatekeeper had.

"Xander!" Giles bellowed. "Give me a hand, here!"

With a curse, Xander moved. But he was too late.

As Giles cried her name, Buffy tumbled toward the broken marble floor, where the Sons of Entropy waited to destroy her.

# Chapter 17

*So, this is how I die,* Buffy thought fuzzily as the hard marble floor rushed up to shatter every bone in her body. Robed men rushed toward the spot where she was going to land, arms outstretched as if they were going to rip her to pieces.

*And it's gonna hurt . . .*

Then, in a blur, a figure, not robed, barreled through the crowd of men and ran deliberately beneath her falling body. She could make out a smear of color on its shirt—dark brown, green, red—and then she slammed against its back with a bone-jarring crack. The figure went down and she rolled to the right, smacking against the floor. Stunned and bruised, she crumpled in a heap.

The Sons of Entropy rushed for her. With a grunt, she rallied almost immediately, rolling onto her back and then flipping to a standing position. The person who had blocked her fall lay motionless on the ground. She glanced quickly at him.

"Oz," she whispered, horrified.

She grabbed his wrist to drag him out of the range of the fighting.

A voice shouted, "Buffy! They're coming for you!"

She glanced up and saw Angel, in full vamp face, as he knocked one of the Sons of Entropy out of his way. His face was smeared with blood.

She was alarmed, but she had no time to worry about him. Acolytes rushed her from both sides. She spun into a high kick, connected with the jaw of a thickly muscled man with a crew cut, and he went down hard, unconscious. Then she was being rushed from behind, and she brought her fist up, stepping back, ready to break his nose . . . and he was too fast for her. From behind, the acolyte grabbed Buffy's wrist and began to reach for her hair.

Buffy ducked, turned under her own arm, and grabbed his restraining hand with her own free one. She pulled, dropped, and flipped him over her. His head struck a marble column, and he, too, was out of the fight.

But there were too many of them.

"Don't kill her!" shouted a white-haired man in a robe from across the room. "Il Maestro wants her!"

"I hate being so popular," Buffy grunted, as she rammed her heel into the face of a surprisingly short man.

"Buffy, get the old guy!" Xander shouted down to her. "He's the leader."

Buffy parried the blows of another assailant and sent him unconscious to the floor as she sized up the white-haired man. The hood of his robe was thrown back, and he smiled grimly at her as he pulled up his sleeves.

"Surrender, Slayer," he urged. "I'll let your friends live."

"Promises, promises," she retorted, dodging yet another attacker. "For some strange reason, I'm having a little trouble trusting you. Possibly because nobody in your little group has shown much interest in letting my friends live before."

He shrugged. "Then have it your way."

He lifted his hands. A sphere of magickal blue began to form between his palms. His voice rose in a singsong chant.

The burning sphere flew from between his hands. Buffy flinched.

It hurtled upward.

Overhead, Cordelia let out a wild shriek.

The white-haired man glanced up. Buffy took advantage of the momentary distraction to charge him. He jumped backward and gestured with his hands.

Just as she was about to grab him, she slammed into an invisible barrier. A violent shock ran from her skull through her spinal cord and down to her toes. It hurt. A lot.

She was jarred, and might have collapsed, except for the smug smirk on the white-haired man's face. Anger boiled inside her, and she gathered up her strength to try to get at him again.

There was an explosion above and behind her. Her instinct for survival screamed at her not to look away from the white-haired sorcerer, but she couldn't stop herself: Giles, Cordelia, and Xander were up there.

The Gatekeeper, propped up by Giles, stood on a

re-created landing, hovering in midair. Green energy crackled from his hands as remnants of the blue fireball sputtered and sparked like a burned-out Roman candle. Then he pointed at the invisible barrier and closed his eyes.

"Try now, Slayer," he said in a shaking voice.

Buffy ran toward the barrier.

It held fast, sending jolts of energy through her body. This time she fell to her knees as two of the Sons of Entropy grabbed her arms.

"No, Buffy!" Angel called, as a hooded acolyte grabbed him around the knees and another raced at Angel with a long, sharp knife.

"Angel!" Buffy cried out, straining to free herself and help him.

One of her captors slammed his fist into her face, and for a moment everything went black.

When her eyes flickered open, she saw something impossible. Angel was flying.

"What are you doing?" Xander demanded of the Gatekeeper as he drew Angel toward them. "The whole reason we needed him here was because the son of a bitch is so hard to kill! Buffy can't win this thing on her own. You're leaving her defenseless down there!"

"It's all I can do," the Gatekeeper said with great effort. Xander could barely hear his voice over the sounds of fighting. The man looked terrible. His face was the color of concrete and he could barely stand up. Giles caught hold of him and slung the man's arm over his shoulder. "We must perform the Ritual of Endowment if we are to save her."

"You don't care about her at all," Cordelia flung at him, pounding his shoulder and pointing as Buffy freed herself, only to be grabbed by three more hooded men. She fought them off and looked anxiously up at the landing. "Or you'd help her now!"

They watched as Angel was drawn up and onto the landing by the Gatekeeper's magick. The old man coughed and wheezed.

"My strength is fading," the man said, wheezing. His forehead was beaded with sweat. "There are too many of them. She is the Slayer, but she's not a magick-user. Left to this battle, they will defeat her."

"Then let me go back and fight with her!" Angel shouted at him as he was unwillingly deposited beside the Gatekeeper. Still in vamp face, he grabbed the man by the shoulders and gave him a hard shake. "Or have you lost your mind along with your strength?"

"Angel," Giles remonstrated sternly. "The Gatekeeper's right. Buffy will be defeated and the Gatehouse plunged into madness. Unless, that is, we perform the ritual as soon as possible."

The Gatekeeper doubled over in a fit of coughing. When he straightened back up, Xander saw blood on his fist. He began to panic. The man was dying where he stood.

Regnier said to Angel, "You have cried tears of blood. That's excellent." He looked to Giles. "Follow me, all of you. We will need to concentrate."

"I'm not leaving Buffy," Angel announced.

"Me, neither. This is wrong." Xander looked hard at Angel. "In fact, if I can get down there without breaking my legs, I'll do my best to break some of theirs."

"Oz is down there, too," Angel reminded them, and looked meaningfully to Xander.

Xander tensed as if to jump.

"Excellent, excellent," the Gatekeeper murmured. "This is what she needs. This is what she must have. Your loyalty. Your willingness to die for her."

"Well, let's not get carried away," Cordelia said anxiously. "Dying wasn't exactly on my to-do list for today."

"Come," the Gatekeeper urged, gesturing for them to follow him. "You can save her only if you do as I say. Otherwise, she will die. And so will all of us."

"No," Angel said, gripping the landing and nodding slightly at Xander. "I won't leave them down there. I won't leave her."

Giles grabbed Angel by the shoulder and the vampire turned on him, snarling, yellow eyes blazing. But Giles was not deterred. He gripped both of Angel's shoulders and met his gaze unwaveringly.

"Listen to me now! I know what your brain is telling you, but listen for a moment! They are too powerful. They are using magick as their weapon and only with magick can we hope to defeat them! The Gatekeeper is failing fast. If he does not perform the Ritual of Endowment now, he may be too weak to ever perform it.

"You want to save her? So do I! I would give my own life if it would buy her another moment to continue this fight. But there is another way! It's our only hope, Angel!"

The Watcher spun on Xander, glared at him. "It's the only way."

"Yeah, right," Xander said angrily, also placing his hand on the banister. "Who died and made you Obi-wan?"

"Half the reason we sent Oz to retrieve Angel was that this ritual might be necessary. It calls for those who love Buffy to endow her with their strength, to give up part of themselves for her. I thought everybody understood what we need to do."

"That was before the ten thousand maniacs down there crashed the party," Xander said, his anger rising to fever pitch. "And I'm *not*—"

"Look out!" Cordelia shrieked.

Long tendrils of crackling blue energy whipped into the air like the tentacles of an octopus, paused, and then shot straight for them. Raising his hands, the Gatekeeper prepared a counterattack, a sword and shield of electric green springing into his hands. Blue collided with green, and showers of energy ricocheted off the ceiling and walls. Everyone but the Gatekeeper hit the floor.

The ghost of Antoinette Regnier appeared beside Xander and whispered, her eerie ghost voice somehow audible over the noise, *"The house is beginning to crack, Jean-Marc. We're running out of time."*

The air was shattered by a round of explosions. Bits of plaster rained down on Xander's head and he yanked Cordelia into his arms as a huge chunk of wood plummeted from the ceiling, narrowly missing her face.

Behind them came a deep, low growl, and something said, in a weird half-human voice, "Gatekeeper, I hunger."

*"The binding places are breaking down,"* Antoinette Regnier announced. *"The monsters and demons walk."*

"Go back," the Gatekeeper commanded in a whisper. As Xander squinted up at him, the dying sorcerer made motions in the air. "Go back, I command you!"

Xander raised his head. A large, black panther was

slinking down the corridor of the east wing of the house, headed directly for the landing on which they stood, overlooking a long drop down to the first floor, now that the staircase had been completely removed. The landing was a T-junction of three corridors, with the deadly drop the fourth side of the junction.

Another round of explosions shook the house. Glass shattered. The panther crept closer.

Her face pressed against his neck, Cordelia clung to Xander and said, "What's going on? What's happening?"

"What's not?" Xander asked, holding her as close as he could. He could feel her heart thundering against his chest.

A low, savage growl echoed down the hall. Xander swallowed hard. He said, "Cordy, I want you to run when I tell you to, okay?"

*"What?"*

There was the screech of something large, something horrible. A violent flapping buffeted the air.

"What's that?" Xander shouted. To his astonishment, the Gatekeeper paled and covered his eyes. "Hey! Super Mario! Don't check out on us now! Talk to me!"

Jean-Marc Regnier knelt beside Xander and gripped his shoulder. He looked terrified. "It's a demon sent to carry her away," he said. "We must act *now.*"

Buffy heard unearthly shrieks as she fought three hooded acolytes at once. Pieces of wood and plaster showered the battle arena.

A large shadow, almost a fog, unfurled from a place high above Buffy's head and spread across the room.

*Now what?* she thought.

"Mr. Regnier?" she called. "What's happening?"

There was no answer. She looked up.

She couldn't see her friends. She was alone.

For a moment she panicked. Then she shook her head hard, once, and set her jaw. It didn't matter.

She was the Slayer.

And then the sound of huge, leathery wings filled her ears, and Buffy was plunged into bone-chilling cold as blackness engulfed the room.

The Gatekeeper murmured something, and the landing and the corridor went completely black. He'd drawn the darkness around them.

"All of you, rise and walk," Jean-Marc said. "Take the main corridor. Go toward the back of the house."

"Gatekeeper, it doesn't matter if I can't see them," growled the subhuman voice, much closer now. "I can smell them."

A frisson of icy fear washed down Giles's back as he sat up in the blackness and slowly got to his feet. "You've got to bind it," he said. "Buffy ran into them before. She killed the female."

"The female what?" Cordelia's shrill voice asked. "Xander, what's down there?"

For once, Xander was silent. Giles felt for Buffy's two friends. He half crouched and said, "I want you to get up very slowly. No sudden moves."

"I have energy for the ritual, but not for binding as well," the Gatekeeper wheezed. "If I bind the panthers—"

*"Panthers?"* Cordelia wailed. "Now there are panthers?"

The Gatekeeper said, "If I bind the panthers, I shall die."

*"We'll fetch the Cauldron to strengthen you,"* Antoinette whispered. To Angel, she said, *"You must get around the panther. It's in a room—"*

"No, Mother. It's for the ritual," Jean-Marc said, and then he collapsed in Giles's arms.

*"No, for you,"* she pleaded. *"My son, you cannot die."*

Giles was more than alarmed. He had no idea how to perform a Ritual of Endowment. Buffy was fighting for her life, and the house was destroying itself.

"Don't argue, *chère maman.* I haven't enough energy for it," Jean-Marc wheezed, struggling to stand. "Just to keep this landing intact, I must exert myself more than I should."

Giles blinked. He had forgotten that the landing was a magickal re-creation. He said, "I've an idea," and dropped his voice as low as he could and still be heard over the tumult.

Oz opened his eyes with a groan. For a second, he thought he was at the multiplex at the Sunnydale Mall, watching a movie. Shapes strobed in a low-level blue light all around him.

But it was no movie. Slowly he got to his feet.

It was then that he saw the hideous birdlike demon soaring down toward him. Part bird, part lion, part something so very totally else he could not describe it, it caught him up in its talons and darted its huge beak toward his face.

"Yeow!" Oz shouted.

"Oz!" Buffy cried.

But she was completely surrounded by Sons of

Entropy thugs, several of whom had decent holds on her. Buffy was not going to be much help at the moment. In fact, it looked like she could use Oz's help.

So Oz began to fight back as best he could.

Cordelia and Xander inched their way into the corridor. Their backs were pressed against the wall. Xander held his breath. Cordelia couldn't seem to catch hers.

Bathed in a soft blue glow, Giles and the Gatekeeper stood on the landing, facing the panther as it crouched mere feet from Xander and Cordelia. They were in the main corridor, which ran north to south, and it moved toward them along a side corridor. Angel stood on the other side of the junction in a fighter's stance. As Cordelia swallowed, the panther flicked its huge head in his direction.

"Come for me, and spare the young ones," the Gatekeeper urged, from his perch atop the magickal landing. "Come for me and this man. He is a Watcher."

The panther cocked its head and let out a huge roar.

"A Slayer killed your mate, did she not?" Giles said. "I taught her everything she knows. If you desire revenge, come for us."

The panther roared and lurched forward at Cordelia and Xander, swiping the air with its paw. Cordelia couldn't stop herself from screaming, even though Giles had told her not to.

"Stop toying with us," Giles called. "As soon as the Gatekeeper is dead, you will be free. He is all that keeps you here." He turned his head toward Jean-Marc. "Perhaps it doesn't understand us."

"Oh, it does," the sorcerer said. "It's prolonging the moment. It's savoring the victory."

The panther roared again, this time in Angel's direction. Then it burst forward in a flash of black and charged straight at Giles and the Gatekeeper. Cordelia screamed.

Angel flung himself after it, tackling it, slowing it down. It swung its head around and bit Angel's hand, and he shouted in pain. Then it dragged Angel along as it made for the sorcerer who had imprisoned it in his house.

The Gatekeeper shouted, "Now!"

He and Giles dove past the panther, one on either side of it, so that it had a moment of indecision. Angel let go. In a flash, the landing disappeared.

With a howl of frustration, the panther sailed over the ledge.

"C'mon," Xander shouted, pulling Cordelia back down the corridor.

Giles was clinging to the edge of carpeted floor with one hand while he strained to hold the Gatekeeper. Angel grabbed his hand and Xander reached for the Gatekeeper. Cordy pulled on Xander to give him an anchor. Below, she saw the panther land, claws out, on top of an enormous, horrible, birdlike thing that was attacking Oz.

"Take his feet," Giles said.

Angel grabbed the Gatekeeper's ankles while Giles took his hands. Antoinette Regnier led the way down the hall and through several passages. Then they clattered into a room.

The place was circular, with a wooden floor and

dozens of gold-framed mirrors covering the walls. Shapes were draped by pieces of heavy white fabric.

In the center of the room were several objects the Gatekeeper's ghostly mother had apparently gathered, perhaps aided by her son's magick: the Cauldron, a spear, a dish of salt, a bowl of water, and a heap of white belts or sashes. The Gatekeeper had already fallen unconscious. Not a good thing.

Beyond the room, there was a crash, followed by a cheer. Angel almost dropped the Gatekeeper. Everything inside him told him to leave this room and help Buffy.

"Lay him down," Giles said. "Xander, make a sacred circle around him." He pointed. "Use the salt."

"Roger that." That made sense to Angel. They'd used salt for sacred circles before.

Xander picked up the dish.

"No." Regnier's eyes flickered, opened. So he wasn't completely out of it yet. "Blood. From each of them."

"Excuse me?" Cordelia said, shocked.

"How must it be collected?" Giles asked quietly.

Cordelia looked fearfully at Angel. "Collected?"

"I will officiate." Regnier's hand shook, and then he looked at Cordelia. "Young lady, fetch the Cauldron of Bran."

"Yes, sir," she said, racing to a large black pot of cast-iron metal. Its three feet were the claws of a griffin. Otherwise, it was unadorned.

The suffering man clasped Giles's hand. "You must use a sharp blade on each of them, and a true one. The Spear of Longinus."

*"What?"* Cordelia said, touching her neck.

"At this very moment, the life of the Slayer is all that keeps the world from tumbling into the abyss of chaos. She cannot hope to win on her own, but neither can any of you be of physical help to her. Thus, you must share your life with her. Your life, yes, but more.

"From each of you, she will require life's blood, and love, and fealty, and trust, and even that may not be enough. It is clear that you all care for her, but if there are any whose love for the Slayer might still be untapped, we may yet need to call on that love."

The Gatekeeper paused, flinched, and closed his eyes a moment. When he opened them again, he seemed slightly more aware.

"Now, the blood," Regnier said. "The vampire's blood will be the truest. He has wept scarlet tears. Most precious." He looked hard at Angel. "For whom did you weep, monster? Yourself, or your victims?"

Angel blinked, glanced at Giles, but kept silent. He did not know what to say. He wasn't even certain that what he'd seen on the ghost roads had been Jenny Calendar. But now was not the time to discuss it.

"To Angel, it's rather the same thing," Giles said, and Angel felt a rush of gratitude. He knew that Giles could not quite forgive him for killing Jenny, the woman Giles loved. But Angel knew that he tried.

"I thought the Watcher was the one closest to the Slayer," Regnier managed. "But now I see her face in your golden eyes. I hear her heartbeat in your veins. You love her. All here love her." He gestured to the pile of objects. "Make the cuts," Regnier said to Angel.

"No," Cordelia said anxiously.

"I'll do it," Xander volunteered. "We, um, have some issues with Angel and blood."

Jean-Marc shook his head. "Bloodletting is not for you. The circle must be drawn by a pure-hearted youth. That is you."

Xander grunted in frustration. "Later, I'm going to think about that, and I'll probably be insulted."

The Gatekeeper looked up at Giles. "If I die before we finish this work, the best we can hope for is that the madness of my house will possess the Sons of Entropy."

"As it did us?" Giles asked quietly.

Regnier slowly shook his head. "The Slayer stands for order, and so you were able to impose order on the house. These are the minions of Chaos. They serve madness."

"So they impose madness on the House, and your little freak zoo escapes into Sunnydale, and there's some big blastorama and the Otherworld comes into our world, and school's out forever," Xander said in a rush. "Not a good idea, Mr. Keeper, sir."

"We must do what we can," the Gatekeeper said. He nodded at Angel. "Cut them across the palm, and pray to your gods—if you have any—as you do it."

"I don't think he's allowed to pray," Cordelia piped up.

"For Buffy, I can do anything," Angel said grimly.

He picked up the Spear of Longinus. A sharp burn sizzled his skin as he carried it back to the others.

Giles straightened his shoulders and held out his hand. He gazed levelly at Angel and whispered, "On the road of the dead, the ghost road. Who did you weep for?"

Angel dropped his eyes a moment, and murmured, "You know who."

Giles's eyes welled. He held out his hand.

No one spoke as Angel drew the blade across Giles's palm.

"Collect it, quickly," Jean-Marc told Cordelia. He coughed, and in his throat there was a rattle. Angel knew death was knocking at the threshold.

He moved to Xander, and took his blood.

The panther and the demon fought, claws flashing, talons slicing. Each howled in fury. The demon was bleeding badly, the panther faring only slightly better. The white-haired sorcerer had tried to intervene, but for some reason his magick did not work on the panther.

Fascinated by the struggle, Buffy's captors began to loosen their grip. Beside her, Oz, also now a prisoner, turned to her and raised an eyebrow.

She gave him a little nod.

The house shook around them. Monsters walked the halls. The Gatekeeper was barely conscious.

Xander had drawn the circle in blood. The mingled scents filled the air, combining with their fear.

Angel held on tightly to Cordelia's hand. It was bound to his with one of the white sashes. His other was tied to Giles's. Each of them had been bound to the other.

And they were all bound to the Slayer.

His ghostly mother cradling his head, the sorcerer chanted in Latin, which Angel knew:

> *Behold, those who would belong to the Slayer.*
> *These are her followers, those by whom she is*
> *beloved above all else.*
> *Though they part from her a thousand leagues,*
> *their spirits stay with her.*

*Their hearts stay with her.*
*Their souls stay with her.*

Suddenly, the Gatekeeper's face twitched, and he opened his eyes wide.

"What?" Giles snapped. "What's wrong?"

"It isn't enough," the Gatekeeper replied.

Cordelia whimpered. Xander swore loudly.

"What about Oz?" Giles asked quickly.

"The ritual has found him already. Though he does not realize it, he is contributing as well. It isn't enough."

Xander's eyes lit up. "Cordy!" he snapped, "Give me your phone!"

Cordelia looked at him as though he were crazy, but she went for her bag and dug out the phone without arguing.

"Listen, we've tried using this thing from in here, but the signal can't get out of the house. You've got to make it go through," Xander told the Gatekeeper.

"I will try to . . . I will manage," he said weakly.

"Xander," Giles said, "what are you . . ." and then he got it. "Willow!" he said excitedly.

Xander started to dial.

"She's not home!" Angel said suddenly. "Oz told her to go to Buffy's mom's house. Try there."

Xander swore, disconnected, and began to dial again.

Willow sat staring at the television in the Summers living room, but was only tangentially aware of what was happening on-screen. She was tired, and had started to nod off several times before her mind strayed into areas she'd rather it stay away from. Joyce had called Willow's mother to say that she was going to help at the gallery, unpacking for an exhibit. The excuse had worked, but Willow didn't know how long she could stay before it would become obvious that she was doing something else.

Together the two of them had watched meaningless cable gibberish until Joyce had drifted off. The woman was not sleeping comfortably. She murmured in her sleep, and the way her face scrunched up from time to time, Willow thought she was having a nightmare.

Maybe a series of nightmares.

But she didn't want to wake Mrs. Summers. She only wished she could get some sleep too. But though she had closed her eyes from time to time, sleep would not come.

And then it did. Simple as that.

Several minutes after Willow had finally dropped off, the phone rang and pulled her roughly from her dreams. On the second ring, with Mrs. Summers still barely stirring on the sofa, Willow reached for the phone. She glanced at the clock: not quite late enough for her mom to be calling to complain.

"Summers residence," she said, still slightly groggy from her interrupted descent into unconsciousness.

"Willow, thank God!" Xander shouted over the phone.

"Xander? What's wrong? What's happening?" Willow cried, deeply frightened by the tone of his voice.

Mrs. Summers was up now, and she came across the living room toward Willow, reaching for the phone.

"That's Xander?" she asked. "What is it? Has something happened to Buffy?"

Willow shushed her angrily, held up one hand to prevent further interruption.

She listened to Xander, her face draining of all color, eyes growing wider by the moment. Joyce kept gesticulating at her, and after a moment, Willow held her hand over the phone and looked at Buffy's mom.

"You'd do anything for Buffy, right?" Willow asked.

"I'm her mother, Willow," Joyce said anxiously. "I'd die for her."

Willow only nodded. With a frightened expression on her face, she said, "Find something sharp."

The cellular phone lay, the line to Sunnydale still open, on the floor at Xander's feet. They had rejoined hands. Three thousand miles away, Joyce Summers and Willow Rosenberg were bleeding for Buffy. Somewhere downstairs, Oz fought at her side.

The Gatekeeper began again.

> *Behold, those who would belong to the Slayer.*
> *These are her followers, those by whom she is beloved above all else.*
> *Though they part from her a thousand leagues, their spirits stay with her.*
> *Their hearts stay with her.*
> *Their souls stay with her.*
> *To one another are they true, for the sake of her.*
> *Their loyalty is one living thing among them, no matter the future, no matter the past.*
> *This is their bond, and this is the Slayer's strongest weapon. Beyond battle, beyond force, this is their greatest gift.*

"You must know this in your bones," the Gatekeeper whispered. "Over and beyond your ability to fight the darkness, you must be her light. You have proven your prowess and your courage against monsters and demons, but now you must surrender. You are the Slayer's, and you will always belong to her."

He closed his eyes. "Even if you never see her again."

Giles, Angel, Cordelia, and Xander stood tall and steadfast, hands clasped. Blue light crackled around the cellular phone and seemed to leap into the air toward the Gatekeeper. A fierce, searing wind howled through the room.

Cordelia's hand jerked and her eyes widened. Angel gave her hand a squeeze. She closed her eyes and murmured to herself, "I'm not moving I'm brave I'm not moving."

As the wind burned Angel's face, the ceiling crashed down around them. Snakes wriggled from the floor.

Ghostly specters writhed in the mirrors. The mirrors shattered in their frames, and a dozen dark creatures stepped into the room: trolls; a skeleton heavy with rotting flesh; a headless woman, her neck spouting gore; another panther.

Cordelia whispered, "Buffy Buffy Buffy Buffy."

The creatures began to converge on the circle.

"Stand fast!" the Gatekeeper commanded. "Do not falter."

There was a scream.

It was a voice Angel knew well.

It was Buffy.

As Angel watched, Xander reached for the sash to untie himself.

"Stand fast!" the Gatekeeper shouted, in surprisingly strong and ringing tones.

"But she needs us!" Xander protested.

"That's right, she does," Angel said. "And that's why we have to stay here, Xander. This is our battle. *This* one. The other is for her."

"He's right, Xander." Giles looked pale. "We must believe this. We must know this."

Another scream.

Angel's eyes bled.

The panther lay dead at the feet of the winged demon. Shouting in triumph, the white-haired sorcerer pointed to Buffy and said to the monster, "Take her to Il Maestro!"

Dripping with blood, the huge black thing flapped its wings and rose into the air, fighting a blast of fiery wind that cascaded from the ruined hallway above.

Then it dove for Buffy. Unnerved, her captors let go of her and she screamed once, in surprise. She raised her fists as the creature approached. She barely heard Oz's shout of warning as it tilted its body backward and grabbed her in its talons. Where it dug into her waist, it drew blood.

But although her mouth was closed, the scream reverberated throughout the room. The demon clutched her ever more tightly and now she couldn't even breathe. It rose into the air and crashed through the ceiling. Night had fallen, and when Buffy threw back her head, she could see the moon.

"Fly!" the sorcerer shouted.

Below, a wild parade of evil creatures began to leap into the room. The hooded figures blasted them with magickal energy. Within seconds, it was a free-for-all, and Buffy looked mutely for Oz, down amid the chaos.

She saw him then. Fighting. Bleeding. Staring after her with a fist in the air. And he screamed to her.

"Fight, Buffy! You can beat it!"

In Sunnydale, Willow and Joyce cried together.

"My God," Joyce whispered. "What's happening? Oh, God, please let my little girl come home."

They held on to one another, and each of them felt a tug, as though part of their minds, their inner selves, were being spirited away. They hugged even more tightly.

"She'll win," Willow said to Buffy's mother. "She'll come back."

The rotting skeleton grabbed Cordelia around the waist. She shrieked and said, "Xander, stop him!"

"Do not move," the Gatekeeper ordered. "Do not falter."

"But—" Xander said, reaching once more for the sash.

"Do it, and Buffy dies," Giles said. "Believe in us. Believe in all of us, Xander. But most of all, believe in Buffy."

Xander closed his eyes. He saw Buffy as clearly as if she were standing next to him. Saw her big blue eyes. Her smile. Saw how much he loved her, and would always love her.

Cordelia screamed, over and over again.

The wind howled.

The monsters walked.

He heard Buffy's scream.

He saw how many times she had risked her life for

him. Saw how many times she had wanted to quit. How torn she was between duty and desire. Between her responsibility to the world and to herself.

Saw that he was part of all that.

The wind howled. The creatures descended upon the circle, grabbing at each one of them. Even Giles shouted with fear.

"I believe," he whispered.

And there was silence.

Just as the demon had flown almost completely through the hole in the roof, the ceiling reformed.

The demon's legs and claws were instantly severed. The dead talons released Buffy, and she angled her fall to land on the upper story, where the landing once had been.

Tucking forward, she landed hard, but whirled around.

The white-haired sorcerer looked up, shouted, "No!" and fire arced from his fingers at the demon's remains as they plummeted toward him. His magick did nothing; still the sharp talons and huge legs fell. Buffy watched, riveted. The sorcerer tried to run. Too late. As he looked fearfully over his shoulder, the sharp, curved claws pierced his back and impaled him.

Magickal blue energy crackled around him. It gathered in force, and as Buffy watched, it snapped and buzzed like a live wire.

It leaped to the nearest hooded figure and enveloped him. The man cried out, then collapsed.

It left him and went to the next figure. The next. The next. And Buffy knew then that it was not the sorcerer's own magick, but the power of the Gate-house. Cleaning up.

By the time Buffy's friends reached her, all the Sons of Entropy lay dead.

From the carnage in the stairwell below, Oz slowly rose, blinked, and said, "At some point, if it's not too much trouble, can someone get me out of here?"

# Epilogue

They stood in the foyer of the Gatehouse. The marble sparkled. A cool breeze slipped through windows throughout the house. The chandelier high above them cast an eerie glow down on them, and on the newly restored grand staircase to the second-floor landing.

The Gatekeeper had done it all.

Now he lay once more in the restorative Cauldron of Bran the Blessed. Giles had spoken with the ghostly Antoinette Regnier only moments earlier, and with spectral tears streaming down her face, the long-dead woman announced that her son would likely have to remain in the Cauldron for several days before he would be reinvigorated enough to fend off any further attack. With a proper rest, and with a soaking in the Cauldron at least once or twice a day, he would be able to go on, at least for a little while. But the Cauldron would not keep him alive forever. If the heir was not recovered, chaos would still prevail.

Giles had found it odd that the ghost would not look forward to her son finally joining her in the afterlife, and said so. Antoinette's spirit smiled at that. It was not his impending death that saddened her, but the pain he suffered each moment that he clung to life.

That had been enough to silence Giles.

Until now.

"We really only have one choice," the Watcher explained. "We must go to Europe, and somehow find young Jacques Regnier, and return him to this house before his father dies."

They stared at him.

"Well, I don't like the idea any better than the rest of you," he said huffily.

Which wasn't entirely true. For Giles had not forgotten about Micaela Tomasi, and the mystery of her disappearance. He hoped that this trip might solve that mystery once and for all.

"Well then?" He turned his gaze upon the Slayer.

Buffy smiled affectionately at Giles. Glanced around at the others. She knew what they'd done, and how it was done. Knew that they were all there for her. Even Cordelia, which a part of her still found amazing. They would never discuss it after this, Buffy knew, but in spite of all her carping and haughty attitude, Cordelia was a courageous and loyal friend.

She would never have imagined it.

"Fine," Buffy said, and idly picked lint off her sweatshirt. They'd all changed into clean and comfortable clothes after the chaos had ended. "Someone's got to stay here, Giles," Buffy said. "And I'm not leaving Willow alone back in Sunnydale, so someone's going to have to go home and back her up. As for the rest of us . . . I don't know how long the search for the heir is going to take, but it doesn't really matter. Either we find him in time, or it just won't matter anymore."

They all stared at her. One by one she searched their faces. Giles. Cordelia. Oz. Xander. And Angel. Dear Angel. They'd rarely been this close, and rarely this far apart.

"First we sleep," Giles said. "None of us will do anyone any good unless we get some sleep first."

Buffy nodded her agreement.

So, that would be it. Sleep. Just a little. And then the madness would begin again.

Once upon a time, the vineyard had been the pride of his villa. But Il Maestro ages ago had lost interest in grapes. In wine. Power was the only substance upon which he could become drunk. Power, and chaos.

"Il Maestro?"

The voice was quivering with fear. Taking his eyes off the lights of Florence in the distance, turning his back on the ravaged and overgrown remains of his vineyard, Il Maestro turned to find Brother Aldo standing at a respectful distance, eyes downcast.

Il Maestro chuckled dryly, and black fire burned almost invisibly at his fingertips where they hung at his sides. The Frenchman who had taught him to access that darkest of sorceries had called it *La Brûlure Noire*. The Black Burn. Even now, it began to creep up his arms, enveloping Il Maestro in a sheath of blazing darkness.

"You've come to tell me that the Gatehouse still stands."

Brother Aldo said nothing, but he began to cry.

"That the Slayer is still free."

Aldo started to sob.

"That we still do not have the heir."

He nodded slightly, bit his lip.

"That the Hellmouth has been put . . . in *order.*"

With a whimper, the young magician turned to run, screaming, through the remains of the vineyard.

Il Maestro snickered. He didn't bother to expend the energy it would take to raise his hand. He'd never been melodramatic. Black lightning coursed from his body, crackling as it reached shadow tendrils across the dead vineyard and lightly caressed Brother Aldo's body. He froze in place and began to shudder. Black tendrils danced across his skin and his clothes.

Aldo erupted in an explosion of charred flesh and bloody cinders.

Il Maestro shook his head. "What a waste," he whispered to himself.

He never expected to hear the voice that was now raised behind him.

"My sentiments exactly," said the voice.

Perturbed, Il Maestro turned and peered through the night and the dead vineyard at the figure who even now stepped closer. The hair was as white as white could be. Though slender of frame, he held himself with a power and arrogance that was slightly off-putting, even for one so powerful as the master of the Sons of Entropy.

"You haven't come through with your part of the bargain," the visitor said dangerously.

"I want the boy," Il Maestro replied, his tone meant to brook no argument.

The other, the visitor, only smiled. Showing fangs.

"You promised us the Spear of Longinus," he said. "A trinket, you said. A toy, in the grand scheme of things. My baby doesn't like to be disappointed. Her man promises her something, he delivers."

As the wind he moved, and stood beside Il Maestro, ignoring the black fire that surrounded the master sorcerer.

"That'd be me, by the way," he whispered.

Then he backed off, with a grin and a laugh. "I don't much care for babysitting. We're gonna have stew à la Gatekeeper Junior before long. You get us the Spear of Longinus, we'll give you the boy."

Il Maestro was enraged, but logic dictated he must remain silent. He wanted that boy. The heir of the House of Regnier was hidden from his magickal senses by virtue of his heritage. Thus had the vampires been able to hide the boy from him. As he had done quite often in the past, he had used them as his tools to abduct the boy, in exchange for that little trinket. It had been an agreeable bargain at first. But then, he had thought he would have the spear in hand by now.

"How long do we have?" Il Maestro asked.

The white-haired vampire shrugged his shoulders nonchalantly. He took out a cigarette and a metal lighter, flipped it open, and lit up. There was a long pause as he sucked smoke into dead lungs.

"Way I figure it, you've got until I get bored, or Drusilla gets hungry," he said casually.

A moment later, Spike was gone.

# About the Authors

CHRISTOPHER GOLDEN is a novelist, journalist, and comic book writer. His novels include the vampire epics *Of Saints and Shadows, Angel Souls & Devil Hearts,* and *Of Masques and Martyrs;* the recent hardcover *X-Men: Codename Wolverine,* the upcoming *Strangewood,* and six *Buffy* novels written with Nancy Holder. His latest project is a series of young adult mysteries for Pocket, the first of which, *Body Bags,* is on sale now. Golden's comic book work includes *The Punisher,* as well as *Punisher/Wolverine, The Crow,* and *Spider-Man Unlimited,* and a number of *Buffy* comic book projects.

The editor of the Bram Stoker Award–winning book of criticism *CUT!: Horror Writers on Horror Film,* he has written articles for *The Boston Herald, Disney Adventures,* and *Billboard,* among others, and was a regular columnist for the worldwide service BPI Entertainment News Wire. He is one of the authors of the recently released book *The Watcher's Guide,* the official companion to *Buffy the Vampire Slayer.*

Golden was born and raised in Massachusetts, where he still lives with his family. He graduated from Tufts University. Please visit him at www.christophergolden.com.

NANCY HOLDER has written three dozen books and over 200 short stories. She has worked on nine *Buffy* projects, including six novels and *The Watcher's Guide* with Christopher Golden (with assistance from Keith R.A. DeCandido), as well as *The Angel Chronicles,* volumes 1 and 3, and *The Evil That Men Do. Gambler's Star: Legacies and Lies,* the second book in her science-fiction trilogy for Avon Books, is available now. She also writes novels based on the TV show *Sabrina the Teenage Witch,* for Archway/Minstrel.

Holder is a former editor with FTL Games, as well as the author of comic books and TV commercials in Japan. She has also taught writing. Recent short story appearances include "Little Dedo" in *In the Shadow of the Gargoyle,* and "Appetite," in *Hot Blood X.*

She has received four Bram Stoker Awards, one for her novel *Dead in the Water* and three for short stories. She also received a sales award from Amazon.com for *The Angel Chronicles. Volume 1.* She has been published in over two dozen languages and is a former trustee of the Horror Writers Association.

Holder lives in Southern California with her husband and daughter. A former ballet dancer, she graduated from the University of California at San Diego.

Golden and Holder started working together when Holder sold an essay to Golden's *CUT! Horror Writers on Horror Films.* They write together via the Internet, and to date have collaborated on seven books as well as short fiction, including "Hiding," for *The Ultimate Hulk,* and "Ate," which appeared in *Vampire Magazine* in the U.S. and Canada, and *Vampire Dark* in France.

# BUFFY

## THE VAMPIRE

# SLAYER™

## THE WATCHER'S GUIDE

The official companion guide to the hit
TV series, full of cast photos, interviews,
trivia, and behind the scenes photos!

**By Christopher Golden and Nancy Holder**

POCKET
BOOKS

Published by Pocket Books

1492-01

## Buffy the Vampire Slayer
# OFFICIAL FAN CLUB
www.buffyfanclub.com

1 YEAR MEMBERSHIP INCLUDES:

* 4 Issues of the *Buffy* Official Magazine

* Official I.D. Membership Card

* Exclusive Cast Photos

* Exclusive *Buffy* Poster

* Official *Buffy* Bumper Sticker

# JOIN
# NOW!

# Everyone's got his demons....

# ANGEL™

### If it takes an eternity, he will make amends.

Original stories based on the
TV show created by Joss Whedon
& David Greenwalt

Available from Pocket Pulse
Published by Pocket Books